PRAISE FOR *1066, WHAT FATES IMPOSE*:

'An extremely promising debut – highly recommended.'
Historical Novel Society

'Highly Commended.'
Words for the Wounded

'An epic story set in the eleventh century beautifully transferred
into fiction.'
Carol McGrath, author of The Daughters of Hastings Trilogy

'A fascinating look at a fascinating time.'
Gold Medal Winner The Wishing Shelf Award for Adult Fiction

'A tremendous five star read.'
The Book Magnet

'This is a great book for anyone interested in the history of
early England ...
Awesome Indies Reviewers

'The 11th Century as if it were yesterday.'
Breakaway Reviewers

'In all, this is a bloody tale of grasping and greed that set the island
nation off on a round of desperate struggles for dominion and rule that
lasted for many hundreds of years.'
Internet Review of Books

'This is definitely a meaty slice of well-pitched and sometimes
astonishing factoid heaven.
The Book Bag

'This is probably my favourite historical novel so far.'
Book Traveler

'Give yourself a treat and delve into the world of eleventh century life, warfare and history in this well written tale.'
Hoover Book Reviews

'History aficionados, you'd better get your hands on this one ASAP.'
Serious Reading

'Novelists lie awake at nights desperately trying to think up new plots, yet meany of the best stories have happened in real life. Here, Holloway has taken the events of the twenty-one years leading up to 1066 and they have provided a dramatic book that I could not put down.'
Whispering Stories

'A book I wish I'd read when studying A Level history.'
Bookmuse

'I highly recommend this insightful, fascinating and brilliant historical novel.'
Bits about Books

1066

WHAT FATES IMPOSE

G. K. HOLLOWAY

Matador
9 Priory Business Park
Kibworth Beauchamp
Leicestershire LE8 0RX, UK
Tel: 0116 279 2299
Email: books@troubador.co.uk
Web: www.troubador.co.uk/matador

ISBN 978 1783062 201

British Library Cataloguing in Publication Data.
A catalogue record for this book is available from the British Library.

Typeset in Aldine401 BT Roman by Troubador Publishing Ltd
Printed and bound in the UK by TJ International, Padstow, Cornwall

Matador is an imprint of Troubador Publishing Ltd

For Alice

With Best Wishes

[signature] Halloway

LIST OF MAIN CHARACTERS

Royalty
Edward King of England, son of Emma
Edith, Queen of England, daughter of Earl Godwin
Emma, Dowager Queen of England, King Edward's mother and great aunt of Duke William of Normandy

Wessex
Godwin, Earl of Wessex
Gytha, Godwin's wife
Sweyn, son of Godwin
Harold, son of Godwin
Tostig, son of Godwin
Edith, daughter of Godwin
Gyrth, son of Godwin
Leofwine, son of Godwin
Wulfnoth, son of Godwin
Beorn, Godwin's nephew
Edyth Swanneck, handfast wife of Harold
Godwin, son of Harold
Magnus, Son of Harold
Edmund, son of Harold
Gytha, daughter of Harold
Ulf, son of Harold

Mercia
Leofric, Earl of Mercia
Godiva, Leofric's wife
Aelfgar, Leofric's son
Aldytha, Aelfgar's daughter
Edwin, son of Aelfgar
Morcar, son of Aelfgar

Northumbria

Siward, Earl of Northumbria
Aelflaed, Siward's wife
Osbern, son of Siward
Waltheof, son of Siward
Cospatric, Earl of Cumbria, grandson of King Ethelred
Gamel Ormson, great grandson of King Ethelred
Oswulf, grandson of Earl Uhtred, King Ethelred's son-in-law

The Church

Edmund, a monk, Harold's friend
Stigand, Archbishop of Canterbury from 1052
Eadmear, Archbishop of York
Wulfstan, Bishop of Worcester

Normans

William, Duke of Normandy and great nephew of Emma, Queen of England
Matilda, Duchess of Normandy
Robert, Count of Mortain, brother of Duke William
Odo, Bishop of Bayeux, brother of Duke William
Robert de Jumieges, Archbishop of Canterbury
William Malet, Norman knight and friend of Harold Godwinson
Eustace, Count of Boulogne, brother-in-law of King Edward, ally of
Duke William
Guy, Count of Ponthieu, ally of Duke William
William Warenne, knight and close friend of Duke William
William FitzOsbern, knight and close friend of Duke William

In 1066, England had a population of about two million people. Adults stood as tall as the English do today. By 1166 the population had halved and the average adult was three inches shorter. There had been neither famine nor plague. What happened was that half the Saxon population died at the hands of the Normans, and those who survived worked longer, paid more taxes and ate less. The English, under an apartheid-like regime, were denied access to positions of power and ownership of substantial amounts of land.

William had conquered; Norman civilisation had arrived.

ROUEN, NORMANDY 1087

In his bed the King, who can never be killed, lies dying. The old hag was right after all. He would not die on the battlefield. So, here he is, inside the church at St. Gervase, sixty years old, white haired and corpulent, waiting for fate to find him, while his courage deserts him and terror creeps through his being.

Six weeks previously, at the height of battle, the Conqueror's horse bucked and threw him high into the air. He dropped back onto the pommel of his saddle, splitting his pelvis and puncturing his bowel. The infected wound turned his insides putrid.

As he lies in his sweat-soaked sick bed, his fevered mind flits back and forth to deeds both past and present. The old king feels his life slowly slipping away. He urgently needs to make his peace with God. Only the Almighty can help him now.

Around his bed a few dignitaries are gathered, including the Conqueror's sons, Robert, William and Henri; their fates too, will be sealed this day. Henri, the youngest, sits at a fine oak table. He knows he will inherit nothing from his father and so he counts out, one at a time, the five thousand marks bequeathed him by his late mother.

Outside in the pale blue sky, a raven circles; inside Robert stares vacantly at the bedroom wall. William Rufus, his fingers stretched out before him, inspects his nails. He appears quite satisfied with his manicure and so busies himself with running his hand through his fine long red hair.

Their father turns towards them, no expression in his bloodshot eyes, his face an explosive red. Blotches like bruises have formed all over him. A few silver hairs grow like onion roots from the end of his bulbous nose. His once powerful body is drained of its strength and virility.

Long forgotten memories buried deep in his mind, revived by guilt and foreboding, form familiar characters; wretches who parade mockingly through his semi-conscious. In his delirium he watches a parade of aberrations. They jeer at him waving handless arms, some hobbling about on the stubs of their legs, their feet hacked off long since. With perverse delight the miserable creatures beckon him towards them, greeting him with rotten-toothed smiles. Something about their diabolical welcome is irresistible to him. He cannot help but stare. Tears flow down his face. This is his first display of emotion since his coronation twenty-one years before, when he sat newly crowned on the throne at Westminster, trembling before the eyes of God.

Now though, he must face the enormity over which even he, a king, has no control. He must pay the price.

As he gazes down the bed, he is surprised to discover it is not a warrior's sword he holds but a beautiful, leather bound, gold-inlaid, jewel-encrusted Bible – there to comfort him, to reassure him of the existence of God and the hereafter. It offers no reassurance; it is simply a reminder that he will soon be called to account, a quick and violent hero's death denied him, as he has always known it would be. After a sigh of resignation he turns in the direction of his priest, Bishop Gilbert de Lisieux.

'Father, hear my confession.'

With difficulty Gilbert forces his gaze away from the jewel-clad tome. The bishop nods sagely to the Conqueror, who then begins the last of his confessions.

'I have persecuted the natives of England beyond all reason,' gasps William. 'Whether gentle or simple, I have cruelly oppressed them. Many I unjustly disinherited. Innumerable multitudes perished through me by famine or the sword.'

After a short struggle for breath he continues, 'I fell on the English of the northern shires like a ravening lion. I ordered that their houses and corn, with all their implements and chattels, be burnt without distinction and great herds of cattle and beasts of burden were butchered wherever they were found.'

He stops for a moment to pause for breath and to reflect on his actions. He lowers his eyes; he sees only the Bible.

'In this way,' he continues, 'I subjected a fine race of people to the calamity of cruel famine and so became the barbarous murderer of many thousands of men and women.' He pauses and breaks down, tears mixed with perspiration running down his face. The onlookers remain motionless, voyeurs at a grim display. No one steps forward to help the old man. Contrition is something they had not expected to see.

Slowly William regains control, reaching inside for his last remnants of strength while William Rufus tries hard to suppress a yawn. To his credit he succeeds.

The King continues, 'Having gained the throne of that kingdom by so many crimes I dare not leave it to anyone but God.'

Rufus and Robert exchange startled glances. At his desk Henri smirks.

The King then utters the following words to the room: 'I appoint no one as my heir to the Crown of England, but leave it to the disposal of the Eternal Creator, whose I am and who orders all things. For I did not attain that high honour by hereditary right, but wrested it from the perjured King Harold in a desperate bloody battle.'

He feels none of the expected relief from the burden of guilt that weighs him down, just remorse. 'I declare amnesty on all those I have imprisoned, that they may once more enjoy their God-given freedom.'

Still fearful, still full of dread, he lies there in his hot, damp bed, breathing sour air, hoping for what, exactly? He does not know. No matter what he says, the burden of guilt continues to weigh him down. He is convinced the fate he has dreaded since childhood now awaits him; he will go to hell and burn there for all eternity.

He has made amends, adhered to the Christian faith, built fine churches. What more is he supposed to do? He needs a sign, a sign from God, to know all is well, that he has been forgiven his transgressions. Is it too much to ask?

With the very last of his strength he raises his head to look around the room. There are his sons, his brother, the bishop, and ...'Oh God, oh God Almighty. No, not him! Not him! Not now!' his voice rasps in his constricted throat, his eyes bulge as he is gripped by terror. Before him, unseen by the others, stands a blood-drenched warrior, tall and proud as an oak, fresh from the battlefield, his lank and sweat-soaked hair hanging down his shoulders, his once handsome face made ugly by an eyeless socket. More blood runs from a wound to his throat and another from his chest. As though to steady himself, he leans on his battle axe, resting his hands on its iron head. He stares impassively at William with his single eye, blue and deep as the ocean; a stare made all the more intense by its singularity.

William has seen him, or thought he has seen him, a number of times over the years, glimpsed in crowds or spotted in enemy lines but never before has he seen him so clearly, so close and for so long as he does now. The first time he saw him after Hastings was in York, while burning the city to the ground. Later, he thought he saw him outside Stafford, amongst a party of refugees. Over the years Harold had come back to haunt William at the most unexpected times; he knows this is their final meeting on this earth.

A chill floods William's body, making him raw, shaking him to the core.

'What do you want? What are you doing here?' he gasps.

In response the warrior says nothing.

'Is this a trick?' the King growls.

The onlookers think him delirious.

'You need rest, my Lord.' It is the kindly John de Villula who speaks, stepping toward his patient.

'Can you see him? Can you?' William croaks.

Villula stops in his tracks as though punched; such is the force of the King's question.

'See who, my Lord?'

'There! There,' rasps the old man, pointing with a trembling finger.

'There is no one there, my Lord, it must be a trick of the light,' comes the embarrassed response.

William is not reassured. This is no trick of the light. The warrior stands there just as before, his expression unchanged, although the King now thinks he perceives dark humour in the face.

'Have you come for me?' he ventures.

A trace, fleetingly brief, of a smile appears on the face of the apparition. He turns, swinging the axe over a shoulder as he does so, and steps, with a swift backward glance, silently out of the room.

Hopelessness descends upon King William. The chill leaves him and he feels hot again. His temperature rises as though he is being poached in his own perspiration. He wants to break free from the heat but escape is impossible. Pain washes through him. He closes his salt-stung eyes and sees scarlet as bright and vivid as fresh-spilt blood. Horror floods through him. The demons have returned. He hears their raucous laughter and feels their dirty, hot, sweaty hands all over him, pulling him downward, ever downward. Was he, like a pagan king of old, to be consumed by fire?

Then all is hot, black and silent.

THE BEGINNING, WINCHESTER, JANUARY 1045

In the King's great hall, disturbed by sounds of early morning, Edmund the young priest opened his eyes. Like many of the other men he had slept all night in his chair. Looking round, he noticed the heavy wooden shutters remained closed against the cold morning air; a few torches and the glow of embers in the braziers still provided the only light in the dark hall, which was permeated by the smell of wood smoke, stale beer and mutton fat. On the tables lay the remnants of last night's meal; plates, goblets and drinking horns, carelessly strewn about.

Close to the remnants of the fire sat Godwin, Earl of Wessex, a great bear of a man, and four of his sons. They were discussing the day's forthcoming events and were in good cheer. This was King Edward's wedding day and at last England would have a queen: Edith, Godwin's daughter was the bride and with God's grace she would produce an heir to the Crown. Godwin looked up, noticed Edmund and beckoned him over.

'Come and join us, Edmund,' he called genially.

Edmund rose slowly to his feet, stretched his stiff limbs and after a few cursory scratches walked past the ornately carved oak columns, on which creatures, real and mythical, chased each other to the heavens. Stepping gingerly through a group of sleeping dogs he joined his friends, who sat discussing the day's forthcoming events.

Godwin, Earl of Wessex, his hair grizzled at the temples, had dark blue bloodshot eyes under heavy eyebrows, strong features, a ruddy colour, thick lips and a square chin. He was broad shouldered and thick set. Sweyn, at twenty-five years old, was Godwin's eldest and favourite son and he sat on his right. He was bigger built than his father though his features were less angular and his muscles not so well defined. His hair was darker, his eyes green and deep set with an unnatural glint to them. He had a smooth complexion and the blubbery lips of his ever-open mouth always seemed wet. Edmund, like most people, always felt uncomfortable near Sweyn.

To Godwin's left sat his third son and Edith's twin, Tostig. Sweyn and Tostig were aged three years apart and were not at all close. Tostig was not quite as tall or as strong as Sweyn. He had long blond hair tied back with an amulet so the body of it fell down his back. Beside him sat another brother, Gyrth, and asleep across the table was the youngest of the boys at the table, Leofwine. All of them had the dragon of Wessex tattooed on their right forearm.

Neither of Godwin's two other sons was present. Wulfnoth, only four years old, was still asleep in the bowers with the women and other children. Harold, the second oldest son, had disappeared the previous evening with his cousin Beorn, looking for excitement.

'Here, have some breakfast, Edmund,' offered Godwin, leaning closer and pushing forward some bread, cheese and a mug of beer towards the still sleepy monk.

Edmund sat down, produced his knife and helped himself to breakfast.

'Are you looking forward to the great occasion?' enquired Godwin.

'Yes, I am. This is a great day for England. The King will soon have a queen...'

'That'll be three of them, then,' interrupted Sweyn.

Everyone tried his best to overlook the remark.

'Three of them,' Sweyn repeated, 'our Edith, Emma the King's mother and Edward, that's three,' said Sweyn, appearing proud of his mathematical ability.

'We'll also have three new loyal earls, won't we, boys?' said Godwin.

In return for supporting Edward's claim to the throne, Godwin had required earldoms to be found for Harold, Sweyn, and their cousin Beorn. The seeds Godwin had planted four years previously were about to bear fruit. After spending the previous twenty-five years in exile, Edward needed the family behind him. Now into the fourth year of his reign, he still had no powerful friends in England. In fact the country and its people were still something of a mystery to him and he still struggled with the language.

The talk continued as they ate their breakfast and the women and children joined them. Godwin's youngest son entered first, followed by two of his three daughters and his Danish wife, Lady Gytha. She was a tall, elegant woman in her early forties. Her physique belied her nine pregnancies. Her long blonde hair, striking blue eyes, high cheekbones, full-lipped mouth and noble demeanour had no match at court, and she easily outshone Lady Godiva, whose austere good looks made her cold and unapproachable. Lady Gytha sat down to breakfast with the children and their nurse.

'Good morning, Godwin,' she said, giving her husband a light kiss on the cheek.

'Good morning, my dear,' he replied, squeezing her hand gently in return, 'did you sleep well?'

'Yes, thank you,' she replied, looking around the table. 'Isn't Harold here?'

'No. He's gone somewhere with his cousin Beorn,' Godwin replied.

'You need to have a word with him, my dear.'

'I have. Do you think he listens to anything I say?'

'Yes, but this is the King's wedding.'

In his room King Edward was preparing for the day ahead. He picked up a silver hand mirror and gazed with admiration at his reflection. In his early forties, he was tall, and apart from a few Normans and clerics, the only clean-shaven man at the English court. He made an imposing regal figure, resplendent in his fine blue woollen mantle, which he wore over a linen tunic drawn in at the waist. The softest of woollen cross-gaiter leggings covered his spindly legs; his feet were comfortable in red doe hide shoes. His cloak and tunic were edged with broad bands of intricate design, gold threads woven among the silks of vivid reds and blues, the garments pinned together with splendid jewel-encrusted brooches. Finally, perched on his head was a slightly oversized gold crown studded with precious stones.

His servants were helping him with a few finishing touches. Not so long ago he had been simply Edward, son of the late King Ethelred, living in exile, reliant on the good will of others. Now, he was in his rightful place, continuing the glorious Cerdic line of Saxon kings into its sixth century.

After once more checking his appearance he continued his train of thought. He had expected to die an old man in Normandy, forgotten just like Alfred, his greatly missed brother, murdered by a man who worked in the shadows.

After King Knut died, Edward and his brother Alfred had received a letter from their mother, Queen Emma, inviting them to return to England. She told them they could easily seize the throne and support would rush to their aid. Their mother, in the hope of gaining more personal power, had deluded herself and misled them. Support for the sons of Ethelred was nonexistent – Edward discovered this on a visit to Winchester and fled the country immediately. Alfred was less fortunate. On King Harold Harefoot's orders, he was apprehended by Earl Godwin and handed over to the King's custody. Harold Harefoot had Alfred stripped naked and bound, mounted on a donkey then led to the abbey at Ely. Once there the young prince's eyes were burned out. Harefoot did such a bad job that Alfred died of his injuries.

Edward held his mother responsible for the letter enticing them back. Emma always claimed it to have been a forgery of Harefoot's. Edward was never sure whether to believe her or not but whoever had sent the letter, he still held Godwin ultimately responsible for Alfred's death. One day he would take revenge.

Calming himself, he let his thoughts drift back to his forthcoming marriage. He had never been married, and in fact had always remained aloof from women, but Edith, in spite of being Godwin's daughter was, it galled him to admit, the finest eligible lady in all the land. She was refined, cultured and educated to the highest degree. She could speak more languages than he and she knew more about fashion, art and literature. She was even a competent musician but, he reassured himself, she did not possess the innate wisdom and divine insight always present in one appointed king by the Almighty.

Suddenly the door burst open and his thoughts were interrupted. Looking away from the mirror Edward saw his mother bustling toward him.

'Not ready yet, Edward?' she asked.

'Almost, mother,' he answered meekly.

Emma, the dowager queen, brushed the servants aside and started making adjustments to his dress.

'Are you well?' she asked.

'I feel quite calm.'

'Good. It will be a long day,' she said quite seriously.

'And how do you feel today, mother?'

'I feel well, very well.'

'I was thinking, today will bring a big change for you too, mother.' He looked at her. She was tall, thin and possessed of an austerity made all the harsher by a frame of dyed black hair. Her pale skin, now creased like cracked lime, covered a face where a smile had to work hard to break free.

'When she is queen, Edith will fill the position now occupied by you,' Edward continued. 'What will you do then, mother?'

'That is for you to decide,' she answered flatly.

'Not entirely, one has to consider custom. I am told that in England, it is befitting for a widow to tend her husband's grave. Tell me mother, whose grave will you tend? I was forgetting for a minute that you have a choice.'

'Ethelred was a good man but Knut was great.'

'So you favoured his son over me?'

Emma brushed his shoulders and turned to go, but stopped. 'Edward, I wish you luck in your marriage and I wish you success as king. So far you have done quite well, but you'll find trials and tribulations ahead. You will have to make decisions you do not wish to make but nevertheless, you will have to live with the outcome. You will discover that it is not easy to be a king and neither is it easy to be a queen. Events have a tendency to unravel, not as you have planned, but as God intended. After the wedding I shall stay here in Winchester. Now you need to go to the church, for we can't have a wedding without a groom.' Having said this she turned and left.

Lady Gytha stood back from her daughter, looked her up and down thoughtfully, smiled proudly and announced, 'You look wonderful, Edith. No bride could look lovelier.'

'Fit for a king?'

'No one can rival you. Don't concern yourself with Emma, my dear; Edward is as keen as you are to put an end to her interfering.'

'He seems unable to control her.'

'Your father and the other earls will change that.'

Edith made some last minute adjustments to her appearance and when satisfied that she looked presentable, the two ladies left the room, followed by the bridesmaids. A minute later the ladies walked with decorum into the great hall where Godwin was waiting with the rest of the family and guests.

Godwin smiled proudly at his daughter and nodded to himself. Embracing Edith, he lifted her veil and kissed her on the cheek. He exchanged looks with his wife and saw in an instant she was as proud and pleased as he. Looking round, he called out to the gathering, 'Is everyone ready?'

'Yes!' came the hearty reply.

'Then leave now, and I'll follow, with Edith.'

Gradually the guests made their way through the doorway. Soon enough, with the exception of a few servants hurrying to prepare the hall for the afternoon, Godwin and his daughter were alone.

'How are you feeling?' he enquired. He could feel the tremor of her hand in his. 'In an hour or so you will be the Queen of England.'

Edith smiled to keep herself from crying. She looked up adoringly at her father. 'I suddenly feel quite afraid.'

'Edith, you've been rehearsing this for weeks. Everyone knows his part by heart. Everything will go so smoothly that it will be over before you know it.'

'Well, where is that man?'

'The monk, Herman? He'll be here in a little while. Look, here are the rest of the maids.'

With that, five bridesmaids entered the hall and took their positions with the bride. Edith gave a sigh of relief, for it seemed everything was going according to plan. The next step was to make their way over to St. Peter's and the altar.

'Where in God's name is that monk?'

Outside, people thronged the streets and hung out of every window; some sat on rooftops, others had climbed trees to get a better view. Earls, thanes and their ladies, all in their finest clothes, made the onlookers gasp in awe and squeal with delight, as they made their way to the wedding.

The front of the procession was entering the church when two handsome young men appeared from nowhere, out of breath, and with casual expertise slipped in through the crowd and took their places amongst the family. Apart from the amount of mud spattered on their boots and cloaks, a casual observer would never have guessed that only an hour ago they had been miles away, in the beds of an inn keeper's daughters. They were Harold Godwinson and his cousin Beorn Sweinson. They were just getting their breath back and feeling quite pleased at getting away with their late arrival when they heard a voice from behind them.

'I am glad you could spare the time to join us.'

'Ah, mother. You would not believe the trouble we had getting here!' said the older of the two, an easy smile spreading across his handsome face.

'You are right, Harold, I would not. You can discuss it with your father later,' Lady Gytha replied sternly.

'I'll look forward to it, Mother. You look wonderful, by the way.'

In the king's hall, Herman the monk had finally arrived to lead Edith, her father and two sisters to the church. With the monk leading the way, the little group made its way through the cheering crowd, leaving behind them a small army of attendants preparing the tables. In the hall, youths laden with armfuls of tablecloths, shuffled along under the weight of their burdens from one table to another. Others took the cloths and laid them expertly on the tables in well-practised fashion. First the frontals, which covered the table and hung down to the floor at the side away from the diners, were laid. Next, a long cloth large enough to cover the table and reach down to the floor at either end was placed over the first cloth; finally, a cloth large enough to cover the top of the table and hang down just a little on all four sides. When the tables were ready, draw-cloths were placed where the diners would sit, and bread, goblets and bowls would stand. They had until the wedding ceremony was finished to complete their tasks. Woe betide anyone who had not finished his job.

On the way to the Old Minster, the sound of organ music greeted them. This was a great relief to the monk Herman, who at the last minute had had to find beer for the seventy bellows men before they would set to work. Now, by the sound of it, the beer had arrived, the bellows were being pumped and the organ was working. Even so, as he entered the interior he had to have one swift glance just to make sure he was not hearing things. There, sure enough, he could see two monks completely absorbed in the operation of the largest organ in Europe. From its four hundred pipes breathed music as heavenly as a thousand flutes as the two clerics, with great agility, moved this way and that to push or pull the sliders to change the notes. Why they never bumped into one another he would never know.

There was a stir as the group entered. Godwin's family stood at the front of the church on the right, with the sheriffs and thanes from all the counties of Wessex behind them. On the left was Edward's family; his mother Queen Emma, his sister Countess Godgifu with her second husband, Count Eustace of Boulogne, their two sons and their wives. Behind Edward's family stood the earls and ladies of the land, and the remaining spaces were filled by the most powerful thanes in the kingdom.

At the altar, looking pale, stood the ailing Archbishop Eadsige of Canterbury and the number of anxious glances in his direction confirmed there were many who thought he would be lucky to survive the day.

The King, with Earl Leofric, whose eyebrows always gave him the look of an owl, was waiting patiently at the front of the church as his bride entered with Earl Godwin. As the choir sang, father and daughter, followed by the maids, walked down the aisle to Edward. When they arrived, Archbishop Eadsige welcomed the guests at length and after what seemed an eternity, began the ceremony.

By this point in the proceedings some of the younger members of the congregation found their attention wandering, and the Godwinsons were no exception. Harold's eyes fell on a young woman whose beauty took his breath away. She stood behind and across from him. He had to crane his neck to see her properly. He nudged Tostig, 'Who is the girl with the long chestnut hair, dressed in blue with the old couple?' he whispered.

'I've seen her before somewhere,' Tostig replied, turning around for another glimpse.

'I declare you man and wife. You may kiss the bride.' said Archbishop Eadsige with an indulgent smile.

To cheers from the congregation, King Edward gave his beautiful new bride a quick peck on the lips. The applause focused the brothers' attention back to their sister and the King.

Now they were married, Edith was taken to kneel before the altar where Eadsige anointed and crowned her, placing the crown on her head with shaking hands. Edith rose, turned and made her way over to Edward, who gave her a beatific smile. Now they had come to a part of the proceedings especially for the benefit of the crowd. Arm in arm the royal couple climbed the stairs out on to the balcony on the second floor of the six-storey tower. In the bright sunshine Edward showed his wife and queen to the massed crowd. The instant they appeared an enormous roar went up from the spectators who were dazzled by the glistening of gold and jewels in the sunlight. Edward had never felt so popular. Edith's heart soared as he raised her hand high in the air and the crowd responded in adulation. The royal couple waved to the crowd and the crowd cheered and waved back. The city had not witnessed such jubilation for a long time. Here in the heart of winter the King now had a queen and surely by autumn, fruit would be produced.

Proceeding to the great hall for the wedding feast, the guests entered the lobby and first washed their hands in a bowl of water, before drying them on the one of the towels provided. The company then made their way into the hall, where they were shown to their allocated places, to wait for the royal couple. After keeping the court waiting for a few minutes the King, with his new queen, entered from a concealed door behind the dais and they took their places. On Edward's signal the guests took their seats. The clergy, the earls and ladies looked honoured to be sitting at the top table, as did his foreign guests.

Archbishop Eadsige had been taken ill and Edward noted with satisfaction that Robert de Jumieges, Bishop of London, had taken his place.

The King had decided shortly after arriving in England that he wanted this reforming priest to remodel the English church on that of the continent. Robert's crusade against what he considered the scandalous state of English ecclesiastical affairs had won him only one friend in the kingdom — Edward. Robert's sole virtue was patience and this had rewarded him with the position of the King's favourite.

Bishop Robert, for his part, was shocked by the elegance and long fair hair of the men, which he mistook as a sign of decadence and depravity.

In accordance with protocol, the Queen raised a huge drinking horn in her hand before offering it to Edward. The King rose to his feet, thanked his guests and drank deeply from the horn before returning it to Queen Edith.

Edward indicated that Bishop Robert should stand in Archbishop Eadsige's place to break bread. The bishop was thrilled. Of all the nobles and clergy in the hall, the honour had fallen to him. He would make the most of the opportunity.

While the bishop droned on, the girl with the chestnut hair Harold had admired earlier, lifted her head imperceptibly. Looking up at the dais she saw the man who had been craning his neck to see her in church. She knew who he was and knew his reputation. She averted her eyes while grace was said but in no time at all found herself looking at him yet again. But at least she managed to concentrate enough on what was going on around her to realise the prayer was coming to an end and closed her eyes like everyone else, just in time to open them again after saying amen.

The King and his new queen had provided a fine feast for their vassals. Once the drinking horns had passed through each guest's hands and each had taken his sip of ale, paid homage to the King and acknowledged Edith as queen, the feast began in earnest.

As the afternoon wore on the celebrations took on a less formal air; jugglers and magicians entertained, while poets told stories of ancient battles fought by heroes long dead. By evening dancers and musicians appeared, tables were cleared away, music began and dancing started. Laughter grew louder. Conversations flowed in English, French, Gaelic, Latin, and Norse. The promise of a bright future hung in the air. Spirits were high and inhibitions evaporated as the drink flowed. Even the King and Queen got up to dance, Edith with grace and rhythm while Edward pranced like a pixie. His mother Emma, grimalkin and dowager queen, watched them, contempt rising in her like sap.

Further along the table, Lady Godiva, usually quite restrained, wanted to dance. Now she had plucked up the courage there was no stopping her. Wrenching a mutton chop from Earl Leofric's hand and tossing it back on to his plate, she dragged her bemused husband out onto the floor.

No one else would have got away with it.

Before Leofric could find the rhythm, Sir William Malet and his new wife, representing Duke William of Normandy, collided with them. There were smiles and apologies all round. The little accident created no problem; Leofric and Godiva were quite indulgent of the newlyweds and besides, Sir William was the son of one of Godiva's favourite ladies in waiting. She had known him since he was a boy and had a soft spot for him.

But there were a few guests still seated at the high table and not yet dancing. One of them was Harold. While the family talked around him he surveyed the dancers, looking for the girl with the chestnut hair. Then he saw her. She caught his eye and his heart missed a beat as she flashed a smile. In that moment she became the only thing that mattered to him. He watched her as she danced with his cousin Beorn. Harold saw his chance to meet the girl, rose from his chair and headed towards the dancers.

Out on the dance floor, Edward was feeling the strain of the day but showed a growing reluctance to retire to bed. He struggled to prepare for the next stage in the events, the thought of which had his mind seeking any convenient distraction. In an attempt to stay awake he decided to make small talk with Edith.

A few feet away, Harold nimbly dodged the dancers as he made his way towards the girl of his fancy. The music stopped, as did the dancing. He was surprised to discover his heart was racing and his hands shaking as he approached her. The girl appeared engrossed in conversation with Beorn and Ansgar, the wealthiest thane in East Anglia. Harold was close to her now and could see her clearly. He could hear the modulations of her voice. Her beauty almost took his breath away and he could not help but stare. She looked so vibrant, so vivacious, like life itself. Struggling to pluck up the courage to talk to her he was astonished to realise he could think of nothing to say. Feeling utterly stupid, he decided to talk to Beorn and Ansgar in the hope that one of them would introduce him.

'Beorn, Ansgar! Are you enjoying the festivities?' enquired Harold.

'Yes, I am,' replied Beorn. In an instant he knew Harold's motive in joining them. 'It's a truly wonderful evening! Tostig has been asking after you. He's just over there.'

Harold did not even turn his head. 'I've already seem him, thanks.'

'Your father is also looking for you with something important to tell you.'

With a quick glance to see if she was paying him any attention, Harold, sounding as casual as he could, said, 'I'm sure it can wait. Will you introduce us?'

'No,' Beorn replied with a grin. 'Why should I, when I know that if I do, I'll probably never see her again?'

'Beorn, don't you trust me?'

Beorn smiled, 'No. Not where women are concerned,' then he turned to the woman and with a big smile said, 'Edyth, this is my cousin Harold. Harold this is Edyth.'

'And I'm her uncle Magnus,' boomed a voice from behind Harold's shoulder.

'Pleased to meet you, Edyth,' said Harold, then turning to the huge bearded stranger, 'and pleased to meet you too, Uncle Magnus.'

'This is my cousin, Harold Godwinson,' said Beorn.

'You're Earl Godwin's son, aren't you?'

'That's right.'

'I had the pleasure of accompanying your father to Denmark to fight with Knut against the Norwegians. He's a fine man.'

'Thank you.'

'A very honourable man, especially where the ladies are concerned,' Magnus added.

'Yes, and like father, like son,' chipped in Ansgar.

'We'll see,' Magnus replied.

'I wonder if you would allow me the pleasure of a dance with your niece?' enquired Harold, with a disarming smile.

'You are most welcome, as long as she wishes to dance with you.'

Then turning to Edyth, Harold asked, 'Would you care to dance with me?'

She looked into eyes as blue and deep as the ocean and a shiver ran through her.

'Thank you,' she said. 'I would.'

At the reply, Harold felt fire tear through his veins. Excitement grew within him as he took her hand. She smiled and a flush came to her cheeks and he knew he wanted so much more than a dance. He wanted to walk her straight across the floor, right out of the door, back to his room and throw her on his bed but somehow, he thought, not even he would get away with that. Not yet, anyway.

He led Edyth on to the floor and they took their positions just in time start the next dance. The musicians struck up and everyone took their steps, the men forming the outer circle and the women the inner, each couple facing in alternate directions. As they made their way among the couples, moving this way and that, passing here and there, Harold snatched every opportunity to talk to Edyth. When he discovered she was an East Anglian, he was delighted and asked her questions about exactly where she came from. And all the while he had a manic grin on his face. By the time the dance was over Edyth was beginning to think him a little mad.

By coincidence, another Edith was beginning to wonder what was going on in the head of her partner. She was keen to make a start on her wedding night but King Edward, who usually disliked dancing, was showing an obstinate reluctance to leave the dance floor.

'Edward, if you're ready, perhaps we could retire before we're both exhausted.' She smiled seductively.

The allusion struck a note of tension in the King and for an instant he was lost for words. In that instant Edith struck. With Edward's arm in her grasp, she turned him so he was close by her side, then looked up to him and smiled. The King was still speechless as the rest of the company stood in anticipation. No one would begin another dance until the King permitted. All eyes were fixed on the royal couple.

'Good people, the time has come for me to bid you goodnight.' The King's announcement was greeted with a bawdy cheer. 'Please continue the celebration for as long as the fancy takes you,' he continued, counting the likely cost of the festivities in his head. To cheers, the newlyweds made for the bedchamber.

'Would you care for another dance, Edyth?' Harold asked.

'I would like that, but I promised my uncle Magnus that we would stay only as long as the King was present.'

Harold was about to persuade her to change her mind when he noticed Edyth's attention wander. He followed her gaze to see Magnus giving her a meaningful look.

She walked over to Magnus and as Harold watched them leave, his eyes moved up and down the length of her body. She turned to see if he was watching her just as he looked away, distracted for an instant by Beorn, and for a moment disappointment swept over her.

Still at the feast was Harold's older brother, Sweyn. He had been standing to one side with some of his cronies getting drunk. He hated this kind of occasion, being happier in the confines of a tavern, where he found life less complicated than court.

Sweyn and his few friends slipped away unnoticed, looking for a livelier party. There were plenty of places down by the quayside where a pretty woman was not averse to a good time with a fun loving man like himself. Staggering about in the dark, he found himself down by the river with his men.

Clambering onto the first ship he came across, he started looking for anything that might contain drink. With the luck of a drunk, in a moment he found what he had been looking for; a barrel. It was small but he tested it and it was full. He was about to lift it when a sailor, who had been left on board as night watchman, challenged him.

'Who are you and what do you want? ' snapped the sailor, appearing out of the night.

'Oh, in the dark, I confused this ship with my own,' slurred Sweyn casually.

The sailor was still suspicious. 'That's all right, friend. It's an easy mistake to make. Why don't you put the barrel back where you found it? Perhaps I can help you find your ship. What's it called?'

'What's it called?' repeated Sweyn, stalling for time.

'Yes. What's it called?'

Sweyn stared at the sailor with cold, blank eyes that in the darkness were the colour of the night. He tottered back slightly as he searched his drink-addled head for an answer. The sailor, thinking the stranger was about to topple over, moved forward to grab him. Sweyn whipped his head forward, butting the man square on the nose; the sailor fell over backwards, groaning with pain. Sweyn now lifted the barrel above his head and brought it crashing down on the sailor's skull as hard as he could. There was a pop as the bone smashed. The sickening sound seemed to spur Sweyn on and he stamped on his victim's face several times before looking down at the body and remarking with contempt, 'He didn't even put up a decent fight. Come on, lads, give me a hand.' His men, used to his sporadic outbursts of violence, stepped over to help. They tied up the body with a rope, weighted it and dumped it overboard. No one other than the little gang heard the splash.

Sweyn grabbed another barrel of beer to consume at his leisure. He and his men clambered back onto the quayside as Sweyn got the bung out of the barrel. He was now drinking from it, holding it above his head and pouring the beer straight down his throat and all over himself as he did so. 'Come on,' he said, 'let's go and have some fun. The drink's on me,' giving a loud guffaw. His men followed suit, laughing raucously. He and his gang wandered down a street to where they saw a light and heard laughter — a tavern. Sweyn rapped hard on the thick wooden door with his knuckles and was pleased when a good-looking young woman opened it.

"'ello 'andsome. Come in,' she welcomed him with a smile.

When he left the following morning, Sweyn had enjoyed a night of pleasure. But the woman would ever after be wary of men and distrustful of nobility in particular, left scarred in mind as well as body.

NUPTIALS

Edward climbed the stairs to his bedroom like a man heading for his execution. He felt no better when he and Edith entered the bedroom and were greeted by the aroma of dried flowers and the warm glow of beeswax candles. As the servants undressed them, Edith was disappointed that Edward appeared not to notice the undergarments she wore specially for the occasion. He stared straight ahead, transfixed like a cat, by something only he could see, hanging in the air. He bade the servants leave. The two of them were alone for the first time that day, she naked and he in a nightshirt.

Candlelight caught on golden threads in the wall hangings and glittered in the semi-darkness. Edith, her strawberry blonde hair hanging loose to her breasts, a beautiful young virgin, her skin soft and creamy, her curves accentuated by shadows, waited patiently in silent anticipation. She saw Edward, her king and husband, standing before her, older, mature and masterful. He was bound to know the ways of love. What would he do to her? What, in return, would he expect of her? Her cheeks were reddening and the flush spread down her neck, across her shoulders and down to her breasts. Her heart pounded and her blood raced through her veins. She could barely repress the urge to throw herself on the bed and let him take her there and then.

Edward moved towards her, attempted a smile, leaned over and with a trembling hand, pulled the bedclothes back for her to climb in. His heart was also beating faster. His breathing too was shorter and quicker. Edith kept her eyes on his face, all the time trying to detect an emotion. When would he pounce? She sat on the bed and turned as she lifted up her legs before slipping them under the covers. As she did this, Edward shuddered. He had caught a glimpse of what looked like an ugly wound. As he walked slowly round to his side of the bed a picture of her imagined injury ran through his mind. He had seen an evil-looking cut, which looked sore and could not have healed. Worse still, she had hair!

As he made his journey round the foot of the bed, Edith watched Edward closely. She thought about the consideration he was showing her. He was taking his time; putting her at ease before sharing his passion, prolonging the anticipation. How considerate he was.

Edward climbed gingerly into bed beside her. Edith wriggled over toward him expectantly, like a puppy wanting to play. She smiled and put her warm hand on his white, hairless chest. She looked at him with sparkling, doe-like eyes. He returned her look but recoiled as his senses reached saturation point. He had had enough. He had seen her disfigured body, felt its touch and now he could smell, at close proximity, the womanly fragrances emitted by her and it disturbed him. This was all too much. Godwin, he was convinced, had palmed him off with a freak.

'Edith, excuse me, my dear,' he said earnestly, 'I need spiritual guidance.'

'What?'

'I must seek spiritual guidance?'

'What, now?'

'Yes, now.' Edward jumped out of bed and dressed faster than he had ever done, then left the room as though escaping a fire.

Later that night, after she had finished crying, Edith lay in the nuptial bed wondering whatever had she done wrong but she had a growing awareness that perhaps the fault lay in Edward. This feeling would be confirmed during her lifetime. But for now, echoes of overheard whispered conversations and recollections of some of Sweyn's jibes, jibes she had thought odd at the time, flew through her weary mind.

Edward's spiritual guidance took the form of a visit to Robert de Jumieges. Robert was surprised to see Edward and greeted him with a warm welcome and offered him wine.

'This is a calamity, Robert, a complete calamity. You must know something of these things. Surely you can advise me.' With an imploring look he asked, 'Can I have the marriage annulled?'

'Annulled? This is all a little sudden, my Lord. Take a deep breath and compose yourself. Perhaps if you sat down here,' he offered, indicating the bed. 'There, now you can relax and tell me everything.'

Edward told de Jumieges all about how Edith had looked naked. 'She's not like you and me, Robert,' the King complained, the disappointment welling up inside him.

'All women are like that,' spat Robert in reply. 'They are the devil's work. It was they who had us cast out of Eden. Remember they are the daughters of Eve. To be charitable, they can't help themselves but are nevertheless best avoided.'

'You mean Edith is not a freak?'

'No more so than the rest of them.'

'Oh my God, it's worse than I thought. Does this mean I will never be rid of her?'

'Only for the time being,' and then as an afterthought, 'some more wine, my Lord?'

Edward accepted de Jumieges' offer. His goblet refilled, he sat and talked with the bishop. Edward was glad he had come to see his friend; he was a good man, a Norman, someone he could trust, someone to whom he could open his heart. And so he did. Then the two men prayed to God for guidance. It was dawn before they had finished talking and it was during this time de Jumieges became the first person in England to realise there was still a succession problem.

The new day brought a fresh, more positive mood to Edward and he returned to his chamber to greet his new queen good morning.

'You've been praying all this time,' observed Edith bitterly. 'You must have done wicked things, to be on your knees in front of de Jumieges all night.'

'What do you mean?'

'Edward, do you think it appropriate for a man who has been in confession all night to act so innocent?'

'What are you trying to say?'

'Given the choice between spending the night with your newly wedded wife or the Bishop of London, you choose the latter. Do you think it any way for a man to behave?'

'I am the King. It is for me to decide how I behave. I am not like other men.'

'I'm well aware of that!'

'What do you mean?' he replied.

Edith sighed. Looking him in the eye she saw a man in hiding.

'It was our wedding night, Edward. Why would you wish to spend it with anyone but me?'

'I had spiritual matters to attend to,' he said in his defence, realising even as he spoke how weak he sounded.

'The Kingdom desperately needs an heir to the throne. It is our duty to provide one.'

'God will provide a successor to the Crown.'

'And how do think that will happen?'

'I spoke with our Lord the Creator last night and I am to remain chaste and he will provide. Come to breakfast, my dear.' He smiled and bounced out of the door.

THE EARL HAROLD

A month later, Harold Godwinson, the new Earl of East Anglia, was out hunting in the Cambridgeshire countryside, accompanied by half a dozen of his men, a hawk and a couple of dogs. His friend Ansgar, a powerful landowner, had been instructed by King Edward to act as guide and mentor for the new earl. Ansgar too was fond of hawking and introducing the new earl to the county was more enjoyable than he had hoped.

Harold was also looking for a place to live, ideally not far from London, with easy access to the sea and with good hunting. This was not the place. He never intended it to be but it was close to someone he was contriving to meet. While he prepared his bird for the hunt, two of his men approached on horseback.

'Well, what did she say?' asked Harold, sensing from the look on the rider's faces all was not as it should be.

'She said she would be pleased to come, but it would have to be another time.'

Harold mulled things over for a moment and then looked pleased with himself. 'Let's try another field where we might find better hunting,' he said, moving off.

Half an hour later, Harold and his companions arrived at West Wickham. 'Let's see how good the sport is here,' said Harold, pointing his horse into the light breeze. Searching around for a few moments, he spotted a couple of rooks in a small blackthorn tree. Checking his dogs had also seen them, he signalled to make chase. The two hounds raced, barking and yapping, towards the tree. Harold's men, on horseback, cantered after them. With about ten yards to go the rooks took flight.

With expert skill, Harold removed the hood from his falcon's head and pulled the leash. By the time the rooks had left their shelter his bird was ready to fly. Taking a second to adjust to the situation, she saw the rooks in flight and took off from Harold's leather-gloved fist.

The rooks rose from the tree and turned to head downwind as they climbed. They saw the falcon and wheeled round, back into the wind. By now the falcon was already above them, climbing fast so as to make her first stoop. She had already singled out her intended victim. As she dived the rooks shifted, twisting and turning in the air to avoid the deadly sharp talons of their hunter. Succeeding, they turned back downwind to gain more speed and head back to the rookery. The falcon came back up above them and stooped again, this time coming much closer to its ducking, diving, dodging quarry. The rooks evaded two more stoops before the final attack, just yards away from the shelter of their home, but they were too late. The falcon took her prey, ripping her target out of the sky and down to the ground in an instant; then bobbing up and down in some grim parody of mating, she kneaded her victim with her talons.

Beneath the birds, racing on horseback, the men followed the scene as they chased across the fields in pursuit. They approached the falcon and Harold dismounted, producing some meat from one of his saddlebags, which he offered to the bird. The falcon climbed back on his glove and took the titbit. When she had finished, Harold hooded her and remounted.

Sitting astride his horse he spotted two riders approaching at the gallop, their long winter cloaks trailing in the air behind them. One was a man, the other a woman. He was tall and powerfully built and wore a quilted leather-studded tunic, and from his belt hung a sword and a long dagger. The woman was dressed for riding, wearing loose-fitting linen breeches, a thigh-length tunic and a long cloak; her long chestnut hair was tied back in a single tight plait. Harold recognised her the instant he saw her.

The riders brought their mounts to a halt facing Harold's party. They were both red-faced and out of breath. Harold could not help noticing the way the woman's chest heaved.

'Good morning, Lady Edyth, what a surprise it is to see you here!'

'Really? And why is that?'

'Well, I didn't expect to find you wandering in the country.'

'I'm not wandering in the country. This is my land. It would seem it is you who are wandering.'

'My Lady, please accept my most profound apologies,' said Harold, with a broad grin. 'I thought I was on common land. I can assure you I made a genuine mistake and meant no harm by it. Perhaps I can make amends by offering you a place at my table this evening?'

'Your table?'

'Yes, I have been made a gift of Sawston.'

'It's beautiful; I trust you like it. You must have done something very special to have been given so fine a place. So, will you be living there now?'

'Not permanently. I have business in Cambridge tomorrow and thought I might do well to make the acquaintance of my neighbours. It's such a piece of good luck to find you like this.'

'So, you're not living here?'

'I regret it's too far from the centre of things. Waltham in Essex is where I'll probably live.'

'Oh, I see. Well, while you're here and as you're new to the area, I should offer you hospitality. You will be my guest. I insist, and you too, Ansgar.' Edyth turned to her companion, who had remained quiet but observant the whole time. 'Come, Finn, I'll race you back.'

The two turned and immediately their horses took off at a gallop, leaving Harold to continue his sport. As he watched them ride away he could not help but admire her horsemanship. She rode well and with obvious pleasure. He watched her until she disappeared over the brow of a ridge, enjoying the sight of the back of the saddle slapping her buttocks, the slight wobble caused by the shock accentuating their firmness.

It was dark that evening when Harold, Ansgar and their men arrived at Edyth's home in West Wickham. The stars twinkled brightly in the cold clear sky and a wolf howled in the distance. Edyth's companion of earlier that day stepped out from the house, greeted them and showed them where to put their horses before escorting the guests through to a modest hall.

As he entered, Harold was surprised to find quite a few other guests. Although he had had no introductions, it was evident that he was known to everyone there because they all rose when he entered and called out in greeting. Harold made his way to the top table, one of five being used for the evening; he smiled and acknowledged everyone present. His men were offered places on the bench at a lower table. Skalpi joined Harold and Ansgar with Edyth at the top table. A huge scar ran in a crescent round the right side of Skalpi's face. It started in his hairline and ran across the edge of his temple, just missing his ear, then down the edge of his jaw to his chin. It was a fearsome thing to behold but for the most part was covered by his hair and walrus moustache.

The hall, though modest, was warm and cosy. Shutters kept out the cold winter night and the fire provided warmth and added light to that provided by the candles. There were about thirty guests in all. As far as Harold could tell, they were local thanes, with their wives and families. Apart from Ansgar and Skalpi, with him on the top table were Finn, Edyth and an older couple. He recognised the man as Edyth's uncle, Magnus. He sat down and was offered a goblet of mead.

'Welcome, Earl Harold.'

'Good evening, Lady Edyth.' Harold took her hand and kissed it.

'Welcome to you too, Ansgar,' she said with a smile and nodded a welcome to Skalpi. 'You remember my uncle Magnus.'

'It is a great pleasure to meet you again, Magnus.'

'The pleasure is all mine,' said the old man, greeting his guest with a hug. 'Ansgar, what a pleasure it is to see you again,' and subjected him to the same treatment.

'And this is my aunt Wulfgith,' Edyth continued with the introductions. 'Welcome to our home, Earl Harold, it's a privilege to have you and your companions with us tonight.'

'Thank you, Lady Wulfgith, but the privilege is mine,' responded Harold, before kissing her hand.

'Harold, would you grant us the favour of a few words before we continue with the evening?'

Magnus turned to face the hall and requested everyone's attention for Harold, Earl of East Anglia. To enthusiastic applause, the new earl rose as though he had been born to public speaking. He thanked his audience and complimented them on their industry, their abilities in agriculture and commerce, their renowned seafaring skills, the quality of their products and their fine reputation at home and abroad as virtuous God-fearing people. What is more, he sounded absolutely sincere in everything he said. All were convinced that now Anglia had its own earl to represent it at court, its people would be so much closer to the King. They were happy to welcome their new earl but most importantly for Harold, Lady Edyth was impressed. He knew it and this thrilled him more than the cheers and acknowledgement of his audience.

He sat down and the food was served. The ideal guest, Harold gave kudos to the house and the assembled guests, making conversation easily with anyone, on his or her own level. He joked and laughed but listened as well as he talked. He spent a considerable amount of time talking to Magnus and Wulfgith and had a positive impact on them both.

As the evening progressed and the novelty of being at supper with a nobleman began to wane, people started to converse in their own little groups, always keeping an eye on the top table for any change of mood. Harold took advantage of the change of focus to turn his attention to Edyth. He told her that becoming an earl would entail big changes and that his parents expected him to take a wife, perhaps a noble lady from the continent.

She told him of the death of her parents from plague. She had no brothers or sisters; after giving birth to Edyth, her mother was never able to have any more children. The two relaxed and talked until it was late. The women and a few children retired to the bowers. The men were given blankets to wrap themselves up in when they chose to sleep, in whatever spot they could find in the hall. Edyth's uncle and aunt let it be known they were about to retire for the night. After they left their guests, Edyth told Harold she too would be leaving him.

'It is time, too, for me to go to bed. A room has been reserved for you, naturally.'

'Thank you, but I had hoped we might have some time alone.'

'Why?'

'Well, to be honest, I thought tonight might have been a little more…'

'Intimate?' she suggested with a smile. 'I thought you were keen to meet people who live in the area.'

'I am.'

'You must be glad of this opportunity, then.'

'I am.'

Edyth returned his look in silence. The upturned corners of her mouth betrayed her amusement at his predicament.

'I am. I am. I'm very glad,' he said, trying to sound earnest.

'Good. I'm happy you're glad,' she replied with a grin.

'Well, then I'm glad you're happy,' he laughed.

They both felt foolish.

Suddenly a serious-looking woman appeared, walked briskly over to Edyth, and whispered, 'I'm sorry to interrupt, my lady, but Thorkell is upset. He's had a very bad dream and can't be calmed by anyone. He's insisting on seeing you.'

Edyth nodded, 'I'll be along in a moment.' Then turning to Harold she excused herself and bade him goodnight.

Harold asked Finn about the child. He discovered the boy was an orphan taken into care by Edyth after his parents had been killed in a pirate raid. He was touched by her kindness.

The next day, Harold and his men stepped out into the cold morning air. Their horses were already tacked up and waiting to go. As Harold was about to mount his horse, Edyth came out of the house towards him.

'Were you going to leave without saying goodbye?' she asked.

'I have to attend to some business in Cambridge and we must make haste. I didn't want to disturb your household.'

'That's considerate of you.'

'Perhaps we will meet again. I will be in London for the King's court at Easter. Perhaps I'll see you there?'

'Why would I be there?'

'You were at the King's wedding.'

'Only to keep uncle Magnus company.'

'Then come and keep me company.'

'I don't think it's your place, grand though you are, to invite me to the King's court,' she replied.

Harold tried once more, 'If you think it unseemly to attend the Easter court, will you agree to visit me at Whitsuntide? By then I should be at Waltham.'

'I would have to ask my uncle and I'm not sure what he would think.'

'I'm sure he wouldn't mind a bit.'

'You seem quite sure of that.'

'Oh, I am. I invited him and your aunt last night. I'm sure they'll be delighted to have you accompany them,' he said, smiling that prepossessing smile of his that she found more attractive each time she saw it.

'In that case,' she replied, 'who am I to argue?' all the time wondering what she had let herself in for.

'Good, until Whitsun, then. Farewell and God be with you.'

'And God be with you too, Earl Harold.'

A VIKING PROBLEM

Earl Godwin, having been summoned by the King, was in Edward's private chambers. He and the king exchanged pleasantries before Edward enquired of Godwin, 'I suppose you've been wondering why I asked to see you?'

'Yes I have.'

'King Magnus of Norway has sent me a letter in which he reminds me of the Gota River Agreement. He's decided he, not I, should be the rightful King of England. I think we can look forward to an invasion attempt in the summer.'

The problem raised by the Gota River Agreement concerned Edward's right to rule England. Several years before Edward had come to the throne, Harthacnut, King of England and Denmark, had agreed with Magnus that he would recognise the independence of Norway as a separate kingdom and it was agreed in a second compact that when one of them died, the other would inherit his kingdoms.

A few years later, when King Harthacnut died, in accordance with the agreement, Magnus claimed Denmark as his own. But King Swein and the Danes had other ideas. Magnus set out to take his new kingdom by force. To Edward he wrote that out of compassion for his harsh early life in exile, he would withhold his claim to the English throne for Edward's lifetime but reserved his right to claim it on his death. Now a series of events had caused him to change his mind. He was engrossed in a war with Denmark and wanted Edward's help. Edward had refused. Magnus was now preparing to invade England, believing that with the combined resources of England and Norway, he would be able to deal Swein a fatal blow. In his letter, Magnus announced his intention to claim the English throne as his own. Should he acquiesce, Edward would be allowed to return to Normandy or any other country of his choice. On the other hand, should he fail to agree to the request, he could expect a Viking army to cross the North Sea before the end of the summer.

'Well what do you think?' enquired Edward, tentatively, knowing Godwin would support Swein, who was his nephew.

'Have you replied to this letter, my Lord?'

'No, I want to put it before the Easter Court.'

'As you wish, my Lord.'

'Another matter I wish to discuss with you concerns your son, Sweyn. The Bishop of Worcester in particular is quite disturbed by his behaviour. He runs wild. There are stories about abuse of power and privilege, pocketing fines imposed on transgressors, running amok on hunting parties. They say he was out hunting a boar, which was eventually cornered but he'd used up all his spears so leaped off his horse and killed the beast with his bare hands. Broke its neck, apparently.'

'That sounds like Sweyn,' Godwin laughed, 'but surely killing a boar with his bare hands is cause of celebration, not condemnation.'

'But he did it in the grounds of Hereford Abbey on Sunday morning.'

'Oh, oh I see,' said Godwin, his laughter quickly subsiding. 'Yes, he is spirited and sometimes a little thoughtless but he doesn't mean any harm. I'll have a word with him. Is there anything else, my Lord?'

'No.'

'Until next week then.'

'Until next week.'

Around the tables in the great hall sat the finest in the land. King Edward and Queen Edith, with the old dowager, Queen Emma, sat at the head table. Most of the earls were there: Siward of Northumbria, with his nephew Malcolm Canmore, the exiled claimant to the Scottish throne, Leofric of Mercia, Godwin of Wessex, Harold of East Anglia and Godwin's nephew, Beorn of Hertfordshire. Of the earls only Sweyn was missing. He claimed to have urgent business in Wales.

Invited sheriffs and thanes were present, though few in number. Leofric and Siward were unhappy now the Godwin family outvoted them. Robert de Jumieges, the newly appointed Bishop of London, represented the clergy.

The meeting progressed more or less as Godwin expected. King Magnus would be informed that Edward was regarded by all as the rightful King of England and would not recognise Magnus's claim to the throne. If Magnus were to recognise Edward, the English would send no help to Swein. The court expected a flat rejection of its offer and in anticipation of a Norwegian invasion would gather the English fleet at Sandwich.

There was dissension over the policy. Godwin wanted to aid his nephew against the forces of Magnus and stated his case. 'If we help Swein and he is successful, we have an ally against Magnus should he make any future claim to the throne of England. If Magnus defeats Swein, then he will be able to use the resources of two countries to mount an invasion against us.'

Edward was not impressed with Godwin's argument. 'On the other hand, we might provoke Magnus even more and who knows, Swein might invade us once he has disposed of Magnus and tell me, where will we be then?'

'We could make Swein a loan of a few ships and some fighting men.' Godwin countered.

'Isn't that the same thing? I think we ought to let them fight it out and in the meantime guard our coast. What does the council think?'

With the exception of Godwin, Harold and Beorn, the council favoured Edward's plan, if only because Godwin did not.

Next was the appointment of clergy, which went smoothly enough. The monk Herman was nominated by Edward as Bishop of Ramsbury and the appointment went through unopposed.

Regenbald was appointed Chancellor and welcomed by all at court. There was not a sharper administrative mind in Europe and it was seen as only fitting that he take up the vacant position.

After the council meeting, Godwin, Harold and Beorn went back to Southwark to discuss events. A few minutes' ride took them across the Thames to Godwin's Southwark residence. As the three rode across the courtyard and up to the hall the servants sprang into life, performing their assigned duties with vigour. It was easy to see Godwin's anger and no one wanted to incur his wrath. The earls dismounted and Godwin strode into his hall with Harold and Beorn hard on his heels.

'What's the point in having relatives if you don't have alliances with them?' Godwin was seething and kicked over a chair. 'What does he think the point of marriage is? He seems to have forgotten that now he's married to Edith, all of her relatives are now his. He could use this to England's and his own advantage. Swein is his family now, and yet he seems to think he has no obligation. My God, there's an opportunity here to bring Denmark and England together again and to make us both the stronger for it, yet he's passing up the chance. Who knows, some time in the future we could have a united kingdom of England, Denmark and Norway, just as we did in Knut's time. Think of that!'

'You think he's against this because he hates the Danes?' Harold asked tentatively.

'Of course.'

'But surely, a king wouldn't allow his personal feelings to cloud his judgment when the matter is so important.'

'Not in Edward's case and I'm afraid that might always be so. But still, we won't give up, eh, lads? One day we'll win him round.'

Neither of them was optimistic enough to think Edward would ever see eye-to-eye with a Godwin over the Danes or Denmark. They waited for him to resume speaking.

'Anyway, I have another happier matter to discuss,' he continued in a lighter tone. 'Harold, you would never let your heart rule your head in matters politic, would you now?'

Harold was on his guard in an instant. He had fallen foul of his father's traps too often and was alert to any danger that might lie in an innocent-sounding remark.

'You know me, Father, my heart rules my head every time,' he replied.

'Harold, you are too modest. When it comes to politics you have a reputation for being most astute. That's why I know you'll be glad to hear your mother and I have at last found someone for you. She has everything a nobleman could want in a woman – a fine genealogy and a good education in the finest nunnery in Flanders. She is a sparkling conversationalist, a great beauty and what's more, has a fine dowry. She is none other than the Lady Judith, sister of Count Baldwin of Flanders.' Godwin was beaming his roguish grin, happy that something has worked out that day.

'Well that's a great honour and I thank you for it.'

'Good, I'm glad you're pleased. Your mother is delighted.'

'I didn't say I'd marry her.'

Silence descended on the room. Few defied Godwin.

'May I ask why?'

'I've never met her and I don't know her.'

'I have told you about her. What more is there to tell?'

'I haven't seen her for myself. We might not make such a good match.'

'I'll be the judge of that.'

'Father, I'm not saying I won't marry her. What I am saying is that I won't marry someone I don't know.'

'I don't think you understand, Harold. It's taken months to arrange this.'

'Why didn't you consult me?'

'We didn't want to disappoint you in case negotiations fell through. Anyway, there seemed no need.'

'Why not?'

'Harold, a lot of preparation has gone into this; to back out now would be an insult to Baldwin. It will bring disgrace on our family and think how much you'll disappoint your mother. You have to marry Lady Judith. It's all arranged.'

'And if I don't?'

'You will, Harold. It is your duty as a son.'

'Do you think it the duty of a son to marry a woman of his parents' choice?'

Just as Harold knew it would, this final comment stopped Godwin in his tracks. Lady Gytha's parents had not welcomed his attentions all those years ago. They had had hopes for someone better but little say in the matter of whom their daughter married.

'Times have changed, Harold. We are a highly respected family. This marriage will bring power to us and where there is power, there is security. You know that.'

'Yes, but I haven't said I won't marry her, just that I can't promise I will.'

'I need to give Baldwin a date for the wedding. Harold, I think it best you give this some serious thought and when you are calmer, come to me with your answer. Take as much time as you need.'

'Thank you.'

'Let me have your decision by the end of the week.'

'It will remain the same.'

WHITSUN AT WALTHAM

So abundant was the May blossom that year that its weight forced boughs to droop to the earth. In the woods the last of the spring bluebells carpeted the ground. The trees flushed fresh green, the new season's leaves bright against a clear blue sky. Everywhere the scent of early summer hung heavy in the air. Through the sultry air four riders were seen approaching Harold's hall, which lay on the edge of Waltham. One of the riders blew his horn to signify he was coming in friendship. Harold watched them approach and instantly recognised Edyth, Magnus, Wulfgith and Finn. He walked round to the front of his hall to greet them.

The four dismounted and their horses were led away by a servant, while another servant took care of their baggage. A maid appeared and took Magnus, Wulfgith and Edyth to their rooms. Once she had unpacked, Edyth changed into her finest dress and waited until she heard Magnus and Wulfgith before opening her door to greet them in the passage. The three of them then made their way to the hall to join the rest of the guests.

Edyth was feeling a little nervous. Finn was talking with Harold and she recognised Ansgar and Skalpi but the others were unknown to her. She could not help but notice there were several other women there, all of whom seemed better dressed than her. She glanced quickly round the room and noticed there was food and drink in abundance. The hall itself, though spacious, seemed rather bare. Perhaps Harold needed more time to do something with it, she thought.

Harold caught sight of Edyth the instant she entered the room and went over to join her, taking Ansgar with him. A servant appeared with a tray, some goblets and a jug of wine. Ansgar engaged Magnus and Wulfgith in small talk, enquiring about their journey. As Edyth sipped her wine Harold said, 'I'll introduce you to people as we take our places.'

'Do you have many guests staying here, Harold?'

'About forty have travelled here and there are some local people. Why do you ask?'

'I had expected something more... ' she hesitated.

'More intimate?' he suggested mischievously.

'Yes,' she smiled.

'Come, join me at the table,' he invited, as he started heading toward the dais.

As he took his place at the high table, Edyth took hers beside him. Ansgar led Magnus and Wulfgith to their places and the steward guided everyone else. Once they had sat down, the conversation continued.

'Is Waltham yours now?'

'Yes. It was a gift from King Edward when he made me an earl. The land and buildings belonged to Tovi the Proud. He and the King had a difference of opinion and what was once Tovi's is now mine. I am told Tovi has gone to live in Denmark.'

'That was fortunate.'

'For me, yes. It was Tovi who had the Holy Cross brought here from Somerset.'

'The Holy Cross?'

'According to the story, a carpenter in Somerset had the same dream for three nights, instructing him to dig on the hill above his village. At first he ignored the dream but each night it returned and so eventually he decided he had better start digging. He dug a great hole in the place he'd been shown in his dream and there he found a marble slab broken in two and under it a huge cross with an image of Christ cut into black flint. Beneath the crucifix were a book, a bell and a smaller cross. He was amazed but unsure of what to do, so he went to Tovi, who at that time was the lord of the village. Tovi thought the best place for the relics was a religious centre but was undecided, so he had the treasures loaded onto a cart which was hitched up to two oxen. He stood in front of them calling the names of every abbey or minster he could think of until the oxen moved.'

'Who told you this?'

'Leofgar.'

'Leofgar?'

Harold indicated, with a nod, a huge man like a Norse seafarer dressed in a cleric's garb. 'I introduced you earlier.'

Edith looked over. 'Ah yes, I remember, he stood next to Ansgar. And it was not a joke?'

'No, I assure you, it was not. To continue the story: Tovi called out the names of the grandest and greatest places in the land but the oxen refused to move until Waltham was mentioned. Only then did the cart begin to trundle forward and so the cross was brought right across the country to be here. Tovi had the church rebuilt to house the relics and people came from far and wide to see their wonder.'

'It must have brought trade to the town.'

'I suppose so, yes.'

'That was fortunate for Tovi.'

Harold gave her a stern look.

'That the oxen insisted on bringing it here is almost a miracle,' she said, with an impish look in her eyes.'

'Quite.'

Sitting next to Harold at the high table that evening was a real honour for Edyth that both flattered and embarrassed her. The evening was much grander than Harold had experienced at West Wickham and she was flattered because she was treated as an esteemed guest, but embarrassed at the humble fare they had offered the earl. But as the evening wore on and she and Harold talked, she relaxed. Harold appeared naturally gregarious and seemed to enjoy entertaining. Ansgar was getting on very well with Magnus but Harold was careful to include as many guests as possible in conversation.

After a wonderful evening of food, wine and entertainment the women went to bed, leaving the men telling tales that grew wilder and bawdier as the night wore on.

The next morning a cock crowed to announce daybreak. The church bell rang and Harold and his guests made their way to church. The party, with everyone dressed in white as was the custom at Whitsuntide, made its way to the crowded church. Entering with Harold, Edyth approached the altar, noticing with each footstep beautifully coloured frescoes depicting scenes she recognised from the Bible. And there, in pride of place to one side of the altar, standing against the wall was the holy cross of Waltham.

'Do you like our little church?' asked Harold.

'It's beautiful.'

'I have plans for something much greater.'

'That is a pity. This seems perfect.'

'Well, I think the Holy Cross deserves something more.'

Their conversation ended as Leofgar entered to take Whitsuntide mass. After celebrating, the congregation collected their weapons from the porch where they had left them before returning to Harold's hall to change for a visit to the local fair.

An hour later, after they had changed, Harold and his guests were making their way back to the village when they were greeted by laughter and good-natured shouting. Peddlers, musicians, jugglers, magicians and anyone with a talent for entertainment had arrived, hoping for rich pickings from the extra crowds who had turned up to see the new earl. Some of the more accomplished hoped for an invitation to perform at Harold's home that evening and for a few, their efforts were rewarded.

Joining in all the games, enjoying all the distractions, Harold and Edyth fell into easy laughter. She admired him when he won an archery competition. He found her confidence in his abilities flattering. When the time came, he was reluctant for them to leave.

But the evening lay ahead and in good humour the party made its way home, knowing the pleasure would continue. The only shadow cast over Harold's day was the thought that he might be sickening for a cold.

That evening, Edyth once again sat at the high table with Harold, as did Magnus and Wulfgith. Finn was there, of course, sitting with Harold's housecarls, who had welcomed him warmly.

'What is planned for us tomorrow, Harold?' enquired Edric of Laxfield, landowner and shire reeve, one of Harold's guests for the holiday.

'I thought we might go hawking... '

'Harold,' Edyth interrupted, 'do you know that man?'

Harold and the shire reeve followed her gaze to a tall man moving from table to table. Neither of them knew him. 'Why do you ask?' said Harold.

'He has a great many pockets in his cloak and most of them are stuffed with food from your tables.'

'Let's see who he is.' Getting to his feet, Harold called out, 'You there!'

The thief, like everyone else, looked round. Everyone else had the luxury of following the earl's gaze; the stranger did not.

'Who, me?' was the meek reply.

'Yes, you. Come here.'

The man complied and nervously approached Harold's table.

'Who are you and what are you doing here?'

'My name is Herfast, my Lord.'

'And who speaks for you?'

There followed a silence.

'Well?'

'No one, my Lord, at least, no one here.' He slouched and had difficulty meeting Harold's gaze.

'Then what are you doing here?'

'I'm a peddler, my Lord, from Ipswich, here for the fair. I heard that the entire village was invited to the feast and I thought it churlish not to come too.'

'You knew, did you not, that the invitation was meant for those who lived in the village and on my land?'

'No I didn't, my Lord,' Herfast lied.

'You thought you'd join in the celebration with everyone else?'

'That's right, my Lord'

'So tell me, Herfast, why are you lining your pockets with our food? Is that an Ipswich custom?'

The thief would have to think fast now.

'No, no, my Lord. No, it's not an Ipswich custom, my Lord. It's my wife, she's... err, she's ill, you see.'

If it came to the ordeal he knew he could not stand it. Pulling an iron rod from coals or lifting hot stones from boiling water to prove his innocence had no appeal for him. He knew his hands would blister and bleed; the sure sign of a transgressor.

'You're sure of that, are you?'

Images of infected wounds and damaged hands shot through Herfast's mind.

'I am, my Lord, I am.'

'Usually when people are ill they lose their appetite but I'd say by the contents of your pockets, your wife is voracious.'

'Well, she's making a bit of a recovery, my Lord. I just wanted to help her along.'

'You know, Herfast, I'm glad to hear it.'

'Thank you, my Lord. That's very kind of you, if I may be so bold as to say so.'

'Tell me, Herfast, I am, as you may know, not from these parts; I am in fact from Wessex. Do you know anything of me by reputation?'

'I do indeed, my Lord. It is said you are a kind and generous man, my Lord and honest and fair, it's said. And very forgiving,' he added hopefully.

'Quite,' said Harold, reaching for a flagon of beer, everyone in the hall watching closely to see what would happen next. 'You know, I wouldn't want to ruin my reputation so soon and have you or your wife think me mean,' he continued, rising to his feet. 'With all that food you have for her, your wife will work up quite a thirst,' he said, walking right up to his uninvited guest. 'So it's probably best if you take her something to drink.' And with that Harold pulled on the stranger's coat, exposing a hidden pocket, and poured in the entire contents of the flagon. The thief stood shamed, drenched down his front. Everyone erupted into raucous laughter.

'Which do you find more humiliating, Herfast, getting caught or looking a fool?' said Harold quietly.

The man's face was crimson. He looked fit to cry and yet full of fury but he said nothing.

Harold looked more serious now. 'Tell me, Herfast, what do they do with thieves in Ipswich?'

The man remained silent.

Harold stepped towards Herfast until their faces were only inches apart.

'I'll ask you again, Herfast, if that's your name. What do they do with thieves in Ipswich?'

'They cuts off their hand, my Lord,' came the choked reply.

'The hand that committed the theft?'

'Yes, my Lord.'

'Then swear to me you won't steal anything again.'

'I swear I won't steal anything, ever again, my Lord, I swear.'

'Then you'd better get back to your wife.'

Herfast made his way to the door where he was stopped by the steward who relieved him of his plunder and sent him on his way with a cuff round the ear.

Despite an unsuccessful day's hawking, Harold and his male guests returned in good spirits. The women had remained indoors catching up on news and their embroidery. For Edyth the time had dragged. Pleased though she was to make the acquaintance of so many fine ladies, she just wanted to see Harold again. It was the dragging of the time that first alerted her to her feelings towards him, that and her inability to concentrate on anything for more than a minute at a time. Magnus knew nothing of his niece's feelings but Wulfgith noticed how her behaviour changed whenever Harold was present. To her it seemed almost as if Edyth's entire vocabulary consisted of only one word and that word was Harold. She said as much to Magnus that evening before they went down to eat and he dismissed the idea as wishful thinking. But later that same evening, after he had observed Harold and Edyth together, he was inclined to agree with his wife.

The following day the guests were dismayed to find Harold was not with them. He had still not stirred from his bed when the guests began to leave. The task of bidding farewell was left to Wynfrith, Harold's steward. Edyth was concerned when she heard of Harold's illness. His steward explained Harold's symptoms and Edyth immediately decided to stay. Magnus and Wulfgith would return to West Wickham and Finn would stay at Waltham with Edyth as the eyes and ears of Magnus. Against Wynfrith's protestations, Edyth made her way to Harold's room.

'Earl Harold is not well, my lady, and I'm afraid it must be serious if he can't leave his bed.'

'I'll see him.'

'He wants no visitors, my lady.'

'But I must see him. Where is he?

Wynfrith led her to Harold's room where the earl lay in a hot fever, delirious, complaining of cold and dreadful pain from an ulcer on the back of his hand. He was also suffering cramps and vomiting. She placed her hand on his forehead and felt him burning. Taking his hand, she was alarmed to see it red, swollen and badly ulcerated.

'How long has he been like this?'

'It must have come on in the night, my lady. One of his falcons pecked his hand a couple of days ago, just where the ulcer is'

'Are you giving him anything for it?'

'No, my lady. I've just given him something for the fever.'

'I'll make him something to help. Where do you keep your herbs, Wynfrith?'

In the kitchen Edyth began mixing herbs with a mortar and pestle. Her aunt had taught her the healing arts and she had a remedy for everything. Edyth used a knife to beat an egg, the better to cut through the pain. She mixed the egg with mugwort, plantain, chamomile, nettle, crab-apple, chervil, fennel, betony and finally some ash, all the while muttering a charm to herself as she did so. Edyth finally had the salve prepared, which she insisted on carrying up to Harold's room herself. She persuaded him to let her apply it to the ulcer on his hand while she whispered her charm.

Edyth stayed with him awhile, talking to him when he seemed in need of reassurance, calming him when he was confused and nursing him like a mother would her child. But the fever grew worse. After two days, in desperation she called for Leofgar, in the hope that he might be able to help. He arrived promptly.

'You look exhausted, my lady,' he said. 'You need rest too. I'll send for some of the brothers who will take him to the abbey, where we can care for him night and day.'

'No. No. I can take care of him. I thought you might know of some remedy for his ills.'

'Edyth, if we don't take care of him in the abbey, I'm afraid you too might become ill. May I suggest Earl Harold stays with us, where we will take care of him? You may visit whenever you choose.'

She acquiesced; surprised that someone who looked so fearsome could be so gentle.

Within an hour the earl was in the abbey. A monk sat with him at all times but his condition continued to deteriorate, despite the prayers that were offered for him without respite. The next morning Edyth went to see him and was alarmed to find that he had swellings on the elbows and under each armpit, though the ulcer on his hand was no worse. Harold's fever was extremely high and yet he shook with chills. She could not bear to leave him, though the monks insisted she spent each night at his hall. The days passed; she and the monks fed the sick earl with brews, broths and all manner of herbal concoctions but his condition was gradually deteriorating.

As May turned to June, the lumps on Harold's elbows and armpits grew bigger, burst and then drained. All this time he lived in a fever.

After three weeks Harold was still suffering. The egg-sized swellings that had plagued him so much were gone, only to be replaced by pains in the chest each time he breathed. He was also coughing up blood. His illness seemed to stretch on for an eternity, until he could barely remember ever having felt well. Then after another three weeks, Harold's fever faded, the chills disappeared, the coughing stopped and he regained, if only slightly, his colour. He survived, but only just. Recovering but completely debilitated, he had to rest to regain his strength.

Eventually Harold was well enough to venture outside to walk a few steps in the warm summer air. When he and Edyth had time on their hands, they would sit and talk for hours, taking shade from the harsh summer sun beneath a walnut tree that stood in the abbey grounds.

She told him of her life, her childhood spent on the coast, how she became orphaned, how her father had died defending her mother from pirates and how her uncle and aunt took her in. He told her of his life of privilege and hardship, learning English, Latin, Norse, mathematics, theology and history, not to mention military training and his childhood fear of his older brother Sweyn. 'It was a blessing, having him for a brother. If you can stand up to Sweyn, you can stand up to anyone,' he told her.

Gradually, as Harold recovered, they walked further afield. Soon, Harold was able to resume his duties and needed less help. Finn had already made his way back to Magnus and Wulfgith, recalled for the harvest. He was unhappy to leave his charge but soon she too would return home; besides her aunt and uncle were sure nothing untoward would befall her while she was in the earl's care. But Magnus and Wulfgith had not seen Harold and Edyth together since his illness.

One day when Harold was feeling quite well he and Edyth went for a walk and were caught in a sudden summer shower. There was only one cloud in an otherwise unspoilt blue sky. It was not particularly large but it was black as night and seemed to make straight for them, opening up directly over their heads.

'Quickly,' said Harold, taking Edyth's hand, 'let's make for that tree.'

The two ran the short distance to a beech tree and took shelter under its boughs in silence while they got their breath back. The pitter-patter of the rain washed the dust from the air and released a thousand fragrances from flowers and blossoms alike. The gentle whoosh of the wind drew their attention upward, where they noticed leaves fluttering like the wings of a thousand butterflies. The effect was hypnotic.

'It looks wonderful, doesn't it?' he remarked. A few raindrops fell on her face and the eyelids of her lightly tanned face flashed white, which he found entrancing.

'Yes, it does,' she replied smiling. 'But I must confess, I am a little cold.'

Harold put his arm round her shoulder and pulled her close to him. 'I'll keep you warm.'

The shower was heavy, but short and extremely localised. After it had passed they continued to shelter under the tree, talking, for another hour. It was only when a cart passed close by, filled with labourers heading out to the fields, that they came back to earth and realised where they were.

'Afternoon, my Lord, afternoon, my lady,' came the cheerful calls from the cart.

Harold looked around sheepishly, giving a start when he saw them passing by so close. 'Good afternoon,' they called in response.

The cart carried on its way, chuckles and laughter following in its wake. They watched the cart for a moment then turned to each other and laughed.

They stepped out from the cool shade of beech tree into the heat and dazzling sunlight of the hot summer afternoon. There in the crowded countryside everyone was helping with the harvest. They would be hard at it for a month, men with scythes and women with sickles, leaving behind rough golden stubble, the swishing sound of sharp iron blades cutting through the grass, the sweat-soaked swarthy faces fighting against time and a change in the weather.

The pair were decidedly hot when they reached Harold's home, empty and with no one likely to return until the end of the day. It was with obvious relief that Harold entered the cool of his home. He sat in a chair by the table in the sunroom.

Edyth fetched some cider and poured some for them both. The stoneware goblet kept the drink cool and refreshing and he was glad of the cold touch of it on his lips.

'How do you feel?'

'I am glad to be out of the sun. I felt if I had walked into a cobweb I'd be stuck forever.'

Edyth took a drink of the rose-coloured liquid and enquired through wet lips, 'But you're all right now?'

'Yes, I'm all right now.'

The room was filled with silent excitement and anticipation. Harold stood and put his drink down on the table. Edyth did the same with hers.

'I hardly know what to say, Edyth.'

Her eyes fixed on his but she remained silent.

'You've been so very kind these last months,' he continued.

'You nursed me and stayed here much longer than need be. You saved my life.'

'It was the least I could do. I might have nursed you but the monks saved you.'

'Well, thank you all the same. I'm very grateful.'

'And now you're fully recovered?'

'Yes, almost. I only wanted to thank you.'

'Now you have done that,' she said with a smile.

There was a moment's pause. 'Don't make it hard for me.'

'What do you mean?'

'Look into my eyes and you'll see how I feel about you.'

'Look into my eyes and you'll see how I feel about your reputation. They say you've had your wicked way with every woman in Wessex.'

This time it was Harold who remained silent.

'You have nothing to say to that?'

'It's not true. It's simply not true.'

'You mean that you missed one?'

'No. No, that's not what I mean. Why are you mocking me?' He was confused, hurt and starting to feel exasperated.

'I didn't mean to mock you, Harold. That wasn't my intention. Only...'

Not knowing how to say what she felt, she stopped.

'Only...?'

'I am not sure...'

'Not sure of what?' He was calmer now and gentle.

'Not sure that I can trust you...'

He looked directly into her eyes, made all the more alive by the blaze that had started in her cheeks and had now spread now across her face down her neck to the top of her breasts. His head started to swim.

'You can trust me, take my word for it,' he said in a voice that did not seem to be his own. He felt driven now, he felt propelled by a force more powerful than the two of them, a force to which he had to submit.

She returned his gaze. 'I want to trust you but I don't know what to think.'

'Then I'll help you to decide.'

He could wait no longer. They were inches apart. He had never seen a woman more beautiful in his life. She was irresistible. Just looking at her intoxicated him. Letting go of her hands, he reached up to her face and kissed her with a long, deep, loving kiss. She felt his tongue on hers and her heart raced. Her kiss was as sweet as fresh blackberries. He wanted to suck the air from her lungs, so desperately did he want to fuse the two of them together and he set about fulfilling his desire without any further hesitation. Gently he pushed her back onto the table.

Edyth felt a yearning but her ardour was edged with reserve. She would have liked time to think, to have given consideration to what they were doing but her head spun as waves of pleasure swept through her. Harold's hands found their way through her clothes to her body. She knew she should resist him but her natural responses urged her on. Her limbs grew weak. She couldn't think, didn't even want to think; she abandoned her thoughts and let her heart have its way. Her eyes closed and her head filled with a swirling darkness. She lived in a world of overwhelming touch and bursting sensation. Excitement coursed through her, reaching every corner of her being. It was all so new, so much to handle. She let him guide her while she fervently followed wherever he led.

Harold too had travelled to another world, soaring skyward, higher and higher, rising in spirals, flying upwards, reaching beyond the clouds, beyond anything he had ever known until in bliss, in heaven amongst the stars, feeling huge and mighty, like some gigantic entity and yet still a tiny part of the vastness of creation, he had exploded in a blaze of fire and blinding light, before returning slowly, gently, earthward, like a feather, settling effortlessly, like a bird in a tree.

Afterwards, the couple held each other. Golden summer light formed shadows on their bodies, emphasising their contrasting contours and smoothness of flesh. On the clothes-strewn floor, where shards of a broken goblet lay scattered amongst pools and droplets of cider, the lovers lay and laughed and talked and time slipped by. Both of them understood the importance of the moment whose warmth still lingered on. Neither of them wanted to dress or even be the one to suggest it, neither wanted to break the spell, to bring an end to the enchantment. They wanted to suspend the moment for eternity; each knew that was the other's desire. Neither foresaw the eventual outcome of that golden afternoon. They simply knew that in each other they had found happiness and that nothing would ever be the same again.

As the heat of the afternoon subsided and gave way to a gentler, cooler evening breeze the two heard a commotion outside and before they could get up a tall blond-haired man burst into the room. His face, bronzed by the fiery sun and darkened by dust, ran with rivulets of sweat; he looked down at them, surprise spreading over his handsome face.

'Harold, I see your health is much improved!' he joked, through a wicked grin.

'Tostig, this is a pleasant surprise,' replied Harold, grabbing his clothes. 'Give me a minute and I'll join you.'

Tostig stood there grinning, his eyes drawn to the naked girl who was also fumbling with her clothes.

'I meant in another room.'

'Of course, brother, of course,' Tostig said as he left.

Once dressed, the pair joined Tostig, who had brought Harold a gift of two peacocks, a male and a female.

'I thought the colours might cheer you,' he said, nodding toward the male.

'Thank you, Tostig. You are very thoughtful. Now tell me the news,' said Harold.

'Edward has spent the summer waiting for King Magnus to invade. He's been sitting in Sandwich harbour with forty ships but all for nothing. Swein fought so hard in Denmark that Magnus became too preoccupied to take on England.' Looking at Edyth he added, 'It's as well Magnus didn't invade. Without Harold we would have been lost.'

'Really?'

'Oh, yes. We'd have been done for.'

'I think you flatter me,' laughed Harold, slapping him on the back. 'Come inside.'

Certain that his brother had recovered from his illness and was in good hands, Tostig left after a couple of nights to help out with the harvest in Wessex. Before he left, he spoke to Harold alone.

'Is this a serious matter with Edyth?'

'Yes, brother, it is.'

'You have forgotten Judith, Count Baldwin's sister?'

'Oh.'

'Oh.'

'There's no hurry, is there? I've heard nothing from Father these last few months.'

'Only because of your sickness. Baldwin would not marry his sister to a man near death. Now that you're quite recovered, and I think we can say that you are, perhaps you will start to feel some pressure.

'Ah.'

'Ah.'

WEDDING PLANS

The early morning autumn sunlight found its way into Harold's room through the gaps round the window shutters. In the half light Edyth stirred, groaned, then leaned out of bed and threw up into a chamber pot beside the bed.

'What's wrong with you, Edyth?'

'Nothing, Harold, it's quite normal.'

There was a moment's silence before Harold responded.

'What do you mean, it's quite normal?'

She wiped her mouth and lay back in bed. 'It's quite normal for a woman in my condition to be sick in the morning.'

'Your condition? What do you mean by "your condition"?'

'I'm not certain, but I think I'm going to have a child.'

Harold looked mildly alarmed.

'Not this minute,' she assured him.

'When?'

'In about seven months' time.'

Harold seemed at a loss as to what to say next.

'Aren't you going to say anything?' she enquired.

'That's wonderful news. Are you sure?'

'As sure as I can be. Are you happy?'

He leaned toward her and kissed her on the cheek. 'Absolutely.'

'What are you thinking about, Harold?' asked Edyth. She knew his moods well now and thought him a little pensive.

'What do you mean?'

'You have a certain look when you're thinking something over. Talk to me.'

'I'm thinking about breaking the good news.'

'Perhaps we should start with our families?'

'Yes.'

'I hear you say, "But".'

'There are some obstacles I must clear, and then everything will be fine.'

'Obstacles? Oh yes, I see. Would one of these obstacles be Countess Judith, by chance?'

'Yes, in part, but not in particular: it has to do with my position and my family. You must understand, as much as I wish it, I can't yet marry you in the Christian fashion.'

'What makes you think I would wish to marry you?'

'Let me explain.'

'What's to explain?'

'Well, I don't wish to estrange my parents. Our union could cause them difficulties. But if I appear to be free for a political marriage in the future, it will quell opposition from them.'

'You think of everything, Harold. I'd really no idea you were so clever. It warms my heart.'

'I don't wish it this way, Edyth, believe me. It's expected. It's my duty to my family and to England. There may come a time when, for the good of the country, I have to marry for the sake of a useful alliance. It would mean nothing on a personal level, of course, and it wouldn't change anything between us.'

'No, of course not! You marry somebody whenever you like. Why should I mind?'

'It's not my choice, Edyth, but a matter of political necessity.'

'I don't see that.'

'You must try to.'

'I can see your hypocrisy. You said I could trust you. You asked me to look into your eyes and you said I could trust you. And where are your Christian beliefs now? One minute you're giving everything you own to the brothers at Holy Cross and practically living in the abbey and the next, you suggest we have a child out of wedlock, just in case the fancy takes you to marry someone else. Is this the offer you make to all the women you bed?

'I do love you and I will marry you.'

'What?' she replied, confused and exasperated.

'You'll see I'm as good as my word. I do love you and I will marry you, if you'll have me. It'll be a handfast marriage, that's all.'

'A handfast marriage?'

'You know what a handfast marriage is; a formal contract acknowledging you as my wife and me as your husband.'

'I would be your handfast wife, leaving you free to go and marry someone else "in a Christian fashion"?'

'But I won't. We'd have a marriage as good as any other; better in fact.'

'And Judith?'

'Her father wishes an alliance with our family: I can save everyone's face by getting Tostig to marry her, leaving me free to marry you in the Danish style. There will be no opposition because I will still be available for political purposes if need be.'

'You're mad!'

'No. It all makes perfect sense.'

'It sounds very calculated.'

'It is to a point but it doesn't alter my feelings for you. My parents have a handfast marriage and they've been together for twenty-five years. So you see, it is possible to have a handfast marriage and still be perfectly happy.'

Edyth signed in resignation. 'Is the story I heard about them true?' she asked.

'What story have you heard?'

'I heard that King Knut sent your father to Denmark with his own death warrant and he came back with a wife.'

'Yes, it's true.'

'What happened?'

'It's as you say. Knut hadn't been on the throne long and he wanted to surround himself with people he could trust. As father had fought for King Edmund, Knut wasn't sure if he could trust him, so he sent him to Denmark with a message. Father knew something was afoot but didn't know what the message said, so he opened the letter, which simply read, "Kill the bearer of this letter". Once he'd read it, for the long-term good of his health he decided to change it. When he had finished, it read, "By order of the King of England, Denmark and Norway, the bearer of this letter shall have his choice of any woman in the country, to be his wife". When he got to Denmark, he presented the letter to Jarl Ulf, who was happy to comply. Father had his eye on his sister, from a previous visit. So he chose her and brought her back to England.'

51

'What did the King say when your father returned safely?'

'He congratulated him on his choice of wife and made him Earl of Wessex. He saw that a clever ally could be useful.'

'Really?'

'Yes. You can ask them yourself if you like, when you meet them at Christmas. You'll come with me to the King's Christmas court at Gloucester. You'd better have some gowns made.'

'I do love you, Harold.'

In response he kissed her and said, 'And I love you too.'

WEST WICKHAM

Magnus and Wulfgith had been expecting Edyth's arrival for days. Harold had found it impossible to refuse an invitation or reject an offer of hospitality and as a result the party was a little late arriving. Edyth's guardians were not unduly concerned. It was the size of the party that unsettled them and first alerted them to the change that was about to come into their lives.

The sound of a greeting horn brought Magnus to his door. He looked out to see half a dozen young noblemen, travelling with fifty or sixty men and two wagons, each drawn by a team of four horses. Edyth and Harold, a falcon perched on his forearm, rode at the head of the column with half a dozen hounds. In their company were Ansgar and Earl Beorn, Harold's cousin, who Magnus had last seen at the King's wedding. Three others at the head of the party who he knew only by sight were Tostig and Leofwine Godwinson and Ralph de Mantes, the King's nephew. There were also two clerics in the party, Leofgar and Edmund.

Such a prestigious party must have a purpose, Magnus told himself. The old man's stomach sank and he turned to look at his wife, who had also come out of the house; he could see she felt the same way. They walked across the courtyard to greet their visitors. Hearing footfalls behind him, Magnus turned to see Finn approaching. The Dane gave little away but it was obvious he too felt apprehensive.

Bringing his horse to a halt, Harold could see a serious-looking aunt and uncle and a particularly stern-looking Finn, awaiting their arrival.

'Welcome, Harold', said Magnus as he approached, hiding his feelings behind a beaming smile. 'Welcome back, Edyth. Harold, are you fully recovered from your illness?'

Finn stepped forward to help Edyth down.

'Yes, fully recovered, thank you, sir. Finn, it's good to see you again.'

Edyth introduced those who did not know each other before her uncle led the party inside to eat and drink. While the men remained with one of the wagons, on Tostig's orders the other was unloaded and servants took in the baggage. Barcwith and Ravenswort, two of Tostig's housecarls, carried the body of a huge male boar through to the kitchen. It was a trophy of Tostig's and his contribution to the anticipated feast.

'It is indeed an honour to have you in my home, Earl Harold, and your friends too,' said Magnus. Wulfgith was worrying about how to cater for all their guests, although the sight of the boar had lifted her spirits.

'We were expecting you some days ago. How was your journey?' enquired Magnus.

'We had an excellent journey, thank you, Magnus. I must apologise for the delay; it's entirely my fault. We were offered the opportunity to hunt and it would have been churlish to refuse. I think you'll agree it was worth it,' he replied, his gaze following the boar as Tostig's men carried indoors.

Magnus glanced at Harold's falcon. 'She must be an uncommonly fine hawk if she can bring a boar home.'

'She's stronger than she looks,' Harold replied, laughing at Magnus's little joke.

Magnus continued to welcome Harold as the guests made themselves comfortable and servants brought drinks. Harold thanked him for the warm welcome and hoped he would accept the gifts he had brought him. As these consisted of the wild boar, some game, several barrels of beer and pots of preserves, Magnus was only too pleased to welcome them. There would be enough food for them all to stay the best part of a week. Beleaguered-looking servants made themselves busy, preparing for the evening meal.

While everyone was busy eating, drinking and socialising, Harold leaned towards Magnus and asked in subdued tones, 'Magnus, may we talk in confidence?'

Magnus led him to a small room off the hall. They sat down together at a fine oak table.

'What can I do for you, my Lord?'

'I'd like to thank you for allowing your niece to stay with me in my time of need.'

'It was nothing, my Lord. It was the least I could do.'

'I think I would not have survived without her.'

'That is kind of you to say. She has a talent for treating the sick.'

'So I understand, but during my illness or rather, during my recovery, we grew very close.'

'Yes,' said Magnus, nodding sagely.

Harold could feel his heart pounding in his chest, took a breath and uttered the words he had rehearsed many times over the last few weeks. 'I feel it a great honour to be here as your guest. I want to make it clear I have the highest respect for your distinguished family, whose reputation has been held in the highest regard by all, for generations. Well, the thing is, would you approve our marriage?

'You and Edyth wish to be married?'

'Yes. Yes we do.'

'I should be delighted, Earl Harold,' answered Magnus, a smile bursting on to his face. 'It would be an honour to have you as part of our family,' he said, reaching out to shake Harold's hand.

As the two men smiled and shook hands, Magnus continued to splutter out his delight at the prospect of the two families becoming united through marriage.

'I've long been a great admirer of your father's. Though I never dreamed that one day our families would be joined. You have my blessing. Tell me, Harold, have you a date in mind? Wulfgith and I married in June; I think that a lovely time of year, don't you?'

'We would like to marry before then — such is my desire to marry your niece, I would wed her right away. We thought next month would be a good time.'

'That is very soon… oh… ' Realisation forced the smile off Magnus' face.

'Would that be all right, do you think, next month?' ventured Harold.

'It would be ideal. We should have enough time to prepare.'

'I thought we could discuss preparations this evening.'

'Yes, my Lord.'

'Magnus,' said Harold, putting his hand on his shoulder and giving one of his warmest smiles, 'there really is no need to address me as my Lord any longer. As we shall soon be related, I think we can dispense with the formalities, don't you?'

'Yes, my Lord.'

Harold gave Magnus a playful look of rebuke.

'Harold.'

'Thank you.'

'I will break the good news to Wulfgith.'

'I'll rejoin the others.'

'Would you mind if I made the announcement?'

'Not at all.'

The two men entered the hall and as Harold made his way back to Edyth, Magnus walked over to Wulfgith.

'You look pleased with yourself, Magnus. What's happened?'

'Harold has just asked for Edyth's hand in marriage.'

'Oh, how wonderful.'

Magnus smiled in response before requesting silence and ordering all the drinking vessels filled. 'Friends, Earl Harold has requested my niece's hand in marriage.'

The announcement was greeted with a hearty cheer.

Magnus raised his drinking horn high, 'To the young couple, Harold and Edyth; tonight we shall feast.'

That evening on the high table Harold sat at Magnus' right hand. Next to the men were their friends and close relatives. The women were banished from the hall until negotiations were finished. The hall was filled to bursting; friends and neighbours who could be reached were there and so were all the men in Harold's party.

Once Harold had agreed a wedding date with Magnus they shook hands in front of the witnesses. There was a long discussion about the morning gift Harold would present to Edyth, on consummation of the marriage. The bride gift that Edyth would bring to the marriage was quite considerable but as the wife always kept possession of whatever was rightfully hers until she died, there would be no personal gain for Harold. However, it did mean Edyth would be independently wealthy and never be a burden to Harold or his family and it would also ensure that she and any children she might have, would not have to beg, if she were to become widowed.

Finally, the handgeld that Harold would pay to compensate Magnus and Wulfgith for their loss of Edyth and also to equalise any gifts her family would make him, was agreed.

The negotiations were carried out in a spirit of fun and laughter, which could be heard ringing round every corner of Magnus's home. Finally when everything was settled Edyth and the other women were called for. To a rousing cheer she entered the hall followed by Wulfgith and the other women. Edyth looked radiant and the sight of her took Harold's breath away. Wulfgith escorted her up to the top table and presented her to Harold.

'Well, Harold, what do you say?'

The couple moved closer together, took each other by the hand and faced the assembled guests. Harold cleared his throat and with a smile spread across his pink face, made his announcement: 'I declare that you, Edyth, arc bound to me in lawful betrothal and that with a handshake you pledge me marriage in exchange for the handgeld and morning gift promised and engage me to fulfil and observe the whole of the oath between us, which has been said in the hearing of these witnesses, without wiles or cunning, as a true and honest oath.'

The two kissed amid much cheering and shouts of encouragement.

'To the bride and groom,' shouted Ansgar, with his drinking horn held high.

'To the bride and groom,' chorused the other guests.

'Here comes the food,' called Magnus with obvious enthusiasm and they sat down to eat, making room for the ladies.

'I must say, I'm a little surprised not to see Earl Godwin here,' said Magnus to Harold, between mouthfuls of meat. There's no problem, is there, Harold?'

'No. There's no problem. In fact I shall call in at Southwark soon to discuss plans for the wedding with my parents.'

'Good. We shall expect to see them at the wedding then?'

'Indeed you shall.'

After two days' journey the brothers and their cousin arrived at Southwark. Ralph parted company with them in London to pay a visit to his uncle, the King. Tostig, Leofwine and Beorn joined Gyrth, who had decided to keep well out of the way when Harold told Godwin of his betrothal to Edyth.

'I'll leave you to unpack while I have a word with father.'

'Good luck,' they said in unison as Harold entered his father's house. He could hear their chuckling as he crossed the threshold.

Without stopping for refreshment or to talk to anyone, Harold made his way to his parents' room. After a brisk knock on the door and a brusque 'Come in,' Harold was in the company of his father. He felt like Daniel entering the lions' den.

Godwin was alone in the room, slumped in a chair, deep in thought, staring into a goblet of wine.

'Harold! Welcome home,' he said, crossing the room to greet his son. The two men hugged one another. 'Sit down,' said Godwin, with a welcoming smile, gesturing to Harold to be seated. 'I've been expecting you for a while now. You look well. Have you fully recovered from your illness?'

'Yes, thank you, father.'

'Good. Your mother and I were concerned for you.'

'Yes, I had a bad fever but I'm well now.'

'Good,' said his father agreeably. 'I understand it was quite serious.'

'I have the monks at Waltham to thank for my recovery. They took such excellent care of me. They think it's a miracle I survived.'

Godwin's face paled. 'Was it so serious?' he asked.

'Yes, it was.'

'Well, we must indeed thank the monks of Waltham, then.'

'And Edyth, we must thank her too.'

'Edyth? Who is Edyth?' asked Godwin in a wary tone.

'Oh, haven't I told you about her?'

'No, I don't believe you have,' replied Godwin.

'Well, she's a remarkable girl,' continued Harold, with as big a smile as he could manage, 'and she did as much as the monks to save me.'

Godwin looked thoughtful and a silence descended on the room. Over the years he had learned to be on his guard at the sight of Harold's huge grin; it was genuine enough most of the time but his son had learned how to use it to disarm any reaction to bad news. Godwin expected an announcement any moment. 'Who is this wench?' he asked.

'She's the daughter of Alwine Egwinson, Thane of Wickham. Her name is Edyth but all over East Anglia she is known as Swan-neck for her elegance, her great beauty and the delicate colour of her skin.'

'You always were a fool for a pretty face.'

'She has more than a pretty face; she's educated and refined.'

'And what about her family, are they of any importance?'

'Her parents are dead but you know her uncle, who took her in when she was a child. He is Magnus Egwinson, Thane of Fulbourn.'

'Magnus! He fought alongside me in Denmark, with Knut. I saw him at Edward's wedding. Ah, I remember now. He came with his niece. Was she the girl with the chestnut hair and bright blue eyes?'

Harold nodded.

'Mmm… her family's quite wealthy, I believe? Well known and respected in half a dozen counties.' Godwin slipped into quiet thought for a moment. 'And?'

'And, what?'

'And are you serious about this Edyth Swan-neck?'

'Very. We wish to marry straight away.'

Godwin was amused by Harold's impatience; he suppressed a laugh but not a smile. 'I can see why you find her attractive and ordinarily I might think it a good match but why the hurry to marry her?' For an instant Godwin froze in his movements as the answer to his own question flashed through his mind.

'She's with child, that's it! That's it, isn't it? She's with child,' his piercing grey eyes cutting into Harold.

'Yes, and we are to be married. Will you offer us your congratulations?'

Godwin looked aghast; his face turned white with rage.

Harold continued before his father could speak, 'Have no fear; we're to have a handfast wedding, and so a Christian marriage, at some time in the future, will still be possible.'

'Have you gone mad?'

'I've met the woman I want to spend the rest of my life with. I want her to feel sure of that, to know I'm serious about her.'

'Tell me, exactly what is it I'm to say to Count Baldwin?'

'Can you not tell him you've changed your mind?'

'Don't be a fool!'

'Not about the marriage; about the groom.'

'What?' seethed Godwin.

'Well, none of my brothers is married.'

Godwin took a deep breath. 'You don't seem to realise the importance of this, Harold. The family needs to consolidate its position, not just for itself but also for the country. Sometime soon Edith must produce an heir. That future king will be a part of our family. Imagine the power we will have then. You will be the King's uncle. If you marry Judith, England will in good part be tied to Flanders. Between the two of us, we will control the English Channel. Eventually, if Edward and Edith's son were to marry a Danish princess, we could dominate the North Sea. We already have a family link with the Danish royal house but Edward refuses to acknowledge it, let alone exploit it. Can't you see my frustration, Harold? I have great plans for all of us but I'm being thwarted at every turn.'

'Listen to me, father, as long as one of us marries Judith, it's still possible to have your alliance with Baldwin. Do you agree?'

Begrudgingly, Godwin agreed.

'So if Sweyn or Tostig marries Lady Judith, all will proceed as you planned. And as I will be married to Edyth, with her powerful family connections in Anglia, I'll have the kind of support we will need in the east, if we're to control the North Sea, as you suggest.'

Godwin rolled his head and looked skyward. 'Look, there may be something in what you say but I need time to think it over.'

'I'm glad you approve, father.'

'I didn't say that.'

'Oh, then you disapprove?'

'I didn't say that either. But the situation is a lot less bleak than I thought. Will you have more wine?'

'Not at the moment; I haven't unpacked yet.'

'Did you think you might save yourself some time, if I'd decided to throw you out?'

'It did cross my mind, yes.' Harold was smiling again now.

'Quite wise, Harold, quite wise.'

In Wickham, preparations were moving forward hastily. As custom demanded, Harold would be presented with a new sword at the wedding. Magnus went to Lyfing the smith to have it made. There by the riverside they talked at length about how the smith would go about making it.

The sword was to be three feet long plus an inch. As was the custom, Lyfing made the weapon from five iron bars; when he had made three flattened bars he welded them together side-by-side and twisted them repeatedly. He did this not just to remove the slag, which could weaken the weapon, but also to produce a strong, unbreakable sword and form the beautiful pattern that would emerge on the blade when he later beat it flat. The three bars would form the core of the blade and he would weld two more iron bars to either side before grinding them down to form the cutting edge.

Throughout the process, Lyfing would heat and then cool the sword in water from the river with its special powers, to harden it. After two and a half weeks the blade, gleaming with the marks of the fire along its fullered tapering length, was finished. The hilt was made in three parts, the lower guard, the grip and the upper guard. These three sections were fitted over the tang, the end of which was hammered out over an iron bar to hold them all in place. The lower guard extended just under an inch, offering some protection to Harold's hand.

The hilt itself was of fine oak inlaid with an intricate gold pattern and fixed with brass rivets to the tang. It was ornamented with gold plates riveted to the upper and lower guards and a gold pommel inscribed on one side with the name Harold, while on the other a wolf and a dragon were intertwined. When finished, the sword had perfect balance and great strength. Lyfing boasted it was a work of art and the finest sword he had ever made. When Magnus held it he felt it full of life; he could feel its power racing into him, invigorating him, making him feel like a young warrior.

The scabbard was a purely practical affair, made of ash, lined with fleece and covered with leather. To protect the neck from wear, an ornate bronze casting of intertwined serpents was fitted and the bottom of the scabbard was protected with a cast decorative figure of a Wessex dragon. Other than that there was no ornamentation whatsoever.

Finally, Magnus had a fine shield made from alder, strong and light. Circular and around three feet in diameter, it was half an inch thick. The finest red leather covered it front and back and the golden dragon of Wessex was emblazoned boldly across its front. The shield boss was made of iron, shaped like sugar loaf and kept in place by six rivets. To hold it there was an iron grip enclosed by a wooden handle, bound with woven leather and straps to allow Harold to carry it on his back when not in use.

Eventually the day came when Harold's wedding party arrived in Cambridgeshire. To maintain the time-honoured tradition of the groom not seeing the bride on the eve of the wedding, Harold stayed at Sawston with all the other male guests. All the women stayed together with Wulfgith at Magnus's hall. Conspicuous by their absence were the other earls and the King and Queen. Edward had declined the invitation, as he did not wish to be seen approving an unsanctified wedding.

On the morning of the wedding Harold led the party over to Magnus's with Tostig at his side, followed by Leofwine and Gyrth, then Ralph and Earl Beorn. Ralph was there despite the King's disapproval. Next were Harold's parents, guests of honour and finally the housecarls. It was almost mid-day by the time everyone had arrived.

As tradition demanded, Edyth had already had her hot stone bath in the small wooden bath house. She and her three maids had sat naked in the hot steamy room, any impurities perspiring from them. Hot rocks brought out of a fire, which had been burning all night, had been placed in the centre of the room and a bucket and ladle provided to produce steam on demand. The young women, lost in their misty world of excitement and laughter, had to be reminded more than once by Wulfgith's lady-in-waiting that soon Harold would arrive and they really ought to get on with things.

When the women considered the ritual purification complete, they moved out of the bathing room to the drying room next door. After Edyth's attendants had dried her and themselves, they all dressed in their finery. Edyth's dress was of the deepest blue. The wreath her maid of honour had specially made was placed on Edyth's head. When they were ready they slipped back into the main house.

Harold also attended the act of purification, going to the stone bath and bathing with Ralph, Beorn and his brothers. Once through, they dressed in their wedding attire and Harold strapped on his ancestral sword, brought up by his father for the occasion.

Following tradition, when Harold left the building, Edyth and her maids were outside waiting for him. He and his groomsmen chased after them, Harold trying to reach Edyth, the maids keeping him at bay until they reached the door of Magnus's hall, where Harold took her hand before they entered together, followed by the maids and groomsmen. They all fell in through the door in riotous laughter. The hall had been prepared for the wedding feast with all the gifts on display. The women were awed into silence but only briefly. Soon they were passing comment on everything before them. There were cloaks from Magnus and Wulfgith with fine golden shoulder clasps as well as a leather belt with a gold buckle with niello inlay. From Harold, golden amulets, bracelets and a brooch, all with a motif of a Wessex dragon and Anglian wolf entwined. He had been generous with his gifts, though not so generous as to hurt the pride of his hosts.

At the top of the hall were Magnus and Wulfgith, with Earl Godwin and Lady Gytha. Each one turned to see the magnificent looking couple; the sight of them immediately put smiles on faces. Standing between their parents was the wedding thane, dressed all in green, Edmund, who was to give a blessing and Finn, who was bearing the new sword Magnus had had made, to be presented to the groom.

When Harold and Edyth arrived at the top of the hall the wedding thane flicked water over them, looked from Godwin to Magnus, to Edyth and Harold and when he ascertained they were ready, began the ceremony

Handgeld and bridesgift were exchanged and Harold presented Edyth with his ancestral sword, which she accepted and passed to Magnus. Finn handed her the new sword her father had had made and she then presented it to Harold.

The wedding thane spoke: 'Harold, I have not the right to bind you to Edyth, only you have this right. If it is your wish, say so at this time and offer the ring.'

'It is my wish.'

Tostig handed Harold the ring, which he in turn offered Edyth. It was made of the purest gold and bore the dragon of Wessex. She took it with her left hand before placing it in the palm of her right. Harold picked it up and pushed the ring on her finger.

The man in green spoke again. 'Edyth, if it is your wish to be bound to Harold, place your ring on his finger.'

Magnus presented Edyth with a gold ring fashioned in a style with two wolves, a mirror image of each other, ready to pounce across its face.

Edyth placed a ring on Harold's ring finger.

'Who will bind the couple?' asked the wedding thane, producing a leather cord from somewhere behind his back.

Magnus and Godwin stepped forward. Godwin took the cord and together with Magnus bound the couple at the wrists, Edyth's right to Harold's left, crossing the twine over so that a knot was all that was needed for the binding to stay in place and they stepped back to their places.

'Harold, will you tie the knot?'

'I will.'

With that, Harold tied the knot binding himself and Edyth together in marriage. As they kissed a cheer went up and barley seeds, thrown by the guests, rained down on them. After Harold and Edyth had signed the marriage contract the county shire reeve added his signature to it and then Edmund stepped forward to bless the couple.

'Feast!' yelled Magnus.

'Feast!' yelled the guests in unison.

Doors flew open as servants brought platter after platter of food to the tables. Horns, goblets and glasses were filled with mead and a toast wishing the happy couple the best of heath and fortune was offered by Magnus.

'It's as well you like it, Harold; you'll drink nothing but honey mead for a month,' laughed Tostig.

Harold, Edyth and the other guests made their way to their places, music began to play and a minstrel began to sing. Even Godwin was happy. Arrangements had been made for Countess Judith to marry Tostig. Lady Gytha was happy too, pleased to see Harold with a woman of whom she approved. She had presented Edyth with a book on estate management, *Rectitudines Singularum Personarum*, of which she had persuaded Edmund to make a copy. 'You may find this useful, my dear, I wouldn't be without it,' she had said, as she handed it over. Edyth was delighted.

The couple danced. The music was the song that they danced to on Edward's wedding night.

The feast went on into the night and as each guest left they were given a slice of cake to put under their pillow, so that they could dream of their own true love. Whether each man dreamed of his wife and each woman her husband could never be told.

The next morning Edyth and Harold were, as was fitting, the last to enter Magnus's hall for breakfast. When everyone had eaten, Harold gave Edyth a gold jewel-encrusted necklace. Leading her outside with everyone following behind, he presented her with a fine, bridled white horse of breathtaking beauty.

'She's fast and can gallop all day, but in case you're wondering, she is always very calm,' Harold added with a swift glance at her belly.

Edyth mounted the horse sitting astride with her skirts trailing either side of her.

'Are you ready for a ride, Edyth?'

'What, now?'

'Of course.'

With that Ansgar, Tostig and Skalpi appeared mounted on their horses and a servant came with Harold's.

'I'll see you all in Waltham tonight,' called out Harold, as he climbed into the saddle. Waving farewell, they all rode off.

'I expected this,' said Magnus with a crafty grin. In an instant his groom appeared with two horses, one for him one for Finn. They mounted and gave chase.

Godwin and Gytha watched with Wulfgith as they all rode off.

It was Godwin who spoke first. 'I should have realised that too,' he said. 'Come, let's get our horses.'

Godwin, on Wulfgith's behalf, barked commands, organising the servants who could ride and get their hands on a horse. There was no doubt in his mind that Harold would reach Waltham first, thus making it the job of Magnus's household to serve the evening meal. But the servants were prepared and were at Magnus's side racing towards Waltham in moments. There was quite some distance to cover before nightfall so he hurried the servants on, hoping to make a good race of it.

Harold's group had a slight lead on Magnus and Finn, who were doing all in their power to catch up. Racing full gallop through villages and across fields, taking shortcuts across rivers and streams, each rider was doing his best to reach Waltham first. Ansgar was the winner, closely pursued by Finn. The others, with the exception of Skalpi and Edyth, were all bunched behind him. Dismounting and running up to the door of the hall as fast as he could, he was first to reach it. Finn, seeing his chance to win disappear, dropped from his horse and strode over to Ansgar. Through short breaths he congratulated him on his ride.

'I thought I was a good rider.'

'You are.'

'I thought I had a good horse.'

'You have. That was as close a ride as I've had in a long time and horses are my life. Have you seen the others?'

'They're not far behind.'

Sure enough, within a minute or so Harold, Tostig and Magnus came into view. The three were galloping hard, whooping and laughing as they went. They barely got through the gate, riding three abreast, and each horse had to drop down on its back legs as they slid to a halt outside the hall.

Harold called out and servants appeared with refreshments. The riders dismounted and chatted outside for an hour until Edyth and Skalpi arrived. Harold helped her down from her horse and carried her, to the cheers of his friends, across the threshold and into Waltham hall. That night, in the company of the same wedding party, Harold and Edyth enjoyed a feast served by Magnus and Wulfgith, with many of the same toasts and more of the same camaraderie as the previous evening.

During a quiet part of the evening, Harold took Ansgar aside and asked him for his opinion of Magnus's housecarl, Finn. The next day Magnus was disappointed to lose such a valuable man but he agreed that he could stay with Harold if he chose to. Finn was practically Edyth's man these days anyway, that was how Magnus saw it, so he might as well stay, as a kind of wedding gift.

ANOTHER WEDDING

In Earl Godwin's home at Bosham, Tostig and his bride-to-be, Countess Judith, welcomed Harold, Edyth and their new son Godwin. He brought added joy to the occasion: Godwin's sons were pleased to be uncles and young Wulfnoth, now aged six, took particular pride in his new status, as he saw his new position in the family somehow putting him on the same footing as his older brothers. What Sweyn's feelings were, no one knew. He had sent word that he had important business in Wales to deal with. Cousin Beorn, never one to miss a feast, had arrived in good time.

Earl Godwin and Lady Gytha were overjoyed at becoming grandparents, especially as Harold and Edyth had named the boy after his paternal grandfather. The King and queen, present for the prestigious Christian wedding, viewed the infant coldly. He was and always would be a living reminder of their failure to produce an heir and of the coldness that dwelt in the heart of their relationship. The uninvited Robert de Jumieges was cool to Harold and Edyth for reasons of his own. Furious, the outraged de Jumieges took the first opportunity to express his feelings to the King, whom he had taken to accompanying everywhere.

'Don't you think it a disgrace that they've brought their bastard child to a Christian wedding?'

Edward's left eyebrow raised as it did when he registered something he found mildly ridiculous. 'What do you suggest I do, Robert?'

'Banish them from court as an example to your subjects.'

'Would you have me ban everyone from court who had a child out of wedlock?'

'Exactly! It would be a Christian act worthy of praise from the Pope himself.'

'Then what do we do when no one is present at court?'

'What do you mean?'

'It's not just Harold and his woman who haven't had a Christian marriage. The same goes for most of the court.'

'This is a more disgraceful state of affairs than I'd thought. You know the Church condemns fornication. All that fleshly meddling, we should do more to discourage it, much more.

'Yes, Robert,' said Edward wearily, 'you're right.'

'Discipline,' de Jumieges stammered through lips, which by now had small flecks of foam in the corners, 'this country needs discipline, and plenty of it.' Then as an afterthought he added, 'And to be rid of all those whores,' indicating with a jerk of the thumb some of the noblest ladies in the land.

This had been a poor start to the festivities but next day the wedding was one which nobody would forget. Countess Judith was everything Godwin had said she would be: erudite, gracious, wealthy and in her physical appearance tall, fair, elegant and, to Tostig's relief, attractive, if a little austere looking.

But as the perfect day was coming to an end the arrival of the King's messenger would change the mood of the evening. Entering with minimum fuss and directly approaching the King, he whispered hurriedly in his ear for up to two minutes. Edward's serious expression conveyed the importance of the news and the looks cast Godwin's way informed him that whatever had happened, it would have a direct bearing on him. When the messenger had finished, the King stood and the hall fell silent.

'My noble friends, there is bad news. It seems King Magnus of Norway is on his way with a massed fleet to invade us. Let us continue with the celebrations now but we must rise early in the morning and travel with all possible haste to Sandwich, where we will make preparations to greet our northern friend in a manner he will never forget.'

A deep murmur ran round Godwin's Bosham hall.

The King continued, 'There is some good news. Earl Sweyn, with the help of Gruffydd of North Wales, has routed the South Welsh and put an end to their raids, at least for the time being.'

A cheer went up at the news.

'Now I will continue to enjoy the festivities and I suggest you do the same.' The King then sat down, beckoning for Earl Godwin to approach.

'I have some more news of your son, Sweyn. It seems he's been busy in Wales.'

'I knew Sweyn could deal with the Welsh.'

'Yes, he did and he found another use for his time too,' replied

Edward. 'It seems he's abducted Abbess Eadgifu of Leominster, from her abbey. If my information is correct, then your son will be in as much trouble with the Pope as he is with me. Heaven only knows what he's going to do with her.'

Godwin knew only too well what Sweyn would do with her.

'My Lord, I'm sure there has been a mistake …'

'Yes, Earl Godwin and your son Sweyn has made it.'

'I'll make amends. I shall seek Sweyn out and have him brought before you and I shall also have the Abbess returned.'

'Intact,' said Edward, by way of an order, rather than a request.

'I shall do my best to have her restored without scandal, my Lord.'

'You had best start right away.'

TWO YEARS LATER

Two years had passed since Tostig's and Judith's wedding. Both appeared happy and Ketel, their first son, brought them immense joy.

Magnus's threatened invasion never materialised.

Sweyn Godwinson had not been seen by anyone in England for three years. He had released the abbess Eadgifu but only after he had been threatened with excommunication. She was taken to Bosham for her confinement; fearful that her assailant's kin might murder her and bury her along with the scandal at sea, and having heard such terrible things about Godwin, she scarcely slept for the first week. She was eventually able to trust her hosts and gave birth to Sweyn's child the following spring in a thunderstorm and a flood of tears. A week later, Eadgifu left Bosham for good. As agreed, the Godwins took her son in and brought him up as one of their own. She never saw her boy again and did not even know his name. She knew nothing of his character but she thought of him every day in the cave where she lived as a hermit for many years until her eventual demise, long after his own tragic death.

As Sweyn had incurred the wrath of the Pope, Edward had the excuse to banish him and had divided his earldom equally between Beorn and Harold.

Harold and Edyth had become parents for a second time and chose to call their second-born son Edmund, after East Anglia's most venerated saint and Harold's good friend, the priest. It was a choice that went down well in the earldom. People saw it as a demonstration that their new earl, though a West Saxon, had respect for them. They were also pleased to see a small college opened at Waltham. It was there to educate the children of East Anglia's thanes. A lot of trouble had been taken to find the right college chancellor and a Suffolk abbot by the name of Adlehard had been appointed. He proved an excellent choice and soon won respect and affection. Harold, one way and another, won more friends as each month went by. For most, his only faults were his leniency and his dallying.

Earlier in the year messengers had arrived from Zealand with news of King Magnus's murder by his uncle Harald Sigurdsson, who had recently returned from his fabulous adventures in Byzantium. Swein returned to Denmark and was elected king. He had at last begun what was to become his long reign over Denmark.

That summer most of Europe, including the Pope, was at war with Count Baldwin of Flanders. Not surprisingly, the war was not going well for the count. The Holy Roman Emperor, Henry III, requested Edward to prevent Baldwin escaping from Flanders by sea. Edward responded by moving the English fleet to Sandwich to await news of any sightings of him. For the English, this had been a quiet time. The weather had been pleasant and the nobles had enjoyed many a fine day's hunting. Returning late to their camp one afternoon, all in good spirits after another successful day's deer hunting with the King, Godwin, his sons and nephew Beorn were exchanging good-natured banter while the grooms led the horses off to the stables, when completely unexpectedly Sweyn appeared, as if from nowhere.

'Father, I'm home!'

'Sweyn, my son, it's so good to see you again!' Godwin greeted his son with a great bear hug; the two men were thrilled to see each other.

'And it's good to see you again, father.' Then turning to the others he enquired, 'What's the matter? Isn't anyone else going to welcome me?'

Harold was the first to speak: 'You'll have to forgive us, Sweyn. It's not every day we have a visit from an exile and it's unlike you to make a social visit. To what do we owe this unexpected pleasure?'

'I've had enough of banishment and thought that I'd like to come home, back in the bosom of my family. There's no harm in that, is there?'

'That's great news, son,' interjected Godwin. 'We'll see Edward at the earliest opportunity. I'm sure he'll agree to your returning.'

Godwin's other sons were astonished.

'Wouldn't you like Sweyn back, boys?'

At first no one answered. Each looked to the other.

'Well' snapped Godwin, 'Sweyn has returned from his travels and you don't have anything to say to him. What kind of a welcome is that?'

'Join us for food and drink,' offered Harold.

'Yes, son, you must be in need of refreshment after your journey,' added Godwin, indicating to a servant.

'Well, this calls for a celebration; the prodigal son has returned,' beamed Godwin, slapping Sweyn on the back. 'Let's hear your news. Join me in my tent, everyone.'

The men made their way to the tent, Godwin and Sweyn chatting all the way.

'I've just come up from Bosham,' Sweyn volunteered.

'Did you see your mother?' enquired Godwin, keen to hear news of his wife.

'Yes. She's well and sends her love.'

'And Haakon? Did you see him?'

Sweyn was unsettled by this question about his son and mumbled a reply.

When they reached the tent they made themselves comfortable. Godwin's servants arrived with drinks. Godwin ordered one of them to take a message to the King.

'Tell him that Sweyn Godwinson has just ridden all the way over from Bosham and requests an audience at his convenience.'

The food arrived and they all began to eat. Godwin soon noticed, that in the awkward atmosphere, only he and Sweyn were talking.

After a short while the messenger returned. 'The King will see you in an hour, my Lord.'

'There, I knew everything would be all right,' stated the ever-confident Godwin, but the atmosphere amongst the men was no less strained.

At the appointed time, Godwin, with all of his sons and his nephew Beorn, entered the King's hall, which was Edward's residence for the duration of the blockade. There was a touching innocence to the way Godwin and Sweyn entered the room. It was as though they were naughty children and thought all they had to do was to say sorry to father and everything would be forgiven. The other members of the family entered as if to do battle, with the exception of young Wulfnoth, who was there only as an observer.

Edward sat impassively, greeting them all as one. He had been at prayer, examining his conscience in preparation for his audience with Sweyn. It was becoming his habit to make important decisions only after a period of meditation and prayer, except when he flew into a rage. Edward could prove ruthless to anyone who caused him offence, though he was never physically cruel: he never killed, imprisoned or mutilated his enemies, but only because he preferred to punish them by making them suffer the misery of exile, such as he had endured in Normandy. But when his rage had been subdued and his anger cooled, he was penitent. He would pray for forgiveness, forgive offenders and sometimes go as far as inviting exiles to return home. Sweyn was hoping that today the King was in a forgiving mood.

'I hear you've ruined yourself with the Danes, Sweyn. Tell me, just what is it you have to do, to be banished by Vikings?'

This was news to the rest of the party, who had assumed Sweyn had returned from exile of his own volition.

'There was just a little misunderstanding and everyone got overexcited. So here I am. But I have gifts for you, my Lord.'

'Really,' responded Edward, looking around the room for treasure.

'Well, I didn't bring them with me. I've come straight from Bosham and ...'

'What Sweyn means, my Lord, is that he was so keen to see you, that in his hurry, he completely forgot the gifts he's brought for you. He let his enthusiasm get the better of him. You know how impetuous he can be,' Godwin interjected.

'Impetuous!' Edward's eyebrow rose. 'Yes, I suppose that's one word you could use to describe him.'

'Well ...' Godwin was about to start to argue the case for Sweyn's reinstatement but changed his mind and looking at Sweyn he said, 'I think he had better speak for himself, my Lord.'

Sweyn stepped forward and said, as if by rote, 'Sire, I realise how wrong I have been in the past and how wicked have been my many transgressions. I am truly sorry for all of the harm I have done to everyone concerned and any offence I might have caused to anyone, not least to you, my Lord. I have been a fool, even to myself. The long years of exile have provided an opportunity for me to reflect on these matters and I see clearly now the error of my ways. I am truly penitent. Please find it in your heart to allow me to return and prove to you my worthiness.'

Edward was thunderstruck. He had never thought Sweyn capable of stringing together more than five words at a time, let alone of making sense. It took him a moment to collect himself.

'Sweyn, much as I would wish to welcome you back into the

kingdom, the decision is not entirely mine. You have upset, even outraged, too many people, including the Pope. It would be no easy thing to reinstate you. Can you honestly see yourself living a quiet life over in Bosham?'

'Bosham? Why would I want to live in Bosham?'

'Isn't that your family home?'

'Yes, but I want my earldom back.

'You want your banishment lifted and your old earldom reinstated?' Edward paused for a moment in order to take in the magnitude of the request and to let Sweyn reflect on just exactly what it was he was asking. 'You must have discussed this with your brothers? What do they think?'

It was Harold who replied: 'My Lord, it is only now I have been informed of my brother's desire for the reinstatement of his former position and property. But the earldom is now mine. He relinquished any rights to it when you banished him. I will give up to Sweyn nothing that you gave to me as a gift. He has neither my agreement nor support for his return.'

'What! What do you mean?' snarled Sweyn.

'Thank you, Sweyn,' interjected Edward. 'You will have your chance to make your contribution to the proceedings in a short while. Thank you, Earl Harold.

'Earl Beorn, what do you have to say?'

'I agree with my cousin Harold, my Lord and I have nothing to add.'

'You as well? You bastard!' yelled Sweyn, fury getting the better of him.

'In my court you will refrain from that sort of behaviour,' Edward remonstrated.

Sweyn was livid and stepped forward to protest.

'You have four days to leave the country. If you are seen in my kingdom at any time after that date you will be treated as an outlaw. Do you understand?'

'What! That's not fair!'

'I said, goodbye,' snapped the King.

Godwin reached forward and grabbed Sweyn's arm, at the same time thanking Edward for the audience. The family took a few steps back as they bowed, then turned and left.

'Bastards,' hissed Sweyn. He could barely repress his rage. 'You treacherous bastards! How could you do that to me? You mangy curs! How could you do that to me?'

'Sweyn,' replied Harold calmly, 'what do you expect?'

'I expect loyalty!'

Godwin had to hold his incensed son by both arms now. They were out in the open, everyone around them looking on.

'Then you expect what you never give,' Harold replied. 'Where's your loyalty to our family? You bring nothing but shame and disgrace on us all.'

'Bastard! I'll kill you, dog!' snarled the enraged Sweyn, still struggling violently. Tostig, Gyrth, Leofric and Beorn, as well as Godwin, were now holding him back while Wulfnoth gawped at the scene before him. Even with five of them holding him, it was difficult to control Sweyn.

'I'm ready for you Sweyn, let's finish this now,' said Harold, calmly pulling his sword from its scabbard, 'or are you all talk?'

Sweyn struggled harder than ever.

'Let go of him,' snapped Harold.

'Put your sword away, Harold, and get out of here; this is only making matters worse,' ordered Godwin.

'Let him go. I'll finish him off. He's a mad dog and the only thing to do with him is to put him down.'

'I'm head of this family and what I say stands. Now put your sword away and be gone,' snapped Godwin.

Harold thought for a few moments, looked coldly at Sweyn and said, 'You have another reason to be indebted to our father. He's just saved your life.'

Harold put his sword away and sauntered back to his ship. With the help of his other sons, Godwin dragged Sweyn, cursing, swearing, ranting and raving, in the opposite direction, shouting at Harold what he would do to him, if they ever should meet again.

When Sweyn eventually calmed down, he left for Bosham, embittered by what he considered his unjust treatment.

Next morning, Edward received news from a messenger that enemy ships had been seen in the Channel. Godwin took forty-five ships, including one commanded by Harold and his younger brother Tostig. Ralph and Malcolm Canmore went along for the ride. Beorn commanded another ship. As soon as they left harbour the fine day turned sour. The wind rose and so did the swell. Spray blew over the longships; sailors' faces were whipped by their hair, the sky turned from blue through grey to black.

Cold rain fell and it soon became obvious to everyone that to seek an enemy fleet in the storm would be to invite disaster. By the end of the day, they had sailed only as far as Pevensey, where they had become weather-bound.

The wind blew hard and rain lashed buildings and boats alike. In the crowded tavern where Godwin and his sons were waiting out the storm, shutters were closed against the furious elements. Everywhere was dark and deserted while the tempest continued to rage through the evening and all through the night.

Sweyn, on his journey back to Bosham to rejoin his men and ships, had also been caught in the storm. He spent the night with a farmer and his family. The next day, riding along the coast, he could not help but notice the King's fleet taking shelter in Pevensey harbour. Seeing an opportunity to regain his earldom, he turned and made his way down to the seafront. Huddled in his cloak, astride his horse, he drew no one's attention as he rode into town.

Beorn was aboard his ship, which was tied up to a wharf. He was overseeing the checking and securing of its small cargo of provisions. Most of the crew were crammed into an inn to wait out the storm. Sweyn recognised the ship by its distinctive dragon's head prow and the sail, furled around the mast, with gold and red strips that marked it out as Beorn's. Sweyn was unseen by anyone as he dismounted from his horse and stepped across to the boat. He shouted but his cousin couldn't hear him above the noise of the wind. Sweyn climbed aboard.

Beorn saw him but it was a moment before he recognised him. He was immediately suspicious; a cheery grin and wave from Sweyn did nothing to alleviate his fears.

'Sweyn, this is another surprise.'

'Yes,' replied Sweyn, almost apologetically. 'Beorn, I need your help,' he began. 'I need you to come with me to see the King.' He could see the shock register on Beorn's face but pressed on. 'I dearly want to improve my relations with him. You're the only one who can help. I know if I can just see him, he'll allow me to swear friendship to him and I can take oaths to reassure him of my loyalty.'

'Sweyn, do you really think that will work? You heard what he said; you have four days' safe passage.'

'Well, that still leaves me with three. Please come with me,' he pleaded, 'please.'

The conversation was growing intense and the three other members of Beorn's crew who were still on board, gathered around their captain in case he should need assistance.

Eventually Sweyn persuaded Beorn to hurry with him to the King. Having commandeered four horses for Beorn and the sailors, the party rode off towards Sandwich. They had travelled less than two miles when Sweyn called a halt.

'We must go to Bosham first.'

'What for? It's forty miles away and in the wrong direction.'

'I have to make sure my crew doesn't desert me. If I don't return soon they might think the King has had me killed.'

'It's a long ride on a day like this and then we've got the journey back.'

'Don't worry about that. A warm welcome awaits you in Bosham and this storm will soon pass, then we can sail back to Sandwich.'

'If you say so,' Beorn reluctantly agreed.

And with that the party made its way to Bosham. They rode through the gale until soaked through, cold and wet, they reached Bosham as sunset approached and where at last the rain stopped and the wind was not so wild.

Sweyn informed the party he intended to go the ships straight away, to see his crews.

'Come with me, Beorn. Come and see my fleet. I think you'll find some handsome ships amongst them.'

'Can't this wait until tomorrow? It's late and I'm cold and wet. Besides, I can see them from here.'

'Come on, Beorn. It won't take a moment. You can have a closer look at the ships and I'll see the crew are all right.'

'As long as you're quick.'

The riders made their way down to the little harbour at Quaymeadow. They had been spotted and some of Sweyn's sailors stepped out of their ships and on to the quayside to meet them.

'Welcome back, my Lord. I trust the news is good?' one of them shouted over the crashing of the waves.

'No. No, I'm afraid it's not good, not yet anyway. I am still banished. But we're going to see the King once more and Earl Beorn is going to help me change his mind. Aren't you, cousin?' he smiled.

'I'll do all I can.'

'Good, let's climb aboard, then.'

'Don't be ridiculous. I told you, I'm wet, tired and hungry. Besides, we can't sail to Sandwich while this east wind still blows. Let's go up to the hall.'

'I said, get on board!'

'I said, no,' and with that he turned and headed for his horse. Sweyn leaped towards him, followed by his sailors who had now drawn their swords. One of them let out a shrill whistle and sailors emerged from all the ships. In no time, Beorn was overpowered and at least twenty armed men had arrived in support of Sweyn, who now had the upper hand. Looking menacing, he addressed Beorn's companions. 'I'd advise you to back off before there's any blood spilt. This is a family matter and not your concern.'

The three men looked to Beorn, who needed no convincing of the futility of resistance. He ordered them back, instructing them to get word to the family.

By the time they had mounted their horses and made off towards Godwin's hall, Sweyn had given orders to set sail. Sweyn's ship led the way and the others followed. The sea was still quite rough away from the calm of Bosham harbour, so they made their way down the Solent, between the mainland and the Isle of Wight. They sailed through the night, making their way westwards with no particular destination in mind.

Beorn had been dragged on board, bound and tied to the mast, where he had been kept all night while the ships sailed west. His anger had turned to frustration, to exasperation and finally to resignation. He believed his cousin was going through a deranged phase and would hopefully respond to a calm voice and sensible talk. Just after dawn, Sweyn awakened and approached his cousin.

'Good morning, Beorn.'

'Sweyn, this doesn't make any sense. Why are you forcing me away like this?'

'Why? Isn't it obvious? I want my earldom back.'

'And you think you're going to get it this way?'

'Why not?'

'Well, what do you intend to do? If you want your earldom back, you'll have to see the King in Sandwich. We're not even sailing in the right direction.'

'Never mind about all that. I want you to agree to my reinstatement.'

'You've forfeited your earldom and it now belongs to Harold and me. I've no intention of giving it to you, especially now you treat me so disgracefully.'

'What's mine is mine and you will return it.'

'I will not. Harold will not. And nor will the King, especially now that you have added kidnapping to your sins.'

'Who says you've been kidnapped?'

'My men saw what happened.'

'Your men are liars and troublemakers. Besides my men saw you come aboard voluntarily, didn't you, lads?'

There was a resounding positive response from Sweyn's crew.

'There, you see. You've merely come for a short sea trip with your cousin. But you must be careful. We wouldn't want any accidents, would we? It's so easy to fall overboard.'

'What do you mean?'

'If I don't get my earldom back, you'll be going on another trip, this time to the bottom of the sea, or shall I sell you as a slave at Dublin market? My brother and father wouldn't want that and neither would the King. So he will return my earldom. You see, it's as simple as that.'

'If you believe that, Sweyn, then you're mad.'

'I'm not mad,' he yelled. 'I know exactly what I do and I will have my earldom back!'

'Over my dead body.'

'If that's the way you want it,' bellowed Sweyn, reaching for his sword.

Unable to move, Beorn stared in disbelief as Sweyn brought the weapon down hard across his belly. Tied to the mast he could do nothing but cry out in agony as his guts spilled on to the deck, as again and again Sweyn slashed the blade into him.

'There you are, you fucking bastard. Happy now?' snarled Sweyn.

Finally, the mad man lunged at his cousin's chest, puncturing the young man's heart, forcing what was left of his life to spurt out of him. Beorn's golden head flopped down in final submission. Sweyn, blood-spattered, still ranting, stabbed him three more times. The crew were staring in silence. There was not a man amongst them who was not appalled by what he had seen.

Sweyn turned to face them and recognising the look of condemnation on their faces, yelled at the dumbstruck sailors, 'Did you see that? Did you? Did you? The bastard wouldn't give me my earldom back!'

He turned to Beorn's body and plunging the sword into it once more yelled, 'You bastard,' at the corpse. Sweyn turned again to his transfixed crew and meeting their stares he addressed them, 'Well, what else could I do? You saw what he did! He asked for it,' and then stamping his foot on the deck, his spit-flecked lips curled back. He wouldn't give me my earldom back!'

Sweyn, silent except for his breathing, looked once more at his dead cousin and then turned his attention back to his crew. 'He deserved that,' he screeched, with his arm stretched out behind him, his forefinger pointing at the dead hostage. The silence of his crew, the sound of the sea and the calling of the gulls were all that greeted him. The ship rocked in the waves as though trying to calm a troubled baby. But there was no calm on board that particular crib. The uneasy atmosphere quickly turned to one of revulsion, as though some evil spirit had settled on the ship. Sweyn felt distant from his crew, marooned on an island, set alone in an ocean of contempt and loathing.

Growing calmer but still edgy, in a quiet, gentle tone for the benefit of those who seemed unsure, Sweyn reiterated, 'He had it coming to him, didn't he? He had it coming to him.' No one seemed convinced. 'I tell you what,' he said, with an uncertain smile quivering on his lips, 'we'll give him a decent Christian burial. What do you say?'

This was Sweyn's idea of appeasement but as his crew was pagan, his offer had little impact. Sweyn could feel the danger in the hostility of the men and decided to do everything he could to keep them with him. He knew full well if a leader lost the respect and loyalty of a Viking crew, it was only a matter of time before he lost his life. Sweyn, looking along the coast, recognised the mouth of the River Dart.

'Look, Dartmouth's just over there. There's a nice church where we can give him a send-off,' he smiled reassuringly, nodding his head, his eyes wide in a caricature of innocence.

The steersman pulled on the helm and the ship headed toward the river. Sweyn started to relax a little. Now we can dump the body, he thought. He would be glad when this blew over. Sweyn's spirits were lifting, though his crew remained silent.

The threat from Baldwin's fleet had passed; most of his ships had been lost in the storm and Edward felt free to dispatch Harold to intercept his wayward brother. With Tostig at his side and ten other ships, Harold left Pevensey and sailed along the coast until just outside Exmouth, he met two of Sweyn's ships heading towards them. Given the order to prepare for battle, the King's ships closed in on the Danes. It soon became obvious Sweyn's men did not intend to fight. When they had closed to within a few feet of each other, the captain of the first boat explained to a grief-stricken Harold what had happened. He went on to say that the murder of Beorn had been no part of any agreement to sail. The crew were so revolted by the heinous killing of one kinsman by another, they felt compelled to leave Sweyn to his own evil ends.

Following the directions given to them by the Danes, Harold and Tostig sailed down to Dartmouth, exhumed Beorn's body and sailed on to Winchester, where they gave him a Christian burial, finally laid to rest beside the body of his uncle, the late King Knut. After several months, word came from the continent that Sweyn was living in Bruges, where he was enjoying the protection of Count Baldwin. Edward sent word that should he return to England, it would be on pain of death.

PLANS IN THE MAKING

King Edward and Bishop Robert were returning from a visit to the site of the new abbey at Westminster. The master mason, a Norman, had supervised the building of the abbey at Jumieges and had been brought over from Normandy especially to oversee the construction. He was proving to be an astute choice.

'Well, what do you think, Robert?'

'It will be a truly wonderful building, my Lord.'

Edward was pleased a start had been made on what he hoped would become his mausoleum and was in good spirits when he and de Jumieges reached his private chamber. They made themselves comfortable and a servant brought them wine. Edward opened the conversation.

'I hear Harold and that woman of his have had another son. Do you know what they've called him?'

'I dread to think, my Lord.'

'Magnus. Magnus, can you imagine it? Why would they call him Magnus after all the trouble we've had with Norway?'

'I've absolutely no idea, my Lord. No idea at all.'

'No, I don't suppose you have. Well, it's one more of Godwin's brood to grow up and give me trouble. We've rid ourselves of Sweyn and not before time. You'd think Godwin would be glad. Even his own sister, the Queen, calls him a gulping monster. But no, at every opportunity Godwin is there to persuade or cajole us into taking him back. He murdered his own cousin, for God's sake, and Godwin still wants him back. We can't have that, can we? You know, Godwin's other sons aren't so bad.'

'Really?' replied de Jumieges, startled by Edward's remark.

'Oh, yes. Tostig is a boy any father would be proud to call son. He's tall, strong and handsome; very religious too, a man of great faith. He and Lady Judith are such good company. I enjoy the time we spend together. Winter evenings spent talking by the fireside, the days spent out hunting. He's so good in the saddle, you know. You really ought to see him ride.

He's like a Norse god galloping through the country with all that long blond hair of his flowing behind. Ah, it's a splendid sight.'

Images of Tostig flooded into the King's mind, filling him with joy, until he suddenly caught the curious look in Robert's eye and continued, 'Harold is a good fellow too, but there are so many of them. There's Gyrth, he's twenty-five now. Leofwine must be twenty-four and Wulfnoth, how old is he?'

'About fourteen, I'd say.'

'Well, he'll want a slice of the cake when the time comes, as will all the rest. They'll all want an earldom and if that happens, I'll be completely outnumbered at court, and it's bad enough now.'

'What do you suggest, my Lord?'

'I need powerful friends in the right places. Friends I can rely on.'

'Like your nephew, Ralph.'

'Exactly.'

Robert, having a feeling his moment was about to arrive, waited with bated breath to see what Edward would say next.

'Saddened though I am that Eadsige has passed away, his death has provided a heaven-sent opportunity that cannot be missed. Robert, you have excelled as Bishop of London and you are more than a mere chaplain to me; you are a friend I can trust and rely on, which is why I want you to replace him as Archbishop of Canterbury.'

'My Lord, this is indeed an honour,' effused Robert, trying to project a picture of saintly calm through his excitement.

'You will be my ally at court and I hope, if you are not too busy, you will find time to reform the church.'

'That will be a pleasure,' said Robert.

The King continued, 'I'll announce my decision at the mid-Lent council. I'm sure it will be agreed. You see, I have the support of Leofric and Siward in this. They are anxious, especially Leofric, to save a little money. By reducing the size of the fleet we'll be able to cut taxes. As King Magnus is no longer a threat and Harald Sigurdsson and King Swein are too busy fighting each other to bother us, we don't need so many ships. Fewer ships mean fewer taxes.'

'So in return for their support of my nomination, you will reduce the tax burden. That should be popular with everyone except Godwin.'

'Yes, but he can strut and squawk all he likes, he'll still be outvoted.'

'Very clever, my Lord. He'll lose some of his military support, but don't you think he'll still be too powerful?'

Edward let out a loud sigh, and then confided, 'You know, I've been thinking what it would be like to be a king in England without Godwin and his family to block me at every turn? Heaven knows I'm under pressure to produce an heir. If we got Edith out of the way perhaps I could remarry and resolve the succession problem.'

'Do you have another lady in mind, to take her place as queen?'

'Godwin decide.'

'Why should Godwin decide?'

'What?'

'My Lord, you said, 'Godwin decide."

'I said no such thing. What I said was' 'God will decide'.'

'I apologise my Lord. I must have misheard,' said the red-faced bishop.

'Indeed you did!' snapped the King.

MID-LENT COUNCIL

The council members bustled into the great hall of Westminster; they exchanged greetings and smiles laden with false sincerity. There was a tension in the air which the Godwins noticed immediately.

Robert de Jumieges sat in quiet anticipation. His mind was barely able to contain the thoughts swimming in his narrow head. Soon he would be the most powerful churchman in the land. That would not be the only change. Today Godwin's fate would be sealed.

Robert's bulbous eyes swivelled in his head, darting from one face to the next, trying to fathom the thoughts that lay behind their owners' expressions. His eyes settled on Godwin, deep in conversation with his son, Harold. Godwin, so wise, all powerful, the kingmaker. He was at the pinnacle of his career but about to take a fall. Who would catch him?

He shifted his gaze to the English clerics, looking at them with utter disdain. What a rabble they were, like shepherds, overly concerned with their flocks; too busy looking the wrong way, paying attention to the bleating of their woolly-minded parishioners to concentrate on what truly mattered: papal reform and the rule of Rome. These were the important issues of the day and for these England needed a united Church, where everyone spoke with the same voice, in Latin, and read from the same bible, in Latin, and the people came to church and prayed, in Latin. Why couldn't these fools see it was the rule of Rome that held us all together and protected us from our enemies? There were wolves prowling around not far from these shores and what did they do? They sat here wittering on about poverty, the needs of the homeless, the plight of orphans, the concerns of mothers struggling to bring up children on their own, without the help of a father. These weren't problems to be solved by the Church. These poor people were gifts from God, here on this earth so that those more fortunate could be charitable, just as women were here so that we might pursue chastity and drink so that we might abstain. Life seemed full of paradoxes.

And so Robert sat through the ecclesiastical meeting, offering less than his usual contribution of pearls to the swine. Looking from one to the other, he made up a list of who would stay and who would go after the great upheaval. His train of thought was broken by the King's voice. De Jumieges had no idea how long he had been talking but he was making an announcement.

'... bid a special welcome to our new Earl of Hereford, my nephew Ralph.'

Cheers and shouts of congratulation boomed in the hall, even though everyone there had been expecting the appointment for weeks. The new Earl of Hereford might be French but he was not a Norman, something that was beginning to count for a lot in England. Ralph was quiet and modest to the point of earning for himself the nickname of Ralph the Timid. Many, especially Harold, liked him for his modesty, openness and optimistic outlook. There was not the mildest objection to his appointment from anyone. It was a good choice to make this the first announcement.

Edward's second choice on the agenda was popular too. He proposed Regenbald, from Lorraine, for Chancellor. This was no surprise to anyone as the royal clerk was liked and had a reputation for prudence in all matters. The appointment was unopposed. As the mood grew more relaxed, Edward introduced the third item on his agenda.

'The next matter we need to discuss is paying off the fourteen foreign ships which we have been retaining to bolster our fleet,' announced the King, with a certain amount of glee, looking positively mischievous.

This came as a complete shock to Earl Godwin and his family. Now he understood the atmosphere; conspiracy was in the air.

King Edward continued, 'Who has something to say on the matter?'

Godwin stood up. 'Does the King think it wise to reduce the fleet? Does this not make us appear weak to an enemy? Would it not invite attack?'

The King seemed almost bored. 'Does anyone else have anything to say?'

Earl Leofric put forward his argument: 'Now peace has returned the English navy is too large; would we not profit by ridding ourselves of the foreign squadron? It's my opinion that we're over burdened by the crippling tax levied to support these idle foreign mercenaries.'

Siward and Ralph, keen to reduce taxes, came in straight away in support of Leofric, as it would be at the expense of their neighbours to the south.

Harold stood to speak. 'Have the other earls considered that England enjoys peace only because the navy is large? Those who would seek to profit by attacking us are deterred by the size of our forces and go elsewhere to look for easier spoils. I believe my father is right; to reduce the navy is to invite trouble.'

This time the King spoke. 'That is something I have already considered, Earl Harold and Earl Godwin. And I agree with you; if we simply reduce the size of the navy we might invite trouble but if we had an alliance with Normandy this would give us the control of the Channel we enjoy and cost us nothing.'

Godwin jumped to his feet in an instant to address the court again. 'My Lord, the Normans have no navy to speak of and that being the case, what possible use is an alliance with them?'

'Earl Godwin,' replied the King quite sternly, 'the Normans could deprive any enemy fleet of access to its ports. Our fleet could roam at will and if by chance it ran into trouble, our Norman friends would be there to offer shelter.'

'Why should we have to rely on them, my Lord? Why rely on foreigners?'

'Aren't we relying on foreigners now?'

'But they are Danes and we have close ties with them.'

'Some of us do,' replied Edward, 'and some of us have ties with Normandy.'

Godwin and Harold continued to argue in vain but when a vote was taken it was determined that the foreign fleet would leave.

Edward addressed the council hardly able to suppress a smile. 'We have the business of the vacant see of the archbishop of Canterbury, and I would like to announce that my preferred choice is Robert de Jumieges, Bishop of London.'

'I'll support that,' called Earl Leofric in an instant.

'Are there any other proposals?' enquired the King.

One of the Canterbury monks called out, 'My Lord, as representative of the monks of Christchurch, Canterbury, I am authorised by my fellows to propose one of our own number, Athelric, to succeed Archbishop Eadsige.'

Athelric was Godwin's cousin and close enough to the earl to have been chosen to preside over Tostig's and Judith's wedding. Godwin had supported Christchurch in its temporal business since Archbishop Eadsige had become too infirm to do it himself. Athelric had taken over Eadsige's clerical duties and had impressed Godwin with his abilities. Several times Earl Godwin had spoken to the King on Athelric's behalf but this had only made the King more determined to offer the archbishopric to de Jumieges.

'Will anyone second this proposal?' asked the King.

'I will,' answered Godwin.

'And why would you do that, Earl Godwin?'

'It would seem only natural to me that Athelric, who has been acting archbishop these last six years and has the support of the monks of Christchurch, should step into Archbishop Eadsige's shoes. Has he not performed his tasks well?'

Edward looked down at Godwin as if considering his answer. 'Athelric has performed his tasks admirably, which I am sure nobody would deny. However, I feel it is time we moved towards a reformation of our Church, as we did in Dunstan's time. We need a change of course and that means a new steersman at the helm, someone who has experience in these matters; in short, Bishop Robert.'

Leofric, Siward and Ralph all agreed, as did those of the clergy who were to benefit from the appointments Edward would make later in the day. By the time the council finished its business, de Jumieges was appointed Archbishop of Canterbury and the views of Godwin and the monks of Christchurch were disregarded.

Edward was now beginning to assert his independence. He appointed as Bishop of London the Abbot of Abingdon and royal goldsmith Spearhavoc, even though De Jumieges favoured William, a Norman and a royal clerk.

Cynsige, a royal clerk who had wormed his way into Edward's affections, was appointed Archbishop of York. Ealdred had hoped to get this position, for the tradition was that the Bishop of Worcester was first in line to the northern metropolitan see, but he was disappointed.

Stigand, Bishop of Elmham and Winchester had remained in the background. Like most bishops he too had designs on Canterbury, but told himself he could afford to wait until another day; in the meantime, he would work to build up allegiances.

Edward was pleased the promotion of Robert de Jumieges brought the feelings between the bishop and the earl into the open. Robert could fight the King's battles for him and Godwin would see the King's favourite, whom he loathed, reach the highest position in the English Church. De Jumieges, from his exalted position, thought he could attack the earl whenever the fancy took him.

Within a week of taking up his new office, de Jumieges returned to Westminster to visit Edward and accuse Godwin of usurping lands belonging to Christchurch. This was just the sort of thing Edward wanted to hear and came even sooner than he had hoped. He summoned Godwin to explain his actions at a private meeting. Godwin had assumed the meeting would include himself, de Jumieges and Edward. To his surprise, apart from de Jumieges, there were four other men waiting with the King. They were Spearhavoc, the newly appointed Bishop of London, Rothulf, the newly appointed Abbot of Abingdon, Earl Ralph, the King's nephew, who was now growing his hair long in the English fashion and the monk Herman, now a royal clerk.

After a few formalities, Edward opened the proceedings. 'Earl Godwin, you know why you've been summoned to see me?'

'I understand I am to answer questions about irregularities concerning land I own in Kent, my Lord. I know nothing more than that.'

'Yes, that is correct but this is not a trial. This is merely an opportunity for you to explain your actions concerning land you say you own in Kent.'

'I see, my Lord. Would you tell me exactly what actions of mine need explaining?'

Edward turned to de Jumieges. 'Archbishop.'

'My Lord, these are the irregularities: Earl Godwin, after the death of my predecessor Archbishop Eadsige, took advantage of the opportunity provided by the grief and mourning of the monks of Christchurch, to usurp church land and use it as his own. Before he was even cold in his grave, Earl Godwin's men were ploughing and sowing the late Archbishop Eadsige's land, church land, in order to seek profit.'

'Well, Earl Godwin, what have you say to that?' enquired the King.

'The lands I believe Archbishop Robert refers to are my estates in Folkestone, my Lord. I made a grant of them for life to Archbishop Eadsige.'

'There you are, he admits it!' snapped de Jumieges.

'If you'll just let me finish, Archbishop,' continued Godwin. 'Thank you. Upon Eadsige's death the estates would revert back to me, or in the event of my death, my eldest surviving son.'

'No. No. The lands should go to the next Archbishop, which in this case is me. Those lands rightfully belong to me. You should deal with Earl Godwin most severely, my Lord.'

'Earl Godwin, what do you say to that?'

'The lands I granted Archbishop Eadsige were not comital estates, my Lord, but held privately by me. The relevant documents are at Winchester and if Archbishop Robert had taken the trouble, he could have seen them for himself.'

'If the lands are his, as he claims, why hasn't he passed them on to me?'

Godwin was beginning to lose his temper now. 'My Lord, I see no reason to make a gift of estates to Bishop Robert. They are my lands and I am free to give them to whom I wish on whatever conditions I choose.'

'Is that so?' snapped de Jumieges.

Ignoring de Jumieges, Godwin continued, 'As a matter of fact, the writ now granting that land to Tostig has already been drawn up. It awaits your seal of approval, my Lord.'

'This is outrageous. That land is rightfully mine,' interjected de Jumieges.

Godwin looked to the King for support.

'If what he says is true I don't see what case Earl Godwin has to answer,' said the King, with disappointment. 'If the land is his, he is free to make a grant of it to whomsoever he chooses.'

'Quite right,' chirped Spearhavoc.

'Yes. Quite right,' volunteered Earl Ralph, rather timidly.

'In that case, unless you have anything to add, you may go, Earl Godwin,' said the King, hoping his father-in-law would leave immediately.

'As a matter of fact I do have something to say. I've been called here today, my Lord, at short notice, away from urgent business. I have had to answer unsubstantiated accusations by, if I may say so, an overzealous hierophant …'

'Archbishop to you, Godwin,' spat de Jumieges.

'…who knows not his business nor for that matter anyone else's. I demand an apology.'

'You will address me as Archbishop.'

'You are not Archbishop yet. You have a pallium to receive, if I'm not mistaken.'

'What do you mean by that?'

'Exactly what I say and you will address me as Earl, as is befitting.'

'Earl Godwin's quite right,' chipped in Spearhavoc.

'What?' spat de Jumieges.

'Earl Godwin is quite right: he should be addressed as Earl,' the bishop repeated.

'Thank you, Bishop Spearhavoc. And now my apology, if you please,' demanded Godwin, glaring straight at de Jumieges.

De Jumieges looked to the King, hoping for a favourable response. King Edward, mortified by the whole business, averted his gaze.

Godwin took a step forward. 'I'm waiting.'

'I'll not apologise to you. You have not yet proved the land is yours,' Robert replied.

Godwin took another step forward; this time his hand went to his sword. De Jumieges was alarmed. 'So, you would strike an archbishop?'

'Not usually, but I would gladly make an exception for you.'

The King, fearing violence, interrupted. 'My Lords, calm please, calm. Why can't you discuss this as civilized people?'

'Because one of us is a Norman and a liar,' answered Godwin.

'That is a gross insult.'

'Is it?'

'Enough!' barked Edward. 'That's enough, Godwin. Earl Godwin,' the King corrected himself. 'The documents will be checked and if they bear out the Earl's account then no more will be heard of this matter.'

'What about my apology?'

'You'll get your apology when we've seen the documents,' said de Jumieges, taking it upon himself to reply for the King.

'Earl. My title is Earl.'

'You heard the King, the matter is closed.'

'The earl is right. You do owe him an apology.' It was Spearhavoc again.

'This is none of your business,' hissed de Jumieges.

'Then why was I invited here?'

'Quiet!'

'No, I will not be quiet,' replied Spearhavoc. Then, turning his attention to Edward, 'I was informed I was to be a witness to events here this morning and so far all I have seen is Earl Godwin accused of a crime, which as far as I can tell, has not been committed and I have seen him treated scandalously by Bishop Robert.'

'Archbishop Robert,' interrupted de Jumieges.

Spearhavoc continued, 'As Earl Godwin so rightly pointed out, you have yet to receive your pallium. Now, why don't you apologise?'

'Yes, why doesn't the Archbishop apologise?' asked Abbot Rothulf, speaking for the first time.

'I think he ought to,' offered Earl Ralph, 'it's only proper.'

King Edward looked studiously at his Archbishop. There seemed nothing else for it. 'I think you owe Earl Godwin an apology, Robert.'

'What! I apologise to him? Never!'

'It would be better if you did.'

'Never!' and with that he flounced out of the room muttering incoherently to himself.

Godwin looked over to Edward; there was a sparkle in the Earl's eyes and the corners of his mouth curled barely perceptibly upward. 'He is more temperamental than I thought. Perhaps the responsibilities of being an archbishop are too much for him. I hope he feels better soon.'

Edward said nothing.

'Is that all, my Lord?'

'Yes, Earl Godwin. You may go.'

Later that day when de Jumieges was alone with the King, he expressed the rage he felt towards Godwin. 'Did you see how he wriggled out of it, the scheming snake?'

Edward, who had had enough of Godwin for one day, started towards the door as he answered, 'My dear Robert, I am afraid we will have to try harder than that to snare that particular snake. He is a clever man and if what he says is verified, and I am sure it will be, then he has won the case very much at your expense.'

'He's made fools of us both, my Lord.'

'Both of us, Robert! Surely not, it was you who made the accusations; I was merely the impartial judge. No, it is you who have been made the fool.'

'Well, it won't happen again.'

'I should very much hope not.'

'You realise it's more than wounded pride that's at stake here?'

'Robert, what do you mean?' asked Edward, now standing in the hallway.

'I think he knows something. I think he suspects we intend to get rid of him and like a cornered rat, he's a danger, a real menace. Being the Earl of Wessex isn't enough for him. His ambitions are limitless, his lust for power insatiable. You do know, don't you, my Lord, Godwin intends to kill you, just as he killed your brother. You can see it in his eyes; he has the black heart of a murderer.'

Edward stared back at de Jumieges, eyes and mouth wide open.

'Make sure you are never alone with him. You are too trusting, which is why you need someone like me to look after your interests. We need to talk more about this at another time. Goodbye, my Lord.'

Speechless, Edward turned and walked away, leaving a seething de Jumieges behind him. There was a heavy thud as the door closed.

Over the next few weeks, Edward's relationship with de Jumieges grew frosty. Forgiveness was not part of de Jumieges' nature and he was enraged by what he considered Edward's act of disloyalty. One evening, as the two men were leaving the King's private chapel, making their way to the great hall, Edward thanked de Jumieges for the opportunity to pray together and explained how he thought he was more skilled in confidential spiritual matters than Spearhavoc, although he did consider the Bishop gifted.

'I appreciate your saying that, my Lord but I'm afraid I've some bad news for you about Bishop Spearhavoc.'

'What is it, Archbishop?'

'I'm afraid I'm unable to consecrate him as Bishop of London. His Holiness has forbidden me.'

'What's has it to do with His Holiness?'

'He has prohibited me from consecrating Spearhavoc on grounds of simony.'

'Simony? Don't be ridiculous. How could he accuse him of simony?' Then Edward stopped in his tracks and repeated his question more meaningfully. 'How could the Pope accuse Spearhavoc of simony? Even if it were true, news would have had to travel very quickly. How could that be, Robert?'

'I'm sure I've no idea, my Lord.'

'Don't you?'

'No, my Lord, I don't.'

'Well, it makes no difference. Since it's unprecedented for the Pope to interfere with episcopal appointments in my kingdom, you can still consecrate him.'

'I fear I can't go against the instructions of the Pope, my Lord, not even for you, especially if you want to reform the Church, so there is nothing you can do.'

'We'll see about that, Robert. If you won't consecrate Spearhavoc because of a papal prohibition, then we must get it lifted. In the meantime, Spearhavoc will remain in possession of London and I shall write to the Pope immediately.'

'Very well, my Lord,' replied the Archbishop. He was not at all unsettled by Edward's threat. King and Archbishop continued the rest of their short walk in silence. When they entered the great hall, everyone stood and the courtiers fell silent. Edward and Robert made their way to the dais and took their places. It was not until they sat down that de Jumieges noticed sitting along the high table next to Godwin, his son Sweyn. Smiling, they sat looking directly at the Archbishop. Robert was livid and sat rigid in his seat, unable to believe his eyes. Godwin and Sweyn could barely repress their laughter.

Godwin was overjoyed at de Jumieges' shock on discovering Sweyn back in court. However, his happiness was soon soured when he discovered his old enemy had refused to consecrate Spearhavoc, especially when it was an open secret that it could not have been anyone but de Jumieges who had made the accusation. De Jumieges had cleared the way for his favourite, William, the royal clerk. The Archbishop had also been busy revealing to the King various murder plots he had uncovered; Godwin was always the mastermind behind them. Throughout July and August tension mounted and by the end of the summer, relations between Godwin and de Jumieges were about to erupt. The Archbishop had found fuel to add to the fire in the form of his new ally from across the English Channel.

THE COUNT OF BOULOGNE

In his private chambers, Edward sat talking with his brother-in-law Eustace, Count of Boulogne and Robert de Jumieges.

'So, Count Eustace, to what do we owe the pleasure of your visit? Have you come to enquire after the health of Earl Ralph?' Edward asked.

'I have no need to enquire of his health, my Lord, I saw with my own eyes how he thrives. You have reason to be proud.'

'So do you, Count Eustace; you're his stepfather, after all, and he did spend his early years with you.'

'Thank you, my Lord; it's most kind of you to say.'

'Not at all. How's my other nephew, Count Walter?'

'He enjoys fine health, my Lord, as does your sister, Lady Godgifu.'

'Good. Then all's well in Boulogne?'

'Let me explain. As you're no doubt aware, Duke William of Normandy is seeking the hand of Matilda of Flanders and you can imagine my court and I are a little disturbed by this news. If Baldwin gives his permission for the marriage, Boulogne will be surrounded by Flanders and its friends and I'll be left with my back to the sea.'

'You will indeed.'

'Naturally, we look to our friends for support. We would not expect help without returning the favour.'

'How do you intend to return this favour, should it be granted?'

'In Boulogne, we think that the English are not in favour of the marriage. If Normandy and Flanders were to grow closer together, they could provide more places for enemies to hide and together they could severely restrict any control England has of the Channel. If they, heaven forbid, took control of Boulogne and Ponthieu, they would have continuous coastline for hundreds of miles. A Boulogne friendly towards England would break that hold. So, you see, you would benefit too.'

'Do you offer anything else, Count Eustace?'

'The atmosphere at court is tense, wouldn't you say?'

'Yes ...and getting worse by the day.'

'You think it might lead somewhere unpleasant, yes?'

'It will if Sweyn Godwinson continues to grace us with his presence.'

'Tell me about this Sweyn Godwinson.'

'He is wild, violent and unpredictable. He has, however, shown remorse and promised to make amends. He's going to Jerusalem on a pilgrimage, seeking penitence. I think he's genuine. Why are you interested in him?'

'Perhaps we can provoke him into doing something rash.'

'You don't have to provoke him, he'll do it anyway,' interjected de Jumieges.

'We may use him to trap Godwin in some way. This Sweyn will provide you with the reason you need to banish him and Godwin too, perhaps.'

'If I banish Godwin, the rest of his family will take his side. What will I do then?

De Jumieges' face split with a malevolent smile. 'Banish them all.'

Edward's expression froze on his face. It was the obvious thing to do, but it seemed too simple. His remained motionless while he considered de Jumieges' remark. 'Is it possible?'

'It's Godwin who stands in your way, my Lord.'

'You will have your alliance, Count Eustace.'

'Thank you, my Lord.'

'If you are successful.'

Edward held a feast to welcome his brother-in-law and as an honoured guest, Eustace sat at the King's side. He fitted in well. He might have passed for an Englishman, with a fine long moustache that ran the width of his long, angular, finely chiselled face, although his hair was a little too short.

Close to the King on the dais sat Queen Edith, Earl Ralph, de Jumieges and the earls and their ladies. As the King addressed his brother-in-law in French, some of those on the dais found themselves excluded from the proceedings. The practice of speaking French at court continued all the while Count Eustace was a guest. In many ways it was as well that people could not understand him, as he did little but criticise England, its court, its weather, horses, farming methods, in fact anything he laid eyes on.

Godwin in particular took a dislike to the Count. On the basis that my enemy's enemy is my friend, de Jumieges courted the Count's friendship. For his part, Count Eustace understood the Archbishop, had the ear of the King and so encouraged de Jumieges' approaches. Like de Jumieges, Eustace had no affection for the English. The only thing Eustace approved of was the English fashion for moustaches worn like his own. He felt slighted on his brother-in-law's behalf that he seemed to lack the power and control exercised elsewhere in Europe. Even relatively small landowners had a say in running the country. It was an anathema to him to see so much interference with matters of state but he hoped he could work it to his advantage. Eustace thought in exchange for offering help to Edward with his fractious earls, some accommodation would be made.

It was not until he was leaving England that he had an idea that would change the course of history. On his return journey to Boulogne, Count Eustace had agreed to spend a night at Canterbury with Robert de Jumieges, so that they could have a word out of earshot of the King. After their evening meal, de Jumieges and Count Eustace devised a plan to dispose of Godwin.

The next day Eustace, with his armed guard of forty men, travelled to Dover. Outside the town they stopped and put on their armour, a provocative thing to do in a foreign country where they were disliked, as Eustace well knew. When they were ready, Eustace led his men through the town gates. As he expected, he and his men were immediately the cause of considerable alarm. One of the townsfolk ran to alert the authorities. In the meantime Eustace and his men entered an inn, demanding food and drink. While the landlord's daughters attempted to supply the soldiers with drinks, a sergeant made his way behind the bar.

'Hey, get out of there!' yelled the innkeeper.

The sergeant muttered and pushed him aside.

One of the customers objected to the sergeant's behaviour and was treated to a punch in the face. At the same time a fight broke out in another corner of the bar after some of the soldiers started to molest the serving girls, just as a burgess was forcing his way into the rowdy bar. He called for order, but had his teeth knocked out for his trouble and he was sent flying into the street, spitting blood everywhere.

Word of the arrival of the armed band of Frenchmen soon swept through the town and in a state of excitement the anxious townsfolk rushed to the Northgate to find chaos. Some of the crowd were holding up a groaning town burgess who was bleeding profusely. There were screams as the landlord of the inn was dragged out into the street surrounded by the soldiers. He was shouting at them. Not a word could be heard above the din of the crowd but everyone saw him run through with a sword and kicked to the ground as screams went up from his wife and daughters. The soldiers laughed and tried to rip the women's clothes off. Like an explosion, the crowd rioted.

Eustace had remained outside the inn with some of his men, looking on approvingly as those who had gone on ahead of them spread mayhem all around. Still on horseback he watched, waiting for his moment to charge into the crowd. When he saw the innkeeper killed and his wife and daughter assaulted, he shouted to the crowd at the top of his voice, 'If the rest of you rabble want to end up like that, then carry on defying us. Do none of you know how to behave? Have you never heard of hospitality? Have you no manners, you English scum?'

Then, addressing his men with his sword held high, 'Let's teach these pigs a lesson in hospitality!'

He spurred his horse forward into the heart of the crowd, his soldiers following his example. They continued flailing their weapons left and right, this way and that, not caring whom they injured or killed. Unable to escape the slashing blades and trampling hooves of the horses, many townspeople were hacked, crushed and trampled. The screams of terrified women and children fuelled the anger of the crowd, who attacked Eustace's troops with anything they could lay their hands on. Overwhelmed by numbers and the sheer ferocity of the locals, Eustace and his men turned and made their escape as fast as they could. They left seven of their comrades behind them.

Four days after the skirmish, Eustace arrived at Westminster demanding an audience with the King and was granted immediate access. King Edward had heard a version of events from Godwin, who was demanding the Count be apprehended and brought to trial. Count Eustace reported his version of the incident to the King. Pacing backward and forward, playing the part of the indignant innocent, he claimed he had been ambushed by Godwin's men and the townsfolk. 'He knew we would return home from Dover and hid his thugs around the town ready to pounce. They took things too far and murdered one of my guards. A fellow soldier, acting with the highest of motives, killed one of the rabble in revenge. It was then that tempers flared. Naturally, my men and I had to defend ourselves from the mob in order to make our escape.'

'That's a lie,' snarled Godwin, unable to contain himself.

'Sit down, Earl Godwin,' commanded the King. Then, turning to Eustace. 'Please continue, Count Eustace.'

'I demand the town be punished with utmost severity, as befits the crime of assaulting a visiting nobleman under the protection of the King. I demand Dover be subject to military punishment!'

'That's outrageous!' bellowed Godwin.

'Is there something you wish to add, Earl Godwin?' asked Edward, sternly.

Struggling to control himself, Godwin defended the people of Dover, describing Eustace's attack in detail.

'What reason would he have, Godwin?' hissed de Jumieges.

'Ask Count Eustace!'

'Tell me, Earl Godwin, do you seriously expect the King to take the word of a rabble of commoners against that of a count? What will people in Europe think when they hear that important visitors to these shores are attacked in the street by mobs?' said de Jumieges, in his loftiest tone.

'What has this to do with you, de Jumieges?' snapped Godwin. 'And who are you to interrogate me? I don't have to answer any of your questions.'

'But you have to answer mine,' stated the King. 'This is a serious business and I think it best if we discuss it at the Gloucester Witan when we meet in a fortnight. Until then I will hear no more of the matter.'

THE GLOUCESTER WITAN

As usual, the September Witan was held in the ancient city of Gloucester. The scene was set for the inevitable showdown between the Godwins and the Normans. Godwin appreciated the danger he was in, so gave himself an edge at the meeting by calling out his soldiers in Wessex. Harold rallied to his father's aid by calling out his troops. Sweyn, Tostig, Gyrth, and Leofwine turned up with their men, as much to show solidarity with their father as to threaten the King.

Edward arrived a week early in order to make plans for the overthrow of the Earl and his family. When the Godwins, with their armed force, also arrived early, Edward was, to say the least, surprised. Eustace, who had accompanied the King from London, was intimidated by the presence of such a formidable force but Edward was made of sterner stuff. Leofric and Siward, who had initially brought with them only a small retinue of followers, called out their entire armed forces and Earl Ralph brought his men from Herefordshire, to protect Edward if the need should arise.

Most of Godwin's men found the arrogance of Edward's French friends overbearing. They were suspicious of their language and customs, which seemed strange and alien. Because Edward indulged himself and spoke French whenever the opportunity arose, many felt they were being excluded in favour of a foreign elite. The French favourites, for their part, thought that Godwin was seeking their destruction. The sophistication of English politics went beyond them; they assumed Edward could rule unchallenged and as for the Witan, they found debates intolerable and unnecessary. Why should matters of government be up for discussion? The King should simply tell them what to do. The involvement of the earls, shire reeves, thanes and the like they mistook for squabbling; the expression of a different view they perceived as disloyalty. They felt confused and besieged.

With Gloucester surrounded by the swelling ranks of armed soldiers, the Witan got under way. King Edward asked Godwin to explain the behaviour of his people in Dover. The Earl went straight on the offensive.

'My Lord, it is not I who need to explain the behaviour of fellow Englishmen but Count Eustace and his Frenchmen, who should be charged for numerous crimes, particularly murder and assault. I demand he and his men surrender immediately and the Frenchmen of Hereford, too.'

Eustace made a counter-accusation. 'That is outrageous. It was Earl Godwin's men who provoked my men into fighting. We had no choice but to defend ourselves. It's Godwin who should stand trial for murder and assault, to say nothing of the crimes he has committed against you, my Lord.'

'What crimes have I committed against anyone, let alone the King?' replied Godwin.

'Rebellion and treason,' answered de Jumieges.

'And murder and assault of my men,' added Count Eustace.

'And complicity in my brother Alfred's murder,' called out the King.

Godwin's face turned white. Now, he realised, there was a conspiracy against him and the King was at the heart of it.

'I refute all charges you have brought against me,' snarled the Earl.

The King responded, 'Then you will have to stand trial. However, before you do, you may find the court takes a more lenient view of your crimes if you punish Kent for the atrocities committed against Count Eustace.'

'But my Lord, it has not yet been established that anyone in Dover committed any crimes.'

Count Eustace jumped to his feet. 'My Lord, you have seen for yourself the wounds my men carry.' Then, turning to look at Godwin, 'We all know how they got them.'

At this, there were shouts of abuse from many of Godwin's men. Quite a few of his contingent were from Dover and the surrounding area and were there to testify on his behalf.

'That has not been established in law, my Lord,' responded Godwin.

'What has been established is this, Godwin,' said the King, oozing satisfaction. 'I have instructed you to punish Kent most severely. Since it was a military party that was attacked it is only fitting a military punishment should be prescribed; burn down houses and ravage the county. That should stop any further outbursts and assure Count Eustace's safe return to Boulogne. Is that clear, Earl Godwin?'

'Perfectly clear, my Lord, but I refuse to commit such an act,' he replied to more cheers from his men. Godwin continued, 'which I consider of unjust cruelty, the decision to do so made unfairly. None of Count Eustace's men were murdered; they were killed by citizens defending themselves and their families. As for rebellion, I would gladly obey the will of the King but it has to be established who is the guilty party.'

Godwin's supporters were growing more hostile by the second. Although Leofric and Siward felt no love for Godwin, they were uneasy about foreigners manipulating the King — that was for them to do. But their distaste for Count Eustace was sweetened by the prospect of Godwin coming to grief. Earl Ralph watched, feeling distinctly anxious as events progressed.

Eustace was denying any guilt. 'That is not true,' interrupted the Count.

'If I might finish!' continued Earl Godwin. 'Finally, I cannot understand why the Archbishop accuses me of treason, nor do I understand, my Lord, why the charge of complicity in the murder of your brother has been raised when I have already answered that charge in the past and been found innocent.'

'I like that,' sneered Jumieges in the King's ear, 'Godwin innocent. The very idea!'

This was too much for Sweyn. 'What has this to do with you, Norman pig? It's none of your business. As for the rest of the French, what are they doing here, I should like to know? This is the business of the English Witan, not the courts of Boulogne or Normandy.'

Sweyn then turned his attention to the French-speaking faction. 'Go to hell, French bastards!' to the cheers and roars of laughter from the Wessex faction. 'This has nothing to do with you. You're only here to cause trouble, lousy Norman curs!'

'I'll second that,' shouted Aelfgar, Leofric's son, much to everyone's surprise, 'and don't come back!'

Once the sons of prominent earls had called out their support, thanes like Ansgar and Azur joined in too, as did a young hot-head from Lincoln called Merleswein.

'My Lords, let's be reasonable about this,' called out Bishop Eadmer, above the din. 'There is no need for unpleasantness. We should discuss matters like civilised men. Let's calm ourselves and this meeting will progress, I am sure, to a proper outcome.'

Count Eustace, Osbern Pentecost and his comrade-in-arms Hugh, had their own ideas as to what would be the proper outcome of the meeting. Behind the scenes they had been urging Edward to take action against Godwin and his family, but it would have been folly as they were far outnumbered by Godwin's men. Earl Godwin pushed for an immediate trial while he held the upper hand and Edward stalled to allow more soldiers to come in from the north. The acrimonious negotiations proceeded slowly. There was a steel-like tension in the air.

Leofric and Siward thought that Edward came down too favourably and too obviously on the side of the French as a result of listening to bad advice. The two earls would protect the King no matter what — he was, after all, their lord. They would also welcome a check to Godwin's ambition but they had no wish to see new men, especially strangers, have things all their own way. But most of all, they dreaded civil war more than the plague, and now its spectre loomed large. Word was spreading around the country about what was happening at the Gloucester Witan. In Wessex, Godwin was fast becoming a hero, while the King was seen as the villain of the piece. In Mercia and Northumbria sympathy also lay with Godwin.

Early the next morning, before the Witan reconvened, Ralph had a brief meeting with Leofric and suggested an adjournment. Glad of a way out of difficult situation, Leofric promised to raise it at the earliest opportunity.

When Edward entered the hall that morning, he was greeted by the sight of most of his nobles looking as though they were preparing for battle. Although no one appeared wearing chain mail, each man seemed to be carrying more than the usual amount of weapons. Throwing axes were tucked into belts, knives as well as swords hung at their sides and most unusually, men had shields hanging on their backs. The King had also been informed that each of the armies surrounding the city was fully prepared to spring to the aid of its lord at a moment's notice. As much as anyone else present, he needed a way out of a situation over which he was rapidly losing control. As Edward sat, Leofric rose to his feet. 'My Lord, would you permit me to be the first to speak this morning?'

As Leofric was usually calm and measured in what he said and had something of a reputation for moderation, Edward was glad to let him address the Witan. He spoke calmly and with great dignity: 'My Lords, you have all been very patient during these difficult days. I thank you all for that. However, I have noticed, as I am sure you all have, that the business of the Witan has been eclipsed by matters connected with the incident in Kent.'

'You mean the murder of innocent English folk,' shouted Aelfgar, not pleased to see his father in the role of appeaser.

There was a murmur of agreement from around the hall. 'If you will hear me out,' continued Leofric. He turned to his son beside him and with a hint of menace instructed him to show his father more respect and to quieten down.

Leofric once more turned his attention to the gathering and continued, 'These matters are preventing the Witan from proceeding with its business, as I'm sure you will all agree. The charges against Earl Godwin are the concern of the law and should be addressed to the court in the form of a trial and not be the subject of endless discussions at a Witan. I suggest a trial in London at some future date.'

Siward was on his feet in an instant. 'I would second that, my Lord.'

'I, too' chipped in Harold.

'And I,' said Earl Ralph.

Edward looked at Godwin. 'I agree,' said the Earl, calmly.

The King surveyed the gathering. The earls were unanimous in their desperation to avoid war, which seemed inevitable if they followed their present course. His mind was already made up when de Jumieges leaned over to whisper in his ear, 'Why not set the trial date soon, say the twenty-first of this month, then if they try and escape across the Channel, they'll face God's judgement in the equinox storms, my Lord.' De Jumieges knew that even if they survived a Channel crossing in late September they would be outlawed. He was jubilant and so was the King, who was better by far at disguising it.

Edward addressed the Witan. 'I think Earl Leofric's proposition is a sound one.' Looking to Godwin he ordered, 'Earl Godwin, you and your sons will appear for trial on the twenty-first of this month at court in London.'

'My sons! What have they done?'

'You heard what I said, Earl Godwin. You and your sons will appear for trial in London on the twenty-first of this month.'

'On what charge, my Lord?'

'You will all be charged before you appear for trial. Now the Witan is dismissed. I will see you in London'

'Hostages. Take some hostages.' It was de Jumieges again, urgently whispering in the King's ear.

'In the meantime you will leave hostages with me.'

'I will not!'

Edward gave Godwin a piecing look. 'Would you disobey me, Godwin?'

'No, my Lord. We will exchange hostages, as you desire.'

'No, Earl Godwin, we won't exchange hostages,' Edward said with a smirk, 'unless perhaps you would like to take the Queen.'

Godwin, though furious, was resigned to his fate. 'I don't think it will be necessary for me to take the Queen as hostage, my Lord. Perhaps you will accept my youngest son Wulfnoth and my young ncphew Haakon.'

'They will suffice.'

With that, the tension eased dramatically. The sound of excited talk filled the hall but it looked as though civil war had been averted, at least for the time being.

Later that day, as the earls and the nobles filed slowly out of the hall, Godwin found himself alongside Earl Leofric.

'Thank you for your suggestion earlier, Leofric.'

'My pleasure, Godwin.'

'He's a fine young man, your Aelfgar. He reminds me so much of Sweyn, all courage and vigour, always speaks his mind. You must be very proud of him.'

Leofric, surprised, simply smiled and nodded in agreement.

The King and the earls gathered up their armies and headed along the north bank of the Thames for London. Eustace and the clergy travelled with them. Godwin and his family travelled with their men to the south of the river.

Before they left, Ralph, Ansgar, Stigand and Malcolm Canmore paid Godwin a brief visit. They would have travelled with him but were too dependent on the King's favour to show their feelings just yet. They did promise their support at the trial. It was reassuring for Godwin to know he still had some friends at court. Godwin shared his thoughts with his family as they travelled to London. 'Edward is behaving like a truculent youth, who on discovering he has some independence, declares his parents useless and attempts to take over the running of the household.'

'Do you think this is because Edward wants to keep all the power to himself?' Harold asked.

'Yes.'

'Then what will happen when we get to London?'

'We'll be tried and we'll all be found guilty.'

'Of what?'

'Rebellion and treason; it will depend on what de Jumieges can dream up.'

'What can we do?'

'Pack our bags. We need to be ready to leave the country at a moment's notice. We need to get as many ships loaded as we can, ready to leave with our best and most trusted crews.'

'They won't be happy putting to sea around the equinox.'

'There's nothing else for it.'

Sweyn, having heard everything, joined in the conversation. 'I shall go to Bristol, then. I have ships and crew there waiting to go to Dublin,'

'May I go with him?' asked Leofwine of his father.

'Yes, Leofwine, go with Sweyn. Tostig, I want you to press on ahead with your men. I want you to gather as many of our valuables as you can at Bosham and be ready to leave. Take the women and children with you. And if you have the time, get someone to organise Waltham.'

'I will, father,' came the reply. He kicked his horse and he and his men set off at a canter for Bosham.

The small party, bitter and with growing despair, continued on its way to London.

Edward eyed the men around him: Leofric, Siward and Ralph and their men at arms, Count Eustace with all of his men, Osbern Pentecost and his comrade Hugh. Then there were the thanes and shire reeves he had called in. There must be three thousand men at arms. There were so many that they lined the riverbank between the Thames and the city wall for half a mile on either side of him. The clergy were also present to offer impartial advice, de Jumieges amongst them. Edward's gaze drifted across the river to the small party on the other side. There were about a couple of hundred of them and Godwin himself appeared to be standing on a table calling to him, his words blown away on the wind like autumn leaves.

Seeing Stigand amongst the clergy, he instructed him to cross the bridge and summon Godwin to trial. Stigand forced his way through the crowd to his horse. It took the bishop ten minutes to make his way to the bridge, the clattering of his horse's hooves on the wooden crossing sounding like a drum roll.

Stigand arrived hot and flustered, pink-faced and out of breath. He delivered his message haltingly. 'Earl Godwin, you and your sons have been summoned by the King to appear for trial. Treason and rebellion are amongst the charges. I have been instructed to escort you. Will you come with me now?'

'No,' replied Godwin, eyeing Eustace and de Jumieges on the other bank, 'unless I'm promised safe conduct and hostages. If the King complies with my request, I'll gladly obey the summons if, and only if, I'm promised a lawful trial and the opportunity to purge myself of the crimes with which I'm charged. I'll offer the satisfaction that the law demands; I'll undergo the ordeal.' Godwin would have to lift an iron bar from burning coal or take a stone out of a pot of boiling water. If, after three days there were no open wounds on his hands, he would be found innocent. Should his wounds become infected, this would be taken as a sign of his guilt.

The shock of the offer turned Stigand's face white. Dutifully, the ashen-faced bishop returned across the bridge and gave the message to the King, who rejected it outright.

Again Stigand crossed the river, feeling ever more foolish and ever more anxious, the urgency of the proceedings weighing heavily on his shoulders. The tension was rising and as he crossed the bridge the rap of ironclad hoof against wooden plank seemed to announce, more loudly than before, the approach of the intermediary. 'Earl Godwin, I must tell you the King offers no assurances of any kind but demands all your followers offer themselves to his mercy.'

Godwin, crestfallen, turned to his men. 'You heard, friends. I cannot guarantee your safety. The King requests your return and I won't hold it against any man who leaves my side but am grateful for your loyalty thus far. Those of you who choose to stay will be made welcome by my family but I must warn you, I can offer nothing but hardship and danger and no more than a promise — the promise that one day we'll return to our rightful place with our honour and dignity restored.'

To a man, all the thanes bowed their heads and, shame-faced, shuffled off. Only the housecarls stood firm. On the other side of the river there were thanes whose duty lay with their lords but who dearly would have liked to have been with Godwin.

'Harold, make sure all of our horses are ready in case we need to make a hasty withdrawal,' Godwin instructed.

Harold nodded in reply then headed towards the stables, taking Skalpi and Finn with him. By the time Stigand and the rebel thanes had reached the opposite riverbank, all the horses were ready to go. By then even the normally belligerent Sweyn could see this was a situation out of which they could not fight their way. 'What do you think, Father?' he asked forlornly.

'Whatever happens today we can be sure it won't be a fair trial. I see our enemies close to the King and wouldn't be surprised if assassins lay in wait. Edward won't grant us safe conduct and hostages, so it's obvious once he has us, he won't give us up. I had hoped I could meet each charge with my unsupported oath but I fear I should be assigned multiple oaths of an ordeal beyond my capability. Can you think what else we might be offered?'

Sweyn, for once, remained silent.

Once over the bridge, Godwin's thanes were surrounded and disarmed by the King's men. Stigand felt all the eyes of London on him, as he made his way slowly back through the pressing crowd, to the King.

'Well, what did he say this time?'

'You can see, my Lord, he has allowed the transportation of the rebels.'

'I wager he couldn't stop them. I'm only surprised there wasn't a stampede when they heard they could get away. But what did he say?'

'He says he still won't cross without sureties.'

'Ah, did he? Well, tell him this is his third and final summons to attend court and plead to the charges. If he doesn't respond he will be contumacious and liable to penalties. And add that he can have his peace and pardon only if he restores to me my brother Alfred and all his companions. Now, off you go.'

Stupefied by the King's final remark, Stigand carried out his instructions. Sick at heart and powerless to alter the course of events he was part of and yet distanced from, once more he rode his horse across the bridge. When he reached Godwin he wept. Godwin knew as soon as the bishop dismounted that his days as earl and kingmaker were over. Before Stigand could reach him he had climbed down from his table and as the distraught messenger approached him, threw his arm round him. 'Whatever it is, my friend, this isn't the end. Now be brave and tell me what news you have from the King.'

Through his tears Stigand relayed the message. Godwin's head dropped; his chin on his chest, he took a deep breath turned, screamed toward heaven and pushed over the table on which he had been standing. Once he had regained his composure he bade his friend farewell and made for the stables, his sons and his men at his heels. Out of sight of the King they mounted their horses and fled. At Godwin's manor only Stigand remained, weeping like a helpless child. He was still in tears when, fifteen minutes later, Robert de Jumieges and Eustace of Boulogne arrived with five hundred mounted soldiers.

During their flight to the coast, Godwin's family split into two parties: Godwin, his sons Sweyn, Tostig and Gyrth, with Archbishop Robert in pursuit, rode to Bosham and embarked for Flanders. Harold and Leofwine took the road to Bristol, where Sweyn had a ship prepared, ready to sail for Ireland. The morning after the flight, Edward with his council and army declared the fugitives to be outlaws — Godwin and his family had refused to observe the law and were now deprived of its protection. Edward sent Bishop Ealdred in pursuit of those fleeing to the west but the bishop failed to catch the brothers.

EXILE

It took Harold, Leofwine and their men two days' hard ride to reach Bristol, leaving nothing behind them but clouds of dust, rumours and excitement in villages and towns along their way. It was a rare occurrence for a group of mounted men to pass through a town or village at all, let alone in such haste.

News of the family's confrontation with the King had not yet reached the West Country, so once there, Harold and Leofwine felt little need for caution. Making enquiries at the quayside, they discovered Orm Erling, the Norse seaman Sweyn had engaged to take him to Ireland. He was small, with a high forehead, sharp eyes and a small face. He was the ugliest man the brothers had ever seen. As they informed him of the change of plan he remained expressionless, except for the darting of his little pig-like eyes. It was Harold and Leofwine, with their men, who would be sailing to Dublin. Sweyn, in a last-minute change of heart, seeing the family's downfall as further punishment from God for his sins, had decided to set out on his penitential pilgrimage to Jerusalem. Arrangements were made with Captain Erling to meet the following day, just after dawn, to load the ships, ready to catch the morning tide.

After spending most of the night at Sweyn's Bristol estate, organising and supervising the transport of the valuables, they headed down to the harbour. Arriving at the quayside the sight that greeted them came as a shock. The four ships, in which they were to travel to Ireland, were moored in a line. They were almost identical knarrs, all about fifty-five feet in length and fifteen feet wide. Into two of them, wretches the like of which Harold and Leofwine had never before seen were being loaded. One ship was almost filled with women, most of whom were pregnant. Into another were being loaded equally woeful-looking men. They were joined by rope neckties, the tell-tale sign of a slave. The captain was giving orders to his men. He saw the brothers approaching and walked over to greet them, giving them a broad grin through his huge yellow beard.

'Good morning, my lords,' he greeted them and slapped Harold on the back so hard he thought he had been kicked by a horse. 'I see you're ready for your journey. If you get your men and provisions,' he nodded to the carts stuffed with valuables, 'we'll get underway.'

'Good,' said Harold. He then gave orders to transfer the goods onto the ships. In order to draw as little attention as possible to Sweyn's treasure, it had been packed into old chests and barrels, which they hoped would not catch the eye of thieves.

'I didn't realise we would be crossing in so many ships,' remarked Harold to Erling.

'Oh, yes. There's safety in numbers,' came the reply.

'I trust your men are discreet and reliable.'

'I would trust them with my life.'

'You seem very sure.'

'I am. The helmsmen on the other ships are my sons.'

The goods were loaded, half on the ship in which Harold would sail, half on Leofwine's, so at least something would be left if one of the ships sank. The men, closely observed by the Viking, did as instructed and then clambered on board, watched from the quayside by Harold, Leofwine and Orm Erling.

'You look apprehensive,' said Captain Erling to Harold. 'Never been to sea before?'

'Oh, I've sailed once or twice before, Captain.'

'Good. But why do you look so concerned?' asked Erling, following Harold's gaze to the slave ships. 'Oh I see, it's the slaves you're bothered about. Some of them do look a bit scrawny, don't they? Your brother didn't leave any instructions for feeding them. But don't worry, you'll get a good price for them in Dublin if you fatten 'em up a bit before they get to market.'

'I wasn't thinking about that.'

'Suit yourself. We'll sell them as they are, then.'

For a moment Harold said nothing.

'Ah, I know what's troubling you. Don't worry, not one of them is English. Your brother Sweyn is a good man, he wouldn't sell any English into slavery, no. They're all Welsh,' the Viking gave a huge grin of satisfaction and rubbed his hands together in glee. He was convinced he had spotted his employer's discomfort and pleased he had reassured him at once. He was congratulating himself on his insightfulness when Harold asked his question.

'How did they get here?'

'Oh, Lord Sweyn brought 'em from Wales,' he said knowingly. Erling might not have been a Christian but he knew enough about them to avoid any more trouble than he needed. 'They're all legal. Not one of them is to be sold in Wales itself. I know the law. 'No Christian to be sold as a slave in his own country,' he quoted. 'Have to take 'em somewhere else. As there's no demand in England these days, they're going to Dublin, where they'll get a good price,' he said with a grin.'

'Why are so many of the women with child?'

'They make a good bargain, they do! Two for the price of one!' replied Erling, grinning, surprised at Harold's ignorance. 'If the buyer knows they're fertile, he's sure he can use them to breed from. Lord Sweyn's gone to a lot of trouble to prove they're fertile, he has,' the captain guffawed.

'What do you mean?' asked Leofwine naively.

The Norseman looked at the women huddled together in the ship then with a glint in his eye and a grin on his face he turned to the brothers. 'Looks like you two are soon likely to become uncles, ha, ha.'

Harold and Leofwine were shocked and the captain noticed. 'Didn't you know your brother's been making a tidy sum out of this over the years?' he asked slyly.

Leofwine answered, 'I knew nothing of it.'

Erling was amazed at his innocence. 'But this is Bristol; the place is built on slavery, everybody knows that. And that lot down there,' he said pointing to the slaves, 'are Welsh. Welsh means slave; everybody knows that an' all, if you don't mind me saying. So, it's only natural.'

'Well, I didn't realise it still went on,' was Leofwine's limp response.

'Oh yes, tradition dies hard with some. You can make a good living out of this,' Erling said cheerily. 'It's always gone on and always will. Anyway, no time to stand around chatting like old maids, it's time to catch the tide,' and with that he jumped down into the first ship. The women cowered as he landed.

Leofwine, with his men, boarded the third ship and Harold turned to board his to find Skalpi hanging on to an eight year old boy by the scruff of his neck.

'What are you doing with him, Skalpi?'

'Found him snooping around the quay, my Lord.'

The boy sensed danger and struggled to escape. Holding him even more firmly, Skalpi told him to stop struggling.

'He says he's your brother Sweyn's servant.'

'Is that so, lad?'

'Yes it is, my Lord.'

'Then what are you doing here?'

'Keeping an eye on my Lord's treasure.'

'Keep your voice down. Is that clear?' hissed Harold, in a whisper.

'Yes, my Lord.'

'So you're here to look after my brother's things, are you?'

'Yes, my Lord.'

'Well, we're about to take them to Ireland. What do you think of that?'

'When my Lord Sweyn finds out about it, he'll have somethin' to say.'

'You think so?'

'Yes, I do, my Lord.'

'Well, I'm his brother, Earl Harold and that man over there is his other brother, Leofwine and we're going to look after his belongings while he's out of the country. We're going to keep them safe. Understand?'

'Yes, my Lord,' the boy replied but he looked as though he had serious misgivings.

'You'd better run on home, then.'

'Haven't got a home.'

'I thought you said you were Sweyn's servant.'

'I am but I don't really have a home.'

'Where are your parents?'

'I don't have any.'

'So how did you become my brother's servant?'

'He found me in a village after the Welsh had raided. I was the sole survivor. He took me in, God bless him.'

Harold was staggered. He couldn't remember the last time Sweyn had shown anyone a kindness. 'What will you do if we leave you here?' he asked.

'I don't know. I reckon I'll find somethin', though.'

'How do you fancy a trip to Ireland?'

'I don't know.'

'Well, you can come with us and be my servant until Sweyn returns or you can hang around here. Which is it to be?'

'I'll come with you, my Lord.'

'Good. You'd better climb aboard, then.'

The boy did as instructed and climbed into Harold's ship.

'What's your name, lad?' asked Harold.

'Bondi, my Lord.'

'Welcome aboard, Bondi.'

When they were all safely aboard, Erling gave the order and the four ships cast away on the ebb tide. Erling's three sons, each at the helm of his ship, with a crewman at each of the six oars, rowed them comfortably downstream on the fast-flowing river. Harold, Leofwine and most of their men crossed themselves as the ships began to move.

'You'll need to do that an' all,' shouted Erling from the helm of the lead ship. He had turned round to check that all was well with his little fleet. Christians amused him. 'And while you're at it, pray to Odin and Njord. At this time of the year the sea can cut up pretty rough. We'll need all the help we can get.'

As they moved down-river, Harold looked at the ship-load of women heading towards God knew what. Most of them looked like animals going to slaughter. They had never seen a town the size of Bristol or so many vessels or ships so big. Those who were able had crossed themselves; others had made an attempt or mumbled a prayer. They made a depressing sight to Harold, dirty and dressed in rags that hung limply over swollen bellies. They had barely enough to keep themselves alive, let alone nourish a baby. He thought of Edyth and of how she looked when she was pregnant. Where was she now? Safely in Flanders, he hoped.

The miserable little convoy was carried out to the Severn Estuary mostly by the power of the tide. Each ship floated effortlessly with the current. Out in the Bristol Channel the slaves looked even more desperate as the sails were hoisted, unfurled and filled with wind, signalling a final farewell to their freedom.

The powerful tide pushed them westward, along the Welsh coast, with a casual speed that amazed the captives. Looking back at their homeland, the slaves left their hearts behind and a bleak mood descended on them. Most of these unfortunate souls had never before left their village, let alone their country, in their lives.

And so through the late summer's day the voyagers made their way steadily towards Ireland. Two days later Harold and Leofwine were in the court of Diarmait Macmael-Na-Mbo, King of Leinster.

EDWARD'S ENGLAND

The week after Godwin's flight into exile, King Edward celebrated in his great hall at Westminster, sitting on the throne without fear of contradiction or embarrassment. He leaned over to de Jumieges. 'Robert, do you think anyone in England can believe what's happened? How the mighty have fallen.'

De Jumieges was surprisingly quiet; he was well aware that if Godwin should ever make a successful return, he could expect no mercy. Knowing how many times Sweyn had managed to return from banishment, he now urged on Edward measures designed to block the exiles' restoration forever.

'This is what I think, my Lord,' answered de Jumieges. 'Godwin and his sons are no longer earls but his daughter is still Queen. Although most of her family is banished from the country, they're probably planning their return as we speak. They were plotting to kill you and might yet succeed. We need to take steps to ensure this never occurs.'

Edward was surprised. 'What have you in mind?'

'Earl Ralph now holds the shires of Hereford, Gloucester, Oxford and Berkshire. You yourself hold the earldoms of Godwin, Harold and Sweyn. Why not divide the spoils and acquire some loyalty?'

'What do you have in mind, Robert?'

'Odda of Deerhurst has been a faithful servant, my Lord. Why not grant him some of Godwin's shires?'

'Which ones?'

'Cornwall, Devon, Dorset and Somerset would be appropriate, don't you think?'

'Yes that's possible,' replied the King, a little taken aback.

'Earl Leofric's son, Aelfgar, needs more experience in the exercise of power. Wouldn't East Anglia be appropriate for him?'

'It would make Earl Leofric happy but what will that leave me, Robert?'

'You would have Wiltshire, Hampshire, Surrey, and Sussex for yourself.'

'And Kent, Robert. What about Kent?'

'I would love you to have Kent, my Lord, but I think it more fitting for the Church to take possession. The monks at Canterbury are having such a difficult time of late.'

'Oh, well. It always gives me pleasure to help the church.'

'Thank you, my Lord. And about the other adjustments?'

'What other adjustments?'

'Well, there is the Church to reform and as I'm forbidden from consecrating Spearhavoc, I'm afraid he will have to go. We can't have an unconsecrated Bishop of London.'

'But he's working on my new crown.'

De Jumieges gave Edward a disapproving look.

'I suppose you're right,' admitted the King. 'As usual.'

'I suggest William, your household clerk, will make an excellent bishop.'

'You think so?'

'Oh, yes. Then there is the question of the Queen. I had assumed you would divorce her, and then exile her along with the others.'

'What! Divorce her? No, I'll never do that.'

'My Lord is subtle. You have another plan?'

'No. No I don't. I could never divorce her. It's as simple as that. Besides, I have no grounds.'

'I'm sure we could think of some,' replied a perplexed and resentful de Jumieges. He hadn't planned a coup just to have the King lose everything he had strived to achieve.

'No. There has to be another way,' continued Edward.

De Jumieges paused for thought. 'How would you feel if she were to enter a nunnery, just for a while, while we decide her fate?'

Now it was Edward's time to pause for thought. After a moment of contemplation he agreed with de Jumieges. 'We could send her back to Wilton Abbey. She can have a royal escort and all the royal honour that befits her.'

'Naturally, my Lord. Of course she'll have no need of her lands or movables once she's there. Under English law I imagine they would revert to the Crown?'

'Yes, I'm sure they would,' agreed Edward with glee.

'Would she stay there a long time, my Lord?'

'Well, forever, I thought.'

'Oh.'

'What is it, Robert?'

'Well, there is the matter of your successor to consider, surely. If you don't provide one, someone else might.'

'Sometimes I think you worry too much. God will provide, Robert, it has been foretold.'

'Foretold, my Lord?'

'Yes. In the times when the Danes were running amok all over England, Bishop Brightwold fled to Glastonbury for safety. Once there he prayed to God to rid the country of the barbarians and bring peace back to the nation. That night he had a dream in which St. Peter crowned me then told him that God would provide a successor. So you see Robert, God will provide.'

And so England settled into the new order. The earldoms of East Anglia and Wessex were divided amongst Edward's loyal followers. Godwin, exiled in Flanders, sent emissaries to Edward asking for peace and a lawful trial. The Count of Flanders and the King of France interceded on his behalf but Edward paid no heed. Finally, he had things his own way; even court business was conducted in French. Life had never been sweeter.

THE RETURN OF THE EXILES

In England, Edward was planning for the future but it was the death of Queen Emma as much as Godwin's banishment which provoked a break with the past. Oddly enough, Edward laid his mother to rest not beside his father Ethelred but beside her second husband and conqueror of his father, King Knut. Edward saw himself happily burying the last of the connections with the Danish dynasty and at the beginning of a new era, but in Wessex more and more people were coming to look on Edward's removal of Godwin and his family as unjust.

The people of East Anglia were of the same opinion as those in Wessex. It was never spoken of at court but in the great halls across the country many believed Edward was behaving illegally. Unaware of all this, Edward floated on a sea of calm. He felt secure after the expulsions but aware of how much he still depended on the support of Leofric, Aelfgar and Siward, at least for the time being. He also needed the support of other men but these he overlooked, men such as Ansgar and Stigand, who were not a part of the inner sanctum. There were others too whom Edward failed to heed; these were the men in the shires, like Azur in Gloucestershire and Merleswein in Lincolnshire and Edric in Essex. While Edward relaxed in his hall these friends of Godwin worked towards his downfall.

Edward had, by way of securing his loyalty, given Harold's earldom to Aelfgar Leofricson. This, he thought, would probably be enough to deal with any attacks the exiles might inflict on the east coast. Odda and Ralph, neither of them experienced sailors, were to protect the south with the navy's fleet of forty ships. Having discovered Harold and Leofwine were in Dublin, he also arranged a military command to prepare for any attack on the southwest. Edward was happy in his belief that his kingdom was secure.

In East Anglia, Harold's friend, Edric of Laxfield, had been prominent in organising sympathisers and providing shelter for any of Harold's men still left in the country, and Gauti was busy running messages from one group to another. Ansgar, enthusiastic about seeing the return of his friends Godwin and Harold, had many a quiet and subtle word in the ear of Leofric and Siward, as did Stigand. Seeds of doubt were sown in their minds as to how safe their positions would be in the new order. True, Aelfgar might now be an earl but had they not seen with their own eyes just how easy it was to remove a troublesome nobleman from court, even one as powerful as Godwin? The new Norman elite were gaining power in court and in the Church. Was it really for the common good? Did they think that so many foreigners, ignorant of English customs, should have so much control? Where would it all end? Speculation was rife.

Ansgar and Stigand soon realized that the two earls would be very reluctant to take up weapons against fellow countrymen and risk their own lives to defend the new order. Even their sons were in agreement; Aelfgar's and Osbern's hatred of the Normans far outweighed any bad feeling they had towards Godwin. It was evident they would, however, be quick to defend their king, if his person were threatened.

Over the late spring and early summer private armies were raised in Ireland and Flanders. Godwin was busy negotiating with allies in England. Messages came and went this way and that across the English Channel. Godwin's men travelled the roads and rivers of England visiting sympathisers and friends. The response was encouraging and led the Earl to believe he would have a strong following. In late June Godwin sailed with three ships from Flanders. Slipping past the English navy at Sandwich he landed at Dungeness in Kent. Stepping on to English soil for the first time in nearly a year, he received a rapturous welcome and an encouraging response to his propositions.

But Ralph and Odda, if inexperienced, were determined commanders. They moved their ships to attack Godwin and forced him to retreat before them to Pevensey. However, the campaign was halted by a westerly gale which blew both fleets back up the Channel. Godwin returned to Bruges and his adversaries to London, with what was left of the fleet, to claim a great victory. The King summoned them to his chambers.

'Welcome back, my Lords. What have you to report? Total victory? Annihilation of my enemy? A resounding defeat for Godwin?'

'We chased him off, my Lord,' replied Ralph, with what he thought was a winning smile. He just looked foolish. 'We shan't see him again.'

'How many ships were in his fleet?'

'Oh, easily six or seven, perhaps more.'

'How many did you have?'

'Forty, my Lord,' said Earl Ralph. Earl Odda remained silent.

'And you couldn't capture him?'

'We would have, but for the storm.'

'Oh, the storm. And what do you think he'll do now?'

'Stay away, I should think.'

'How was he treated in Kent?'

'It has to be said he's still popular there, my Lord.'

'Still popular! As popular as I am?'

'Oh, I doubt it, my Lord.'

'You doubt it. I doubt if you have any idea at all. Godwin comes back to Kent in a few ships — I understand there were only three — and with the entire English fleet at your disposal you couldn't catch him. You just get yourselves caught in a storm and return leaving half my navy at the bottom of the sea.'

'Less than half, my Lord. I think we came back with lots of ships.'

'Do you? Most of them have sails in tatters, lost oars, broken masts, and that is to say nothing of men overboard and the two ships that capsized in the estuary on the way home! See to it any damaged vessels are repaired and then organise more ships and crews to man them.'

'Certainly, my Lord.'

'You've said nothing, Odda. Why?'

'There's nothing to add to what Earl Ralph has said, except that Godwin must have suffered damage to his ships too. And for all we know, he's at the bottom of the sea.'

'Why did you not follow him and sink him?'

Ralph and Odda turned and looked at each other. Their expressions conveyed their thoughts; they were completely blank. Lacking inspiration they turned once more to the angry face of their king. It was Ralph who spoke. 'We're sorry, uncle.'

'Refit the damaged ships, order another dozen new ones and find crews.'

The two earls were rooted to the spot.

'Well, what are you waiting for?'

They left, red-faced, heads bowed in shame. Soon they would be the laughing stock of all England and Godwin a hero.

'And I'll see if I can find some new commanders,' shouted Edward after them, 'who know what they're doing.'

Ralph and Odda could hear him ranting to himself as they left.

From Bruges, once his vessels were refitted, Godwin sailed directly to the Isle of Wight with a fleet of twenty ships. Once there he helped himself to supplies and provisions. In all his raids not one of the locals came to any harm. From his island base he sent out ships along the southwest to spy along the coast.

In late August, father and sons joined forces on the shore at Portland. Before the ships had even beached, all four sons leaped over the sides and ran towards each other; they were jumping around like puppies by the time Godwin caught up with them.

'Harold. Leofwine. It's so good to see you,' he said, a little out of breath.

'Father!' they called in unison. Letting go of their brothers, Harold and Leofwine grabbed their father in simultaneous bear hugs and squeezed out what little air was left in him. Noticing his colour change, they let go to allow him time to get his breath back.

'It's so good to see you both again,' the old man gasped. 'Let's make camp here for the night. We'll feast under the stars and you can tell me all about Ireland.'

Godwin and Harold signalled instructions to their fleets; the captains turned the longships and beached them on the shore. Rollers were brought out of each craft and laid upon the beach. The crews then hauled the ships up onto the safety of the shore. Shelters were made with the sails. Barrels of pickles, smoked goods, salted pork and preserves were produced as well as beer, mead and wine. Wood was collected and fires started. Half a dozen sheep and a couple of pigs, courtesy of Earl Godwin, were soon roasting. Harold approached him. 'Father, there's something you must know.'

'Go on,' said Godwin.

'Coming over from Ireland we landed in Porlock in Devon to get supplies and the local thane, who took his allegiance to King Edward very seriously, challenged us. He ordered my men to go but told Leofwine and me that we were his prisoners and would be taken to London before the King. I explained to him that soon we would be reinstated and he really ought to go home, which he did before returning with five hundred men.

When they attacked us we defeated them without much effort. The thane and about thirty of his men were killed.'

'Did you lose any men?'

'No, and no one wounded.'

'What else could you have done?'

'Well, nothing.'

'So, it's done now and can't be undone. When we're restored to power we'll compensate the widows. Don't dwell on this, Harold. It wasn't your fault. Now come with me. You must need a drink and something to eat.'

By early evening everyone was ready for a meal. Godwin and his sons, along with the captain of each ship and senior housecarls, sat around a fire. Around other fires sat crewmembers, housecarls, volunteers and soldiers of fortune. There was plenty to drink; the mood was good, the summer evening warm and the sea calm. Everyone, feeling he was amongst friends, was in good spirits. The smell of the sea and wood smoke was in the air, so too was the smell of cooking.

Darkness was falling, as, gathered round campfires, men started to eat. Talking over the sound of the sea as it washed up on to the beach, Godwin reiterated, between mouthfuls of roast meat, the plans he had made over the previous months. He sat there, plate of food in one hand, chunk of mutton in the other, explaining how the family would go about re-establishing itself. His sons were keen to have everything absolutely clear.

The old earl continued, 'Now that we have such a large fleet, the situation is much more favourable.' He paused to take a few chews, juice rolling down his chin. 'We know we can recruit supporters unmolested,' he continued, using his sleeve to wipe the grease off his face, 'and it's time now to sail up the Channel and collect more volunteers. By the time we round the North Foreland we should have assembled enough forces for our campaign.'

The salt in the air had given the men a fine appetite and as they listened attentively they spooned their food from their wooden plates and drank back beer and mead with pleasure.

Godwin continued, 'When we enter the Thames, part of the fleet, given the chance, will slip inside Sheppey and just to show we mean business, burn down the royal manor at Milton. Ralph and Odda are guarding the estuary but I don't think they'll give us much trouble. We should sail straight up to London.'

Harold enquired, 'Do you know where the King's likely to be?'

'The King's staying in London this year. He's expecting us to attack him in the south and so wants to be on hand in case of trouble. The earls should be with him but, as last year in Gloucester, they'll only have escorts. It'll take time to bring all the troops in and even if that should happen, Edward will have no need of them. It'll all be over.'

'You seem very well informed about what's happening, father.'

'Stigand keeps me informed,' answered Godwin, with a twinkle in his eye.

'What about the navy? Won't it be in London? It could be a problem for us.'

'It could be, but Ansgar, Edric and Merleswein are bringing in men from Anglia, and Stigand will arrange for our London supporters to be on the riverbanks. The men of Wessex who support us but who can't join our expedition will travel overland. There'll be a formidable show of strength and support for our cause.'

'I'm surprised so many are willing to rise up against Edward. After all is said and done, he is their king.'

'And ours,' asserted Tostig.

'True, he wears the crown but the Normans make the decisions and what's more, everybody knows it.'

'Even so, won't we be committing treason?'

'Treason! I'll have no talk of treason! I've always been loyal to the King, this king and all the others that have come and gone before him. So I'll have no talk of treason. Some of you may ask, is what we intend legal? I would say it is! The King is the one who is acting outside the law. He's banished us from our own lands without even a trial and refuses to hear our appeal. Does anyone know with what we have been formally charged? No!' snapped Godwin, little globules of spit flying from his reddened face and the wild wind blowing his hair this way and that.

'The Count of Flanders and the King of France have interceded on our behalf,' he continued, slightly calmer now, 'pleading with Edward to see reason and grant us a trial, not a pardon mind you, just a trial. We have been denied even that. Therefore it is Edward who is acting illegally and we cannot have a king who acts outside the law. He must be dealt with accordingly.'

Taking a moment to recompose himself Godwin continued, 'Now, I take the view that if a man acts outside the law, then he shouldn't enjoy the protection of the law. For instance, supposing someone acted outside the law against you, wouldn't you take the same view? What if you discovered a man attacking your wife, what would you do? You'd take action, wouldn't you? If you found a man stealing what was yours, what would you do? You'd take action, wouldn't you? And if in the course of that action the villain got hurt, would you then expect to compensate him? No, you would not.'

'Not that I intend for this particular villain to get hurt, even though the man himself might seem undeserving of our loyalty. He's still the King and as such it's not for us to remove him or cause him injury of any sort. That's in the hands of God Almighty,' said Godwin, looking heavenward for effect.

With that, Godwin took another swig of wine from his drinking horn and when it was drained, pushed it back into the sand. 'The King, if he's wise, will back down from our challenge and we'll be reinstated, Edith will be back at Edward's side and Wulfnoth and Haakon will be returned to us. But let me make it quite clear, just in case there are any doubts, we are also returning for the sake of England; we have to rescue Edward from the Norman beast that, against the nature of things, seems to have manipulated the King into acting against his will. What if this continues, where will it stop? How many families will live in misery, paying increased taxes as a result of Norman greed, or be driven from their lands? Is it England's future to suffer foreign rule? No! Remove the Norman and free Edward. Free Edward and we free ourselves. But he must listen to reason and reinstate us.'

'You make it sound simple, father.'

'Harold, this will work. I'm convinced.' Then as if signalling the end of the conversation, looking around at no one in particular, he took his horn from the sand and without checking to see if it had been refilled, drank deep. Godwin's servants knew better than to keep him waiting.

'My only regret is that Sweyn won't be with us when it happens.' The old earl looked deeply saddened by the thought. 'And I've had another idea but I'll tell you all about that when we're safely installed in London,' he said gruffly.

Now a chill sea air blew on to the beach and the men huddled deeper into their cloaks and blankets. Some crawled into their leather sleeping bags, others edged closer to the fire.

In the clear black summer sky the stars and the golden moon shone brightly. On the breeze, the chords from someone's lyre floated on the night air; the music mixed with the sound of the gentle breaking of the waves, forming a lullaby to send the warriors to sleep. Godwin and his sons were still drinking, singing, reminiscing, telling new riddles and stories of bold adventurers and solving the problems of the world long into the night.

The next day Godwin with his sons and their men, after a blessing by Edmund, set sail for London, stopping off to pick up followers at their home town of Bosham, before sailing eastwards along the coast to gather supporters in Pevensey, Hastings and Sandwich.

When they arrived in Dover they were made so welcome they thought they would never be able to leave. It had been a year since Count Eustace had fought with and slain the residents and memories were still fresh and feelings raw. Since the expulsion of Godwin, under their new lord Robert de Jumieges, the so-called transgressions of the Dover riots had been cruelly punished. There had been rent increases and more taxes and for this the people of Kent had seen nothing in return, except for one injustice after another.

Now Godwin had returned and brought an army with him, they saw him as their saviour. The roar of the crowd was deafening; Dover had seen nothing like it and rather than make a speech, Godwin gave up and allowed himself to be carried to the town's great hall to be entertained with his sons and some of his men. The whole town joined in the celebrations and the party continued until the next day when, amid the cheers and best wishes of the townsfolk, the exiles, with a bigger force than the one they had arrived with, left for London.

Half way up the Thames Estuary, Earls Ralph and Odda lay in wait with fifty of the King's ships but as the invaders' formidable fleet advanced, made what they later called a strategic decision to withdraw. Edward had received news of the invasion when the exiles passed by Sandwich. He calculated a battle would be fought and won well downriver from London. It was a shock for him when his fleet returned, without any sign of having engaged the enemy, to moor just upstream from London Bridge. The shame-faced crew disembarked to the jeers and taunts of the locals.

King Edward saw nothing else for it but to hold London. It was with an acute sense of urgency that Edward gave instructions to send for reinforcements. As Godwin had predicted, troops answered slowly the call to arms. In the meantime, Harold's followers and Godwin's men in East Anglia and Wessex, who could be spared from the harvest, were already making their way to the city.

Unhindered, Godwin's fleet sailed up the Thames, heading straight for London Bridge. When they came into view a deafening cheer went up from the crowd that had gathered there for the spectacle. Godwin, in the lead ship, heard the roar and his face lit up with a maniacal grin. 'They're with us lads, they're with us,' he bellowed back to his sons in the following ships. As if in celebration of the earls' return, in the maze of streets sloping away from the bridge and the river, London's many churches were ringing their bells for the feast of the Exaltation of the Holy Cross, as if even the Church welcomed them back. Godwin rushed up to the bow, shouting and waving back at the crowd, which responded with a cheer and began to chant, 'Godwin, Godwin, Godwin!'

The old Earl grew even more outrageous as he realised the strength of his support. He bellowed at the happy throng and, laughing like a mad man, whipped up the crowd.

Just short of the bridge Godwin gave the signal to cast the anchor. Harold and Tostig's ships drew up on his right; Leofwine and Gyrth's on his left. The other ships stayed close behind. Still the crowd chanted.

'Where's the port reeve?' Godwin shouted above the din. Someone must have read his lips because there was no way he could be heard.

Gradually the crowd began to chant 'Aelfsige!'

The port reeve appeared on the bridge, looking a little flustered. He looked down to see Godwin smiling up at him. 'Aelfsige, do we have your permission to enter port?'

The port reeve caught the gist of the request and nodded his head. What else could he do? Another roar went up as Godwin beamed an enormous smile at the port reeve before performing an elaborate bow. As the noise of the spectators grew ever louder, Godwin ordered the crew of his ship to put out the oars. Out of each side of his ship thirty oars appeared.

'What's he doing now?' shouted Tostig to Harold.

'I don't believe it. He's going to walk the oars.'

'What!'

The crowd, seeing what he intended, yelled encouragement at Godwin. A band of minstrels now struck up and began playing popular folk songs, mostly drowned out by the mob. Enterprising tradesmen sold beer and pies.

'He's going to walk the oars,' Harold replied.

'Let's just get under the bridge while we've got the chance. Tell him, Harold, he might listen to you,' Tostig bellowed as loud as he could.

'I don't think there's much chance of that.' Harold turned to see his father cast aside a drinking horn, clamber out of the ship and start walking along the outstretched oars. 'Walk' is hardly the right word to use to describe the tradition still popular with English and Scandinavian seafarers. In order to celebrate a successful voyage an entire crew of a longship might walk the oars of their ship, which would entail the oarsmen keeping the oars protruding out from the ship. Starting with the captain, each man would stride or rather leap from one oar to the next, from the stern to the bow of the ship. As each oar was spaced slightly more than anyone could stride this meant the oar walker would have to bounce from one oar to the next. Once started, it was practically impossible to stop. The only way to stay dry was to make it safely back to the bow of the ship where the successful crewman would be presented with a horn full of ale. Naturally he would have to drink this before getting in line to make a second attempt. This past-time was best not entered into at Godwin's time of life. But what did he care? Wobbling about, he managed over five of oars before he lost his balance. He was laughing even as he entered the water. His helmsman, Eadric the steersman, threw him a line and hauled him in, while all the time Godwin shouted to his sons to join him. Leofwine was the first out on to the oars and the first to complete the walk. The crowd roared encouragement.

King Edward, watching from his vantage point on the riverbank, felt his heart sink. De Jumieges, by his side, saw how dismayed he was. 'Don't be concerned, my Lord,' he said by way of reassurance, 'what you see is the reaction of the rabble to the promise of a little entertainment and the opportunity to get drunk. They will celebrate just as much when you banish Godwin once more. Mark my words.'

Stigand, overhearing the conversation, said nothing. Leofric and Siward remained silent but watchful, calculating how far Godwin would go and how they would respond.

On the river the scene was mayhem. After Leofwine, Harold, Tostig and finally Gyrth had performed the walking of the oars, Godwin had the idea of them walking the oars of their ships together, which they did successfully, to the delight of the onlookers, who much to Godwin's joy started jumping off the bridge to join them.

Upstream, on the other side of the bridge, Earls Odda and Ralph looked on, the questioning eyes of their crews seeking orders. The two men had none.

As the tide turned, Godwin's longships started to drift upstream. Acting quickly, the crews steeped the masts and the vessels manoeuvred under the bridge. Once they had passed under they knew they were home.

When all the ships were safely under the bridge, Godwin led them to Southwark, where he immediately set about taking up residence in his old home. No one on the south bank put up the slightest opposition to him; he was greeted with deafening cheers and shouts of encouragement wherever the crowd caught sight of him. On the north bank and the bridge, the crowds, organised by Stigand and Ansgar, cheered and waved. The people were with them. Godwin's army disembarked and arrayed itself along the riverbank. Reinforcements were pouring in from Kent, Surrey and Sussex. As every minute passed by, Godwin's strength increased.

Edward again, as he had done the previous year, had had his throne placed on a wagon and taken out along the riverside, close to the bridge. Archbishop de Jumieges was at his side as they jolted and jarred on their riverside journey. The rest of the court was in close attendance and the men in arms followed in turn.

The King's court and housecarls surrounded them; all around the excited crowd was gathered. As they came to a halt by the bridge, Edward addressed his earls.

'Malcolm,' the King called out, 'come up here and join me.'

As instructed, the young Scot dismounted and approached the King.

'Watch me and learn well a lesson in kingship,' Edward told him, 'it will stand you in good stead in the future, my boy.'

'If you want lessons in kingship, keep your eye on Godwin,' muttered Ansgar, as his friend passed by.

'So, my Lords, do you have the stomach for a fight?' asked Edward.

Edward's nephew Ralph, timid as ever, said nothing, Odda likewise. Earl Aelfgar was not going to speak before his father and so Edward waited for Leofric or Siward to answer the question.

It was Earl Siward who replied, 'My lord ...'

'The answer's no, isn't it? If it is, just say so. Let's not beat about the bush.'

'Let's see what he wants,' said Siward flatly.

'See what he wants!' seethed de Jumieges, who was standing next to the King.

'Isn't it obvious? He wants to be reinstated. In fact he probably wants more than that, he wants the crown. And what are you going to do about it?'

Siward met de Jumieges' gaze. 'We don't know what he wants until he tells us.'

'I've just told you what he wants,' yelled de Jumieges, fear driving him to fury. The fog in his suspicious mind was clearing; he could see now, only too well, which way the wind was blowing. The other Normans at court looked decidedly unsettled.

'Are you privy to information of which the rest of us are ignorant?' enquired Siward calmly, somewhat enjoying de Jumieges' distress.

'It's obvious! It's obvious,' hissed the incensed Archbishop through gritted teeth.

Turning away from the Archbishop, Siward addressed the King serenely. 'My Lord, if your counsellors were to advise you, they might suggest sending someone to enquire. Should we see exactly what Godwin wants?'

'Very well,' the King replied. 'Bishop Stigand, please find out why Godwin is here.'

'Yes, my Lord,' answered Stigand, suppressing a smile.

History repeated itself as Bishop Stigand mounted his horse and cantered across the bridge to convey the King's message, the clatter of hooves on the wooden structure echoing the past, adding a drum roll to heighten the tension. On the other side, waiting patiently, were Godwin and his sons.

'Stigand old friend, how are you?' called out Godwin.

'Earl Godwin,' replied Stigand, dismounting, 'welcome back. And you too,' he added, throwing his arms around each of the sons in turn. 'Edmund, it's good to see you again,' he said, hugging the monk.

Edward, showing more than a little consternation, watched the Bishop from the opposite bank.

'Is that how we welcome back traitors?' asked Edward, of anyone who could hear him. 'I didn't think he would be so pleased to see them,' exclaimed the King, looking perplexed and noting Leofric's and Siward's expressions. 'You know something, don't you? What is it?' Edward demanded.

The two earls did their best both to look innocent and perplexed by the King's question; they remained silent and looked awkward.

Back on the south of the river, much to the amusement of the onlookers, Stigand and the Godwins were drinking wine together, seated at the very same table Godwin had toppled over the previous year. Calls and chants broke out from the crowd but were drowned out by the sound of church bells. It was as though all of London, every man, woman and child, every beast and every building was celebrating the family's return.

'This is a nice homecoming you've arranged for us, Stigand. It's wasn't necessary to go to these lengths, you know.'

'What? Oh, the bell ringing. It's the feast of the Holy Cross.'

'And I thought they were celebrating my return,' Godwin joked.

'They are. Have you seen the turnout?'

'Have I seen the turnout? I can't see anything else! Thank you Stigand, I won't forget this. How many of our men are on the other side?' he asked in a more serious tone, nodding towards the north bank.

'Over a thousand. Just about enough to overcome the King's men. You could force your way across the bridge if you had to.'

'How many men does Edward have?'

'He has two hundred housecarls, plus the earls and their escorts, then there are the thanes at court and any men they might have with them; probably five or six hundred in all but more are arriving all the time and I understand many more are on the way.'

'How willing are they to fight?'

'If the King's threatened, they will fight to the death to protect him.'

'But there aren't that many of them.'

'No, but their ranks are growing. Time is against you, Godwin.'

'Well, let's get on with it, then,' he said, rising to his feet.

'What shall I tell the King?' asked Stigand, also rising, as did the others, following their father's lead.

'Tell him my demands,' Godwin responded.

'Which are?'

'They are what they have always been. I, that is to say we,' indicating his sons, 'demand the restoration of everything of which we have been deprived. And when I say we, I'm including Queen Edith. It's as simple as that.'

'De Jumieges says you want the throne to yourself.'

'And I thought he wanted it! Tell Edward my demands,' then as an afterthought he added, 'and tell him I want de Jumieges' head on a spike.'

'That'll go down well.'

'But tell him I mean him no harm and make sure everyone hears you. It must be clear to everyone that the King is in no danger from any of us.'

'Everyone who needs to know already does, my Lord.'

'I had a feeling that was so,' retorted Godwin with a wicked grin. 'But it won't hurt to remind them.'

The family walked over with Stigand to his horse and for the time being, bade him goodbye.

Edward and his party watched as Stigand climbed into the saddle and put his horse into a slow, loping canter across the bridge. Edward had to dampen the anger that burned inside as Stigand's features became clear and he picked out a smile. The heat of the mid-September afternoon wore on.

Stigand dismounted and approached the King. Before he could say anything Edward called out, 'Well?'

'It is as we thought, my Lord. Earl Godwin wants nothing more than what was his returned to him. The same goes for the rest of the family.'

'It's a trick, my Lord,' interjected de Jumieges. 'He means to take the throne for himself.'

'I can assure you, King Edward, Earl Godwin wants no such thing; all he wants is the reinstatement of his family and himself,' Stigand paused for effect, 'oh, and Archbishop de Jumieges' head on a spike.'

'What!' shrieked de Jumieges and Edward simultaneously.

Leofric and Siward hid their smiles, as did some of the thanes. Others were not so considerate of the King.

'I'm afraid so, my Lord,' Stigand confirmed. 'It seems Earl Godwin and his sons, have less than charitable feelings towards our beloved Archbishop.'

Edward turned and bellowed, 'Siward! Leofric! What are you going to do about this?'

The two earls looked at each other, each waiting for the other to reply; as Siward had done most of the talking, Leofric left him to answer for them both.

'My lord, as you know we have only our escorts. For you we would gladly give our lives and we will always ensure your personal safety. Earl Godwin has given his word he means you no harm. You are in no danger, my Lord.'

'But what about me? What about me?' screeched de Jumieges in alarm.

'Ah, now that might present us with some difficulties. Perhaps a stealthily executed withdrawal might be your best course of action, Archbishop.'

There was something about the way Stigand emphasised the word executed, which disturbed de Jumieges.

'A what?' demanded de Jumieges.

'Well, for the time being, a pragmatic approach to your difficulties might best serve your interests.'

'You do mean for me to run away?'

'You would live to fight another day.'

'And what if I don't? What if I stay and choose to fight today?'

'Then I am afraid there's nothing to stop Earl Godwin sticking your head on a spike if the fancy takes him. Our duty is to protect the King.'

Edward then addressed Stigand: 'I think your good friend Godwin is bluffing. He wouldn't dare risk attacking me. It's just more posturing, more histrionics. He's just a cockerel crowing and strutting on the riverbank, nothing more.'

Stigand's face grew pale.

Edward continued, 'This is just a show and he thinks I'll back down. Well, go and tell him and his pack of thieving dogs to get out of here at once. I will not meet their demands. They'll leave on the next tide or they will never leave at all, unless to enter the next world. And if they choose to stay, their departure will be all the sooner.'

'Are you certain that's the message you want me to convey, my Lord?' the gravity of Edward's response settling in his stomach like lead.

'It is. Now go.'

'Very well, my Lord,' Stigand responded sombrely. He turned, walked over to his horse and remounted. Within two minutes he was talking to Godwin.

'The King will meet none of your demands. He wants you to leave on the next tide or you will all be killed. He thinks you're bluffing.'

'Does he? What if we won't go? What will he do?'

Stigand shrugged resignedly.

'You know, my friend, I think it's Edward who's bluffing.'

'He seems set, my Lord.'

'Well, we'll soon see about that.'

Godwin made a signal to the captain of his leading ship. Instructions were shouted down the line and a frenzy of activity followed. Within moments, oars were produced, ships cast off as one and Godwin's fleet encircled the King's navy.

Above the sound of the bells, above any other yelling, above all the noise of the city, again the chant was taken up on both banks of the river, 'Godwin! Godwin! Godwin!'

Archbishop de Jumieges stood upright in the cart, proud and erect, and started chanting, 'Edward! Edward!' No one joined in. For the first time since taking the crown, King Edward felt truly vulnerable. This rendezvous with reality turned his mind into a whirlpool of thoughts and fears, none of which served any useful purpose. He turned to speak to de Jumieges but the Archbishop had slipped away. Looking around he noticed all the other Norman members of court had disappeared. In the warmth of the late summer sun, sitting on his throne, the King looked decidedly uncomfortable.

'Siward! Leofric! What are we to do?'

'Perhaps, my Lord, you might reconsider your offer to Godwin,' answered Earl Siward, above the din of the chanting crowd. Spotting the King's reluctance, he drove the point home. 'What would be your alternative, my Lord?'

'Godwin! Godwin! Godwin!' chanted the crowd, drowning out any other sound.

Realising his cause was lost Edward beckoned his nephew to approach him. Climbing up on to the wagon Earl Ralph leaned over, the better to hear.

'Go over, Ralph, and tell Godwin I'll meet his demands. Tell him the Witan will meet tomorrow, here, where we are now and I'll talk with him then. Stay over there as a hostage so that he will know I'll keep my word. Don't worry, I'm sure you'll come to no harm,' Edward reassured Ralph, noticing the look of woe on his face.

No one in the Godwin camp was aware of the rapid departure of most of the court's Norman contingent. No one had any real idea if the campaign was going their way or if Edward would call their bluff but when a rider was spotted crossing the bridge, everyone guessed there had been a major turning-point in the proceedings.

'Can you make out who it is?' asked Godwin of everyone in general.

'It's Ralph,' answered Harold, 'I'd know that riding style anywhere.'

'Yes, you're right, it is Earl Ralph,' agreed Godwin.

'He rides very well, doesn't he?'

Godwin eyed the rider, noted the position of the legs, the hands, the way he sat in the saddle and the ease in which he controlled his mount. He also noticed the way the horse responded; he had to agree. 'Yes, he's a fine rider. It's a pity he can't do anything else so well.'

'He's still young and has a lot to learn. He's a kind-hearted and generous man, father.'

'It's you who's a kind hearted and generous man, Harold, to express so high an opinion of him. You do know he's called Ralph the Timid, don't you?'

'I'd heard he'd acquired a nick-name, yes.'

As father and son continued, almost absentmindedly, to discuss Earl Ralph's merits, he grew ever closer; the horse's hooves' drum roll on the bridge now almost seemed a natural part of the proceedings. Earl Ralph brought his horse to a halt before them and dismounted, handing the reins to one of Godwin's servants.

'Good day, Earl Ralph.'

'Good day, Earl Godwin,' responded Ralph, looking a little wary. He was unsure of the welcome he might receive as one of the commanders who had tried to intercept Godwin in the Channel. Would he be seen as an enemy?

'I take it you have some news.'

'I do, my Lord. King Edward will call the Witangemot tomorrow. He requests your presence. He'll meet your demands.'

The family cheered, jumping for joy and laughing as they hugged each other.

'I knew he would come to his senses,' Godwin exclaimed.

'In the meantime, I am to be your hostage.'

'Consider yourself our guest, Ralph,' welcomed Godwin.

'Care for some wine?' offered Harold.

Sensing Godwin's victory, the crowd let out a mighty cheer. Relief and happiness spread throughout the city; Godwin was back and there would be no war. Everyone was happy, save one. Edward's friend, Robert de Jumieges, had slipped away, leaving Edward humiliated and despondent, an island of sorrow set all alone in a sea of joy. Amidst the happiness that flowed all around, he sat in misery upon his throne.

At about mid-morning the following day, after Edmund had blessed them, Godwin and Harold left their home in Southwark with an escort of a dozen housecarls. Feeling confident, if vigilant, they rode across the bridge. Looking down at the river below they could see the navy still encircled by their ships. Behind them, lining the riverbank, their soldiers looked on.

The party approached the Witan through a quiet and expectant crowd. It was as though no one could believe his good fortune; as though the natural order had been restored without bloodshed. Could it be true? Through the morning rumours had spread like wildfire through the dark and narrow streets, from house to house, inn to inn. The rumours told of the return of de Jumieges, with a large force of soldiers. Some people were said to have seen omens while others had claimed they had seen a fleet heading up river.

Godwin and Harold approached the Witan, which was meeting in the open air. When they were just outside the city walls they could see other earls waiting for them, as were the church hierarchy and the King. Edward sat in state, white-faced and anxious-looking upon his throne, raised above them on a plinth. Before him and a little to his right, standing on the bare ground, was Bishop Stigand. In his hand he held the shaft of the ceremonial axe; the head rested at his feet.

The Witan remained hushed, not a word of greeting passed anyone's lips. Godwin and Harold dismounted, as did Skalpi, Finn and Gauti. The rest of the housecarls remained on their mounts at the edge of the scene. Father and son approached the King but Edward indicated with his hand for Harold to halt; he did so and Godwin continued on his way, stopping when he was level with Stigand, who presented him with the ceremonial axe.

Godwin, with both hands outstretched, supported the axe across them. He took five paces forward and laid it at the King's feet. Kneeling there in homage, he then raised his head and begged to clear his sons and himself of all charges.

In response Edward said nothing but sat impassive, stone-faced on the throne.

'My lord,' implored Godwin, 'I beseech you, in the name of the crown you wear and the highest and greatest signs that makes up its ornament, the Holy Cross of Christ. Will you grant my sons and me a hearing before the Witenagemot?'

It pained Godwin to grovel like this and he hoped the onlookers took his actions as a genuine sign of respect of a subject for his king. It galled Godwin all the more because Edward was his son-in-law and owed his position to him.

Collecting himself he continued, 'I put it to you that my sons and I have never been formally tried as the law demands. I am convinced, my Lord, you have been badly counselled and I hope you will hear what the family has to say in its defence.'

From just within earshot Harold heard everything his father said and could detect each minute change of expression on Edward's face; by the look of it, Edward in his own way felt just as humiliated as Godwin. The Witan's decision was a foregone conclusion. The crowd welcomed Godwin's return and the English earls preferred him to the King's foreign faction. Edward overlooked the illegality of his own actions and put his present situation down to Godwin's audacity. He saw himself coerced into going through some bizarre ancient ceremony, all in order to facilitate the reinstatement of a scoundrel and his family of rogues.

Edward, rigid faced, looked down at Godwin. He thought how much he'd like to kick him in the head and then began to wonder if he could get away with it. Something made him look up; there was Harold looking at him studiously, reading him like a book. It made things worse. Now he felt embarrassed, as well as trapped.

But Harold was more concerned about his father and what he was suffering than any urges Edward might have to restrain. A proud man humbled before the King, before everyone, as he supplicated for a fair hearing for his family. Harold had never so admired his father as in this moment; the King he abhorred.

It was soon clear that Edward was swayed by the argument; there were no charges against the Earl or his family who, all that time ago, had acted in the best interests of the people of Dover. Edward knew in his heart he had been the victim of a conspiracy; he had taken bad advice and this was the result. He also knew things might have been far worse.

The King reverted to wearing the countenance of the gentle, saintly man of popular acclaim. It was with an air of resignation he rose out of his throne, took up the axe and laid it before Godwin in a token of friendship. There was an enormous cheer from the crowd, hats flew in the air, smiles broke out on all the faces and the relief felt by everyone was tangible. Once again London was filled with the sound of bells ringing in joyful celebration.

The King and Earl exchanged the Kiss of Peace. Edward stepped back up on to the dais, turned and addressed the Witan.

'It is with great joy I pardon Earl Godwin and his family from any crimes or misdemeanours of which they might have been accused and I ask you, members of the Witan, to endorse this pardon, so that Earl Godwin and his family might resume their rightful places in our court and in our society.'

The Witan endorsed the royal pardon with barely a word said. Once more Godwin was Earl of Wessex, Harold was Earl of East Anglia and Queen Edith returned to court. Now the dispute had been resolved, the King and Earl Godwin walked along the river to the palace at Westminster, and London looked on in glee. Godwin asked the question which above all he wanted answered. 'Can you tell me, my Lord, when I might see Wulfnoth and Haakon?'

'I am sorry, Earl Godwin; I fear they're with Robert.'

'De Jumieges! What are they doing with him? They were entrusted to your care.'

'I delegated the responsibility.'

'But why de Jumieges?'

'While you were away he was so very helpful. He's a very capable man and his offer to educate them seemed generous at the time.'

'We must press for their return.'

'Rest assured, I shall do all I can to ensure you have them back.'

CROSSING

At mid-morning, three days after his narrow escape from England, Robert de Jumieges was waiting patiently for Duke William of Normandy, along with the rest of the Norman court, in the great hall of Falaise Castle. He was casting a critical eye over the members of court when his attention was caught by a door suddenly flying open as the mud-spattered Duke entered, his spurs clanking on the floor. As usual he was flanked by his four closest companions – William Warenne, like a faithful dog, always at his master's side, William fitzOsbern, who like Warenne was nearly always in the company of the Duke, Walter Gifford and Hugh de Grantmesnil. They too were covered in mud spats from head to foot.

The Duke marched over to his place at the dais, slapping his gauntlets into his left hand as he did so. His companions followed after him. 'Excuse my lateness but I've been out hunting', the Duke explained. 'Had no luck, though.'

Duke William stared around at the gathering as if looking for quarry as he and his comrades strode over to the ducal throne. He and his companions placed their gauntlets on the table, each taking a goblet of wine from a servant as they sat down. The Duke took a sip of the drink and reclined. All heads were bowed, the eyes of their owners looking toward the hard stone floor. Only Robert risked a peep. No one spoke.

Duke William looked much more imposing than the last time they had met. Then he had been a lad of fourteen, tough admittedly, but still a lad and one with an uncertain future before him. He was now almost six feet tall and powerfully built. His shoulders were broad like a bull and muscle bulged on the back of his short, stout neck, upon which his turnip-like head rested. He wore his hair after the Norman fashion, cut straight across the brow in front, shaved around the sides and right up the back to the crown. The style did nothing to enhance the appearance of most men but particularly suited the Duke. His roughly sculptured face seemed a strange place to house a pair of the brightest blue eyes de Jumieges had ever seen. They were like a clear, bright, frosty winter sky.

The Duke's body looked fit to burst through his leather tunic; he exuded a powerful physical strength and athleticism. Action came as easily to him as his appearance suggested. He possessed great cunning and an implacable will. He appeared rough to de Jumieges, almost crude, as if in some way not quite formed. The youth he had known so many years ago was gone; it was a battle-hardened man who sat before him now. He was impressive here in his own court where he ruled supreme, although outside Normandy he was of little importance.

The Duke took another delicate sip, the goblet looking fragile in his big, strong hands. He swallowed slowly, put the goblet down and steadily surveyed the hall.

'What business do we have this morning?' he enquired brusquely, addressing everyone in general and no one in particular. 'If it's all right with everyone, we shall discuss business while we eat.'

This was the Duke's way of telling everyone they could look up. 'Robert, won't you join us? I trust you were well received and offered a bed?'

'Thank you, my Lord.'

'Bring another chair over for our guest,' ordered the Duke. A chair was brought over immediately and by the time it had travelled its short journey, two chevaliers on the Duke's left had made space. Servants scurried around laying plates of food on the Duke's table. The court stood around while the Duke and his friends tucked in heartily.

'It is both a surprise and a pleasure to see you, Robert,' said William, good-humouredly. He scooped a chunk of braised lamprey, one of his favourite foods, from his plate. With his mouth full of food he continued to speak with an eloquence not to be found in any court outside Normandy, his speckled table a testament to the quality of the dish. 'It's only a pity it's not in different circumstances.'

De Jumieges was taken aback. So he knows, he thought. 'Yes, my Lord,' he replied.

'It's not every day we have the honour of an archbishop's company.'

'I'm no longer an archbishop, Duke William.'

'You're an archbishop until the Pope says you're not. Has the Pope told you you're no longer an archbishop?'

'No, my Lord.'

'Then you're an archbishop.'

The two talked about Robert's journey and his experience of England while servants continued to bustle around with food and wine. William listened to Robert complaining about England in general and the Godwins in particular before he tired of the griping and interrupted, 'That's all very interesting, Robert, but I understood you had something you wished to discuss with me.'

'Yes I do, Duke William.'

'What is it, Robert? Pray tell.' The gruffness in his voice betrayed his impatience.

'As you know, I'm an exile.'

William conveyed not the slightest hint of surprise.

'If there is such a thing as a man being an exile in his own country. I am in need of a home and I wonder whether you can help me?'

'Of course, Robert, of course. Make yourself at home here in the castle. I will talk to Bishop Odo and we'll see what he has to offer you. But rest assured we'll find a place that befits you and we'll not rest until you're reinstated.'

'I've another favour to ask, my Lord.'

'What is it, Robert?'

'I wonder if you might take care of two hostages for me,' Robert whispered.

'Hostages?' William whispered, in reply.

There's something he didn't know, thought de Jumieges. 'Yes. Although I had to leave England in somewhat of a hurry, I managed to bring two hostages with me.'

The conversation continued in hushed tones.

'Who are they?'

'Godwin's son Wulfnoth and his grandson Haakon.'

'What would you have me do with them?'

'The choice is yours, my Lord,' said de Jumieges, stating the obvious with a smile.

'Consider them a gift.'

'I think Earl Godwin would give a lot for their safe return.'

'I agree, my Lord and they might be worth more than just a few trinkets.'

'What are you getting at, Robert, what do you mean?'

'There's a crisis in England.'

'Your presence here testifies to that.'

'Begging your pardon, my Lord but I do not refer to the present state of affairs in the kingdom.'

'Go on.'

'There is a succession crisis. The English talk of little else. There's no obvious successor, or atheling, as the English would say.'

'How does this involve me?'

De Jumieges leaned close to the Duke. 'Aren't you King Edward's cousin?'

'Yes, but I'm not the only one.'

'That might be true for the moment, my Lord but circumstances, like the weather, have a habit of changing; who knows which way the wind will blow in five, ten or fifteen years from now?'

'You think the hostages might one day make some sort of bargaining counter?'

'Exactly so, my Lord.'

'What does Edward think of your absconding with Godwin's kin?'

'It was his idea, my Lord.'

'Really?' said William, growing suspicious.

'Yes indeed. Edward fears Godwin might wrest the throne from him and so he instructed me to bring you his son and grandson.'

'To deter Godwin from making any attempt to grasp the throne for himself?'

'Exactly so, my Lord. You are perceptive.'

William replied with a nod of his head. 'Do you have a letter from Edward explaining all this?'

'King Edward cannot tell you himself because if Earl Godwin found out what is afoot, there would be trouble. He dare not send a message for fear of interception. Subterfuge and subtlety are called for when dealing with the snakes that surround him, those cunning vipers that scheme day and night for their own ends. The Godwins are like beasts who prowl up and down outside the city gates looking for an opening, waiting to get in and devour whatever they can get their teeth into. They are like …'

'Yes, I understand,' interrupted the Duke, 'they're dangerous and can't be trusted.'

142

'Exactly so, my Lord.'

'Thank you for the warning — and the news of course, thank you for that.'

'But that's not all, my Lord.'

'There's more?

'Yes. As I said earlier, there's a succession crisis in England and Edward thinks you're the solution to that problem, my Lord.'

'How am I to solve his problem?'

'He has no son to succeed him but as we said earlier, he does have a cousin.'

'As we agreed earlier, he has more than one cousin. There's also Earl Ralph and his brother, Count Walter. Surely Edward must consider a nephew first?'

De Jumieges looked around to make sure no one could hear. 'Yes but he wishes you to succeed him. You are his heir designate. You have the qualities to rule England …you look surprised, my Lord.'

'You have not said why my dear cousin Edward would prefer me to succeed rather than Earls Ralph or Walter.'

'King Edward is very fond of his nephews and loves them dearly.'

'But?'

'But Earl Ralph doesn't command the respect of his subjects in a way befitting a king and Walter is unknown to them.'

'So am I.'

'Yes but you have strength, Walter does not. He's timid like his brother. He can't command men or rule a people. And Ralph, he's an excellent farmer, a loyal friend to men and the Church but he's ineffectual as a soldier and as a politician. He's known the length and breadth of England as Ralph the Timid, my Lord.'

'So Edward thinks he might not be able to stand up to Godwin when the time comes and England will need a stronger man?'

'That's Edward's thinking exactly, my Lord. How well you know him.'

'Do you think Edward would like a response to his offer? After all, I might not want to be King of England.'

'I don't think the King expects a refusal, my Lord.'

'Then the King is quite right. How could anyone refuse a crown?'

'Exactly so, my Lord.'

'Would you care for some more wine, Robert?'

'Thank you, my Lord.'

After the meeting, the Duke pondered on everything the Archbishop had told him. Was it credible that he, the bastard son of a duke, could rise to become a king and King of England at that? Then again why not? Edward was nobody just a few years ago. If it could happen to Edward, it could happen to him. King William I of England. Yes, he liked the sound of that. He liked the sound of that very much.

The Duke felt his heartbeat quicken, his breath grow just that little bit short. He thought of his late father, Duke Robert the Magnificent, who had made an attempt to take the throne of England but as his fleet sailed across the Channel the wind changed and blew him to Brittany, so he fought there instead. William hoped to leave a strong, united and enlarged Normandy for his heir whenever he produced one but to leave your heir a kingdom – now that was another matter, and something his magnificent father had failed to achieve.

A NEW ERA

Though suffering ill health, Godwin worked hard to re-establish his position at court. His hopes for the family's future still lay in a grandson yet to be conceived. As time passed Godwin grew restless, his ambitions unfulfilled, but at least he had an alternative plan to secure the family's future. In the meantime he would reconcile himself to Edward.

Godwin showed no animosity to Earl Ralph or Earl Odda. Those Frenchmen who were innocent of conspiracy and who had been loyal to Edward were allowed to stay. William, Bishop of London, who had left the country with de Jumieges, was recalled. He had made no enemies and was one of the few Normans genuinely liked in his adoptive country. No one could discover the whereabouts of the newly rich Spearhavoc or the King's new crown.

Godwin had seen to it that Stigand, Bishop of Winchester replaced de Jumieges at Canterbury. The Normans, Osbern Pentecost and his comrade, Hugh, were banished from the Kingdom. Earl Leofric allowed them to pass through Mercia on their way to Scotland to join King Macbeth, a warrior much in need of brave soldiers.

Late that autumn, on a bleak November day, it was an ailing Earl Godwin who greeted Lady Gytha and the other women and children when they returned home from Flanders. It was a bittersweet reunion for the family. The strain of the previous year seemed to have aged the earl. After Godwin had welcomed his family, he and Gytha exchanged news right there on the quayside where they met. Gytha could tell straight away something dreadful had happened.

'What is it?' she asked.

'Wulfnoth and Haakon are gone. De Jumieges took them with him when he fled the country and I don't know when we'll see them again,' he told her as he held her tight. Tears of sadness and joy flowed together. Happy as they were to be together, Gytha was the bearer of news even more harrowing.

'Husband,' she said. He knew she had something bad to tell him; she

145

never addressed him as husband otherwise. 'It's Sweyn.'

'What mischief has he got himself into this time?' He looked at her face, pale as death. 'Come on; tell me it can't be that bad.'

'He was on his way back from his pilgrimage to Jerusalem,' she could hardly bring herself to continue.

'What happened?'

'He was caught in a snowstorm.'

Godwin now feared the worst.

'The snow fell very early this year. Sweyn walked to Jerusalem barefoot, so I assume he was walking back without boots too.'

'Go on.'

'He was caught in the open and perished of the cold,' she cried.

'No. No. It can't be.'

'A pilgrim who journeyed with him told me. There were twelve in the party and eight died.'

The old man was devastated. 'My boy, my beautiful boy is dead,' he sobbed.

The couple went into the house and straight to their room. There was no celebration in Godwin's hall that evening.

Sadness settled on Southwark. The Earl and Lady Gytha had regained everything they had asked for but in return suffered losses for which they had not bargained. On their minds played the perpetual questions: what had become of the boys, were they alive or dead, who had them now? The questions seemed endless and without answer. It was a mystery that dispirited them throughout the winter.

Harold, Edyth and the children were reunited at Southwark shortly after the rest of the family but it was not until they reached Waltham that Edyth discovered the true nature and the full extent of the changes in the royal court since the family's return. As she sat with Harold and the children in front of their own fire, in their own home, she began to appreciate just how much they had lost.

'Isn't it good to see Leofgar again?' she remarked.

'Yes, it is. And it's good to have you home. Aelfgar left the place in a poor state but all's well now.'

'I'm so glad.' She smiled and squeezed his hand, holding it on her bulging stomach. Another child was on its way.

'You've taken good care of the children. They're all thriving.'

Little Godwin, now six, was attacking Edmund. Magnus, now four and armed with a wooden sword, had come to his aid. All three boys were similarly armed and all had wooden shields. Only the clattering of the children's swords rivalled the tremendous noise of their shouting. Gytha, just a toddler at eighteen months, seemed unperturbed by the clamour. For the children the events of the past year or so were way behind them; they were just happy to find themselves at home, all together with their mother and father and the people and places they loved.

They continued to discuss the children and at first Harold seemed attentive but then his mind seemed to wander.

'Harold?'

'It's this matter of Stigand. He was very useful to us when we were in exile but father decided to reward him for his loyalty with an archbishopric. Now he's ensconced in Canterbury there'll be no prising him out. Father thinks he's a loyal friend but Stigand's only loyalty is to wealth.'

'You have strong objections to him?'

'I do. And if you think my reactions are strong, you ought to speak with Tostig, he's in a rage and he's taken the King's side. So has Edith. Loath as I am to say it, Stigand has no right to the position, certainly while de Jumieges is alive. It's a matter for the Vatican to decide, not just the King. Pope Leo has refused to recognise him, saying the appointment was uncanonical. Stigand says he wears the pallium, so he's within his lawful rights to exercise the functions of archbishop. It's absurd, he only wears the pallium because he found it on a peg. De Jumieges was in such a hurry to get out of the country he left it behind when he ran away.

'Athelric should have been appointed; he is a true man of God. He has the most support at Christchurch; it was he who father supported and now he's arranged for him to have some land in Kent, but that's not the same thing. I discussed this with Stigand – you know what he said? "You're too principled, Harold. You worry about Rome and what Rome will think and what Rome will do. Do you imagine Rome gives a fig about what you think?" He went on to say, "I've been to Rome and seen nothing but corruption everywhere; everything has a price, everything is for sale, holy relics, everything. Do you know I've seen enough fragments of the true cross to build a barn?" '

'I can't believe his audacity.'

Harold paused for breath and then continued, 'He started to complain that Rome was like Sodom and Gomorrah. "London is a more holy city than that place. Why can't an Englishman be Pope? Do you think we'll ever see that day dawn?" Then he went off on a rant for a while.

'I must admit he's got a point about an English Pope. He asked me, "Are we not as holy; are we not as pious? Is our faith any less, do we not adhere to the ways of the one true Lord? Or is there some other reason why Rome is so distrustful of us?" Well, I can think of one. I don't think it helps our relations with the rest of Europe when we have an archbishop who's a bigamist. Of course he claims this is not a problem because he divorced his first wife but he performed the divorce himself. Rome has difficulties accepting that. For them it's bad enough a man having one wife, let alone two. In the case of an archbishop, well, words fail me.'

'What do the other earls think?'

'They take the attitude it's not really their business. Ealdred is Archbishop of York, so Mercia and Northumbria are happy with that. Because Stigand is at Canterbury, which is in Kent, which in turn is in Wessex, then it is the concern of the Earl of Wessex. They're washing their hands of the whole affair.

'That's not all. While we were out of the country, Gruffydd ap Llewelyn ravaged Herefordshire. The King and Earl Leofric have taken a hard line and they're looking for revenge. As a lesson to Gruffydd, his brother Rhys will be executed. If, after that, his depredations continue, then it'll be his head that rolls.'

'Why his brother? I don't understand.'

'He's almost as bad but easier to get to.'

Harold was right. Soon after his conversation with Edyth the head of Rhys was brought to Edward on the eve of twelfth night. In retaliation a band of Welsh raiders killed a large number of villagers in Westbury, Gloucestershire. Tensions on the border were mounting.

DIVINE RETRIBUTION

That Easter, the royal court moved, as was usual, to Winchester to observe the holy day and was enjoying the celebrations in Winchester's Great Hall. After working his way through twelve courses, Edward felt replete. Judging by the mood and inactivity of his guests so did the rest of his court. Surveying the scene, seeing the smiling faces, hearing the laughter and the good-natured banter above the sound of music, Edward wished he could feel more part of it all. He spoke English well enough now not to feel isolated through the limitations of his language but still he felt lonely. True, Godwin and his sons were much warmer towards him now the old status quo had been resumed. The people seemed to have forgiven him for his little transgressions and welcomed him as warmly to Winchester as they had ever done. But still he felt alone. How he missed Robert. Two letters were all he had written; they were kept hidden safely in a casket in a trunk by his bed. A monk, Hugh Margot, who was based at Steyning and frequently crossed the Channel to Normandy, had brought them to him secretly and taken letters to Robert in return. This exchange was his only contact with his dear old friend and the thought that he might never see him again gnawed away at him. His misery, he concluded, was all the fault of the hated Godwin.

For the other members of the court, the feast had reached one of those pleasant moments when everyone was full and there was only wine and customary bread left on the tables and the men looked for easy conversation. Seeing Edward looking pensive, Godwin thought to lift his mood. As the serving men passed to and fro the earl called over to the King.

'I have a new riddle for you, my Lord.'

Mother of God, another riddle, he thought. 'Do tell me,' he said.

'What am I?'

A bastard, thought Edward.

The King sat patiently waiting while Godwin told his riddle, the hall falling silent so everyone could hear.

'I am a wondrous creature,' said the earl with a lecherous grin. 'To women I am a thing of joyful expectancy, to close-lying companions serviceable. I harm no city dweller excepting my slayer alone. My stem is erect and tall – I stand up in bed – and whiskery somewhere down below ...' Bawdy laughter broke out all around.

'Sometimes a countryman's comely daughter will venture, bumptious girl, to get a grip on me,' Godwin continued. He had everyone's attention and it delighted him. 'She assaults my red self and seizes my head and clenches me to a cramped place. She will soon feel the effect of her encounter with me, this curly-locked woman who squeezes me. Her eye will be wet.' He finished to guffaws and ribald laughter all round.

'What did you say?' a voice called out. 'I didn't quite catch it.'

'I don't think we need to hear that again,' said Edward, who hated lewd humour.

'I think I know what it is,' called out Aelfgar. 'Our stallion's got a big one.'

'Never mind that, what's the answer?'

'Is it a church tower?'

'A church tower! Whatever makes you think it's a church tower?'

'Well, it sounds like an erection of some sort.'

'Is it a beard?'

'No. It's not a beard. Let me know when you've worked it out.'

Two or three others stood up and told a riddle. The court was huddled in clusters as solutions to the riddles were sought out, gossip exchanged, conversations continued or conspiracies whispered until an awkward silence fell on the tables. At that moment a servant, attending to drinks, stumbled over some rushes on the floor but saved himself from falling by throwing the whole of his weight upon one foot.

Godwin laughingly drew his table's attention, pointing out, 'We should all be like that, one leg helping the other, one brother readily coming to the aid of the other.'

'Yes,' Edward replied, 'it's always pleasant to see one brother help another and if my brother Alfred were alive today, he would help me now.'

A deathly silence fell across the hall. Godwin jumped to his feet; a plate clattered to the floor as if heralding an announcement. All heads turned, all eyes focused on Godwin in the silent hall.

'So, my Lord, you still believe me guilty of Alfred's murder, after all this time? If I am guilty of Alfred's death,' he cried, 'may God choke me with the next morsel of food that I put in my mouth.'

He reached across the table and grabbed a piece of bread, put it into his mouth and started to chew defiantly. It was so quiet his breathing could be heard quite distinctly the length and breadth of the hall. Then all at once his shoulders started to rise and fall and his face turned red as he gasped for air. His eyes bulged, his face turned purple and he reached to his throat. Choking and gasping he crashed into the table, upsetting food, plates and drinks as he fell sprawling to the floor.

'No! No! No!' Lady Gytha cried out. She threw herself at Godwin, grabbing him, trying somehow to force life back into him. Wailing and crying, tears streaming down her contorted face, she had to be pried off her husband by Harold. Throwing his father over his shoulder, he carried him from the hall. Startled guests stared as Harold made his way to the King's chamber.

Unnoticed by everyone but Leofric was the smile on the face of Aelfgar. 'What bad luck, now we'll never know the answer to the riddle,' he said.

'It's an onion,' was Leofric's curt reply.

In a second, Aelfgar had calculated that he would be the prime beneficiary of Godwin's death. Harold would take his father's place in Wessex, leaving East Anglia without an earl. It would be fair of the King to honour the house of Leofric, as he had the house of Godwin, by restoring the earldom to its son. He looked at his father, who he could see was sharing his thoughts. They both turned their heads to the King, who looked startled by the event. They misread him; he was excited. If only Robert had been here to see this, was his thought.

After collapsing at the King's table, Godwin was taken to his bed where he lay in a fever. At times calm, at times disturbed, on the third day he screamed out, 'Sweyn!' This would be his last word.

Thinking he held the reins of state firmly in his hands, Edward decided to steer his own course. While Godwin was dying in his sickbed, Edward hatched his plan. He summoned Tostig to Queen Emma's old house, where he was staying until such time as Earl Godwin no longer required his private chambers.

The King sat at a table with his queen. When Tostig entered he was

151

invited to sit with the royal couple. The servants were dismissed so they could talk, overheard by no one.

'Tostig, how is your father?'

'Much the same as he's been for the past two days.'

'And what do the physicians say?'

'They're hopeful of a recovery.'

'Good. That is good news.'

'Mmm.'

'You're not so sure.'

'We can but hope and pray to God.'

'Very wise, Tostig. Very wise. It's painful for me to have to have this discussion with you but I'm afraid it is something that must be done.'

Tostig looked at Edward quizzically but remained silent.

'For the country's sake I must prepare for your father's demise.'

Tostig looked him in the eye impassively.

The King continued: 'In the unfortunate event of your father passing away, it's my intention to make your brother Harold Earl of Wessex.'

Tostig simply nodded his head. This was to be expected; Harold was the eldest surviving son and already had experience in East Anglia.

'Aelfgar will be reinstated as Earl of East Anglia.'

'I protest,' replied Tostig firmly. 'Surely …'

The King silenced his brother-in-law with a graceful gesture of the hand. 'Tostig, I have plans for you which will make you far more important than Earl of East Anglia.

Tostig simply stared at him like a befuddled child before responding. 'As Harold's younger brother surely it is I who should be Earl of East Anglia. My wife is the sister of the Count of Flanders; you can't expect her to be a thane's wife forever.'

It was obvious Tostig did not understand the politics of the move, but the King assured him. 'Something will come up, Tostig, you will see. God will provide.'

'God is going to provide me with an earldom?'

'Stranger things have happened. Lead a good Christian life, Tostig and you will see these things will come to you.'

'I must wait for Leofric to die until I get something? My family's position demands I have East Anglia!'

'All things in good time, Tostig.' Edward was not to be moved. Not in a way that anyone would notice. 'You may go now and remember what I've told you and tell no one, absolutely no one at all.'

After Tostig had left, Edith turned to her husband. 'What did you mean by that, Edward? Tostig is confused and disappointed and rightly so. I think he might have led Judith to believe he would be made an earl after his return from Flanders. I must admit, I too expected he would have been offered something before now.'

'I love your brother dearly and I will do all I can to help him. It's awkward that your father sired so many worthy sons; positions will have to be found for all of them.'

'I'm sure you will, Edward; you have the wisdom of Solomon.'

'Thank you my dear.'

Earl Godwin was buried by his family in the old Minster at Winchester, next to Knut and Emma. While the Queen wept, Edward remained silent. He concealed well his pleasure in seeing the ground swallow up his old adversary. He knew instinctively the instant he saw Godwin struck down that England would enter into a new era without the sly old fox around. But Edward badly underestimated the value of a sly old fox.

THE NEW EARL

For a time, life at the English court appeared to run smoothly. There were no threats from Norway; King Harald Sigurdson was far too embroiled in pursuing his claim to the Danish throne. Harold settled into his position as Earl of Wessex with ease. He had grown up in the earldom and knew nearly every worthy south of the River Thames.

He had, in a relatively short period of time, become even more powerful than his father. As well as becoming Earl of Wessex, Harold was now Subregulus and Dux Anglorum. Already fluent in Norse and Latin, he had learned to speak French moderately well; all the better to communicate with Edward and the few remaining Normans at court. It was a gesture appreciated by the King. And so it was in an atmosphere of mutual trust and respect, that Harold broached the subject of succession with Edward, one day when they were alone in Edward's private chambers.

'I'm sorry to burden you, my Lord but the problem of the succession does need to be addressed. If we look to your closest family then Ralph and Walter are obvious candidates. The question remains, are they suitable?'

'You know they're not, Harold. Why do you even ask?'

'Well, there's still Cospatric.'

'Cospatric! I wouldn't have thought you'd put him forward as a candidate.'

'I'm not recommending him, my Lord. He's someone to consider, that's all.'

'Well, I'd say he'd have the country plunged into civil war in no time. At heart he's a Bamburgh and they're full of self interest; all the power will go to the North. The South will resent that and a war will break out. No. Cospatric will have to be content as Earl of Cumbria, I'm afraid. So you see, Harold, what's needed is faith. The Lord will provide.'

'I think you're right. He already has.'

'What do you mean?'

'Edward the Exile, son of the late King Edmund. He's alive and well and living in Hungary at the court of King Andrew.'

Edward was visibly shocked; not so much at the idea of his namesake being alive, he had heard rumours, but at the idea of his being considered an eligible successor. It was the obvious thing to do, of course, and that's why Harold had suggested it. For the life of him, Edward could think of no good reason why he should not be the next king, except of course that he was living on the other side of Europe.

'And he has a son. So when, God forbid, you pass away, England would have a successor to the throne who would already have an heir. If you lived long enough his son could take the throne. Wouldn't that be a good thing?'

Edward had to agree. This idea of Harold's might spoil his plans but for the moment he would go along with it. After all, it was one thing to suggest Edward the Exile be heir to the throne, quite another to install him.

'So, my Lord, do I have your permission to send an emissary to Hungary to make an offer to Edward?'

'Yes, Harold, you do.'

Later that summer Hugh Margot, the monk based at Steyning Abbey who had been conveying letters between de Jumieges and Edward, returned from Normandy bringing news. De Jumieges had been to the Vatican to seek an interdict against Stigand, and the Pope's response had been to name Robert as the rightful Archbishop of Canterbury. But on his return to Normandy, de Jumieges had fallen sick and died. Edward was grief-stricken and gave great sums for the Church to say masses for the Archbishop's soul. Every day, to his dying day, Edward prayed for his beloved friend.

Queen Edith simmered with resentment. Would Edward cry if she died? She watched while her brothers and their families thrived; yet another child had been born to Harold in July, a boy called Ulf. Meanwhile, Edward's failure to produce an heir reflected badly on her, leaving nothing but bitterness eating away at her heart. But at least she was not alone. Tostig was always ready to lend her a sympathetic ear, although she did sometimes wonder if his concern was driven by ulterior motives. He and Judith spent more and more time in the company of the

King. Admittedly, since Godwin had died and Tostig had taken up residence in his father's old hall at Southwark, he was close at hand and so had more opportunity to visit. And whatever his true reasons for being in their company so often, she had to admit his presence made life with the King much more tolerable. When Tostig was around there was laughter in the air and the King was happy. She enjoyed Judith's company, even if she was a little too pious at times. Having them around took her mind off dark thoughts. When left alone she found herself wondering what it would be like to be a widow. Not so bad, she thought; I could remarry and start a family.

BUSINESS IN THE NORTH

That September the court met, as usual, in Gloucester. Absent for the only time since Edward had become King, was Earl Siward. He was away in Scotland with his son Osbern, some of the other northern magnates and an army, sent on King Edward's instructions to assist Malcolm Canmore in his bid to reclaim the crown of Scotland from Macbeth.

Present at court was a subdued Sir William Malet, who was in England to visit relatives and friends. He seemed preoccupied and a little morose. He sat next to Earl Harold, the man at the English court he felt most able to relate to.

As the court sat discussing business it was disturbed by the clatter of horses' hooves amid much shouting and clamour outside. The party could be clearly heard making its way to the great hall. Cospatric, Earl of Cumbria entered, followed by his close friends Gamel and his brother-in-law, Wulf Dolfinson. They made their way to the middle of the hall to face the King.

'You arrive in such haste, Earl Cospatric. What's happened?' enquired the King.

'Greetings, my Lord. It's with great pleasure I bring you news of a tremendous victory over Macbeth. Earl Siward put the pretender to flight at Dunsinane and is now back in England with a vast amount of plunder. Malcolm Canmore is in possession of Lothian and is even now pursuing the enemy for the final battle.'

Space was made for the Earl and his companions on the high table and he sat down on the King's left where he continued his story.

'It was a fierce battle, my Lord, with heavy losses on both sides. The Scots lost many men, including all the Frenchmen who were forced to leave the country with de Jumieges. Earl Siward paid a high price for his involvement. He lost his son Osbern, who fought like a true hero and died bravely amidst a fury of Scottish swords.'

'We must be grateful for small mercies,' was Edward's only comment.

Indeed Edward was grateful; he had every reason to be. True, the plan he had been hatching had not worked out quite the way he had hoped but at least one obstacle was out of the way. It would be interesting to see how the other, older obstacle faired.

'My father has also been killed,' said Wulf Dolfinson. 'He died with Osbern.'

'I am sorry to hear that, Wulf. Your father was a great man and will be sorely missed.'

Cospatric and his comrades continued their stories of battles in the northern kingdom, entertaining the court, well into the night.

Less than a year after Cospatric and his comrades announced the victory over Macbeth, Earl Siward died. Some said he died of a broken heart caused by the death of his son. He was buried in the church he had had built in York. Waltheof, his only surviving son, was too young to take power. In Northumbria, Cospatric, Earl of Cumbria, saw himself as Siward's natural successor but Edward had plans. With the new appointee in mind, he called Tostig to a private meeting.

'Tostig, you and Judith have waited patiently for me to fulfil a promise. Now your time has come... Tostig, Earl of Northumbria! You look surprised,' said Edward, 'but you must have guessed I'd offer you the earldom.'

'I confess the idea had crossed my mind but it seemed too much to hope for. How can I thank you?'

'Before you thank me, Tostig, you'll need to know what's ahead.' The King sat back in his throne, placing his elbows on its arms and interlocking the fingers of his hands.

'As you know, after my father died, a vicious civil war broke out between Knut and my father's son by his first wife, my half brother, Edmund Ironside. One of Edmund's most loyal supporters was Uhtred, Earl of Northumbria.'

'He was one of the Bamburgh family, wasn't he?'

'Yes, he was. Since his death, relationships between the Bamburghs and the court have been a little frosty.'

'I think that's common knowledge.'

'In the winter of 1014, Knut, who was in Dorset, took advantage of a sudden change in the weather to lead an attack on Northumbria. Uhtred rushed north to save his earldom but by the time he got there it was too late to put up any effective opposition and he agreed, through intermediaries, to submit to Knut. Earl Uhtred arranged to meet him in the great hall at Wighill and when the earl arrived, Knut welcomed him as though he were the prodigal son, personally greeting him and escorting him into the hall; the tables were laid out with gold plates and goblets and from the walls hung the finest tapestries. The smell of meat being roasted hung in the air. Uhtred felt both relieved and flattered to be subject to his new lord's protection.'

'Understandably.'

'It was a mistake. Once Uhtred and his guard were seated, a gang of about forty assassins led by Thurbrand, one of Knut's local henchmen, appeared from behind the wall hangings and chopped them all to pieces. They dumped the bodies outside and before the blood had dried on the floor, Knut was feasting with his brother-in-law, Eric of Hlathir, whom he had just made Earl of Northumbria. But Eric was a fool and was really nothing more than the Earl of Deira, while Eadwulf, Uhtred's son by Sige, his second wife, became Earl of Bernicia.'

'Did Eadwulf look for revenge?'

'No. He was a fat, lazy coward. He had no fondness for Knut but it made no difference what he felt because he was dead within a couple of years; murdered by one of Knut's men.'

'Siward?'

'Yes, Earl Siward! Though he wasn't an earl at the time; the earldom was a reward for the murder. Eadwulf was succeeded as Earl of Bernicia by his nephew Ealdred, who was Uhtred's son by his first wife, Ecgfrida. Ealdred was not as easy-going or as forgiving as his uncle. To avenge his father's murder, he killed Thurbrand, the leader of the assassins who had killed Uhtred all those years before.'

'What became of Ealdred?'

'Well, Thurbrand had a son called Carl who became Earl of Deira after Eric Hlathir died, oddly enough of natural causes.'

'So the son of Thurbrand, the murderer of Uhtred, has the earldom neighbouring Ealdred, the son of Uhtred, Thurbrand's victim?'

'That's right. How complicated it all is. They spent some time trying to kill each other but eventually Carl killed Ealdred.'

'Now you will tell me Ealdred had a son who killed Carl?'

'No. It's not as simple as that. Ealdred had no sons but he did have daughters.'

'I know! Aelflaed, Siward's wife, is one of them.'

'That's right. Siward had impressed Harthacnut with his demonstration of loyalty but to make his position as Earl of Northumbria appear more legitimate, he married Aelflaed.'

'So when he murdered Eadwulf he killed his future wife's uncle. What did she have to say about that?'

'Nothing.'

'Nothing?'

'Well, perhaps she saw the wisdom of silence. When I became King I left Siward to govern Northumbria with a free hand. It suited us both. He resented any kind of interference and I had to consolidate my position in the South.'

Tostig nodded in agreement. 'So that was the end of the feud?'

'No. What do you know about Cospatric?'

'I know more or less what everyone at court knows about him and that is Uhtred's third wife was Aelfgifu, the daughter of King Ethelred, so therefore your half sister. Uhtred and Aelfgifu had a daughter called Edith, who is Cospatric's mother. That makes him King Ethelred's grandson. I know when he was a child he was kept away from court in case anything should happen to him. He was a claimant to the throne, one that King Knut might have liked to see out of the way. I understand he was made Earl of Cumbria at Siward's request, in order to buy off any claim he might have made to Northumbria.'

'Cospatric is one of the last surviving males in the line of the great Earl Uhtred.'

'And in the line of Cerdic.'

'Yes,' Edward replied uneasily.

'So why not offer him Northumbria?'

'Because he embodies the worst of the North and I want you to change all that. I want you to bring the North properly into the Kingdom: the same laws, the same taxes. You must have heard the stories; Northumbria is lawless. If a party of travellers makes a journey there without the protection of an earl they're likely to be robbed. Any women amongst them will probably be raped and perhaps murdered. It's well known that local notables are corrupt; most of them are involved in petty crime in one way or another. It can't go on. I want Northumbria to be like the rest of the country. That's why I need you, a God-fearing man with more loyalty to the crown than to his pocket, a man who has respect for the law and who takes his office seriously. It will be a difficult path to follow, Tostig. Do you have the strength for it?'

'Yes, I have the strength for it, if I've your full support, my Lord.'

'That you do, Tostig. That you do.'

'Then I'm adamant in my resolve to root out corruption and I'll deal with perpetrators fairly but mercilessly.'

'Good.'

'You said Cospatric was one of the last surviving males. Who are the others?'

'There are two: Gamel Ormson – not only is he the son of Orm, he is also the son of Aelflaed's sister. His grandfather was Ealdred and so he is great-great grandson of Ethelred. Not so close to the throne or the earldom. Then there is Oswulf, son of Eadwulf.'

'So, when I'm Earl of Northumbria, I'll have to keep an eye on them?'

'You will, Tostig. Beware: in the North; whatever their differences, no matter how much they feud with one another, if you move against one, they'll close ranks and move against you. It would be like attacking a pack of fighting wolves; they'd be on you in an instant.'

In London, at the great mid-Lent council, Edward called on the court to help him deal with the problem of succession to the earldom of Northumbria. Their participation in the invasion of Scotland, which he had so readily sanctioned, had brought about the situation Edward had hoped for. Earl Siward and his eldest son were dead and Tostig would fill the vacancy and learn how to wield power effectively, before being handed the crown.

The council deliberated and Edward announced his decision. 'My friends, never before can any king have been better advised by his court and I thank you sincerely. I will keep you waiting no longer; the new Earl of Northumbria is to be Tostig Godwinson.'

'But my Lord, surely you jest?' protested Earl Cospatric, up on his feet in an instant.

'Why would I jest, Cospatric?'

'No doubt Tostig is a worthy man, but he's a West Saxon. Would he understand our ways?'

'I've no doubt of that,' Edward replied, meaningfully.

'But surely the earldom is mine by right?'

'No, the earldom is not yours by right but I do recognise the reason for your misapprehension.'

'Then why not choose Gamel Ormson? Or am I to take it that you think there is no one in Northumbria worthy of the title of earl? Do you think none of us man enough?'

'I think it's time the winds of change blew across Northumbria …'

'The winds of Godwin, you mean,' shouted Aelfgar, looking the worse for drink.

'Aelfgar, if you have an opinion to express, do so in the proper manner.'

'What do you call the proper manner? You want to set your catamite up in Northumbria and you expect everyone here to agree to it!'

'You had better rephrase that remark, Aelfgar,' Edward snapped.

'I'll rephrase nothing.'

Leofric had his head in his hands, hiding his shame and embarrassment.

'Tell me you're not going to offer Northumbria to Tostig, and then I'll start rephrasing my remarks.'

'I think you had better leave.'

'If you're not going to give the earldom to Waltheof because he's too young, why not hand it to Cospatric?'

'I've said all I intend to say to you on the matter, Aelfgar. Now leave my court.'

'You can't give Northumbria to Tostig! If not a Northumbrian, then why not give it to me? I'm already an earl. I have experience. If you're not going to give Northumbria to Cospatric, why not give it to me and give Cospatric East Anglia? Wouldn't that make sense?'

Aelfgar's remarks emboldened the northern faction, who rose out of their seats and stood as one.

'I think we need a better explanation than the one we've had so far, my Lord,' asserted Gamel Ormson. 'Earl Aelfgar has put forward a very strong case.'

'Here's your explanation. Tostig Godwinson is to be the next Earl of Northumbria because I have chosen the best man.'

162

'You're allowing the Godwinsons to take over the country!' shouted Earl Aelfgar, extremely agitated.

At this point, in an attempt to calm the atmosphere, Queen Edith interjected, 'I think, Earl Aelfgar, you need to consider your words more carefully.'

'And who is the King's real consort in this hall, eh? Tell me that?' Aelfgar leered as he spoke.

'Earl Aelfgar, you are banished from the country forthwith.' Edward spoke.

'What?'

'You heard me. In your place the new Earl of East Anglia shall be Gyrth Godwinson.' Edward had made the choice out of sheer spite.

'What? I told you! Godwin's bastards are taking over the country.'

'Guards, escort this man out,' ordered the King.

'Watch, Father. Mercia will be next. Watch your back. Watch your back, especially if there's a Godwinson about.'

Even while Edward's housecarls were dragging Earl Aelfgar out of the building, he could still be heard shouting. His wife, Lady Aelfgifu, left the hall, shamefacedly scurrying after her husband with her three young children, Edwin, Morcar and Aldytha, in tow.

In the great hall an air of astonished silence had fallen over the council.

'I'm sorry for my son's behaviour,' said Leofric, looking quite drained, 'He's not been well lately.'

'Let's hope he recovers soon,' replied Edward, good-naturedly. He had got his way and he was happy.

'Does anyone have any opinions they wish to add?'

Nothing was said. With the approval of Queen Edith and Earl Harold, their brother Tostig was appointed to succeed Siward. Earl Aelfgar was outlawed and sought refuge in Ireland. In Earl Aelfgar's place, Gyrth Godwinson was appointed Earl of East Anglia. But the ranting of Earl Aelfgar as he was dragged from council was not the last that would be heard of him.

Within a few days of his appointment, Tostig took Countess Judith and his sons, Skuli and Kettle, to York. From there he ruled Northumbria firmly from the outset and the changes he introduced were resented by the old ruling families. Earl Cospatric soon emerged as the leader of the malcontents. Gamel Ormson, Wulf Dolfinson and Oswulf were his staunchest allies. To make things worse, Tostig left his capable deputy Copsig in charge during his frequent absences from Northumbria. The Bamburghs hated Copsig even more than Tostig, who in their eyes was at least a nobleman, whereas Copsig was a jumped-up Saxon thane. They saw Earl Aelfgar's banishment as an attempt by the House of Godwin to extend its power across the entire country, even though it was the King who had banished Aelfgar. Earl Leofric, for his part, had understood and supported Edward's decision but although he would not miss his son much at court, both he and Lady Godiva pined for their grandchildren.

Across the Irish Sea, Aelfgar was planning his return.

THE WELSH PROBLEM

It was a damp November morning when Harold arrived at Westminster in answer to the King's summons. He found Leofwine and Gyrth already in attendance and Leofric sitting silently on his own. Edward looked a little flustered.

'Harold, there is bad news. Gruffydd has allied himself with Aelfgar and they've ravaged Herefordshire. Last week Ralph met Gruffydd's forces two miles outside Hereford and offered battle. It was a calamity. You know Ralph was so keen to try the European way of fighting on horseback?'

'Using cavalry, yes.'

'His men fled the field before a spear was thrown. Gruffydd's saying the English fight on horseback the faster to run away. Afterwards, the Welsh raced to Hereford and killed about five hundred people, then put it to the torch. St. Aethelbert's, the new minster, was looted and burned to the ground and the clergy defending it were butchered. The survivors were taken as slaves.'

'Do you think they intend a full scale invasion?'

'No.'

'How is Ralph coping?'

'Not very well. I'm putting you in command of the army, which has been summoned to report at Gloucester. I want you to lead a force to Hereford and destroy Gruffydd and Aelfgar if you can. Otherwise, secure the border. It's too late in the year to mount a campaign now. You shall have men from all the corners of the kingdom.'

'Very well.'

Leofric looked alarmed by this. 'My Lord, I beg you, please excuse the men of Mercia. They know Aelfgar well and it would be like brother fighting brother if they were called upon to help.'

Harold was not sure he wanted Mercian help if they could not be relied on. The force led by Gruffydd and Aelfgar was relatively small and did not require all the resources at the King's disposal.

'I understand, Earl Leofric. You may be excused. Earl Harold, how long would it take you to get an army to Hereford?'

'A week. What of Cospatric, Orm, Gamel and Wulf?'

'They say this is not a Northumbrian problem. You will have to manage without them.'

'Very well, my Lord.'

Harold and his brothers arrived in Gloucester to find Azur had organised food and accommodation for the army. Earl Ralph was there to greet them looking very ill at ease. The following day Harold quickly moved the army to Hereford. Although it was Harold's first major campaign, Gruffydd, rather than test him had retreated into the hills. Harold was completely unprepared for the devastation he found. Bodies lay in the street where they had been butchered. No one had been spared. Even the animals had been killed. But the worst sight to greet them was of hundreds of corpses that lay strewn in the ruins of the once fine minster of St. Aethelbert's, fallen in the flames, trapped in the church where they had sought sanctuary. Charred roof beams lay scattered among the corpses. All around, the remains of buildings were scorched black as if in mourning. The stench of the slaughterhouse hung over the town.

Harold gave orders for burial of the dead while he and his brothers, along with Ansgar and Azur, inspected what remained of the town.

After fortifying Hereford against future attacks, Harold made arrangements to open negotiations with Aelfgar and Gruffydd, at a place outside the little town of Billingsley. The two armies of about equal size met in the fields just outside the town.

Gruffydd, with Aelfgar at his side and a dozen of their men as escort, rode out to meet Harold and his brothers, accompanied by a small band of their housecarls. As they approached each other, Harold could make out Gruffydd's features. Beneath his helmet curly brown hair emerged, spewing this way and that. His round, freckled face gave him an innocent, boyish appearance but his demeanour was betrayed by the trace of a sneer and a disdainful look in his eye. Aelfgar simply looked smug. Harold couldn't help noticing how much like his father he looked: the same wide, thin-lipped mouth, square jaw and deep-set eyes but there was none of the humility of Leofric. Instead Aelfgar carried with him an air of recklessness.

Both parties dismounted cautiously, alert to any unpleasant surprise that might be sprung upon them by the other. Considering the circumstances, though, the negotiations were quite relaxed.

The terms reached at the meeting at Billingsley left Aelfgar restored to his earldom of East Anglia but at the price of accepting Tostig's retention of Northumbria. Gruffydd gained some territory on the border, including Archenfield. In return, he swore never to raid English territory again and in return for his recognition as King of all Wales, Gruffydd recognised King Edward as his overlord. The deal done, the parties went their separate ways. As they rode away, Earl Ralph could hear Gruffydd and Aelfgar laughing. The entire party felt angry and humiliated.

'This seems a poor return to me,' hissed Tostig to Harold, as they rode back to Hereford.

'Patience, Tostig, patience,' Harold remarked. 'Things aren't as bad as they seem. Gruffydd might still be a threat to England, but at least we've broken his alliance with Aelfgar. And your succession to Northumbria has been resolved peacefully.'

'What about my succession?' enquired Gyrth.

'I'm afraid you'll need to be patient for a while, brother.'

As those on the border struggled to resume a normal life, the raid on Hereford continued to take its toll; later that winter Bishop Athelstan of Hereford died – many said it was the burning of his beautiful church that killed him. Harold persuaded the King to appoint his personal chaplain, Leofgar, from Waltham, as Bishop of Hereford in Athelstan's place. The gentle giant would be killed a few months later in a Welsh raid.

ROME

Bishop Ealdred brought back news from Europe that Edward the Exile was happy to return to England and accompanied Harold across the cold winter continent to meet the future king. In Ragenburg, at Christmas, Harold met King Andrew I of Hungary and opened negotiations for the return of Edward. While awaiting a response, Harold accompanied Pope Victor, whom he had met in Cologne, on his return to Rome.

The party passed through the snow-clad Alps and Dolomites in time to arrive in Rome for Easter. After weeks of hard travel, Harold and Ealdred were glad of the opportunity to rest and recuperate in their lodgings at the English College in the Borough. The Borough was a part of the Holy City, which the Italians called the Borgo, granted to the English in King Alfred's time as a haven for tired pilgrims. Away from England for so long, they felt quite at home. They had a break of a week or so while the Pope presided over a council at the Lateran.

After the council, Harold had a formal meeting with Pope Victor and Cardinal Hildebrand, a German Benedictine monk. Harold had never before seen anyone so ugly as the cardinal, who was a short squat man, aged about fifty. He had a wide mouth and a double chin, which hung like a bag from his great square jaw. In contrast to his huge head, his hands looked too small and delicate for an adult. His dark, bulbous eyes added to the toad-like quality of his appearance. Beneath his cardinal's robes, his stubby legs propelled him around in quick, short steps, so that he appeared to glide across the floor. But the cardinal's looks belied his forceful personality and ferocious intellect; by cunning, willpower and an unshakeable belief in his view of the truth, he had thrust himself to the top of the church hierarchy.

The cardinal was a great reformer and as a stickler for sexual rectitude, he had insisted that the sexual appetites of priests be curbed and that celibacy and abstinence were to be the rule. These notions were either challenged or ignored by the many priests who kept wives or concubines, or both. Hildebrand was determined to deal with them and the other wider reaching reforms he intended to pursue.

For quite some time the German kings who ruled the Holy Roman Empire had dictated the selection of popes. In this way they controlled the worst excesses of the Church, caused in part, they believed, by the Vatican holding too much power. Hildebrand thought it held too little. What irked the cardinal more was the kings' insistence they were the rightful successors of the Roman Empire. Hildebrand was determined that the power to name the Pope would, in his lifetime, be placed in the hands of the cardinals. But his plans went further than that; his goal was to have popes appoint kings, including the emperors of the Holy Roman Empire itself. Hildebrand was the driving force in Rome; his sole ambition was to enhance the power of the Church and in England's succession crisis he saw an opportunity.

Harold's audience with Pope Victor was more like a friendly welcoming chat than a religious discourse. Weeks in the saddle, riding across mountainous terrain, meant the two men were already familiar with each other's views. Cardinal Hildebrand was in attendance and very keen to know about Harold's serious illness and remarkable recovery at Waltham. Pope Victor had grown to like Harold on their journey together to Rome; now Cardinal Hildegard was enjoying his friendly disposition too.

'So what do you think of the Vatican, Earl Harold?'

'I can only marvel at the sheer magnificence of it.'

While Harold felt overawed, Cardinal Hildebrand saw the opportunity to strike.

'Would you care to accompany me on a stroll around our humble city, Earl Harold? You might like to familiarise yourself with our simple abode during your stay?'

'It would be my pleasure, your Eminence.'

'Then come.'

The two men rose and Hildebrand escorted Harold from the Pope's chambers.

'It is a pity King Edward is unable to visit in person.'

'The King is most disappointed but he really is such a poor traveller over water.'

'It is a shame that he lives on an island.'

169

'Indeed. But King Edward is building a fine new abbey at Westminster. When it's finished, perhaps your Eminence would like to visit?'

'I should love to. I do so enjoy travel and it's always a pleasure to meet an Englishman; I'm sure I'd find your country delightful. You know, your people have such a reputation for generosity; King Knut's splendid gifts are still remembered and talked about to this day', said Hildebrand, sure that his hint would not go amiss.

As they toured the holy city, the Cardinal showed Harold artefacts and row upon row of rare books, all bound in leather and embossed in gold.

'You know, over the years many scholars have visited us from many parts of the world; several were from England, including the blessed Bede and of course, Dunstan. Your great King Alfred is also honoured here.'

Harold felt flattered but nevertheless saw in Hildebrand's expression an ulterior motive.

The Cardinal continued, 'Wasn't it Alfred who said, 'He may be no king of right under Christ, who is not filled with booklore; letters he must understand and know by what right he holds his kingdom.'?'

'It was.'

'Alfred was a man of great learning; that's a rare quality in a king.'

'I think you'll find in England that scholarship has always been valued and not just by the clergy; all of the earls, the shire reeves and most of the thanes are literate in English, if not Latin.'

'So I understand and that is to the credit of your countrymen. England is such a civilized country. Other countries sometimes stray from the path of righteousness. It's not simply the rulers of these countries. It has to be said, there are those in the Church who have, shall we say, also strayed from the path. There is great need for reform, Harold, I'm sure you agree.'

'Please continue,' replied Harold, noncommittally.

'Great moves are afoot to purify the church at every level.' Hildebrand paused for effect. Harold did not miss the remark; one word flashed though his mind: Stigand.

'As you are aware, the Holy Father is combating, with untiring zeal, simony and clerical concubinage. Bishops have been deposed and kings threatened with excommunication, such is his commitment to the cause of reformation. I'm sure you approve.'

'I think you'll find challenging times lie ahead.'

'You must agree the Church is in need of reform?'

'Who am I to decide?'

'Quite true and that's as it should be.'

Harold remained silent, waiting for the Cardinal to continue.

'My dear Earl Harold,' said Hildebrand, in an intimate tone.

'Your Eminence?'

'What would you say to the proposition that his Holiness should decide the fate of kings?'

'What do you mean, exactly?'

'All power, whether in the hands of your humblest thane or a mighty king, is derived from God. Therefore, all these thanes, nobles and kings, what you will, should be united under God. Naturally, supervision would fall to His representative on earth, his Holiness the Pope, don't you think?

'Consider this, Harold. It may be that the blessing of a king, by his Holiness, would make succession less troublesome. Take your country's recent history, for instance: didn't a succession of civil wars break out after the death of Ethelred? Is this the way to organise a succession? Think how much less blood would have been spilled if it had been recognized by all that only the Pope could decide who should be king.'

'You think it should be for his Holiness alone to decide who should be king?'

'Naturally, candidates would be submitted for papal approval and each court would select who those candidates should be.'

'And what if the Pope were to reject all the candidates?'

'Do you foresee such an eventuality?'

'Suppose it happened.'

'In that unlikely event, then, more would have to be found.'

'But supposing the court and the country were not prepared to consider any more candidates? Isn't this the road to conflict between the secular world and the clerical?'

'I'm surprised to see in one so young such a pessimistic view.'

'Perhaps, but surely the role of a king is to look after the wellbeing of his people – their secular interests, if you like. The Archbishop's role is to care for their souls. Wouldn't papal selection of kings reduce the power and authority of one who should be above challenge? In the case of

England, you might as well ask the Archbishop of Canterbury to rule the country and have done with it.'

'No. No. No, Harold. You have completely the wrong idea,' beamed Hildebrand with a broad yellow smile. 'The King would have full control of secular matters, just as now. But don't you see, he would be in a much stronger position if he were legitimised by papal approval.'

'He has that already, surely? After all, it's an archbishop who anoints him at his coronation.'

'Yes,' Hildegard was beginning to feel frustrated now, 'but this would be a binding contract. In return for the King's fealty, his Holiness would offer recognition, legitimisation and support. He who would challenge the King would challenge Rome. He would face excommunication and find his allies cursed, while his enemies would be blessed and supported by His Holiness. Could any king be more secure than that?'

'English laws are ancient and were for the most part laid down by King Alfred, whose praises you have previously sung. It's not my place to agree to change them. I'm one among many. Amendments may be made with the consent of the Witan but only so long as they do not fundamentally alter the wishes of King Alfred.'

'But aren't we entering a new era? This is a time of great reform. Consider my words carefully, Earl Harold.'

'You can rest assured I'll give them all the consideration they deserve.'

'Good. Now perhaps you would like to come and view one of our most treasured possessions. It is a piece of the true cross.'

Harold could not conceal his surprise.

'Prices can be negotiated. But let's not rush into that just yet, let's go and appreciate it for what it is.'

A week after his audience with the Pope and his meeting with Cardinal Hildebrand, Harold left Rome and made his way to Bavaria, where he collected Edward the Exile and his family before escorting them back to England. In his baggage, along with other relics, was a piece of the true cross, mounted on gold and surrounded with jewels. It had cost a small fortune but Harold thought it worth the price. It would adorn the Abbey at Waltham and demonstrate his gratitude to and faith in God.

Arriving at Bosham on a hot September day, he was greeted with the warmest of welcomes by a family he had not seen for nearly a year. Staying for just one night, he left the next day for London, taking his family with him. They had been apart too long for him to leave them so soon. As always, Thorkell accompanied them and so did Bondi, the boy Harold had met in Bristol and taken to Ireland, who had become part of the household.

When they reached London, instead of going straight to Westminster they stopped at Southwark and it was there that Edward the Exile simply dropped dead. Three days later he was buried in St. Paul's with great ceremony, by courtiers he had never met. It was a sombre time. The succession crisis appeared to have come back to life like some curse that could never be shaken off. At least, as Leofwine reminded Harold, there was still little Edgar.

Bad news visited the court again in the autumn of that year. Lady Godiva woke up one morning to find her husband, Earl Leofric, dead in bed beside her. His heart had given out in the night. Two months later, Earl Ralph was killed in a riding accident. No one saw what happened but it was believed something had startled his horse and made it bolt, which was an odd way for such an accomplished horseman to die.

At the Christmas court, Edward deftly handled the reshuffle of the earldoms. Aelfgar was allowed to succeed his father in Mercia and in an attempt to build a new alliance, he married off his daughter, Aldytha, to Gruffydd. Gyrth Godwinson was made Earl of East Anglia and Leofwine was given a specially created earldom made up of some of the south-eastern shires.

After many years of calm, Scottish raids on Northumbria had resumed. It was incumbent upon Earl Tostig to resolve this problem. Preferring diplomacy to war, Tostig made the decision to meet his good friend Malcolm, now King of Scotland, at Edward's winter court at Gloucester, with a view to arriving at an amiable settlement. The Bamburghs, less keen on diplomacy than their South Saxon earl, were watching closely.

THE KING'S WINTER COURT

After the usual round of celebrations, thanksgiving, feasts and hunting trips, Tostig took the opportunity to approach King Malcolm about his concerns in Northumbria. As if just passing, Tostig knocked on the door of Malcolm's room.

'Tostig, how good it is to have a few moments alone together. You know it does a man's heart good to sit and talk with his oldest and dearest friends. I must say, your earldom suits you. You're obviously one of those men born to hold high office. Rather like my good self.'

'Yes,' replied Tostig, through a smile. 'And I would think men naturally respect you.'

'Aye, they do.'

'So perhaps you can help me. You see, more and more often my fellow countrymen are complaining to me about raids from across the border.'

'Is that swine Gruffydd troubling you again?'

Tostig greeted the remark with a wry look. 'No, Malcolm, it's not from across the Welsh border that raiders are coming; it's from Scotland'

'Are you sure they're not Viking raiding parties?'

'I'm absolutely sure. You see, these raids are undermining me, Malcolm. What am I to say to nobles who complain of rape, robbery and rustling? How should I answer when I'm asked, 'Do you think England sheltered your friend Malcolm all those years and helped him back onto the throne, just so he can show his gratitude by raiding us?'

To his credit Malcolm looked a little shame-faced; for good measure Tostig added, 'Many of the thanes want to follow the raiding parties back over the border and pursue them until they're caught. That would mean fatalities. If there were to be any serious developments as a result, I would be obliged to provide assistance; in turn the King would be obliged to support me, should the occasion arise. You see, what to some of your high spirited countrymen is an entertaining pastime might have more serious repercussions for us both.'

'Look, if it's anyone I know, and I'm not saying it is, mind, I'll have them put a stop to it immediately. You have my word on it. No more Scotsmen will raid Northumbria while you're there looking after things, my old friend.'

'Good. I'm glad we could come to a friendly agreement.'

'And why shouldn't we? Aren't we like brothers?'

'We are, old friend, we are.'

'Then let's seal our friendship with blood,' said Malcolm producing a knife.

Tostig produced his dagger and together the two cut across the palms of their hands then gripped them firmly together and the blood of the two warriors mingled together.

So the two friends resolved the border problem. Later, King Malcolm, having paid his respects to King Edward and the English court, left for Scotland accompanied, as he was on his outward journey, by his new brother Tostig.

CONSECRATION

Harold felt a thrill of delight as he showed Sir William Malet around the abbey at Waltham, which had taken him so long to build. It was to be consecrated the following day and Sir William had come from Normandy especially for the occasion. Because of Stigand's dubious status, Ealdred, Archbishop of York, would be officiating. The King and all the earls would be there to admire the abbey's beauty.

'It's magnificent,' remarked Sir William when they stepped inside. He looked at the two windows high in the wall above the altar; clear, bright spring light shone through. 'You must be doubly pleased, Harold. Your building was started after the King's but it's finished well before. When I last saw it, Westminster looked years away from completion.'

'Will, we haven't spoken about how things are with you. How's your family, how's Normandy treating you?'

'The family is well and I spend quiet winters huddled up in the castle and summers on campaign fighting the neighbours. One of the reasons I like England so much is that I can find peace and quiet here.'

'It's not all quiet, Will, as you know. The Welsh can be quite lively at times.'

'Things are much the same in Normandy. We don't have Archbishop Stigand but we have Bishop Odo, who by some strange coincidence is the brother of Duke William. Do you know he's so pious he was consecrated at thirteen?'

'Didn't Rome have anything to say?' asked Leo.

'Nothing: so perhaps, as you say, he's very pious. Just like his bastard son, who's not much younger than he is.'

The next day, at the consecration, Harold began to suspect things were not all they should be in the North. Tostig had arrived with his usual assortment of thanes and housecarls but he also had Earl Cospatric of Cumbria with him. Harold noticed Tostig rarely let Cospatric out of his sight and Barcwith, Tostig's captain of housecarls, was never more than a few feet away. Harold's mind was focused on the consecration or he might have realised why.

Ealdred, the new Archbishop of York, officiated; standing just a few feet away from Harold, he intoned in Latin. By Harold's side the King was quietly seething, furious that work on Harold's abbey was already finished. He could not help but notice how much treasure Harold had lavished on the abbey. Everywhere he looked there were the most beautiful decorations and fittings, including gold and silver plate, candle-sticks and church vestments made of gold and adorned with jewels, all brought back by Harold from Rome.

In front of the King was a magnificent altar of gold and marble, supported by golden lions and decorated with paintings of the apostles. Overlooking all was the famous cross that was credited with healing power so miraculous that pilgrims were flocking to Waltham from miles around. So many had arrived that the congregation had spilled out of the building and there were five times more worshippers outside than in.

Harold had failed to notice the King's envy; he was more concerned with Tostig, who had called in for the consecration before making a pilgrimage to Rome. Harold suspected Tostig was taking a resentful looking Cospatric along with him to make sure nothing untoward happened in Northumbria while he was away. What it was that Tostig suspected Cospatric of, Harold did not know. He decided to question Tostig about this at the first opportunity.

The day flew by for Harold and Edyth. There was much to do and it seemed as though half of England, from the lowliest churl to the King himself, had turned up to help them celebrate. Harold never did get round to asking Tostig why he kept Cospatric so close. The reason he would eventually discover for himself.

RETURN OF THE BROTHER

Tostig returned to England six months later and was met at Quaymeadow by Harold and Edyth. When he was within hailing distance, Tostig ordered the sail to be dropped. He pulled on the helm and, assisted by the oarsmen, brought his ship to a gentle halt by the quayside.

'Tostig, welcome back,' called Harold.

'It's good to see you again, Harold,' said Tostig, leaping from the ship and on to the quay with great agility. 'You look well – and you too, Edyth,' he added, turning to help Lady Judith ashore. Behind Judith followed Ealdred with his new pallium and Earl Cospatric. Both men, for different reasons, looked very pleased with themselves.

'Welcome to Bosham, Archbishop Ealdred, and welcome to you too, Earl Cospatric,' said Harold warmly. Then, looking slightly ill at ease, he added, 'I have news for you all. I'll tell you as we walk back to the house.'

'What's happened?' Tostig replied. 'It's bad news, isn't it? I can tell by your face.'

'Our old friend Malcolm has raided Northumbria.'

'Bastard!' was Cospatric's sharp retort. Ealdred said nothing but visibly paled.

'He raided Cumbria and drove out all the nobles.' Then looking at Ealdred, Harold continued, 'and churchmen too. Worse still, Lindisfarne has been pillaged.'

'That's outrageous!' cried the Archbishop. 'How could Christians behave in such a manner?'

'The only good news is that there have been few casualties,' said Harold, trying to soften the blow.

'This means war!' Cospatric added vehemently. 'What's the King done about it?'

'He thought it prudent to await Tostig's return.'

'What? You mean he's done nothing,' hissed Cospatric. 'Thank you for your hospitality, Earl Harold, you've been most gracious. Thank you for the news; it must have been most difficult for you to have to tell us. Please don't think me churlish but I must say goodbye and head home to my friends and family.'

'I'd do the same myself.'

'Forgive me, Harold,' Ealdred interjected. 'I must go with Cospatric. I will be needed. Could I borrow a horse?'

'There are a few being tacked up in the stables. I thought you might leave in a hurry.'

The two headed for the stables, followed by Cospatric's men. A minute later they all left at the gallop.

'There go two impatient men,' Tostig remarked.

'I'm surprised you're not going with them.'

'I'm sure I can get this business sorted out with Malcolm. If you don't mind, we'll stay overnight and journey up to London in the morning.'

'You're most welcome. Come inside, and tell us how you got on with Ealdred and Cospatric.'

'Ealdred I've always liked… '

'I've always found him easy company… and Cospatric?'

'Interesting… '

'Yes?'

'Yes. On the way back, robbers in the Roman Campagna attacked us. Cospatric was riding at the head of our little band when we were attacked. It was a classic trap. We caught up with a group of people in front of us and another group who were behind us closed in, blocking our way behind. Just as we realised what was going on, more men appeared from either side. They thought because he was so well dressed that Cospatric was me. They asked, 'Are you Earl Tostig?' and he said he was, so they led him away in the hope of claiming a fat ransom. Then they robbed us all and we thought that was the last we'd see of them, so we rode on to the nearest town to raise the alarm.'

'Then what happened?'

'When Cospatric thought I was far enough away to be safe, he told them of their mistake and he said he was a thane in borrowed clothes. They didn't believe him at first; they thought he just wanted to escape. Then when they realised he wasn't me, some of them wanted to kill him but they eventually decided he was a hero for protecting his lord, returned all the stolen goods and released him.'

'That was very good of them.'

'It was very good of Cospatric, too.'

'You look sceptical. What's on your mind?'

'It's a little convenient.'

'And now you're in his debt.'

'Exactly.'

'It could all be genuine.'

'He makes an excellent travelling companion but I'm not so sure I could afford the luxury of trusting him.'

Harold observed his brother studiously before asking, 'Do you think he might have your earldom or some higher position in mind?'

'I'm not sure what he's thinking but he'll have done his reputation no harm at all. Now I'm in his debt, what will they make of that in the North? '

'But what are you going to do about Malcolm?'

'I'll give it some thought.'

'You'll have to do a lot more than that.'

MERCIA: EARL AELFGAR'S GREAT HALL, COVENTRY

That year, as usual, the northern earls met the Mercians in Aelfgar's great hall in Coventry, on the way to the King's Christmas court in Gloucester. On the dais the talk was of nothing but Tostig and his lack of action over the Scottish raids. Cospatric was the most vocal.

'I've lost most of my family's fortune,' he complained. 'Malcolm just came over the border and took anything he fancied. He's supposed to be Tostig's blood brother; they have an agreement to honour the border but what's that worth if as soon as Tostig's back's turned, Northumbria is raided?'

'It's not just the raids,' added Dolfin, 'it's Tostig's inaction. Why doesn't he do something?'

Aelfgar and his teenaged sons, Edwin and Morcar, sat listening silently while the northern nobles spoke disloyally of their lord. It warmed Aelfgar's heart to hear of Tostig spoken of in this way. He thought he might add to the discontent by asking a few well chosen questions of his own.

'Why do you think he hasn't done anything, Cospatric?'

'Apparently, there has been a misunderstanding. Tostig has seen Malcolm, who claims he thought their agreement only applied when Tostig was in Northumbria. As Tostig was out of the country on his pilgrimage to Rome, Malcolm says he thought it acceptable to indulge his men by letting them embark on a few summer raids. Now Tostig has expressed his disapproval of Malcolm's actions and reminded him of his oath, we shall all enjoy peace again. But none of us has had any valuables returned and there'll be no compensation for any losses. It was an honest mistake, Malcolm says.'

Gamel and Hardwulf, who were also present, were nodding in agreement with every word Cospatric said.

The Earl continued, 'This seems to mean nothing to Tostig, nothing to him that Eadwulf and Siward spent years campaigning to win Cumbria back from the Scots and now it's lost. Malcolm should be taught a lesson, one he'll never forget. Tostig should be the man to do it. But where is he? Nowhere to be seen.'

'He's in Wessex kissing the arse of our Norman king,' sneered Gamel.

'He always is,' Hardwulf added. 'Who here can remember when he spent more than three months at a time up here in Northumbria? He leaves everything in the hands of that upstart, Copsig.'

Aelfgar exchanged glances with his two teenaged sons.

Cospatric remarked with some bitterness, 'I risked my life for him in Italy! And what has he done in return? Brought dishonour on our families, on all of us. No Northumbrian would have acted in such a way.'

'Come now,' said Aelfgar. 'Are you not being a little harsh?'

'Harsh! It's Tostig who is harsh, with his swingeing taxes. And what have we ever got for them?'

Although Aelfgar was enjoying all the vitriol, Archbishop Ealdred thought Cospatric had gone too far.

'Earl Cospatric, Earl Tostig is only asking that you pay the same part of your profits, just like anyone else. And you must remember that the taxes are collected in the name of the King. Tostig has the law on his side.'

'That's another thing, his passion for justice, everything legal and above board. We settle things our own way up north. We don't need all these bloody courts and the expenses that go with them.'

'Earl Cospatric,' responded the Archbishop, 'I think you'll find Tostig is acting out of concern for his people.'

'If he's so concerned about his people, why is he never to be found? Why is he always in London with the King? Why doesn't the King come up to Northumbria? Why aren't we fighting in Scotland? The King has never, to my knowledge, been any further north than Shrewsbury and he was probably lost then.'

'Calm yourself, Earl Cospatric,' responded the ever serene Ealdred. 'I'm sure there is a reasonable explanation. Why not talk to Earl Tostig about your concerns at court? You can come with me. There are one or two things I would like to talk over with him.'

'Such as?'

It was now the turn of Aethelwin, Bishop of Durham, to pitch in.

'May I interrupt? Much as I understand and sympathise with your losses, my Lords, I think it proper to express my opinion that King Malcolm's greatest sin was to violate the peace of St. Cuthbert on Lindisfarne, an act which I consider unforgivable. It was the act of a Viking heathen, not a Christian, and he will be damned to hell for it.'

'Now, you might have your problems with Earl Tostig and his tax demands but the Church is more concerned with other issues. There is no doubt about his personal piety or that of Lady Judith. Their pilgrimage was one expression of it, as were the gifts they presented to the church of St. Cuthbert. They are magnificent.'

'They are indeed,' added Ealdred.

'The carvings, the books but most of all, the gospels of Lady Judith – their beauty defies description.'

'That may be so, but not everything's been going smoothly for her, so I hear,' interrupted Cospatric.

'What's that?' asked Aelfgar, hoping to give more bad news an airing.

'Well, Earl Aelfgar,' continued Bishop Aethelwin, 'Lady Judith wanted to pray at the church of St. Cuthbert.'

'That's no crime.'

'Not quite right. She wanted to pray at the saint's tomb. However, women are strictly forbidden to enter that particular church. Now, Lady Judith didn't have the courage to do so herself, so she sent one of her maids to see how she fared. God could strike her down or St. Cuthbert might appear and curse her, who knows? Anyway, the poor girl made her way to St. Cuthbert's and no sooner had she stepped through the doorway than, from nowhere, a powerful gust of wind came along and blew her off her feet.' Aethelwin waved his arms with gusto to demonstrate the poor girl's fate.

'To make matters worse, she struck her head when she fell. Badly injured, she was put to bed but died in the night. Lady Judith, God fearing woman that she is, was terrified. In order to make amends and to placate the spirit of St. Cuthbert, she presented the church with the most fabulous ivory sculpture of the crucifixion, inlaid with gold and precious jewels. When I last saw her, she appeared to be in good health, so it must have done the trick.'

'This is all very well but it doesn't solve the problem of Tostig's unwillingness to retaliate against the Scots,' snapped Cospatric.

Ealdred, as inscrutable as ever, leaned forward and looking directly at

Cospatric, told him, 'That's something you ought to discuss with Earl Tostig. This is not the place.'

Ealdred was right, as Cospatric later admitted. The northern earl did bring the matter up with Tostig at the Christmas court but Tostig was not interested in retaliation or compensation. He assured Cospatric and his friends that Malcolm had made a genuine mistake; that he thought their agreement only applied while Tostig was in the country and he had assured him that nothing like it would ever happen again. Tostig was satisfied with this and had no intention of retaliating. Cospatric and his friends had other ideas and went back to Northumbria seething with discontent.

GLOUCESTER, THE KING'S CHRISTMAS COURT 1062

Just before Christmas, Earl Aelfgar passed away. After going to bed blind drunk, he choked on his own vomit. Now the earldom of Mercia lay vacant. With no one to respond to his actions, Prince Gruffydd began raiding across the border with impunity. Harold regarded the renewed Welsh hostilities as the opportunity he had been waiting for to take revenge for the sacking of Hereford.

King Edward appointed Edwin, Earl of Mercia even though he was only eighteen. Cospatric, Gamel and Wulf were happy to give their agreement. They favoured Edwin simply because he was not of the house of Godwin. Aelfgar had always been sympathetic to Northumbria, Edwin was young and malleable and they did not want to see an end to a great Mercian dynasty.

But Edwin, like his father, had no idea what to do about the Welsh and the border raids. While he celebrated Christmas, others made plans.

In his private chambers, Harold was deep in conversation with Gyrth, Leofwine and Tostig. His three brothers were keen to know what he had in mind.

'I thought I'd take a light force up to Gruffydd's fortress at Rhuddlan tomorrow.'

'Tomorrow? That's a bit soon, isn't it?' asked Gyrth.

'The sooner, the better.'

Now Tostig had a question: 'But it can be really cold in the Welsh mountains at this time of year. Nobody goes there in the winter if they can help it.'

'That's why we're going. No one will expect us.'

'That's true enough. Does the King know about this?'

'Yes. We didn't mention it at the Witan in case word leaked out.'

'Does that mean he doesn't trust Edwin?'

'Not necessarily Edwin. But there are those everywhere who have only their own interests at heart.'

'Why didn't he tell me?' interjected Tostig, looking hurt.

'Because he knew you'd want to come with me.'

'Well, I wouldn't mind.'

'But we want to keep the numbers down, travel at speed and catch Gruffydd by surprise. Small forces can move so much faster than big ones. We'll strike his palace then leave the Welsh to sort the mess out. It'll be a message to them. If they raid again, their next leader will meet a similar fate.'

Tostig chuckled. 'I wish you the best of luck, Harold. When will you be back?'

'Within a week; two at the very most'

'I look forward to seeing you then.'

'And I look forward to seeing Edwin's face when he finds out,' Leofwine guffawed.

After three days' hard ride, Harold and his men made their way along the last stretch of the journey up to Gruffydd's fortress at Rhuddlan. Harold, accompanied by Leofwine, who had joined him with twenty of his own men, had his own and most of King Edward's housecarls with him. With them was Edmund, accompanying them to bless them before they went into battle. All in all, about five hundred men were fumbling around in the darkness of a cold December dawn at the foot of the hill on which Gruffydd had his stronghold. As the sun rose, so Harold and his men climbed the hill.

As they climbed, the early morning sounds of people waking greeted them; cocks crowed, the first of the new-born lambs bleated and dogs barked. In the half-light the men advanced, swords and axes at the ready. They were within fifty feet of the wooden parapet when a great clamour broke out. The sound of men shouting could be heard all over Gruffydd's bastion. Harold gave the order to attack and his troops advanced quickly over the rough terrain.

Five minutes later the main gates were breached. Leading his men through, Harold was astonished to find the Welsh in full flight heading for their boats, which were moored on the River Clwyd. Leaving Leofwine with fifty men, Harold led his men after Gruffydd. They caught and killed a hundred or so of his followers but the rest, along with their prince, either sailed off in their boats or ran away to hide in the mountains.

'Should we give chase, my Lord?' Skalpi asked.

'No. Not today. We did what we came to do; a quick strike and then home. It's unfortunate that we didn't get our man but we'll just have to try again some other time. You can burn the boats, though. And you and the men can help yourselves to anything that takes your fancy. I'll see you back at the fort.'

'Yes, my Lord.'

Harold made his way back up the hill to the sound of women screaming. With no men to protect them, the women were being raped wherever the housecarls found them. Harold passed them by and entered the great hall to find Leofwine with Lady Aldytha, Gruffydd's wife. Leo had his back to Harold, and peering over his shoulder Harold could see her look of fear incompletely concealed. It had been a number of years since he had seen her. She looked magnificent. The Welsh had been caught by surprise and she had not had time to dress. She faced Leo, her two young children hiding behind her as she clutched the bedclothes tightly to her chest. Ringlets of tousled hair fell onto her shoulders; her blue eyes flashed brightly as she looked this way and that, like a cornered animal; Harold thought she might be just as dangerous.

'Hello, Leo.'

'Ah, Harold, there you are.'

'What have you found here?'

'An old friend. You remember, Lady Aldytha?'

Harold's attention switched back to the woman before him. As he looked at her, he felt he could breathe in her beauty. His eyes wandered from her face down the outline of her body and back up to her eyes. He could even tell by the way the bedclothes fell that they hid a curvaceous physique. The silence in the room was broken by the screams of women outside and the raucous laughter of Harold's men.

She read the look in his eyes. 'Do what you want with me but leave the children alone.'

'In Hereford, no one was left alone. Didn't your father tell you?' said Harold, taking steps towards her. 'What about your husband? Surely he must have mentioned what happened? Then again, perhaps he didn't deem it important.'

More screams flooded in through the windows from outside.

'Your men behave like the animals Gruffydd says they are.'

'Gruffydd would know all about men behaving like animals and as for your father, he had a duty to protect the people of Mercia, instead of which he helped your husband put them to death.'

'They did no such thing,' she replied, raising her voice, her cheeks growing red and her eyes blazing.

'You are unlucky with men, aren't you?'

'What do you mean?'

'Your father was a treacherous villain and your husband's a coward.'

'My husband is no coward,' she snapped, feeling at a disadvantage and wishing she were dressed.

'Then where is he now?'

'How should I know?'

'He's sailing off across the Irish Sea. He left you, his children and his people in the hands of his enemies who, according to him, are animals. He abandoned you, left you to your fate.'

Harold was within inches of her, their bodies almost touching, their eyes looking directly into each other's. Even while he was rebuking her, he felt drawn to her. Her pale face, framed by tendrils of raven hair, looked delicate, her cheek bones prominent, her button nose only slightly upturned and her heart-shaped face with a jaw-line that met at a delicate pointed chin. She had a perfectly formed, generously proportioned mouth. He remembered she had always had a dazzling smile. For a moment he considered pulling the bedclothes off her.

They were almost touching now and she thought for a moment he was going to kiss her. She drew her head back.

'You wouldn't.'

'No, I wouldn't. But then I'm not Gruffydd, am I?'

Turning to his brother, Harold asked, 'What should we do with her, Leo, take her with us or leave her here?'

'She'd make a fine hostage.'

'She'd slow us down, though, don't you think?'

'Well, she can't stay here.'

'Why not?'

'Well, after we've burned the place down there'll be nowhere to take shelter.'

'How dare you discuss me as though I weren't here?'

'There'll be a nice fire to keep them all warm, though,' said Harold, ignoring Aldytha.

'You're brutes.'

'No. We'd be brutes if we burned the place down with you still in it. I suggest you pack what you can. You have a long journey ahead.'

'Then you are taking me with you?'

'No, but this place seems a long way from anywhere.'

'You're not just going to turn me out in the middle of winter?'

'Looks like it. I suggest you have a word with your maid, if she's not too busy. Leo, once they've finished what they're doing, get some of the men together and torch the place.'

'And their ships?'

'Skalpi's taking care of them. Just torch this place.'

'It'll be a pleasure.'

'Lady Aldytha, in about an hour from now everything here will be going up in flames. I suggest you're gone by then.'

Lady Aldytha said nothing but turned and left for her quarters.

Harold's eyes followed her as she made her way to a doorway. He could not help but notice the sway of her hips. On impulse he called out after her, 'Shall I convey your regards to your family when I get back to England?'

'Bastard!'

'Merry Christmas,' Harold replied.

There had been a change of mood at court. Edwin had soon noticed Harold was missing and it had not taken him very long to discover why. He felt put out because someone else had been given his job. He felt aggrieved that he had not even been invited along. Yet Earl Leofwine, who had in Edwin's opinion little to boast about, had joined Harold in order to steal some glory. He mentioned this to his brother, Morcar, in a tavern one afternoon as they were discussing court politics. By chance, Earl Cospatric arrived with Gamel and Dolfin. Naturally they joined in the conversation and found they had similar views. Once again Edwin complained about being usurped.

'How do you think I feel?' Cospatric complained. 'My Lord's blood brother ransacked my earldom and I've hardly got a candlestick to my name.'

The conversation continued in the same vein for the rest of the afternoon. Finally, the companions made their way to the King's hall for the evening meal. But before he went down to dine, Cospatric spent some time ruminating in his chambers, staring blankly at the wall, mulling over the day's events. As he lay on his bed with a goblet of wine in his hand, a series of thoughts struck him. He knew Leofwine had decided of his own accord to join his brother and he knew they got on well. But Harold and Tostig were the best of friends as well as brothers. Why then did Tostig not go to Wales?

Cospatric thought about the amount of time Tostig spent with Edward. The Godwinsons never missed a meeting of the Witan but unlike Tostig, the rest went back to their various homes afterwards. Tostig could be with the King for months at a time. True, they both loved hunting, but so did Harold, Gyrth and Leofwine. Tostig enjoyed good relations with his sister, the Queen, but so did the others. Admittedly, Tostig and she were twins but surely that did not account for all the time he spent with Edward. There was something else, he felt sure. The two were more like father and son than friends. Then, like a thunderbolt it struck him. It explained everything; Tostig was Edward's surrogate son! Come to think of it, Edward never had much to do with Edgar the Atheling. The boy might be brought up at court under the watchful eye of Queen Edith but so were most of the earls' children and those of the wealthier thanes. Edward never mentioned Edgar, but Tostig he talked about often.

Cospatric was now sitting bolt upright in bed; on his face he wore the shocked look of a person who has just had a revelation. Edward was grooming Tostig as his heir. Edward loved him like a son and like a son he would bequeath to him all that was his, including the crown.

Cospatric imagined the scene at the Witan if Edward were to name Tostig his successor. If Tostig had Edward's blessing, what would happen then? Harold might oppose him but who would support him? The other two brothers might take Tostig's side but the family, to say nothing of the country, would be split and if it came to civil war, who in the North would support Tostig? He was not popular, as was Harold in the South. Perhaps Harold would take the throne by force. But suppose Harold didn't want to risk civil war, supposing he was content to remain an earl? Tostig would be king and presumably run the entire country in the way he had the North, like a bloody tyrant. But what if Edward named no one and died tomorrow? Cospatric resolved to have a private audience with the King at the earliest opportunity. The following day he went to Edward to ask him to name him as his heir.

'Will you support my claim?'

'There is the Atheling Edgar to consider.'

'Surely my claim is the stronger?'

'Nephew, you are, as we all know, a man of courage and without doubt a fine warrior. Naturally I understand your concern for the country's safety after my eventual demise but whilst you are the great-grandson of a king, Edgar, I am afraid, is the grandson of a king and that makes his claim a little stronger.'

'But I've always lived in England and I'm English. And look at the whelp; what chance has a child of running a country, defending us from our enemies?'

Cospatric's and Edward's eyes met. In that moment Cospatric knew he would never be considered an atheling, at least not by Edward. The question now for Cospatric was what to do about it? On his long journey home he would have lots of time to dwell on the question and time would provide him with an answer.

After the Christmas court he returned home with Wulf Dolfinson and Gamel Ormson as his guests. In a dark room illuminated with the flicker of firelight, Cospatric shared his thoughts with them.

'At Gloucester I had a private audience with the King. I asked him if he would consider me as his successor.'

Both men listened attentively. It was Wulf who asked the question.

'What did he say?'

'Nothing, he won't name a successor.'

'Don't tell me he said, "The Lord will provide".'

'That's more or less the gist of it.'

'But he has Edgar in mind, surely.'

'No.'

'Who, then?'

'Tostig.'

'Tostig! Don't be daft.'

'Just think about it. Who went from nowhere to rule the strongest earldom in the country? Who is the King's best friend and spends most of his time down south, hunting in royal company?'

'Harold's down south all the time.'

'Yes, but he's the Earl of Wessex. And don't forget it was Harold's idea to bring the Atheling back from Hungary and it was he who went to get him. It's Edgar Harold wants to see as king and in return for his support, Edgar will one day have to marry one of his daughters. It'll be just like old Godwin all over again.

'Tostig's plan is a bit more direct. He has no daughters to marry off to Edgar, so when the time comes, he'll take the throne for himself with Edward's blessing.'

'What'll happen to Edgar?'

'They'll probably make him Earl of Northumbria. When the opportunity presents itself, Edward will name Tostig as heir and the Queen will support him.'

'What about his brothers?'

'Nothing would change for Gyrth or Leofwine and Harold would still be Earl of Wessex, although none of his grandchildren would sit on the throne unless he wanted one of his daughters to marry their cousin.'

'Do you think he'll sit back and let Tostig take the crown?'

'What can he do? Mercia won't give a hand to either side and neither will Northumbria. What that leaves is a family feud.'

'With any luck they'll all kill each other and leave the way clear for us'

'Now there's a thought, but like as not, there won't be a feud and Tostig will be king.'

There was a moment's silence while they reflected on what Cospatric had said.

Gamel Ormson broke the silence.

'So why doesn't the King name Tostig now?'

'Because that would give us plenty of time to take action.'

'What, arrange for him to have an accident, you mean?'

'Exactly.'

'I think we need to make some plans.'

While Tostig was in Waltham with Harold, finalising plans for an invasion of Wales, his army stood ready and waiting for his arrival in Chester. He and Harold had made plans and now everything was prepared for a summer campaign.

'So everything's ready?' asked Harold.

'Everything. We can go at any time. What about you?'

'My fleet is ready and waiting in Bristol. Two weeks from now, you can start down the coast and launch an attack on Rhuddlan that should give them something to think about. If it's been rebuilt, you can have fun burning it down again.'

'I'm looking forward to it.'

'At the same time I'll raid along the south coast before making my way inland. Skalpi, in the meantime, will take five hundred housecarls and cross into Wales via Monmouth, where he'll head west, destroying everything in his path until he meets up with us.'

'And when we all meet up in mid-Wales, we'll have Gruffydd surrounded?'

'If he runs away, we'll just stay in Wales destroying everything until we have him.'

'What are we going to do with him?'

'The King wants him dead.'

'Good idea.'

'I thought so, too.'

Now that the two had finished business, Harold asked Tostig if he would like to see his new battle standard.

Harold called a servant and instructed him to tell Skalpi to fetch the new standard. Within a few minutes Skalpi arrived with Bondi, who had finished his training as a housecarl, and Gauti, bearing the banner rolled under their arms. The men eyed Tostig and he could detect a mischievous look about them that he thought inappropriate.

He noticed a twinkle in Harold's eye where he had expected to see reverence.

Tostig watched as the housecarls assembled the standard and then attached the banner to it. It was quite a rigmarole. They had to connect together several brass rods, which, when they had finished, formed the shape of a cross. Tostig was surprised to see it was about nine feet in height and almost six feet wide. The housecarls proceeded to attach the standard to the cross member by means of brass rings that ran along the top of the standard. When they had it all secured they unravelled it and all three disappeared behind it as they struggled to turn it toward Tostig. That was when he discovered what had amused them. Before him, on a green silk square six feet by six, was a perfect representation of the fighting man of Cerne Abbas. He was outlined in silver thread, life-sized and, like the real thing, carried an enormous club and had a huge erection. Skalpi had disappeared; he was behind the banner supporting it. On either side the two housecarls were beaming huge smiles.

Tostig's eyes moved all over the gem-studded banner. Outlining the Cerne Abbas man and making up the edging were purple coloured amethysts representing love and truth unto death. There was chalcedony for fortitude and chrysolite for wisdom. Most impressive were brilliant green emeralds for faith, hope and justice. And to show Harold was willing to spare no expense, there were rubies for valour and azure sapphires to create a reflection of heaven, the emblem of love and truth. Also sewn into the banner were sardonyx for lowliness, mercy and truth and finally yellow topaz for justice. It was a thing of beauty and an outrage at one and the same time and one of the most astonishing things Tostig had ever seen.

'I wonder what Gruffydd will think when he sees it?'

'I doubt if he'll think anything. He'll just run.'

Just over two weeks later, when Harold had finished raiding along the south coast of Wales, he and Skalpi met in Cardigan. The ships were drawn up on the riverbank, the men resting after burning the town to the ground.

'Skalpi! What's your news?'

'My lord, we've had much success and at little cost to ourselves, but we haven't found Gruffydd.'

'Nor have we. Perhaps Tostig has him cornered in the north.'

'Perhaps, my Lord.'

'How did you fare with your new armour?'

Skalpi smiled. 'It works as well as we hoped. It's just what we need for this terrain and this style of warfare.'

After witnessing Gruffydd's narrow escape the previous winter, Harold had adopted a new strategy for the summer. He had reorganised his men, replacing their heavy chain mail coats with tough leather tunics. Battleaxes had been left at home; swords and spears were the order of the day. Instead of remaining static behind their shield wall, the men would act more like light infantry, avoiding pitched battles but attacking swiftly and if all went well, following up and pursuing the enemy. If outnumbered, they would withdraw.

'Have you managed to capture any horses?'

'Yes, I don't think there are any left in South Wales now.'

'Good. Tomorrow we'll venture inland. I suggest you and the men get fed and watered and enjoy a good night's rest. Tomorrow will be a busy day.'

At dawn the next day, Harold led the army past the charred ruins of Cardigan. Wispy columns of smoke made their way here and there towards the sky. An eerie silence hung over what had been a thriving port. Now the only ships and boats in its harbour were at the bottom of the river. Only women and children remained in the town.

For a week, Harold headed further east into the mountain valleys. Everywhere villages and towns had been burnt down; any man caught had been killed, including the priests. In any habitation, no matter how small or grand, once Harold had passed by, only weeping widows and howling children were left behind.

Coming down from the north, Tostig was enjoying similar success. In mid-August, in the heart of Wales, the brothers linked up. Now they were united, Gruffydd was moving even more swiftly to avoid capture. Scurrying from one stronghold to the next, the Welshman's support was rapidly dwindling.

From the heights of hill and mountain the Welsh warriors observed Harold's skirmishers sweep forward across the landscape, out into the blue distance. Those whose homes had not already been destroyed knew that sooner or later they would be destitute. Whenever the Saxons won a victory, they erected a cairn of stones bearing the inscription, 'Here Harold Conquered'. The countryside was littered with them.

Despondent, seeing Gruffydd without an answer to Harold's tactics, there were many who deserted their prince. Gruffydd, with fewer and fewer men, knew his days were numbered. Consequently, he kept up the desperate running battle, until near the end of summer he found himself living high in some nameless hills with little food and no prospect of a future. The English had him trapped and while they debated whether to launch an outright assault or to starve their enemy out, a small group of riders approached from the direction of his camp. Harold, Tostig and Skalpi went to meet them. At the head of the party were Gruffydd's half brothers, Bleddynn and Rhiwallon. When they were within speaking distance both groups halted.

'What do you want?' Harold enquired.

'We have come to negotiate a peace settlement.' It was Bleddynn who answered.

'I wondered when you'd see sense. Hand over Gruffydd or we'll come and get him.'

'I could never betray my lord.'

'Fine words. You'll find yourself dying with him.'

'But, Earl Harold... you are Earl Harold?'

'I am. Who are you?'

'I am Bleddynn, brother of Gruffydd and this is my brother Rhiwallon. Perhaps, Earl Harold, we could come to some arrangement.'

'I've told you the arrangement; hand him over or we'll kill you all.'

'But that's unreasonable! I thought you had come to negotiate.'

'No. You have come to negotiate. I have come to tell you what to do. If you'd seen what I saw at Hereford, and for all I know you did, then you'd understand why I feel the way I do about your highly esteemed leader.'

'King Gruffydd will never surrender to anyone. He is a mighty warrior, descended from mighty warriors. He's bestowed with magical powers which allow him to call up the phantoms of our ancestors.'

'If I get hold of him he'll be calling for his mother.'

'But...'

'I'm going to kill every Welshman I come across until I have the head of Gruffydd on a spike.' Harold leaned forward in his saddle. 'And don't think the winter will save you, because we'll never call off the hunt until we have him. Do you understand?'

The Welshman stared open-mouthed as the reality of Harold's words sank in.

'I can see you understand me. Tomorrow I shall come looking for you and if I find you, you'll die and so will the rest of your motley band.'

Harold waited in silence as the dumbstruck emissary simply sat and stared.

'If I were you, I'd leave before I change my mind and kill you on the spot.'

This seemed to snap the Welshman out of his trance. He turned his horse, put it into a gallop and with his little band of followers struggling to keep up, raced back to his fellow countrymen on the opposite hill.

Within the week, Gruffydd's supporters turned against him. One night, as he lay sleeping with his wife Aldytha, two men crept into his room and slit his throat. As he had no further use for it, they cut off his head, which was duly delivered to Harold by Bleddynn and Rhiwallon. They also brought with them, for their safety, Lady Aldytha and her children. Harold and Tostig, having achieved their goal, conveyed the head and the woman who was once married to its owner, to King Edward.

So wild was the welcome that once through the city gates it took nearly two hours for the brothers to reach King Edward's great hall. Now that the murders had been avenged, English pride had at last been restored.

Tostig's adventures in Wales, which had endeared him to the rest of the country, only served to remind Northumbrians of his neglect of his duty to the Cumbrians, who now found themselves answering to Scottish lords and a Scottish king.

Rumours of their discontent had reached Tostig's ears by the time he returned to Northumbria in late October. The main protagonists, as usual, were Earl Cospatric, Gamel Ormson and Wulf Dolfinson. With a view to dealing with the malcontents and demonstrating to the Bamburghs once and for all that he was not to be manipulated or controlled in any way, Tostig cordially invited them to join him in his hall in York, before they all travelled together to Gloucester for the King's Christmas court. Cospatric sent his apologies; Gamel and Wulf accepted the invitation.

The two men arrived in darkness at the end of a wet and windy afternoon in early December. Through pitch-black streets they made their way to Tostig's great hall, the wind and rain lashing about them as they went. It was with relief they entered the building, knowing a welcome and a warm fire awaited them. Copsig greeted them and a servant took their sodden cloaks.

'Welcome to York, gentlemen. My Lord awaits you in his chambers. Follow me.'

Wulf and Gamel followed Copsig through the great hall where a fire burned and servants ran around preparing for the evening's feast. Through a door, along a corridor and up some stairs they followed Copsig, until they finally arrived in Tostig's chambers to find him busy with some documents.

'Welcome, Wulf. Welcome, Gamel. Welcome to my humble abode.'

'Good evening, Earl Tostig,' they replied, not quite in unison.

Smiling broadly, Tostig offered them both a drink, which they both accepted, helping themselves to the finest wine, much appreciated after their journey. There was a fire burning in the hearth and they could feel its red-hot glow killing the chill in their bones, bringing them back to life. The light from its flames flickered on their faces and danced round the room, losing its way in the corners where the shadows reigned supreme. It made a cosy scene.

Apart from the crackling of the fire there was silence. Shutters closed out the wind and in the gloom away from the hearth the drapes hung lifeless from their rails. The golden light of Tostig's candle illuminated the table on which he had been working and gave his face a golden glow: with his blond hair he looked like an angel.

'Get yourselves warm by the fire, lads. You must be frozen after your ride.'

The two men stayed gratefully by the fire. After they had warmed their hands and the heat from the fire began to feel uncomfortable, they turned to warm their backsides. Warm shivers ran up their spines and their shoulders gradually came to life. After their unpleasant journey they could now relax in comfort.

'I'm glad you were able to accept my offer and pay me a visit,' Tostig said to them, remaining seated.

'We welcome the opportunity, my Lord,' Wulf's replied. 'What was it you wished to discuss with us?'

'Discuss? I didn't want to discuss anything.'

Wulf and Gamel exchanged glances. Each man's look confirmed the other's suspicions.

'Then why did you invite us here?' This time it was Gamel who spoke.

'To say goodbye.'

At that moment, from behind the drapes, Barcwith and Anund emerged from the shadows with swords drawn. In seconds they hacked the two Bamburghs to death. There was a sizzle as some embers spilt from the fire, rolling into fresh blood.

The next morning, two men declaring themselves to be Wulf Dolfinson and Gamel Ormson passed through the city gates, the voluminous hoods of their cloaks pulled up around their heads to protect them from the foul weather. Tostig would say something must have happened to them on their journey after they left. As their weighted bodies lay at the bottom of the Ouse, they were unable to contradict him.

NORMANDY, EARLY IN 1064

Duke William, in a mood of restrained excitement, was ushered by a young monk into Abbot Lanfranc's gloomy private chambers and offered a seat. Flickering candlelight danced demonically in the Abbot's eyes, which were as deep and dark as a well. The cleric offered the Duke some wine, which he refused, then left him alone with the Abbot. The two sat down on opposite sides of a table.

'Good evening and welcome, Duke William. May I say what an honour it is to have you with us?'

'Thank you, Abbot Lanfranc, but the honour is mine.'

William looked at the Abbot, one of the few men he could not fathom and one of the few who could look him in the eye for any length of time. The Duke wondered, for a moment, if it was because he was Italian that he could not really get the measure of him.

'Did you have a good journey?' the Abbot enquired.

'I had a good journey, yes.'

William continued to study his mentor while making small talk. The Abbot sat impassively with his fingers interlocked; they were fat and white like raw sausages. His head was square; his dark hair was peppered with small flakes of skin, which he shed from every part of his body. When he smiled it was to reveal a row of white teeth, perfect except for the gap between the top two at the front. After a brief exchange of pleasantries William got to the point.

'My dear Abbot, I have certain knowledge that I need to share with you.'

'You must do as you see fit.'

'I can trust you?'

'Am I not a man of the cloth?'

William hesitated before speaking. 'I need your advice.'

'Duke William, the advice of a poor cleric like me? You don't need…'

'What I don't need is false modesty, your Eminence. And this is no routine matter of state. Let me explain: many years ago, Edward the King of England promised me his crown.'

The inscrutable Lanfranc looked startled at William's announcement. This was news of which he had heard not even the faintest of whispers and Lanfranc heard everything. Not a bird could sing out of tune anywhere in Europe without his hearing of it. He wondered if the Duke had taken leave of his senses.

William continued, 'I can see this is a shock to you but as I said, I need your advice.'

'My Lord, I am only too pleased to be of assistance.'

'King Edward has made me his successor but succeeding will be no easy matter.'

'May I enquire about Edgar the Atheling and ...?'

'That was Harold's doing,' William snapped. 'It was he who dragged him back from Hungary, not Edward. I will be King of England, mark my words.'

'You must forgive my ignorance but it isn't obvious to me how this will happen.'

'We will make it happen,' answered the Duke, forcefully.

'Do you know how you will do this, my Lord?'

'You are the wisest man in Christendom. You can help me think through a plan, with contingencies of course.'

'Of course, I'm only too glad to help,' Lanfranc replied, still shocked.

'I'm sure you can. That's why I've turned to you now, as I'm sure I will need to in the future, when I'm King.'

Lanfranc was aghast. 'I wonder why Edward hasn't made a public announcement?'

'He wouldn't dare do that. It would be too dangerous for him. If they thought I was to be named King, the Godwinsons would kill him instantly and then they would send assassins to kill me. You don't know how devious the English can be. That's why this business is all so secret.'

'I see,' said Lanfranc knowingly, despite his confusion. The evening was not turning out as he had expected.

'Do you have any idea how you will gain the Crown?'

'That's where I need your help.'

Lanfranc was beginning to suspect the Duke was delusional. 'Please continue, my Lord.'

'I have in my custody a brother and a nephew of Earl Harold of Wessex,' said William, gloating. 'I'm sure we can make good use of them.'

'Indeed... what ideas do you have?'

'I'll use them to entice the Earl here to Normandy. I want you to tell me how to proceed when he arrives. I thought we could find a way to get him on our side. Back my claim to the throne. With him and his family behind me, I can't fail.'

'You're quite right, as usual, my Lord but again you must forgive my ignorance. I cannot understand why the Earl of Wessex would support your claim.'

'It's simple. If he doesn't, we'll kill his brother and his nephew. There, now what do you think of that for a plan?

'Brilliant! Quite brilliant, my Lord. Might I add a few contingencies?'

'Contingencies?'

'Yes, you did suggest I do so.'

'Proceed.'

And proceed the Abbot did, all through the afternoon until at last between the two of them they had devised a trap more subtle than that of any predator in the wild. Just over two-and-a half hours later the Duke left the Abbot's chambers, not as he had arrived, in a state of bewildered excitement, but with the calm assurance of a man who was certain of his future.

Sir William Malet's arrival at King Edward's Easter court had caused a great deal of excitement; rarely did he turn up unannounced. He entered the court grinning from ear to ear, his face red from a hard ride. Impatient to break the news, he started to make an announcement before his name had been called out.

Bowing before the King, he reeled out his message. 'Greetings, my Lord, from myself, your humble servant and from my Lord, Duke William of Normandy. My Lord William sends his best wishes to you and would like you to accept this communication.'

Knowing its contents, Sir William beamed broadly as he handed the sealed letter over to Edward. He watched as the King opened it and was surprised to see not joy but an expression of curiosity appear on his face.

As he read through it, Edward's left eyebrow raised, then, when he had finished reading, he looked up and addressed the court. 'Duke William sends us good news.' Edward paused for effect. 'My brother-in-law Wulfnoth,' he said, looking sidelong at Edith, 'and my nephew Haakon, have through great good fortune, fallen into his hands.'

There was an audible sigh in the court at the announcement and the looks on the faces of those present, especially the Godwinsons, revealed the joy they felt at receiving the news. Only Edward looked uneasy, which Sir William observed and noted.

'Thank you for the good news you have delivered, Sir William,' said the King. 'Come and join us on the dais. I think you'll find you are especially welcome.'

'Thank you, my Lord,' Sir William replied, his smile concealing a certain unease that he felt at the King's reaction to the news.

As Sir William made his way through the excited throng to the high table, the Queen leaned over to Edward. 'Aren't you pleased for us, husband dear,' she purred in his ear, 'our brother and nephew are alive and well in Normandy?'

'I'd be more pleased if they were alive and well somewhere else.'

'Well, at least we know where they are and so there's some hope of return.'

'At what cost? If I know William, there'll be a high price to pay for this.'

'High price or not, we have to do something,' Harold added.

Tostig, Gyrth and Leofwine murmured their assent.

'I know. Harold, I know, Edward responded. 'But why has William picked now to tell us? He's probably held them for years.'

'His letter said they'd only just fallen into his hands and asked one of us to come and collect them,' Leo reminded them.

'Did he say where he found them or exactly how long he'd held them?' asked Harold.

'No,' the King replied.

'Did he say why he didn't just let them return home to their country and their family? They could have come over with Malet,' said Tostig.

Edward considered. 'If I know him he'll expect some form of recompense.'

'I'm sure we can afford it, whatever it is,' said Harold, keen to have the boys back.

'What, Harold, do you intend to do?' Edward asked.

'We could reply, thanking him for his good news. We could suggest one of us goes to collect them. If we send a messenger now, they could be home in a couple of weeks.'

'I suppose there's no other choice but I don't like the sound of this. You heard the news about my nephew, Count Walter, didn't you? He died after the conquest of Vexin, invited to a meal with William, then poisoned.'

'I'll be careful what I eat, my Lord,' was Harold's response.

'Who said you'd be going, Harold?'

'Surely, as Subregulus, it would be appropriate that I visit Duke William?'

Edward looked up to the roof as if for inspiration. None came. 'Yes, I suppose it would, Harold but I warn you, be careful.'

FORTY DAYS AND FORTY NIGHTS

After praying at the church of the Holy Trinity, late on a grey July afternoon Harold sailed out of Bosham, heading for Normandy. Ulf and Thorkell accompanied him as bucket boys; they would gain experience and make themselves useful emptying bilge water out of the ship.

Lady Edyth was there to see them off and smiled as Ulf literally followed in his father's footsteps, plunging his feet into the footsteps his father had left in the sandy mud at the edge of Bosham harbour, as he made his way to the ship, with Thorkell trudging behind. They were glad to be out on the open sea after two days waiting for a storm to clear. Eadric, their steersman, had been taken violently ill, caused apparently, by something he had eaten.

Fortunately, Father Hugh Margot, the same Norman cleric who had conveyed messages between Edward and de Jumieges, was visiting Father Osbern at the church and was able to help. Father Hugh still crossed the Channel frequently, bringing wine and delicacies for the abbot at Steyning Abbey and returning with gifts for the monks at Fecamp. He recommended a sailor who knew the way across the Channel, kindly sought him out and volunteered him for the job. Harold was grateful to start his journey without any further delay. With the new crew member as navigator, Harold and his men set off from Bosham with confidence. Unseen by any of them, Hugh Margot had already made an urgent departure, hurrying with a message for home.

The gusting wind at the tail end of the storm carried their craft swiftly towards its destination across the Channel. The sun was doused in the ocean behind them and left a star-strewn sky to guide them on their way.

The steersman held the helm firm and cast frequent glances heavenward as they sailed into darkness. By dawn the coast was in sight. Knowing their journey would soon be over, the crew stirred, as did all of Harold's men. Ulf and Thorkell, having slept through some of the night, began bailing out the ship with renewed enthusiasm as their shipmates folded their leather sleeping bags and put them away in their sea chests.

'How long now, steersman?' enquired Harold.

'Oh, not long, my Lord.'

'Aren't we too far north?'

'No, my Lord. There's the Seine and Normandy lies either side of it.'

'That doesn't look like the Seine to me,' interjected one of the sailors.

Before the conversation could progress, someone shouted an alarm call.

'Ships! Over there. Ships!'

All heads turned to face the direction in which the sailor pointed. Bearing down on them fast were two ships approaching from the south. Instinctively, Harold looked round for more. Others followed him in turn. Scanning the sea, they saw approaching fast from the west, another two fighting ships.

Looking round at the steersman, Harold could see the face of a deceiver who knew he had been discovered. Rather than incur Harold's wrath, the man jumped straight overboard.

'Someone, put an arrow in him,' Harold commanded, taking the helm. He attempted to manoeuvre between the oncoming ships but his efforts proved futile. He was intercepted and surrounded; there was no escape. All he managed to do was to delay the inevitable. The four ships closed in, their captains indicating to him to make for the nearest shore. But at least the treacherous steersman was dead, killed by an archer.

Half an hour later, Harold ran his ship up on the beach as instructed. They were now just a few miles away from the River Somme and Normandy, which they could see in the distance. As they landed, their four pursuers lay off to sea. Within minutes of their arrival, the sight of an armed force of three hundred greeted the Englishmen.

Skalpi grabbed his sword and shield. 'This is piracy, my Lord, let's fight them.'

The rest of the housecarls scrambled for their war gear but Harold could see resistance would be futile and so made his way from the stern to the bow, moving between the housecarls who lined either side of the ship.

'Everyone stay where they are for now. Let's see what they want.'

On shore, a soldier appeared on horseback at the head of his men. He addressed Harold and the crew in impeccable French. 'I am Guy,

Count of Ponthieu,' then looking down at Harold, 'You there! Are you the leader of these men?'

'I am Harold, Earl of Wessex and Subregulus of England.'

'Well, here you're just another shipwrecked mariner.'

'As you can see, my ship is not a wreck and we are victims of those pirates off the shore.'

Count Guy ignored the protest. 'What are you doing here in Ponthieu?'

'We're on a mission to Normandy.'

'This is not Normandy. You have no business here and you will be thrown into the cells at Beaurain, until we decide what to do with you. Now you and your men will disembark.'

'If you would only listen to me, my Lord, I am, as I said, the Earl of Wessex and I am bound for Normandy as a guest of Duke William. If you think either he or the King of England will have nothing to say about this, you are very much mistaken. Do you imagine that if you lead us off as captives and Duke William finds out, you'll escape with your life? What do you suppose the King of England's reaction will be when he hears his brother-in-law is being treated as a common criminal? Why not release us now and I'll overlook the matter? We'll put it down to youthful exuberance.'

'Get out of that boat, now!'

As if rehearsed, the count's men, in unison, raised their shields a little and lowered their spears slightly.

Harold turned to his crew. 'We should do as he says. He'll probably ransom us, so it's unlikely he'll do us any harm.' Then in a whisper, 'If anyone gets a chance, make a run for it.'

Addressing his captor, Harold called good humouredly, 'Very well, Count Guy, as you are so insistent, we're delighted to be your guests.' He climbed out of the ship and dropped into the sea, wading up to the beach, his men and the dogs following behind him.

'What are you doing with that?' said Count Guy, nodding toward the hawk on Harold's forearm.

'I'm bringing it ashore.'

'What for?'

'In case I feel the need to do a little hunting.'

'I don't think you'll be doing any hunting on this trip.'

'I don't think I'll be here anywhere near as long as you imagine.'

The Count remained silent for a short time then responded enigmatically, 'Perhaps you're right. Bring it along.'

When all the men were ashore and their weapons had been collected, the Count and his guard led them away in the direction of his castle at Beaurain. Past the sand dunes they filed into a bleak, flat landscape. Tall reeds flourished in the marshy fenland and here and there a shrub, bush or miserable little tree struggled to survive. It was in this bedraggled wilderness that Gauti managed to slip silently away, intending to find Duke William and ask for help. He made the perfect getaway and was long gone when at mid-day his comrades found themselves incarcerated in the cells of Beaurain Castle.

Gauti travelled swiftly through the fenland. Late in the afternoon of the day following his escape he entered a Norman town. The appearance of the big man with his long blond hair flowing behind him, alarmed some of the locals, as he ran around the streets, demanding in English, to see Duke William. He was taken to the castle of Robert, Count of Eu, where, as luck would have it, Duke William was staying, enjoying the hunting in that part of Normandy with one of his oldest and dearest friends. Fortunately, Sir William Malet was there and able to act as interpreter as well as vouch for Gauti. The housecarl told of the events that had led to him seeking help. The Duke listened impassively until Gauti had finished.

'Very well. Tomorrow I shall send some men to deal with the matter. Rest assured, your lord will be released from the hands of Count Guy and he will be enjoying our company before the sun sets.'

Gauti found the Duke's confidence reassuring and with lifted spirits allowed himself to be accompanied to the soldiers' quarters for refreshment.

The following day, just as Duke William had promised, two dozen riders appeared at the gates of Beaurain Castle with Sir William Malet at their head. He demanded admittance, which was immediately granted without fuss or ceremony. Sir William made his way to Count Guy's hall, where Count Guy greeted him in restful repose, feet up on a table, a goblet of wine in his hand.

'Sir William, welcome to Beaurain. It is a pleasure to see you.'

'Good morning and thank you for your welcome.'

'Have some wine.'

'Thank you.'

'Have you journeyed far?'

'No, my Lord. I have just travelled from Eu with an urgent message from Duke William.'

'You've not come far then?'

'No, my Lord. Here is the message,' Malet said, attempting to hand over a scroll he had produced from his tunic.

'Read it to me, Sir William.'

'Certainly, my Lord. The message says, 'Greetings from Duke William of Normandy to my friend and Lord, Count Guy de Ponhtieu. I understand you have as your prisoners Harold, Earl of Wessex and a number of his men. You will escort them to Eu where you will hand them over to my protection. Until then I expect you to treat them as if they were your most honoured guests. Naturally, you will be amply recompensed for your trouble. I look forward to seeing you in Eu. Yours etc.'

'Thank you. Will you be accompanying us, Sir William?'

Sir William was taken aback. He had expected denial or some sort of protest. The Count's acquiescence surprised him.

'Thank you, my Lord, I will.'

'Good.'

'Might I visit Earl Harold to give him the news?'

'Yes, of course. How remiss of me. I'd forgotten, you're friends aren't you? Guard! Release the prisoners. Take the men over to the guardhouse and have them fed. Bring Earl Harold to me.'

A few minutes later, Harold emerged through a doorway with a guard scurrying behind him. He looked no worse for wear but was obviously not in the best of moods, that is until he saw Malet.

'Will, now this is a pleasant surprise!' The two men clasped arms around each other in a hug and slapped each other's backs.

'Harold, I trust you've been treated well.'

'No. My men and I have been treated like criminals. That's a fair enough description of our treatment isn't it, Count Guy?'

'Sir Harold... '

'Earl Harold.'

'Earl Harold, you should know none of my actions were personally directed at you. It is the custom here in Ponthieu, to keep salvage and wrecks.'

'And their crews?'

'And their crews.'

'That's not the custom in England.'

'This isn't England.'

'But the goods, the ship and the crew are English.'

'Wherever the ships, their crews and cargos are from makes no matter here in Ponthieu; we treat them the same. It would be unfair to do otherwise. If a ship is wrecked on our shores, it is ours.'

'Tell me, Count Guy, those four ships that chased me onto your coast, are they the full complement of your naval forces? Because I own more ships myself. Would you like me to come back later in the year to collect what's mine?'

'My friend, you lost everything on the beach.'

'Then I'll be back with a search party.'

'Are you threatening me?'

'What do you think?'

'Gentlemen!' interrupted Sir William. 'Let's resolve our differences calmly. I'm sure if Count Guy were to locate any salvage found along the coast belonging to Earl Harold, he would return it and Duke William would be pleased, as a gesture of goodwill, to compensate you for its loss, Count Guy.'

'Very well,' said Guy. Then casting a glance to Harold, 'It pleases me to release your ship and your belongings but that is the only reason I do so.'

'Thank you, Count Guy, I knew you'd understand,' Sir William replied.

It was around sunset that Harold and his men, accompanied by Sir William and Count Guy, rode into Eu and made their way to the grand castle. The Englishmen had never seen anything like it, looking as it did like a brilliant jewel set amongst mature beech trees, overlooking the winding River Bresle as it coursed through the city to the nearby sea. There was an awesome beauty about the building which imposed itself on the landscape, beautiful, entrancing, yet hard and cold as ice.

The huge oak doors of the great hall swung open at the approach of Sir William, Count Guy and Earl Harold. On his feet ready to greet them was Robert, Count d'Eu. On his right, also standing was the Duke.

All the men bowed in turn as Sir William introduced them. Everyone there was conscious of the Earl and Duke appraising one another. Each looked the other in the eye and saw modelled before him the set and bearing of a soldier and statesman. Harold noticed the Duke's build was more compact than his own and somehow ungainly. Something about William hinted at reserve, if not guile. To the Duke, Harold's natural strength was obvious and this he admired. He noticed the Earl appeared genuinely open and warm hearted but perhaps too trusting.

'Come and join us at my table.' Count Robert d'Eu was one of William's most powerful supporters. It was he who had hosted William and Matilda's wedding celebrations fourteen years previously.

The men climbed the dais and joined their host at the high table; Harold was seated next to Duke William.

'Welcome, Earl Harold. I'm pleased to meet you.'

'And I you, Duke William.'

'I understand your journey was quite eventful?' said the Duke, casting a glance in the direction of Count Guy. 'Well, you're here now and your little adventure is behind you. I'll take care of Count Guy and any demands he might make. You are my guest. Whatever you want, it is yours for the asking.' The Duke's mouth produced a smile as his eyes moved over Harold's clothes, inspecting every stitch. They examined his jewellery; he felt inferior by comparison.

'Thank you. For the moment I'm simply glad to be here. My presence is entirely due to your intervention and I am grateful to you.'

'It was my pleasure, Harold, think nothing of it. How is my uncle Edward, by the way? Still dividing his time between saddle and confession?'

'The King is enjoying good health. He hunts at every opportunity and always finds time for prayer and the business of government.'

'Good. I'd hate to think of anything happening to him.'

'Don't concern yourself, William... '

The Duke held up his hand, showing his palm as a sign for Harold to desist. 'You've said all you need to reassure me, Harold and I'm sure you won't mind addressing me by my correct title.'

Harold looked surprised.

'It's for the benefit of my vassals. I think it's best for everyone to know his place. Don't you, Harold?'

'In your court, Duke William, you must do as you see fit. Will you address me as Earl Harold?'

'Why? Do you see a need for it?'

'Surely, if we are to observe formalities, when you are addressed by your title, I should be addressed by mine?'

'But Harold, my friend, you're only an earl.'

'I think you'll find an earl is the equivalent of a duke.'

'Ah, but I alone rule Normandy.'

'In the name of the King of France?'

'That's true but you're forgetting: in this land, only the King is above me.'

'You're forgetting: in England only the King is above me.'

'But you are only one of many earls. I am the only duke.'

'True, but in England I am Subregulus. Should anything happen to my brother-in-law, the King, I would take charge of the country. Would anyone expect you to take charge of France, if anything happened to your king?'

'Enough of this, Harold! It's simple. You are the guest; I am the host. This is my court and I make the rules. Is that clear, Harold?'

The hall was deathly silent now. Everyone's attention turned to the Earl.

'Perfectly,' Harold replied calmly.

'Exactly. I knew you'd understand. Ah, here comes the food. Let's eat.' William's mood changed instantly.

The first course was served up and as everyone began to eat, the atmosphere lost its charge; conversations were resumed but nevertheless, all eyes were upon the Duke, trying to read his exact mood. If he laughed, his court laughed. If he was sad, so were they. There was not one member of the court who did not have to work hard at hiding his true emotions any time he found himself in the company of his lord.

Through mouthfuls, William conversed. 'Tomorrow, Harold, we will travel to Rouen where you shall meet my family.'

'I'll look forward to it. Tell me, will I meet my family too?'

'Your brother and nephew, you mean? We shall see Harold, we shall see. By the way, may I compliment you on your French; you speak the language quite well.'

'Thank you,' replied Harold.

Early the next morning, after mass and a hearty breakfast, the party began its journey to Rouen, except for Count Guy, who returned home.

Because of the lack of horses, most of Harold's men would have to make the journey on foot. Only Skalpi and Gauti would ride with their earl. When Harold and the two housecarls entered the castle courtyard, they saw a midget waiting with their horses. They talked as they walked over to them.

'How are they treating you both?'

'Couldn't be better. Finest hospitality I've ever come across.'

'What about you, Gauti? How are they treating you?'

'Ever since I arrived they've treated me extremely well.'

'Really?'

'Yes. They seemed genuinely glad to see me. I'm surprised really, because Normans have such a bad reputation back home.'

'Does anything strike you as odd?'

'No, my Lord. Why, should it?'

'I fear we might have exchanged one prison for another. If I'm right, we've got another thirty-nine nights here. You know the rules of hospitality. If a nobleman drops in on you, you're bound to entertain him for forty days and nights and the visiting nobleman, for his part, if he were to refuse all or part of that hospitality, would be insulting his host. I'm afraid we're going to have to see this through.'

The ride to Rouen saw the Duke and the Earl become well acquainted. Both loved hunting and although the Duke was a stranger to hawking, he admired Harold's skill. Harold was the better horseman but the Duke, through liberal use of whip and spur, stayed at his side. With them were Sir William Malet and Sir Robert d'Eu, followed by Skalpi, Gauti and a small Norman escort. Harold noticed how few people there were in the fields.

'Where is everybody?' Harold asked.

'Why do you ask?' enquired the Duke. 'Do you want to meet some peasants?' He burst out laughing as though he had heard the funniest joke ever. The Normans in his company followed suit, guffawing with him.

When the laughter subsided, Sir Robert pointed out for Harold's benefit, 'Normandy is not like England. When a man of nobility rides through the land the people go inside as a sign of respect.'

'It's just as well no one's bringing in the harvest, then.'

'Ah, you've noticed. We've had a poor summer here, Earl Harold; as you can see the corn is still green. Anyone would think it was April.'

Arriving at Rouen castle, the Duke dismounted. 'Turold, take care of your horses,' he ordered brusquely, nodding toward the midget. 'My man here will show you to your quarters and I'll see you all in the hall in half an hour.' He indicated with another nod of his head a man Harold took for a steward of some sort. 'You will meet my family and we will discuss how you will spend your little sojourn here in Normandy.'

In the Duke's castle, rooms were quickly allocated. After an hour there was a knock on Harold's door. He bade the caller enter and found standing before him a boy who looked about ten years old. He introduced himself as Robert, eldest son of William and he requested that Harold join them for a feast being held in his honour.

'I would be delighted.'

Robert led him down to the great hall to present him to his father's court. They passed through the entrance doors and Harold was announced.

'Harold, I'm glad to see you again. Please come up to my table,' called William.

Robert led the guest to the dais, past tables crowded with the noblest in the land, to where his father sat. Harold noticed the chill in the air and a strange mustiness familiar in stone buildings. It made him think for a moment of his own hall in Bosham with its fine oak columns and beams with their intricate carvings, a far cry from plain Norman stone. As he approached the high table William stood to greet him. A seat had been especially reserved for him.

'Harold, this is my wife, Duchess Matilda.'

Harold concealed his shock. The woman before him, offering her hand, was barely four feet tall. He had, at first, taken her for one of William's children. After bowing and kissing her hand he assured her it was a pleasure to meet her. And it was. Although diminutive she was otherwise exquisitely formed. She was in perfect proportion and quite beautiful. Her skin was pure white, unspoilt by blemish or even a rogue freckle. Her baby-blue eyes Harold found most alluring, especially when she looked up at him. There was no coy innocence in those eyes, but intelligence and a wicked humour. There was playful mischief in her smile too.

William continued introducing him to the other members of his family. 'Robert you've already met,' he said with a cursory wave of his hand. 'This is Cecilia, my eldest daughter.' A blonde, austere looking nine-year-old was presented. 'This is my second son, William.' The Duke introduced, with obvious pride, an effeminate looking, red-haired boy, about a year or so younger than Cecilia, 'And finally, meet my youngest son, Richard. Tomorrow you shall meet Agatha. She's only four months old but already she has real beauty.'

'I look forward to meeting her,' Harold replied.

'Now, go, children,' ordered the Duke. 'Harold, take a seat while I introduce you to some of the more esteemed members of my court. First meet my brother Odo, Bishop of Bayeux.'

Harold was quite startled; at a glance he could see the man was in his in his mid-twenties.

'It is a pleasure to meet you, Bishop Odo.'

'The pleasure is mutual, Earl Harold. But tell me, what surprises you?'

'Forgive me, but you seem so young for a bishop. In my country you would have to be thirty before you would even be considered.'

Duke William leaned forward. 'It's the same here, Harold, but Odo is gifted.'

The remark raised a laugh from all those within earshot, although Abbot Lanfranc, who was also there, tried hard not to look embarrassed.

Harold was a little puzzled but the Duke simply slapped him on the shoulder and introduced him to this youngest brother, Robert, Count de Mortain. Count Robert was a handsome man with a quiet dignity about him. On first acquaintance, people thought him a little simple but Robert had hidden depths and above all William treasured his steadfast loyalty.

The introductions continued. William laid special praise on his oldest friends, Sir William de Warenne and Osbern, Duke William's steward. Also there were Sir Hugh de Grandmesnil, Sir Hugh de Montfort, Sir Robert de Bellemie, Sir Roger de Beaumont, Sir Roger de Montgomery, Sir Roger Mortimer and Sir William FitzOsbern.

Harold's eyes met de Warenne's and he instantly felt himself in the presence of a formidable man. He was one of the oldest guests present at the court and he was unusual in many ways. He was taller than most and had long, straight grey hair, not kept in the Norman style at all but much more like the style of northern Europe. He would not have looked out of place at the English court but with his steel-grey hair and craggy face he looked hard and cold and he had a twist to his mouth, which gave him a cruel appearance.

The introductions continued and it was with pleasure that Harold saw his old friend Sir William Malet was present. As his goblet was filled with wine, the first of twelve courses was served.

Small talk began and continued for a while but as the wine flowed, the conversation wound this way and that and tongues loosened. Duke William, usually not one to give himself away, started to tell Harold about himself.

'When I was young and still fighting for my inheritance, I met Matilda in Flanders. She had an eye for a fellow countryman of yours, King Edward's ambassador to her brother's court and thought she could do better than the upstart bastard son of a mere tanner's daughter.'

'William, that's not at all true,' said Matilda, in mock horror.

'I couldn't get near her at court, her brother made sure of that. On my return to Normandy I vowed that I would never give up until I had won her as my own.

'When I was twenty-six, I again found myself at the court of Count Baldwin and still not allowed near her. So one evening, I lay in wait for her at dusk, then when she returned home from church vespers, I suddenly rode up out of the twilight, leapt off my horse, gave her a sound thrashing and threw her down into the gutter.'

'William! Why are you telling Harold all this?'

'A man needs to know who his friends are. Anyway, where was I? Oh yes. I remounted my horse and galloped away, leaving her wailing at the side of the road.' William laughed, full of glee: 'It was only after this little adventure that she consented to be my wife.'

William leaned forward to whisper in Harold's ear, 'She must have begged Baldwin to let me marry her. She just loves masterful men,' he confided.

'Don't believe a word, Harold,' Matilda chipped in. 'He paid the dowry, that's all. He tells everyone this tale but only because it makes him sound tough.'

'It's true. If you like, I'll show you. If you look hard enough you can still see the bruises.' Once again William laughed at his own joke.

'So after you beat her, everything went smoothly?'

'No, it didn't, it got worse. No sooner had I got round her brother than the Pope came knocking on my door. Can you imagine it? The Pope! What's it got to do with him who I marry? Still, we all have our crosses to bear; the Pope is mine.

'Matilda and I are distant cousins. Very, very distant! I don't know how long it took to persuade him to grant permission for the marriage but it took a long time. It was my good friend Abbot Lanfranc who persuaded him to give his blessing to our marriage.'

The Abbot smiled and nodded graciously.

'Penance didn't come easily. We each had to build a great abbey and then we had to give alms and forever be friends of the Holy See. That's why we built the abbeys at Caen, the Abbaye aux Hommes for me and the Abbaye aux Dames for her. We dedicated them to St. Stephen and to the Holy Trinity. But it was worth it; they are two of the most magnificent accomplishments in the world and what's more, they will be monuments to Matilda and me for years to come. You must pay them a visit. You'll be most impressed. Do you have any monuments, Harold?'

'I have Waltham Abbey but I don't really see it as a monument.'

'Ah yes, Sir William has told me about it. A warrior like you should have a monument in recognition of your great victory against the Welsh.'

'You've heard of that?'

'Of course, who hasn't? Tell me, Harold, how would you like to accompany me on a little expedition against the Celts into Brittany?'

'Duke William, I would be delighted to accompany you, if you feel you need my help.'

'Yes, Harold, I need your help in this undertaking,' and the Duke, in obvious high spirits, burst out laughing once again. He appeared to have drunk quite a lot of wine, something that was unusual for him.

'Harold, you are lucky. You have a beautiful wife and children. When you were young you had a mother and a father to care for you. You've always had someone to love you but for me life was different. My life was a struggle from the beginning. My life has been spent avoiding the blade of one weapon or another. Since the age of eight I've had assassins queuing up to kill me. But do not concern yourself: I fear no man at all. Do you know why?'

'No, I don't know why. Please tell me.'

'Harold, it is impossible for any man to kill me on the battlefield. What do you think of that?'

'I know of a Scotsman who thought the same thing.'

'Yes, I know of that story. But this is different. I was told by a holy hermit and because there are no conditions or qualifications, I cannot be killed by any man.'

'Then you'd better watch out for a woman.'

'I cannot be killed by women, either,' William said very firmly and with finality before bursting into laughter again. He was swaying now, his eyes unfocused. He leaned back in is seat for a moment, as if in contemplation. Then he leaned forward once more and confided, 'When I was eight my father died and I was made duke-elect. Three of my guardians were killed in the havoc that followed. Do you know what it's like to wake up from a bad dream as a child?'

'Everyone does.'

'Then remember your worst nightmare and what it felt like to wake up from it. Now imagine waking up to discover your nightmare has become real, your guardian is being murdered in his bed before your innocent eyes. You are woken by his screams. You feel his blood splattering all over you, shining like silver in the moonlight, the same moonlight that catches the blade and makes it flash like lightening as it comes down on your protector again and again. You think it's a bad dream. You struggle to wake but nothing changes. The nightmare is real and there in the room with you is a murderer. I would have been next for the assassin's sword but the killer was cut down by my devoted friend, FitzOsbern here. He hacked the assassin to pieces, his blood mingling with my guardian's, into my clothes, on to my flesh.'

William looked down at his arms as he spoke. It was as though after all those years he could still see the blood. His head wobbled as he struggled to gather his thoughts. 'I was thrown out of the window by my saviour who jumped after me and we ran like thieves into the night. For a long time I lived like an outlaw or a leper, hiding in forest huts and hovels, away from the eyes of man. But there were those who stood by me, risking their lives every day. I owe them my life. I never forget those who helped me, just as I always remember those who stand in my way.'

'It sounds dreadful. I thank God I haven't been sent the trials and tribulations you've suffered.'

'Perhaps God, in his wisdom, decided I would rise to these trials better than you. It's as the hermit said; no man can kill me, so I shall never die on the battlefield. Can you imagine what confidence that gives me? Can you imagine how I feel, mace in hand and a powerful horse beneath me, leading a charge against the enemy, knowing I'm invincible? You, Harold, like me, are a warrior but unlike me, you could die on the battlefield. Believe me, I know these things. That is why I know no fear but I do know my destiny. Do you know yours?'

'Only God…'

William, as was his habit, held up his hand to silence Harold. Rising uncertainly to his feet, he bade goodnight to his guests and made an ungainly exit.

'You must excuse him, Harold,' confided the Duchess, 'William rarely drinks more than three cups of wine but I think tonight he enjoyed your company so much he forgot himself. He's been so looking forward to your visit.'

'I'm pleased to hear it.'

'Yes. He has a little surprise for you. I can't say any more and now I must bid you goodnight.'

'Goodnight.'

He watched the Duchess leave then turned to continue conversation with Malet and the others.

The following days were spent gathering an army in preparation for the invasion of Brittany but there was still time for hunting. Harold was flattered to be asked if he would consent to be a godfather to Duke William's daughter, Agatha. Sir William Malet was to be the other. The ceremony had gone smoothly and to all appearances, the Duke and the Earl were growing quite friendly.

The Duke explained his reasons for the expedition. 'Conan must be dealt with. Since his father Alan's death, Conan has ruled under the protection of his mother, Bertha. You see, he's weak and immature, my friend. Over the years, there has been a series of fractious little wars between him and the rebels. All this fighting is making Normandy's southern borders unstable and unsafe. Now Conan is fighting against some of his Breton opposition near Saint-James-de-Beuvron. Riwallon of Dol, do you know him? He's a good man. Well, he has requested assistance, so I'll be helping out a friend.'

The expedition left Rouen with William's gold and scarlet banner held proudly aloft, the Duke full of questions about Harold's men. He couldn't understand the concept of mounted infantry, such as the English housecarls were. He wanted to know all about how they fought. Harold had no objection to enlightening him.

'They ride horses to battle but they don't fight on them?' asked William, perplexed.

'That's right.'

'If they are not going to fight on horseback, like my chevaliers, why don't they walk to battle, like my infantry?'

'So they can get to battle quickly.'

'I don't understand.'

'How fast can your infantry travel?'

'Well, with all their equipment to slow them down, a big force such as this will travel ten or twelve miles a day. How fast can your men go?'

'Depending on the terrain, we can easily travel fifty or sixty miles a day.'

'Impossible!'

'You might think so but quite a few of my men have more than one horse. The housecarl rides on one horse and another carries his equipment. We always travel at the speed of the fastest, so at the end of the day the slow ones have to keep going until they catch up. In the meantime, the faster ones will have made camp. Our horses are different, too. We use fast, strong ponies that have a different action from yours.'

'Action?'

'Yes. Rather than trot with diagonally opposed legs, our ponies move both legs on one side of their body, then the two on the other. They don't go very fast that way but they travel briskly, at a speed they can keep up for a long time. That's how we travel fifty or even sixty miles a day.'

'Very well, you get to the battlefield more quickly but you have less mobility once you're there.'

'But if you arrive before your enemy you can choose the battle site.

With your chevaliers, you might have more mobility but cavalry is no match for infantry, as we discovered against the Welsh in Herefordshire. And mounted infantry is the ideal force, as the Welsh discovered last summer.'

'Well, you fight your way and I'll fight mine but a nobleman should always ride. Only peasants fight on foot and we must never be confused with them. You will see, my friend, I have with me my infantry, my cavalry and my archers and I know well enough how to use them and we will provide you with an opportunity to observe.'

Harold was curious. The only time the English had used cavalry, it had been an absolute disaster, so he was keen to see why the Normans regarded it so highly. He would, he hoped, have an opportunity to see how the Norman infantry performed. He had with him his own unhappy men. Unhappy because William had not provided them with horses and so, like the Norman infantry, they had to walk. The complaints never stopped. Under his command, Harold also had thirty infantrymen on loan from Duke William. They were a quiet, stoical lot, did their jobs efficiently and quickly earned the respect of their English comrades, but they maintained a distance, a natural sort of reserve, which made it hard to really like them.

As the army made its way through Normandy, it travelled through a succession of rich pastures and orchards. The apples were touched with the glowing colours of early autumn. Harold could not help but notice the splendour of the churches, which seemed to compete with the castles; both were built with the need to impress. The churches were built to reflect the splendour of the Lord God; the castle to reflect the splendour of the lord of the manor. To Harold, the buildings seemed to reflect the Norman drive to intimidate.

'You admire our castles, Harold?'

'We don't have castles in England, Duke William.'

'Why's that?'

'England's a peaceful place. Our only threats come from overseas, which is why we have a navy.'

'Forgive me, Harold, but your country didn't seem such a peaceful place at the time of your exile or at your restoration.'

'You might think so, but you might recall civil war was averted.'

'A castle is still the only place for a lord of any substance to live. A castle lets his vassals know who is in control and is an excellent defence against anyone who might wish to attack.'

'Like your neighbours?'

'Exactly. You can trust no one in this day and age, Harold.'

'That might be true here, but in England we have the law of the land to which everyone is subject. Disputes are settled in the courts.'

'And does everyone settle disputes in court?'

'Yes, everyone.'

'Everyone! Even the King?'

'Everyone. The law of England is not the will or the whim of the King; it is independent to itself. The law is sovereign and has been, ever since King Alfred's time.'

'And in England, no one is above the law?'

'No one.'

'Come, we must press on. Conan and I have agreed to do battle on the fifth of the month. If we get a move on and get there early we'll launch a surprise attack.'

They left Avranches, continuing westward at a pace Harold found exasperatingly slow. Finally, they entered an expanse of sandy, flat land that was overlooked by Mont St. Michel, where the River Couesnon marked the frontier between Normandy and Brittany. It was a dangerous spot to negotiate. The river was only passable at low tide and even then, quicksand lay in wait with a slow death for anyone who strayed from the path. Single files of men made their way slowly across the river, each man following the footsteps of his comrade.

How it happened no one knew but suddenly a cry went out; two of the Normans in Harold's company had wandered from the path and were now screaming for help. They were out of reach of their friends, waist deep in quicksand and sinking fast. A small audience of onlookers stood watching them.

Thinking quickly, Harold dropped down from his horse, pulled his shield off his back and ran along the line with it to the two men, Skalpi following at his heels.

'Give me your shields,' Harold demanded of three soldiers among the gathering.

They obeyed their orders and handed over the shields. Taking them, Harold made stepping stones of them and lay flat on top of them reaching out to the two helpless men. Skalpi lay across the path with his arms wrapped around Harold's legs, ready to pull him back if need be.

'Grab my hands,' Harold ordered the nearest.

The man did as ordered and Harold pulled hard, wriggling backward as he did so. After pulling like this several times, the man had his chest on the end shield, which was beginning to sink into the slime. His comrade now hung on to his belt, while Harold pulled hard to get them both out. They struggled and strained as the shields started to sink. The men gathered on the path at last began to help, pulling on Harold's legs. After a few minutes of tugging and straining, the men were safe on the soaking path. With this one act, Harold's status was determined with every soldier in the Norman army.

It took a full day to cross the Couesnon. The next day, William advanced to the relief of Riwallon, who was besieged in Dol. Conan's response was to retreat and make his way to Dinan. Everything, crops, barns and villages, was burned behind him. Livestock was stolen.

The Duke led his men in pursuit; though it was a slow chase for Harold and his housecarls, eventually they came upon Dinan. Conan was hiding in the castle.

Convinced of their invulnerability, some of the townsfolk waved hides over the city wall to remind the Duke of his humble origins. Some of the defenders shouted out obscenities at the Duke, chants of 'Bastard' and 'Herleve the Harlot' rang out. As Herleve was the name of William's mother, the insults were obviously directed at him personally. But in proper military fashion, the Duke organised his men efficiently and soon the town was surrounded.

Duke William and Harold, with four chevaliers on either side, rode up to within hailing distance of the east gate of the town. When one of the local dignitaries presented himself, William prepared to give him an ultimatum. 'You can see how many men we have here and it's obvious your town will fall... ' The Duke stopped in mid-flow, looking perplexed. 'Where's your leader? Where's the mighty Conan? Hiding in the castle, no doubt, like the coward he is. Take a message to him. Tell him I'm willing to spare the lives of the townspeople, on condition that he surrenders this minute or meets me in single combat. If my request is not complied with the town shall pay a heavy forfeit.'

But Count Conan would not indulge William in single combat and if the Duke wanted to see his men die in a futile attempt to take the town then that would be on his conscience.

'So be it,' answered the Duke.

As he led his small band back to the line, a roar went up from those gathered on the wall, once again hides were waved and the chanting resumed. This time, a man who Harold took for the local idiot, displayed his backside to the Normans from the top of the wall before breaking wind at them. Heaven only knew what it was he had been eating but you could hear the rasping sound of his farts fifty yards away.

Acting on the Duke's instructions, the Normans delivered a well co-ordinated attack on the town's gates. On a signal from Duke William, blazing fire baskets were fired from catapults. Chevaliers raced on horseback with burning torches and threw them over the walls, as flaming arrows rained down on the thatched roofs of the town's little houses. Flames spread through the timber buildings and in the chaos created by the fire, the town's defences crumbled. Using battering rams the infantry smashed down the gates and entered, the horse soldiers following hard behind.

'Come, Harold, come and see how these Bretons fight.' It was the Duke, waving his mace aloft with the biggest smile on his face Harold had yet seen.

Following behind William were his brothers: Odo, who was also waving a mace and Robert with his sword held high. Like wolves bearing down on their quarry, they were in their element. Harold, experiencing the novelty of riding into battle for the first time, raced with the chevaliers into the tumult that was Dinan. In the mayhem the screams of men, women, children and animals, the crash of falling buildings and the roar of the flames greeted their ears. Rising smoke climbed heavenward, blotting out the castle but they fought their way through a weak and demoralised defence to their goal, the castle gates. A steward appeared holding out a spear, on the end of which hung the keys to the gates. William snatched them from him. 'Where's Conan?' he demanded.

'Gone to Rennes I'm afraid, my Lord.'

'The coward! The coward!' the Duke yelled, going on to rant about the wretchedness of Count Conan in particular and Bretons in general.

As his soldiers looted the town, William sent some of his men to find the people who had taunted him from the walls earlier in the day. An hour and a half later in the main square, while buildings were still burning, fifteen bound men were marched before the Duke; the prisoners were surrounded by a crowd of locals who had been rounded up and forced to watch by the Norman soldiers. The Duke made a short speech: 'You see fit to insult me and my family. For that you will pay the price. But remember, I am a merciful and tolerant man. I shall spare you your lives.'

The captives remained silent. A few feet in front of them a fire burned beneath a cauldron of molten tar. The Duke nodded to a soldier who produced his sword as he stepped forward. On the nod, another two soldiers walked over to one of the captives and yet another approached the cauldron, into which he dipped a large piece of wood, stirring it and lifting it out when it had a nice layer of tar on its end. He kept turning round to eye the prisoners as he did so.

While two soldiers held up the captive's feet, another methodically lopped them off with his sword and the fourth soldier sealed the wound with tar. They did this with the casual air of well-practised experts. They repeated the procedure with their captives' hands, oblivious to their screams.

Those who did not lose consciousness were made to crawl on their elbows and knees back toward their homes, or what remained of them.

'Go on, run along,' encouraged William, swiping their backsides with the flat of his sword. Then kicking a dismembered foot, he added, 'Now you know what it means to be defeated,' before laughing raucously.

'Ah, what are you going to do to him?' said William, looking towards the idiot who had thought, just a few hours ago, what fun it would be to fart at a duke. The soldiers held him as they had done all the rest.

'We were going to lop off his hands and feet, my Lord,' replied the soldier with the sword.

'No. No. No. We have something special reserved for him.'

'May I ask what it is, my Lord?' answered their leader, a sergeant.

'Look closely at the fire beneath the cauldron. What do you see?'

The soldier studied the area carefully.

'I see a poker heating in the fire, my Lord.'

'That's correct. Now perhaps you can think of some suitable use for it.'

'That I can, my Lord,' answered the sergeant.

With a set expression fixed on his face, the soldier slipped his sword back into its scabbard, stepped forward, picked up the poker and instructed his men to bend the idiot over a horse trough. The men did as they were told, presenting their captive's buttocks to the sky. The piercing scream as the soldier rammed home the red-hot poker was deafening, silencing everything for a mile around. As the soldier withdrew the iron a small cloud of vapour rose from the man's seared wound, 'Now that's what I call a fart,' exclaimed the Duke, once again laughing at his joke.

Whether the idiot died instantly or passed out and died later, none of the Normans ever knew or cared but for the time being he lay prostrate over the horse trough for the entire town to see.

'If anyone touches him, I'll have them flogged,' announced Duke William at the top of his voice. 'He'll make fine food for the ravens. Harold, tonight we'll camp outside the town while my men complete the liberation.'

'Very well, Duke William,' answered Harold, suppressing the anger he felt. This was too much like Hereford for his liking.

So the Duke, the Earl and their men made their way out of the town, back to the baggage train. Confident of victory, people had already lit the campfires and food was being cooked. William and Harold sat at a table with the Duke's half brothers, William Malet and some of the other chevaliers, to enjoy some wine.

The next day Duke William returned home to Normandy. Although the expedition had been an inconclusive affair, the Duke was a happy man. Firstly, his barons had fought foreigners on their soil rather than each other at home; this was a victory in itself. They had looted Dinan and so were all a little wealthier than when they had started out. Secondly, he and Harold had spent a great deal of time observing one another, attempting to gauge relative strengths and weaknesses. William had discovered Harold's great personal courage and the formidable obstacle he was to his ambitions for the English throne.

Harold had learned a great deal about William's military skills and methods of warfare, including his use of cavalry and the employment of castles as strongholds but it was his pitiless strength and unbending will that he had grown to respect most of all. William might be an uncultured illiterate but he had succeeded in a society soured by murderous conspiracy, duplicity and ruthless ambition. He was a force to reckon with.

The army made its way slowly back to Normandy. William promised to escort Harold to Bonneville-sur-Torques, where he would present him with his brother and nephew before he departed for England. Harold was in high spirits at the thought of meeting his kinsmen. The gradually diminishing column made its way through the country where castles were scattered across the landscape intimidating people for miles around. Churches and great cathedrals helped drive home the message: God Almighty supports your landlord. You shall not defy him.

As promised, William took Harold to Bonneville via Caen to give him the opportunity of admiring his two great abbeys there, dedicated to himself and his wife. They were as pompous and overblown as Harold had expected.

The party that arrived in Caen was small now, with only Sir William Malet and the Duke's half brothers, Bishop Odo and Count Robert, as companions, all the leading Norman magnates having departed for their estates. They would rejoin Duke William later at Lillebonne.

At Caen, the monks' hospitality was as lavish as anywhere in Normandy. After being shown to their room, the Duke and his guest made their way to the abbey's great hall. Odo, as a bishop, was made especially welcome and had a room to himself. Sir William had to share with Count Robert. Those men who formed the escort had to find lodgings in town.

Sitting down with the monks on the benches, they ate and drank sixteen courses over four hours. Harold was amazed to discover this was not unusual, as was evidenced by the waistlines of many of the clerics. No one else seemed to pay any attention to this, except for Robert de Mortain, who, unsettled by the conspicuous consumption all around him, exercised restraint.

After the meal, William and Harold retired to their chambers. Bloated from the excess of food they talked a while.

'Harold, a week from now you will return to England. Thoughts of home must play on your mind. I wonder, what are your prospects?'

'My prospects?'

'Yes. Your prospects. You probably expected to spend your life as second-in-command, just as your father did. Now you find yourself ruling the country on behalf of a cantankerous old man and soon, most probably, on behalf of the little boy, Edgar.'

'That would be presuming too much.'

Harold waited for William's response but the Duke seemed lost in his thoughts. Suddenly William turned and smiled benevolently at his guest. 'Did I tell you about my mother's dream?'

'No, you didn't,' replied Harold, perplexed.

'Then I should. Before I was born, my mother had a dream. She saw a tree grow from her womb. It was so tall, it cast a shade over all Normandy and towered up high into the sky, shadowing England and then France.'

Harold did not like the sound of this. 'What do you think it means?' he enquired.

'The French King calls himself my overlord but one day I shall meet him, crown to crown. The day will dawn when the Duke of Normandy no longer has to bow before the King of France. The day will come when he will bow before no man.

'Ruling the country on behalf of an old man or a little boy is a waste of your gifts. I have more to offer than that. I am a man of your own age and our experiences are similar, except as a ruler, I have been proved brilliant. I would make a delightful change from Edward and a more understanding colleague than Edgar. England and Normandy, in a friendly union, would be a very powerful state. Of course, I would be the nominal ruler and you the de facto ruler of England, with more independence than you would have under either Edward or Edgar. I would stay here in Normandy most of the time. You would have free rein. What do you say?'

Harold said nothing; he was agog.

'You look surprised. Didn't Edward tell you he has appointed me his heir?'

'What?'

'Of course we need to bond the agreement. I thought to prove your sincerity, you could marry Agatha.'

'Agatha?'

'Yes. She's young now, I'll admit but she'll be nice and ripe when the time comes. Or if you think she's too young for you, she could marry one of your boys; I'm quite flexible, you know. And your sister, what's her name, Aelfgifu, she can marry one of my boys. What's the matter Harold, you haven't said a word?'

In Harold's mind a picture formed of Wulfnoth and Haakon languishing in a Norman dungeon and the sudden death of Count Walter while visiting William. His instincts told him fate might have a similar future in store for him. All that seemed to matter was for him to get out of the country with all expediency, whatever the cost.

'You must forgive me, Duke William, all this comes as something of a shock.'

'What do you mean?'

'It's news to me that Edward had promised you the Crown.'

'Robert warned me that might be the case.'

'Robert?'

'De Jumieges.'

'De Jumieges! What's he got to do with this?'

'It was he who brought the message from my cousin.'

'Ah.'

'What do you mean, "ah"?'

'You do know that King Edward is not at liberty to promise the throne to anyone?'

'That's why I want your support. You have more power and influence than anyone else in England. You can get me the Crown. And if my eldest son marries one of your daughters, our grandson will be King. What do you think of that?'

'Having a grandson as king is an attractive prospect, I'll admit… '

'There you are, then. And when I'm King I shall do everything you ask of me which can reasonably be granted, I promise you. What do you say?'

'Duke William, as you know, I'm King Edward's man, his foremost earl and Subregulus. I have no right to commend myself to you or make bargains or contracts with anyone concerning the succession. I simply don't have the authority; that rests with the King and the Witan.

'But you could support me at this Witan thing couldn't you?'

'I could.'

'If you did, you would be supporting Edward in his wish to see me as his heir. And if you supported my claim, your brothers would follow your lead?'

'They might.'

'And if you and your brothers all supported me, then that would be enough to carry the Witan and I would be king.'

'Yes, you would.'

'There. You see, it's simple. Thank you, Harold, I knew I could rely on your support. We will discuss the details later. Have some more wine.'

William poured Harold and himself some wine before proposing a toast.

'To our future, Harold,' he said, 'to our future together.'

Their goblets crashed together and they drank.

'Sleep well, Harold. I'll see you in the morning.'

'Goodnight, Duke William.'

After getting into bed, the Duke fell into a deep sleep. He was sleeping like a lamb as Harold turned this way and that in his bed. Awake, he racked his brains for a solution to his problem. Asleep, he would have visions of Duke William in the top of a huge tree, laughing at him, all of his family, all of his men and everyone in England.

A sound from outside woke him from a nightmare. He rose from his bed, went over to the window and pulled the drape aside. In the half-light of dawn he could just make out a naked Odo, chasing after a young wench, pulling her clothes off as they ran. Pursuing her across a meadow as she giggled and laughed, finally the bishop grabbed her, threw her over his shoulder, retraced his steps and put her down on his fallen robes then wrapped them both up in them and rutted her like a great boar.

With the sounds of the bishop's indiscretion carrying on the dawn air, Harold went back to bed. William was breathing deeply, sound asleep.

Several days later, the Duke's party arrived in the small town of Lillebonne. Duke William broke the weary silence. 'At last, Harold, your journey is almost over.'

Harold felt relief wash over him.

'Tomorrow,' the Duke continued, 'you will leave for home. Tonight, we shall feast. In the morning before you depart, there'll be a short ceremony; nothing elaborate, just a formality really. Simply a short swearing of allegiance,' he looked up, his eyes meeting Harold's, 'for all my chevaliers. After which you will be reunited with your family.'

'Are they here now?'

'I don't think so but in any event they'll be here tomorrow. Your ship and its crew are waiting at the harbour to take you home. By this time tomorrow, you will be sitting by your hearth at home with all your loved ones, in your beloved Bosham.'

The day, Harold's last in Normandy, started unremarkably. Just after dawn, everyone awakened and made their way to breakfast. Harold still had no sign of his brother or nephew.

'Good morning, Harold. Did you have a good night?' William greeted Harold at breakfast.

'Thank you, I did.'

'Mushrooms for breakfast, if you like, Harold. I thought you might appreciate them.'

'Thank you, Duke William. I see you're sticking to lampreys.'

'Love them, Harold; I just can't say no.'

Harold was served from the pot which was taken down the table and left to stand. When he had finished, the Duke asked him if he would care for more.

'Yes, I think I will.'

William called for the mushrooms to be sent up to Harold and requested more lampreys for himself. The two chatted over breakfast and when they had finished eating the Duke said, 'I'll see you in the church in two hours?'

'Very well, may I enquire when I will see my brother and nephew?'

'You'll see them in just a few hours, I guarantee you.'

Harold, like the other guests, made his way to his room to prepare for the ceremony. Just under two hours later, Sir William Malet knocked on Harold's door.

'Come in.'

'Hello, Harold, time to go. Are you all right? You don't look at all well.'

'I feel a little strange. Nothing serious, though.'

'Good. Duke William is waiting for you.'

The two men made their way to the great hall and entered to see William seated on his ducal throne. Perched on his head was a golden circlet and in his hand he held the great sword of state. The hall was filled with the nobility of Normandy and the leading churchmen in their full robes and habits. On the dais, in front of William and for all to see, was a chest covered with a cloth-of-gold upon which rested a missal. Bishop

Odo stood close by, his face looking somehow crueller than usual and yet somehow indistinct. Harold felt as though he had entered another world.

'Welcome, Earl Harold,' greeted the Duke.

All eyes turned to the Earl. Suddenly Harold felt extremely self-conscious. A mildly nauseous feeling swept through him and his usual confidence evaporated. Everywhere he looked he could see eyes staring at him vacantly, like so many dead fish. William looked at Harold as though he had the power to read his thoughts.

The Duke beckoned him to walk forward to the chest. Observed by every pair of eyes in that silent assembly, he advanced. Now he felt the urge to laugh and tried hard to suppress a giggle.

'Earl Harold,' enquired Odo, in a whisper. 'Do our Norman customs amuse you?'

Harold looked at Odo's oddly distorted face. It looked as though once he had had a perfect face but over time it had been reshaped by some deep inner emotions. He looked possessed by lust and greed and far from holy.

'No,' replied Harold, weakly. He looked up at William and once more saw his face, almost like a mask, twisted by avarice. Cold shivers ran through him.

'Harold, would you like to see your brother and nephew?'

'Yes please, Duke William,' answered Harold with childlike enthusiasm. He tried hard to suppress another giggle, amused by the sound of his own voice.

'In the gallery,' said William, with a nod.

Harold turned and looked to the gallery. There in the gloom he could make out half a dozen figures. Four were armed men in chain mail and steel helmets with their swords drawn and pointed at two men in front of them. It had been thirteen years since he had last seen them. There was Wulfnoth, now in his twenties but the face of the youth still recognisable in the man. Harold could only guess the other figure was Haakon, who he had last seen as a young boy. Overwhelmed by the sight of his kin, Harold waved, a big grin spread across his face. As he waved he saw his hands leave behind a kind of trail in the air. It was as though he had a hundred limbs blurring in front of his eyes. Small, delicate rainbows appeared out of nowhere, hovered in the air then vanished as quickly as they had appeared. He tried closing his eyes to shut out the images but immediately visions of another type formed in a mind bursting with effortless imaginings.

'Harold, I think you are forgetting yourself.' It was Odo again, stern this time.

'Harold.' Now it was William who spoke but more gently than his brother. 'In honour of your bravery you are to be knighted. After which we'll reunite you with your family,' he paused, 'before you leave for home.'

Harold felt light-headed and a little dizzy, drawn by a vortex into a void.

'Harold,' Odo hissed. 'First the oath.'

Harold moved stiffly toward the chest where the missal sat upon a cloth.

'Good. Now place your hand on the missal.'

As instructed, Harold extended his arm and placed his hand on the missal.

'Now say after me, "I, Earl Harold of Wessex, do solemnly swear allegiance to William, Duke of Normandy".'

Harold repeated Odo's words, his speech growing more slurred with every syllable. He swore to be the Duke's obedient vassal, to do all in his power, to actively support Duke William's rightful claim to the English throne.

Harold felt dizzy and confused and more nauseous by the second. Events were out of his control. His mind addled and his legs weak, he almost lost his balance as he turned to the gallery and saw his brother and nephew, swords at their throats, their fate in his hands. He turned to face Odo.

'S'help me God!' said Harold with his quivering hand touching the missal.

All those gathered in the hall echoed, 'So help me God!' with an abrupt finality.

Even through his distorted perceptions, Harold knew that some balance had shifted, some door had opened but not for him and he could feel the most awful sinking sensation in his stomach.

William rose from his throne and took his place with Harold in front of the chest. Slowly and deliberately, like a magician demonstrating a trick, he removed the missal and drew away the covering cloth.

'Harold, regard this well.'

Harold followed William's gaze. There on the chest was a glass casket, cased in gold, which contained a skull, a dried finger and a fragment of bone.

'Do you know what they are, my friend?'

Harold stared, speechless, his head reeling.

These are the relics of two of your English saints, Revenus and Rasiphus. They are obscure, I'll admit. So obscure you've probably never even heard of them. But nevertheless, they are English and you have just sworn a holy oath on them.'

As Harold's startled gaze beheld the casket's contents he realised some awful mistake had been made. He was bound in a way he did not yet fully understand. He looked around and the fisheyes stared impassively. He felt like some helpless child, conspired against by adults, made to perform some silly trick he did not understand.

Harold looked up to where his brother and nephew were being removed. He looked to William; the one who always knew what was happening, the one who was his friend, his Lord.

'Time to go now, Earl Harold,' said Duke William, softly.

Harold felt a hand on his arm; it was Sir William Malet. 'Time to go, Harold,' he said gently, leading him from the silent hall.

The bright sunlight almost blinded Harold as he stepped outside. He looked down to protect his eyes and saw a huge rust-coloured butterfly, perhaps a foot across, sunning itself in the last of the summer sun. Looking round he saw little rainbows here and there; it was a pretty sight and then he was sick. He heard what sounded like a stampede behind him before Skalpi came into view.

'My Lord, are you all right?'

'Skalpi, I think I've been poisoned. Nothing is all right.'

'You didn't look right in the church.'

'I didn't see you there.'

'They kept us at the back but we saw and heard everything.'

'What have I done, Skalpi, what have I done?'

'Nothing, my Lord, nothing we can't undo, I'm sure,' said Skalpi, looking to Sir William for confirmation.

'I knew nothing about this Harold, I swear.' Malet answered the unasked question.

But it was no time to have a serious conversation with Earl Harold, who was staggering with his arm round Skalpi's shoulder, as he was taken back to his room. He lay on his bed chattering incoherently, until a servant came knocking on the door, announcing that Duke William would like to see him before he departed. The Duke was waiting for him with his nephew, Haakon.

Harold met Duke William, who was on horseback, in the courtyard of the castle. Beside him, also mounted, was Haakon. The two men exchanged greetings.

'Ready to leave, Earl Harold?' the Duke enquired.

'Where's my brother?'

'Your brother will be along later, when you've fulfilled your part of the bargain.'

'What do you mean, when I've fulfilled my part of the bargain?'

'You agreed to support my claim to the throne of England for which I, in return, would deliver up your kinsmen to you. You see how magnanimous I am, Harold? Already I have returned Haakon and you shall have many splendid gifts to take back to England.

'I thought Wulfnoth was to return with me as well.'

'Wulfnoth will remain my guest as guarantee of your integrity. Now, Harold, I suggest you ride with me to your ship, which is ready and waiting to sail.'

When Harold arrived with the Duke at the little harbour, it was to find his ship with its complete complement of crew and as much cargo as it could carry, tied up and waiting. Apart from enough supplies to get them home safely, the cargo consisted of gifts, mostly for Harold, some for King Edward.

'It's been so enjoyable having you to stay, Harold. I look forward to seeing you again soon.'

'Thank you for your hospitality, which I found quite unique. Goodbye, Duke William.'

'*Au revoir*, Harold, and *bon voyage*. Be careful not to get lost on the way.'

The ship cast off and slowly made its way down the river towards home. It was the beginning of Harold's last sea voyage.

BACK HOME

A few days later Harold found himself standing sheepishly before the King in the great hall at Westminster.

'It's been a long time since I was last in Normandy. What did you think of it?'

'Quite different from England.'

'Isn't it?' Edward waited for Harold to respond. When he did not, he enquired, 'And what did you think of the Normans themselves?'

'There are some who have guile and cunning to make up for any lack of education and they're more than a little adept at using their intellect in perverse ways, if it will further their own cause.'

'Oh dear, did someone upset you?'

Harold told Edward everything and when he had finished recounting events, Edward sat on his throne with his head in his hands, murmuring, 'This is not what I had in mind, not what I had in mind at all. Didn't I tell you, Harold, didn't I tell you but you wouldn't listen? Didn't I say what a crafty, conniving bastard William is? He'll stop at nothing to get his way. Leave this with me. I'll see what I can do.'

Harold left the King feeling unsettled. Troubled, he left for Waltham.

Within an hour of Harold's leaving King Edward, Earl Tostig was standing in exactly the same spot where his brother had stood just a short while before. The subject of the conversation was the same as Edward had had earlier with Harold. This time, Queen Edith was present. She and Edward listened keenly to what Tostig had to say.

'Wouldn't it be simpler if you just named me as heir?'

'No, it would create too many problems.'

'For whom?'

'For me, Tostig, for me. This is a difficult business.'

'Then why not make it simple?'

'What about the oath Harold swore, does it mean anything?' the Queen asked.

The King answered dismissively, 'It's worthless.'

'So, my Lord, we can discount William's claim?'

'Absolutely!'

'Then name me,' pleaded Tostig, on the verge of begging.

'Tostig,' said Edith firmly, 'you need to consider our brothers. How will they react? There's also Cospatric to consider.'

'Cospatric! What's Cospatric got to do with this?' Tostig was growing impatient.

'He has a valid claim' said Edward, calmly and authoritatively.

'Not much of one.'

'So what are we to do, Edward?' Edith asked.

'We must bide our time and be ready to take advantage of any opportunity that presents itself.'

Tostig interjected, 'So you won't name me as your heir?'

'Not yet, but I won't name anyone else either. In the meantime say nothing of the matter between Harold and William to anyone.'

'Very well.'

'Now, why don't you stay and enjoy some wine with your sister and me? Perhaps Countess Judith would like to join us?'

It was with genuine pleasure a few days later, that Harold granted permission for Skalpi to leave the housecarls and marry Aelfryth, his sweetheart. The request had been expected for some time and came as no surprise to anyone. Skalpi's time with the housecarls had almost come to an end and his relationship with Aelfryth had been flowering for a while. As was the custom, Skalpi would leave the housecarls after the Christmas court.

'What will you do then, Skalpi?'

'I thought I'd become a miller, like my father, my Lord.'

'All on your own?'

'Aelfryth's brother has experience in the mill. He's going to work with us.'

'Sounds like a sensible decision. Where are you going to live?'

'At Whatlington, my Lord.'

'You'll probably need some land.'

'That might have to wait for a while, my Lord.'

'I don't see why. I've plenty of land around there. Will five hides keep you busy?'

'That's very kind of you.'

'Consider them a wedding gift.'

'Thank you, my Lord.'

'When's the wedding?'

'We thought January.'

'Right after you leave, eh?'

'That's right. We wondered, my Lord, if you'd like to join us in the celebrations?'

'I thought you'd never ask.'

'All the family's welcome, my Lord.'

'We'll look forward to it.'

It was a pleasant distraction for Harold to accept a wedding invitation and hear confirmation that rumours of Skalpi's impending marriage were true, although he would miss him. Another distraction came when Harold was asked by Gyrth to preside over the court in Colchester. He welcomed the routine of the court and accepted Gyrth's request. All he had to do was consider the evidence and pass judgement.

Harold's first case was one of indecent assault. It transpired there had been some confusion, no one had come to any harm and the case was dismissed.

'What's next?'

'We have a man charged with theft, my Lord,' said the shire reeve. 'Call Herfast,' he called out.

A wretch familiar to Harold was brought before the court. He took one look at Earl Harold and knew his fate was sealed.

'You're charged with stealing a pig from the widow Leoflaed. How do you plead?' asked the shire reeve.

Herfast, who had until moments before been considering pleading not guilty, had a change of mind. 'Guilty,' he answered.

There was a gasp from the onlookers. No one had expected a guilty plea. Thieves were usually liars and said anything to escape their fate.

The shire reeve asked if there was anyone there to speak for Herfast. There was not.

'Is there anything you want to say before sentence is passed?'

Herfast looked at the reeve, glanced at Harold for just a moment before his eyes fixed on the codebook. In the codebook were all the law codes, crimes and punishments. He knew the punishment for a theft of this nature. He would have to compensate the victim and he would lose a hand. His eyes settled on the shire reeve for just an instant.

'No, my Lord. There's nothing I want to say.'

The reeve looked to Harold who asked if the owner of the pig would step forward. A huge middle-aged woman presented herself.

'How much was your pig worth, Leoflaed?'

'Twenty pence, my Lord.'

'That seems a fair price for a pig. Herfast, do you have twenty pence you can offer this good woman in compensation for the pig you stole?'

'I don't have a penny to my name, my Lord.'

Harold turned to the shire reeve who had opened the book of codes. He indicated with his finger, Herfast's punishment. The prisoner turned pale and began to shake.

'Herfast', said Harold, 'It is my duty to sentence you to a year of servitude with Leoflaed. After twelve months you should have worked off your debt to her.'

Herfast breathed a sigh of relief; he thought that would be his punishment in total.

'This will be,' Harold continued, 'after you have had your hand struck off as is the prescribed punishment for stealing. You will be led from here to the market place where you will suffer your fate. Tomorrow you will begin to work for Leoflaed.'

CHRISTMAS 1064

As had been the custom for so many years, the King's Christmas court was held in Gloucester, but this year there was a tension in the air. Looking a little wan, Edward appeared less vigorous than of old. At any gathering where the King and the Atheling were present, eyes would flit from one to the other and the same thought passed through everyone's mind; how long did the King have and would Edgar be able to replace him? The eyes would then move to Harold, who was an obvious candidate for the throne. Considering what was at stake, tension between the Earl and the Atheling was minimal.

Speculation as to who would succeed Edward was rife and there were those in the North who favoured a claimant from their own part of the country. In dark corridors there was whispering, which softly echoed round the court. But it was not just in the dimly lit passages that whispers could be heard. In a dark corner of a crowded tavern, talking in hushed tones sat Cospatric, Orm and Hardwulf, discussing England's eternal problem.

'The King must name a successor soon, we can't go on like this,' hissed Hardwulf in what he imagined to be a whisper.

'You must put your case to him again, Cospatric, otherwise we'll be stuck with that halfwit boy or Harold Godwinson.'

'Whichever one becomes king, it'll amount to the same thing for Northumbria. Edgar couldn't control the Godwinsons and Tostig would remain a tyrant. If Harold became king, he'd give Tostig full rein to do as he liked. If not you, it doesn't make any difference to us who becomes king. All the rest have nothing but contempt for us. You're our only hope, my Lord. You must act or we'll all end up the same as Gamel and Wulf. The North is with you and so is Earl Edwin. If Harold and Edgar are the problem, let's get rid of them.'

'It's not Harold and Edgar that's the problem; it's Tostig and Harold. I think I can say we've all had it up to the back teeth with Tostig, so he'll have to go; trouble is, with Harold and the King to support him, he's all but invulnerable.'

'Let's get rid of both of them.'

'Exactly.'

'Tostig first, then Harold.'

'Yes. Then, my Lord, you would be named as Earl of Northumbria.'

'And for Edwin's support, his brother Morcar could later become Earl of Wessex.'

'That sounds like a fine solution to me.'

'When, though, that's the question?'

'Well, there's no time like the present.'

'What, now, you mean?'

'Why not? We've no time to waste. They could easily have a little accident while out hunting.'

'I'll drink to that. Ha, ha, ha.'

'Get some more beer in. I think we have reason to celebrate.'

Little did they realise they had no reason to celebrate at all. Far from discovering a way out of their problems, they had created more. Every treacherous word they had uttered had been overheard by one of Tostig's informants, who went straight back to his earl and explained what he had overheard. Before Cospatric, Orm or Hardwulf had left the inn, word of their plot had reached Tostig and via him, the Queen. The twins took no time to find a solution to the problem.

Later that evening, as the great hall was beginning to fill for the feast, a servant sought out and found Earl Cospatric. The earl and his cronies were already at their table and talking merrily.

The servant approached Cospatric discreetly, whispered something in his ear, smiled and stepped back. Cospatric, looking a little surprised and more than a little pleased excused himself and followed the servant. As the two left, they passed Tostig on his way in. Tostig greeted Cospatric warmly as they passed.

As the servant made his way to the Queen's chamber, he met Hardy, Edith's steward.

'Ah, my lord... Earl Cospatric.' Hardy greeted the Earl as though he were a long lost friend. 'You got the message, I see.'

Before he could answer, Hardy dismissed the servant and bade Earl

Cospatric to follow him. The servant, as instructed, made his way out of the great hall toward an inn on the edge of town. Amund, one of Tostig's housecarls, would meet him there and be the last person to see the servant alive.

Hardy made his way to the Queen's chamber with Cospatric following on behind and the two made small talk as they went. The Earl was desperate to know why the Queen wanted to see him. She had never summoned him before and he could only imagine this meeting must have something to do with the succession.

When they reached the Queen's chamber, Hardy knocked on the door and entered when beckoned.

'Earl Cospatric to see you, ma'am.'

'Show him in.'

Hardy turned and invited Cospatric to enter, indicating with an outstretched arm as though it was not obvious which way he was expected to proceed. 'My lady will see you now, Earl Cospatric.'

As the Earl stepped into the room, Hardy closed the door behind him. Queen Edith dismissed two ladies-in-waiting, telling them that she wished to talk with Earl Cospatric alone. She turned to the Earl and smiled seductively. He returned the smile.

'You must be wondering why I sent for you, Earl Cospatric?' said the Queen, still smiling as she rose to her feet and approached him.

'Yes I am, my lady,' he answered, as she kissed him on each cheek.

'I wanted to have a word with you about the succession,' she said, taking a step back, taking his hands in hers, and holding them gently by his fingertips.

Cospatric was fully attentive as he sensed the Queen was about to give him important news. He stared into her hypnotic eyes, unaware of anything else in the room. He did not hear Hardy come up behind him. It was too late when he saw the blur of a knotted rope flash by his eyes and the Queen was still smiling as the pain from Hardy's knee smashed into his back, forcing him down to his knees. Two men who he recognised as Tostig's housecarls appeared from behind drapes, strode over to him and proceeded to kick him hard in the chest and stomach. The last he saw of Queen Edith was her turning her back on him. The sight of his purple face with its bulging eyes was too much for the lady to bear.

Ravenswort and Barcwith wrapped Cospatric in some old sheets and carried him out of the room. Hardy, ever the gentleman, opened the door for them. When they had left he turned to the Queen.

'Will that be all, ma'am?'

'Yes. That will be all, Hardy,' she answered, pulling back the drapes to clear the air. A little cold, fresh winter night seeped in to her room.

Within minutes Ravenswort and Barcwith were carrying Cospatric's body towards a small malodorous brook, an insignificant tributary of the Severn. His body was relieved of its money and valuables. His throat was then slit to make it look as though the Earl had been murdered on the spot. Cospatric's body was then thrown into the murky water, where he was found the next morning, the victim of a violent and terrible robbery. The main suspect was the servant who had led him away from the hall, never to be seen again.

1065 THE SUMMER OF DISCONTENT

In the great hall at York, Earl Tostig and Lady Judith arrived with the spring sun to an awkward reception. Disinclined to spend the winter in the North, especially after the unpleasantness of the Christmas court, Tostig and Judith had stayed with the King in London. Now, almost like paying a visit to relatives they disliked but were duty bound to see, they were back in Northumbria after the Easter court.

Tostig and Judith could tell as soon as they arrived that the servants were doing their best to welcome them but there was an uneasiness about the way they performed their tasks that communicated perhaps all was not well. Tostig summoned Copsig to his private chambers to catch up on news.

'Welcome back, my Lord. While you were away at Westminster with the King, a dreadful thing happened; the brigand you imprisoned at Durham last November, escaped custody.'

'Which brigand?'

'Alden-Hemel, my Lord. Apparently he escaped with the miraculous assistance of Saint Cuthbert.'

'You mean someone took a bribe. Saint Cuthbert had nothing to do with this, I'll be bound. Anything else I ought to know?'

'Well, after Alden-Hamel escaped, he took refuge in a church.' Copsig continued quite slowly and precisely, as though in an effort to convey the full meaning of his message, before adding with great emphasis, 'It was Saint Cuthbert's, my Lord.'

'Continue.'

'Well, Ravenswort and Barcwith somehow discovered he was in there claiming sanctuary. Ravenswort was all for leaving him there the full forty days and then recapturing him when his time was up but Barcwith, being impatient by nature, went into a bit of a rage, running around shouting and screaming, "Get out of there, you bastard or we'll come in and get you," that sort of thing, but Alden-Hamel wouldn't come out.'

'What happened next?'

'Well, Barcwith, all full of fire and the like, called to his men to break down the doors of the church. He himself was making as if to charge down the doors when he collapsed as if struck by an arrow. Out cold he was and he never recovered, died a horrible death three days later. They reckon he's gone straight to hell for what he did, my Lord.'

'I suppose this is the talk of the North?'

'Yes. The Bishop of Durham wants to see you about it.'

'I suppose he wants compensation.'

'Yes, my Lord. He's furious. He reckons Barcwith was struck down by God for violating the holy sanctuary of Saint Cuthbert and as Barcwith was your man you should pay compensation. It's like Lady Judith's servant getting killed all over again. Perhaps you should pay the compensation Barcwith would have had to pay, had he survived.'

'Did the Bishop say how much?'

'Ninety-six pounds, my Lord,' mumbled Copsig, hoping his lord would not hear him.

'Ninety-six pounds,' bellowed Tostig. 'I could pay less for murder.'

'Exorbitant though it is, I think it advisable to pay up because the Bamburghs are whipping up a lot of trouble. The rumour is that Barcwith was acting on your direct orders. They are saying that you are unholy and you insult the saints and everything that's holy. A few weeks ago, the remains of St. Oswin were disinterred and put on display at Durham.'

'Who's Saint Oswin?'

'One of Northumbria's martyrs. He was betrayed and murdered by King Oswy.'

Tostig's mind flew back to Christmas and the plot he had hatched with Edith.

'Well, we'd better pay the Bishop of Durham his ninety-six pounds right away. That should quiet things down for a while. And start recruiting more housecarls.'

'Is there anything else, my Lord?'

'No. That'll be all.'

'Very well, my Lord,' said Copsig, feeling reassured, now that the Earl was home.

But tensions rose and by the end of the summer things came to a head, as

Tostig found out during a visit to Harold's hunting lodge in Wiltshire with King Edward in early September.

On their arrival at the lodge in Britford, they were surprised to find Harold waiting for them. Harold told them that there had been an attack on another of his lodges, at Portskewet. While he had been out hunting, the lodge had been attacked by a gang of about two hundred men. All the servants were killed and the lodge burned down.

Barely had he finished explaining when a messenger arrived looking for Tostig.

'There has been a rebellion in the North, my Lord. Hundreds of soldiers entered York earlier in the week,' the messenger said, all of a fluster. 'They took everything, weapons, treasure, furniture; anything that wasn't nailed down.'

'But what about the guard?'

'There were too many for them, my Lord. Your housecarls put up a brave fight by all accounts but they were overwhelmed. I'm sorry to say at least two hundred of your men are dead, including Amund.'

'My God, what about Ravenswort?'

'I've no word of him, my Lord. They said if you had been there, they'd have killed you too.'

The King stepped forward, 'So they've taken over York?'

'It's worse than that, my Lord. The rebels have outlawed Earl Tostig and chosen Morcar as the new earl for Northumbria.'

'God's death!' Edward was extremely angry now. 'They must have been planning this for a long time. Where's Morcar now? Do you know?'

'Yes, he's with the rebels. He appeared within a day or two of the revolt.'

'This has been planned, Harold. What are we to do?' the King asked.

'Why do you ask him? I'm under attack, not Harold!' interrupted Tostig.

'Tostig, calm yourself. These rebels and Morcar, what do they want?'

'I don't know, my Lord,' the messenger replied.

'We should go up and see them,' asserted Harold.

'Morcar,' said the messenger 'has appointed Oswulf as the new Earl of Bernicia.'

'The bloody Bamburghs, I might have known,' Tostig exclaimed. Even under the circumstances, the King was amazed to hear him swear, albeit mildly; he'd never known it before.

The messenger continued, 'After they left York, they terrorised Lincoln, Nottingham and Derby. The last I heard they were doing the same to Northampton.'

'Are they planning to move on London?' asked the King, rising to a panic.

'I've no idea. I know Earl Edwin has joined them and a lot of Welshmen too.'

The mention of Welshmen alerted the brothers to where the danger might be coming from.

'Aelfgar's sons,' snarled Tostig. 'They must have got together with some of his old friends over the border. They want the throne, I'll bet. You must name your successor, Edward. Name me now and I'll deal with them. I'll show them what it means to rise up against their king,' seethed Tostig.

Edward turned pale in an instant.

'If I may speak, my Lord?' the messenger asked.

'Go on,' replied the King.

'Although the rebels utterly repudiate Earl Tostig's authority in Northumbria, they claim to be absolutely loyal to the Crown.'

'What, they prove this by running amok all over the countryside? Disloyalty to an earl is disloyalty to me. This must be dealt with immediately. Harold, what do you say?'

'Let's meet them and see what they want.'

'We know what they want,' interjected Tostig. 'We'll raise an army. Get Gyrth and Leofwine. They wouldn't rise against the King.'

'And what if this ends in civil war?' Harold asked, looking to the King, observing the slight quiver that ran the length of his body, noting his increasing frailty. 'Don't you think we're too vulnerable to indulge in something of that magnitude?'

'He's right, Tostig. Harold, I think you ought to see them. Tostig's presence will only inflame the situation.'

Yes, thought Harold, keep him safe. 'That's very wise counsel, my Lord. I'll take a dozen housecarls. If I leave now I'll catch up with them in a few days.'

In the sheriff's hall in Northampton he delivered the King's message: 'You are to lay down your arms and submit your grievances to a full assembly of the Witan.'

This was the day that Aelfgar's sons had long awaited, the day when a Godwinson would be at their beck and call, begging favours, seeking goodwill and asking favour. It was Earl Edwin who answered. Surrounded by his cronies he spoke with confidence, if not contempt, but he was young and knew no better.

'Why should we lay down our arms? Your brother's tyranny has driven us to rebellion. This isn't something we do lightly or something we will stop on a whim.'

'The King would like to talk with you all.'

'Where and when would that be?' asked Edwin, his smile subsiding.

'Oxford, on the twenty-eighth of this month.'

'Very well, we'll see him there.'

Harold returned to the hunting lodge in Britford with a heavy heart. The rebels were not going to back down easily and for the moment they had the upper hand. Gyrth and Leofwine had answered the King's summons and had brought as many men as they could gather at short notice; more were on the way.

After Harold had given his account of his meeting with the Northumbrians, the brothers and the King discussed tactics.

'We can't allow them to get away with this,' said Edward. 'Raise an army then give them the sound thrashing they deserve.'

'Very well, my Lord, we'll invade the North in the spring.'

'The spring? Why wait until then, why not now?'

'We couldn't gather an army of sufficient strength before Christmas, my Lord.'

'Morcar and Edwin have an army.'

'That's true, my Lord but they have had most of the year to plan this.'

'You think so?'

'Since last Christmas is my guess.'

Edward hesitated for a moment before replying, 'This is about Cospatric, then?'

'I think so.'

'Well, if we put our minds to it, why couldn't we raise an army in time to meet them at Oxford?'

'It's important we get this right, my Lord,' Harold continued, calmly addressing the King. 'After all, what would be the result of using too few troops and losing the battle? Wouldn't that leave Edwin and Morcar the victors? And suppose we won but lost so many men in the process that the country was open for a third party to enter unhindered?'

'Then what do you suggest?'

'We can't be sure of success using military means, not just at the moment anyway. Why not try political means, at least for the interim? With any luck it might not come to a clash of arms and perhaps their support will melt away.'

On a miserable October afternoon, Earl Edwin and Morcar arrived in Oxford, ready to air their grievances. They were united in their determination to concede nothing.

Wrapped up in their winter cloaks, the good and the great of England started their discussions, as was customary, in the open, the whole town as witness. King Edward remained out of sight; he had delegated all authority to Harold, a wise move, though Tostig felt slighted.

'Where's King Edward?' snapped Earl Edwin.

'He feels unwell and has requested me to take his place, if there are no objections.'

Edwin looked around. 'Do we have any objections?'

The question was greeted with a barely discernible murmuring.

'What do you have to say, Earl Harold?'

'King Edward seeks to know your grievances and demands.'

'It's quite simple. Since becoming Earl of Northumbria, your brother there has treated us cruelly. He's a tyrant who punishes the slightest misdemeanour with the severest punishment, his taxes are harsh and unfair and his justice prejudiced. He must be banished from the kingdom forthwith and Earl Morcar will take his place.'

'Morcar's no Earl,' yelled Tostig.

'Who are you?' was Morcar's insolent reply.

'Don't pretend you don't know who I am.'

'Ah, I thought I knew your face. Weren't you the Earl of Northumbria?'

'Don't be clever, it really doesn't suit you.'

'Well, when have you ever been clever?'

'My lords, my Lords,' pleaded Harold, walking out between the feuding men with his arms spread wide and high. 'This is no way to solve our problems.'

'Why should the King allow the election of Morcar as earl when he broke into my treasury and plundered it?' Tostig demanded to know.

'It was our money in there,' was Edwin's retort.

'On the contrary, the money in my treasury was tax money for the King. Should treason be rewarded with an earldom?'

'We'll give the King any money that's his but Tostig's not having a penny.'

'And what about the housecarls you killed? Are you going to give them back? You've infringed the prohibitions on killing housecarls.'

'If you hadn't been such a tyrant it wouldn't have been necessary.'

'It wasn't necessary. If you had any genuine complaints you should have taken a petition to the King. And who are you to depose a legitimately appointed earl just to impose your own brother? Appointing earls is the business of the King and the Witan, not yours.'

Tostig was winning the council over; Edwin could see the danger he was in.

'It's your covetousness that's brought this on your head, Tostig.'

'Well, let's ask the King, shall we? Or as the King's not here, let's ask Earl Harold what he thinks?'

'I'm afraid I have to agree with the Northumbrians.'

A cheer of support went up from the crowd. No dissenters were heard.

'Agree? Agree? What do you mean, agree?' Tostig was infuriated. 'How can you agree with this rabble?'

Harold spoke quietly to Tostig. 'The only way I can get you back is by force. That would mean civil war which we must avoid at all costs.'

Tostig answered, hissing through his teeth, 'At all costs? Who will pay the cost? Me. That's who. This suits you, doesn't it? You're behind all this, aren't you, Harold?'

This accusation lightened the hearts of Edwin and Morcar. They had never thought they would live to see the Godwinsons fall out.

'I'll bet this was all your idea to get rid of me. I see it all now. Get Aelfgar's sons to kick me out and in return you offer them my earldom. Now the way is clear for you to take the throne. Does your ambition know no bounds?'

'You've put yourself in an impossible position, Tostig. I can't support you,' answered Harold, remaining calm.

'Won't support me, you mean. It's unnatural not to support a brother. What's the matter with you? Don't answer, I know, you planned all this, didn't you, you and your northern friends.'

'I knew nothing about this, Tostig.'

'Liar! Liar!'

'You'll apologise for that.'

'You'll take an oath.'

These last remarks were greeted with uproar; Tostig's friends and supporters were being yelled down by those of Edwin and Morcar.

There was a brief, quiet exchange between Harold and Bishop Wulfstan, after which the Bishop produced a bible. Then Harold took an oath to the effect that he had had no part in the fomenting of the rebellion.

The assembly became calm and was back under control; Edwin sat looking insolently at Harold, a surly Morcar by his brother's side.

'So, Earl Harold, now we know all this wasn't your idea,' said Edwin, 'what do we do now?'

'You must recognise Siward's son, Waltheof, as Earl of Northampton and Lincoln and he is to hold those lands as his own. All those people who have been driven into captivity will be freed and allowed to return with their goods and chattels. Whatever my brother might or might not have done, the people of Lincoln and Northampton cannot be held responsible or punished. The same conditions apply to all those held in captivity from any of the other shires. In return, Earl Tostig's laws shall be annulled and those of King Knut reinstated. With the permission of the Witan I shall declare Tostig deposed and Morcar elected Earl of Northumbria.'

Harold looked around the faces of the members of the Witan. 'Do you all say, aye?'

'Aye,' was the unanimous reply.

'Then so be it. Is that agreeable to you, Earl Edwin?'

'It is, Earl Harold.'

'Good. Oh, and get those Welshmen out of the country in three days or we'll come after them and kill the lot.'

Edwin knew better than to argue and Morcar's first act as earl would not be to defend Welshmen on English soil against his king.

'Very well.'

'You may leave now. We'll see you at the Christmas court in Gloucester.'

'It's good to do business with you, Harold. Goodbye.'

'Goodbye.'

'And what happens to me, I'd like to know?' demanded Tostig.

'It would appear that you're banished,' said Morcar with a chuckle. 'Goodbye,' he said, and turned and walked away with Edwin, to the cheers and hoots of their men.

'This is outrageous, Harold.'

'Let's see the King.'

'Yes, let's,' snapped Tostig.

They found an agitated king pacing about in his quarters.

'Well, what was the outcome?' he snapped before anyone had time to greet him.

'The Witan voted to depose Tostig and elect Morcar in his place. Tostig is banished.'

'No. No. No.' Edward was heartbroken. 'I can't do that.'

'You see, Harold, at least someone is showing me some loyalty.'

'It's not a question of loyalty... '

'Isn't it? I know your mind. I know what you're plotting. Why should you have the throne? I'm as important in the North as you are down here in the South. Why should you have the throne, anyway? You're not the oldest son, Sweyn was. It was I who destroyed the Welsh, admittedly with some help from you. You claimed all the glory for that. But look at Northumbria; look at everything I've achieved up there!'

Harold did not have to speak.

'I know what you're thinking. I didn't make this mess. Troublemakers did that. Now show me some loyalty.'

'Argh!'

The two men looked round to see the King, right hand on left arm, eyes bulging, slowly collapsing to the floor. He was struggling to remain upright but with no success. The two men grabbed him and lifted him into a chair, calling for aides as they did so. Baldwin, monk of St. Denis and the King's physician was sent for; apoplectic shock was his diagnosis.

After an hour or so the old King came round; he seemed burdened with a terrible sadness. He was suffering a great humiliation and it looked as though the added grief of suffering the loss of a loved one was too much for him.

A scribe entered with the orders for Tostig's exile for the King to sign.

'Forgive me; I have to do this. It's out of my hands,' Edward said, as he sobbed and signed the orders.

The events of the day were too much for Edward. He wept and took to his bed. After an emotional farewell, Tostig and Judith departed for exile at the court of her half-brother, Baldwin of Flanders. King Edward, now a broken man, was taken to Westminster where it was hoped he would make a recovery.

FAREWELL TO THE KING

A great chill fell over the land that Christmas and since Edward was too ill to travel, the court was held in London. The King was desperate to see the consecration of his new church at Westminster, which seemed to be the only thing keeping him alive.

News of Edward's illness had spread and as the greatest in the land gathered, an air of foreboding filled the King's great hall. All around the snow fell and settled deeper each day and when it had reached a foot in depth it stopped, to be followed by freezing fog that hung in the air, shrouding the city, a premonition of mourning.

In spite of the weather, a great concourse from the whole of England assembled at Westminster that Christmas for the consecration and, heaven forbid, if the King should die, to have a say in the election of his successor. Stigand and Eadmer were present, as were all twelve of the bishops, the royal clerks, Ragenbald the King's Chancellor, all seven earls, and too many thanes to mention. Notable by his absence was Tostig. His non-appearance added to the feeling of gloom hanging over the melancholic festivities.

Edward lay in bed feeling the ravens had gathered for a feast. On Christmas Eve, as his subjects celebrated, he had a series of strokes but valiantly staggered through the Christmas Day ceremonies. Exhausted, he spent all of the next two days in bed. But nothing could keep him away from the consecration of Westminster on 28th December, the festival of the Holy Innocents. As soon as it was over he took to his bed for the last time. In attendance were Archbishop Stigand, Queen Edith, Harold and Robert FitzWymarc; other members of the court visited when it was deemed appropriate.

In an anteroom off the great hall, Leofwine and Gyrth were deep in conversation. They knew the King was dying and concerned as they were for him, they had matters of state on their minds.

As the New Year approached, the temperature outside plummeted still further and the King's fever began to soar. The New Year saw Edward drifting in and out of consciousness, sometimes becoming delirious. Once he awoke with a look of sheer horror on his face. Grabbing hold of Queen Edith's arm, he began to recount the horrors of an apocalyptic vision.

'I saw two monks,' he said with staring eyes. His grip was surprisingly strong for someone so weak. 'They told me that all the magnates in England, all of them, not just the earls but all of the churchmen too, they're all servants of the Devil.'

The King struggled for breath as everyone around him looked on with trepidation.

'God has cursed the kingdom!' he blurted, and then sobbed. 'A year and a day after my demise, the Almighty will deliver it into the hands of the enemy. Devils the like of which no one has ever seen will come through all this land with fire and sword. Like a dark black cloud, the havoc of war will descend on this country.

'I told them that I would make my people see the light. I would bring my people to repentance and ask for God's mercy. Surely if I did, His mercy would not be withheld. But do you know what? The monks said that the English would never repent and God would refuse to pardon them. It seemed all was lost and then I had an inspiration. I asked them when God's punishment would be complete, thinking surely he would not punish the kingdom for long.'

'What did they say, husband dear?' asked Edith with watering eyes.

'They talked in riddles. They answered that God would cease to punish the English for their sins when an oak tree in full leaf, having recently been felled half-way up its trunk and the part that had been cut off carried a quarter of a mile away, should all by itself join up with the trunk again, break into leaf and bear fruit. When that miracle happens, God's anger will be calmed.'

'No, dear, no. It can't be true. It was just a dream,' said Queen Edith, trying to calm her distressed husband.

Through tear-filled eyes he assured her it was true. He had spoken with his maker. Now the Queen, as well as the King, was in tears. She was convinced his soul had made the journey to heaven and returned for a short time to bring the news of the revelations. She was sure they were real and thought Edward a true prophet.

Stigand leaned over to Harold, whispering in his ear to reassure him.

'I've spent many a time at a deathbed listening to the ramblings of the dying. Don't worry, just ignore him; he's raving. It's just a pre-death fever. Lots of people do it.'

While Edith was sobbing, the King called for everyone to gather round. 'It's time I spoke and made my will known to you all,' he said, in a whisper.

'I ask the Almighty to repay my wife for her loving and dutiful service.' He then held out his weak and trembling hand to Harold and said the following, 'I commend this woman and the entire kingdom to your protection.'

Harold nodded in acquiescence and the King lay silent for a short time to recover his breath and collect his thoughts before speaking again. Harold turned toward the bed as Edward spoke. The ghostly King's words seemed to come from a distance, as he asked, 'Promise me you'll make my death known everywhere, as is customary, so that at once my people can invoke the mercy of God for me, a miserable sinner.'

'I promise, my Lord.'

The end was upon them now. More and more, the sound of sobbing filled the room. While his vassals wept, the Queen cried unceasingly. 'What will I do now? Whatever will become of me?'

Edward spoke his last words and made his final will and testament. To his men he said, 'Don't weep but pray to God for my soul and give me leave to go to him.'

Then he turned to Edith and tried to comfort her. 'You are not to fear, for by God's mercy I will not die now, but shall become well again.'

Looking straight up at the ceiling he exclaimed, 'May God repay my wife for her dutiful and loving service, for she has certainly been a devoted servant to me and has always been at my side, just like a loving daughter. May God's mercy reward her with eternal joy in heaven.'

With this Edith burst into uncontrollable wailing.

Edward turned and offered his hand to Harold. 'I commend this woman and the entire kingdom to your protection. Remember, she is your lady and sister, and serve her faithfully and honour her as such for all the days of her life. Do not take away from her any honour that I have granted her.

'And I commend to you all my foreign vassals and servants and ask that you shall offer them service under you and should any decline, that you promise safe conduct for them to return home with all that they acquired in the royal service.'

So at last it was said. The King had named his successor in the form of a verba novissima, the customary legal and binding form of will and testament, practised in England since time immemorial.

Harold agreed, as Edward knew he would: 'I shall, my Lord.'

'Good man. Have my grave prepared in the minster.'

'As you command, my Lord.'

Those were the last words the King exchanged with anyone. Drifting off into fitful sleep, he jolted and juddered through the night as he slowly slipped away. The next day, on the cold grey morning of the fifth of January, as snow began to fall around Westminster and the last rites were being administered to him, the King passed away, his suffering over.

All through the eve of Epiphany, Edward lay in state in the great hall. As word spread through the city, more and more of his subjects came to pay their respects all through the day and the long, cold night. The earls took it in turns to keep the death-watch, each standing, sword drawn, hands on the hilt while the point rested on the floor between his feet. They stood by his bier, sentinels in black mourning cloaks, protecting him even in death. When the bells rang midnight, as the monks chanted, Harold left Edyth alone in bed and made his way to confession before taking his place by the King, where he would keep vigil till dawn.

As he made his way from the church to the great hall, snowflakes fell silently from the black night sky, almost as if the stars were falling in on the world. One or two at first, then more, bigger, heavier, faster they fell but still silently. In Harold's eyes they looked like ghosts of autumn leaves. High on the ground they piled, one on top of the other, growing deeper with every passing minute, sucking up the sounds around them. Nothing rustled, nothing stirred; sound and colour vanished, leaving only pure white silence.

The next morning, on the fogbound freezing Feast of Epiphany, the foremost men of the land carried Edward's body on a bier draped in a richly embroidered pall. His face, uncovered, looked heavenward, the crown still on his head. The sceptre was by his side. With Harold, Regenbald, Gyrth and Leofwine shouldering the front poles and Morcar, Edwin, Oswulf and Waltheof shouldering the rear, the old King's body so light any one of them could have carried him alone, the noblemen took their lord effortlessly towards his final resting place.

Through the fog they made their way, clouds of breath rising from them, their feet crunching on the snow. As they entered the western door of the minster, they left behind them nothing but silence. The echoes of footsteps and cleared throats mingled as they made their way through the cold, hard air, the smell of damp fresh cut stone in their nostrils. All were aware of history in the making; this was the first time a funeral procession had entered the building. As the members of the congregation made their way to their places, Harold and the other bearers passed under the massive arches held high by tall pillars that glinted like frost in the semi darkness. In the eerie light the pallbearers made their way to the place before the main altar, where Stigand removed the crown and sceptre. With gentle grace and dignity the King's body was lowered into the sarcophagus. England had a king no more.

KING HAROLD II

That afternoon in the open air, the Witangemot gathered, feet freezing in the icy snow. A cold breeze had risen to blow away the morning fog; it gusted here and there, biting at random, chilling skin and bone. Presiding over the council was Regenbald, standing in the middle of a great circle of men; most of London had gathered around. The Chancellor reminded them of the constitution and their duty under law.

'Before any of you say anything, let me remind you that it is the duty of the Witan, in the name of the people of England, not only to advise the King in his lifetime but also to elect a successor after his demise.

'First, the king we elect should be a man of fit and sober character, someone who will be bold but fair. Second, royal blood should flow through his veins. Third, he must have had the support and enjoyed the trust of the former king.'

All those present knew what was coming next. Regenbald would announce the candidates and everyone knew who they would be; Edgar the Atheling and Harold Godwinson.

Regenbald made the announcement as expected.

'But what about Duke William of Normandy?' ventured Bishop William.

'What about him?' replied the Chancellor, puzzled by the question.

'Surely he has a claim?'

'What claim does he have?'

'He's the King's cousin.'

'He's the King's mother's cousin, which is not the same thing at all.'

'Now you're just being pedantic,' said Bishop William, feeling put out.

'I am simply observing the law. If William were the King's father's cousin then he would have a claim to the throne but as it is, he doesn't.'

'But ...'

'William. Be quiet.'

'But I…'

'Silence,' snapped Regenbald, staring him down.

Bishop William complained to his young companion, Gervicus, the late King's monk.

'Would anyone like to add anything to what has been said?

'I would.' It was Margaret, the Atheling's older sister.

'Then now is the time to speak.'

'I offer my full support to my brother Edgar. It is true that Harold, like Edgar, enjoyed the trust and support of the King. It is also true that Harold, like Edgar, is a fit and sober character but unlike Harold, Edgar is of royal blood. It seems only proper to me that Edgar should be proclaimed king. Who says Aye?'

Nobody said aye. Her enthusiasm was greeted with silence.

'What's the matter? Will no one support the rightful heir to the throne?'

Again she was greeted by silence.

'Why do you think we came all the way from Hungary, if not so that one day Edgar would be king?'

Regenbald responded, 'My dear lady…'

'Don't you my dear lady me.'

'Lady Margaret, please understand that much as we have been looking forward to the day when we would crown Edgar king, that day has arrived prematurely. Another five or ten years perhaps, and I'm sure none of us here would hesitate to support him. But in these troubled times, I'm afraid England needs a warrior king.'

'Well, it's not fair and I'm not in the least happy with it.'

It was noted by all that Edgar remained silent at the Witan. And the question, "what kind of king needs a girl to do his bidding for him?" was in the minds of many.

'Thank you for your contribution, Lady Margaret, I'm sure we all admire your loyalty. So, my Lords, we shall have a vote. All those who support Earl Harold, say aye.'

There was a resounding cry of aye from the Witan.

'So that's a unanimous vote for Earl Harold,' called out Regenbald to many shouts of aye and much waving of hands. The Chancellor noticed that although the northern earls also raised their hands, it was with no real enthusiasm.

'Very well, as today is Epiphany and coronations have to be held at the time of Christian feasts, I suggest we have the coronation today. It might appear unseemly but if we delay, I'm sure our friends in the Church will insist we wait until Easter. This will leave the kingdom without a head for three potentially very dangerous months.'

Gyrth and Leofwine exchanged relieved glances.

Regenbald eyed the Great Council; not a murmur of dissent was heard. 'Very well then, I suggest at three o'clock this afternoon we make our way to the abbey where we will witness the first of its many coronations.'

That afternoon Harold's coronation took place. All the members of the Christmas court were once more in Edward's new abbey, waiting as Archbishop Ealdred led the Earl who looked distinctly regal wearing the crown. At the head of the procession, the choir led in full song. When they reached the high altar, Harold removed the crown and with the bishops, prostrated himself. As Harold and the bishops lay in submission to their God, Ealdred asked in a loud, clear voice, 'Do you, the people and clergy of England, accept Harold as your king?'

'Vivat,' came the response.

'Then sing with me Te Deum Laudamus.'

When the congregation had finished singing the hymn, the Archbishop instructed the bishops to rise to their feet. Harold was instructed to kneel before the altar.

Looking on from behind with the rest of the congregation was Lady Edyth. There was a time when she would never have believed that one day she would look on the sight of her husband being crowned. She found it hard to stifle her excitement and the pride she felt knowing Harold would soon be king. Tears of joy flowed down her face. Even though she felt a little guilty with King Edward dead for so short a time, she was unable to repress a smile as the thought passed through her mind that it might well be her son Godwin who succeeded to the throne. And the thought that she herself might soon enjoy a queen's coronation did not pass her by.

At the front of the congregation Harold's sons, filled with pride for their father, entertained ideas for the future. Godwin in particular had his eyes fixed firmly on the crown, knowing one day it would be his.

There were others in the congregation who could not believe what was happening. Queen Edith had always hoped to see one of her brothers crowned; just not this particular one. The irony that Harold was benefiting from her scheming to clear the obstacles from Tostig's way was not wasted on her. Lady Godiva too, watched with interest the performance before her. Godwin's daughter had become Queen and now his son was about to become king. She thought the Godwinsons were getting a bigger share of honour and power than they deserved and resolved to redress the balance at the earliest opportunity. Her grandsons, Edwin and Morcar, were surely just as throneworthy as Harold, and Aldytha would make a wonderful queen.

Lady Godiva looked over to her granddaughter as if to confirm her thoughts.

Harold was being asked by the bishops to take the triple oath of peace, justice and mercy. Archbishop Ealdred instructed Harold before the entire congregation and admonished him for his own sake and for the sake of all the people of England. In turn, Harold promised the Church and all the good Christian people within his dominion that he would keep true peace; that he would forbid rapine and wrongful acts to all men, no matter how humble and that he would ordain that justice and mercy should be observed in all legal judgements, so that God would have mercy on him and on them all.

The preliminaries now over, they moved on to the heart of the ceremony, the unction. After prayers focusing on the theme of the Christian life and its reward in heaven, Ealdred went on to direct Harold in the duties of Christian kingship, with its duty to defend the Church and its people. Harold was anointed King while the anthem "They Anointed Solomon" was sung. The chrism, the holiest oil known to the Church, was used for the anointing.

Stigand looked on, quietly seething while Archbishop Ealdred performed Harold's benediction, something he saw as his duty. Ealdred placed the crown on Harold's head to deafening cheers from the congregation. With hearty enthusiasm the choir sang the anthem, 'Vivat rex! Vivat rex! Vivat rex in eternum!' Harold rose to his feet, now transformed from an earl to a king. Walking regally out of the abbey, he led a procession back to the great hall for the coronation feast, at which he sat on the dais with Edyth by his side, displaying the regalia, flanked by

Ealdred and Stigand. Homage was paid by the good and great of the land, who acknowledged him as king by presenting him with gifts and offering their fealty and service. Harold, like all the English kings before him, offered gifts in return. Everyone was assured that a kingdom so quickly united was one that could withstand the trials and tribulations of many storms. The omens were good.

NORMANDY

In Duke William's park at Quevilly, near Rouen, the Duke's small hunting party stood silent and perfectly still. Duke William had a young doe in the sights of his crossbow and was about to shoot, when the animal startled and darted for cover. The source of its fear was soon apparent; a rider was bearing down on them at full gallop. The messenger was the young Norman monk Gervicus, sent by William, Bishop of London. He had travelled with the utmost urgency since leaving London, never stopping unless absolutely necessary.

'A message for you, my Lord,' he said, in his innocence handing the sealed parchment directly to the Duke.

Saying nothing, Duke William, without taking his eyes off the monk, handed the parchment to the man on his right. As if he had been handed a hot coal, he in turn passed it on to the next man, who likewise passed it on. Eventually it came back to the monk.

'You read it!' the Duke snapped in the midst of a sea of embarrassment.

Dutifully, the monk followed his instructions. Breaking the seal he unrolled the scroll and proceeded to read.

'The message is to William, Duke of Normandy, from William, Bishop of London,' said Gervicus, with all the seriousness, pomp and gravity that he could muster. This was his first meeting with the Duke and he was determined to make a good impression.

'His eminence The Bishop of London sends you his condolences on the death of your much loved cousin, King Edward of England, who passed away quietly in his bed at Westminster, on the eve of Epiphany. Mercifully, Our Lord granted the King a peaceful death. His body now lies in Westminster Abbey. God rest his soul.'

'God rest his soul,' responded the Duke. What else does it say?'

'May I offer my sympathy too, sire.'

'Yes, yes. Now what else does it say?'

'It must be a great loss to you, sire.'

'Yes! It is. Now get on with it!'

The monk continued, 'During a meeting of the Great Council at Westminster, Earl Harold of Wessex was proclaimed king... '

'What! Harold, king?' bellowed the Duke, startling the horses.

'That's what's written, sire. It's all here, look,' said the monk, indicating the sentence.

'Ahhh!' screamed William and with that grabbed the message from the monk's hand and then punched him so hard in the face he broke the poor man's jaw. Gervicus groaned as he struggled to stay conscious, flopping about on his mount like a rag doll. It would be months before he ate anything but soup.

Outraged, the Duke abandoned the hunt and leaving the monk groaning astride his horse, the party made its way back home. Once there he stormed off into the hall before slumping on a bench with his head against a pillar and his cloak across his face to hide the tears. A quarter of an hour later the rest of the hunting party caught up with him. One of them, William FitzOsbern, approached him in order to offer consolation. William heard his voice and looked up, his staring red-rimmed eyes cutting through anyone in sight.

'There's no use in hiding away, my Lord,' said FitzOsbern, 'There's no time for grieving. We have to do something.'

'I know. I can't accept this news and do nothing, not without losing face. My power rests on my reputation for strength, for action; I can't afford to be made a laughing stock. Everyone in Europe knows Harold swore an oath to support my claim. All eyes are upon me. I must act or be taken for an idiot. What choice do I have?'

'None, my Lord. You must make it clear to all that you are not to be trifled with.'

'That's exactly what he's done. He's trifled with me; humiliated me. After all I've done for him. He had it planned from the start. He shall be punished!'

'Exactly, my lord.'

'Send for my brothers.'

'Yes, my Lord.'

An hour later, Bishop Odo and Count Robert were consulting with Duke William and FitzOsbern. This was one of the most difficult times they had ever spent in his company. His mind still clouded by rage, his ranting continued. His brothers knew better than anyone that Normandy lacked the strength to exact revenge on the English king, no matter how serious his crime. All they could do was humour their brother until he calmed down, saw sense and laid the insult to rest. Until then they would do their best to placate him. Bishop Odo did most of the talking.

'Of course William, you're right. The perjurer must be punished but is that up to us?'

'What do you mean is that up to us? Who else is it up to?'

'You don't believe in divine retribution?'

'I believe in avenging insults, that's what I believe in. Don't you? By God's face, I'll get him for this. You'll see. Well, are you for me or against me?'

It was Robert who spoke now. 'Brother, it's always been a privilege to fight by your side. You are the finest general and the greatest warrior. But Normandy is only so big and we have no navy and the English… '

'We'll build a navy; it can't be difficult.'

Odo spoke now with what he thought was authority. 'You'll need an army and a navy but more than that, William, you'll need a miracle.'

'So you're not with me?'

'You know we're on your side, William, as ever.'

'Thank you, Odo. I knew I could depend on you.'

'And me too, William,' answered Robert, with conviction.

'So you're both with me, then?'

'Of course.'

'Good. I'll call a meeting and we'll see who's loyal and who's not. We'll see who'll avenge his lord.'

That night, after a worrying day, Duchess Matilda and William were at last alone. Now she would have the opportunity to help her husband in some way. She had seen him angry before but never so vexed at this.

'I know this is a monstrous insult to you, my love, but is there really anything you can do about it?'

'Why does everyone believe there's nothing to be done?'

'Because England is much more powerful than Normandy, that's why,' she responded gently. 'Don't you think to make an enemy of such a mighty country would be to invite great danger, greater than we could survive?'

'But we must depose Harold. The throne is mine by right. Everyone knows it. I must reclaim it. I must act.'

'William, do you really want to continue with this or do you think this is something you have to be seen to do?'

'I have to do this,' he snapped.

'Why would you risk everything just to gain a little more? Is it anger that drives you, or hatred, jealousy, vanity or what? Do you even know what it is? Tell me William, tell me; perhaps then I can help.'

He took a big sigh and recomposed himself; he looked down at his diminutive wife. 'A lot of things are driving me, my dear, and one of them is certainly anger.'

'I understand how you feel, my love.'

'Do you? Do you really? Have you ever suffered real humiliation? Have you? Do you know what it's like to be a bastard son? Everyone sniggering behind my back. William the Bastard they call me. Well, I'll give them a reason to call me something else when I'm finished. I'll show them I'm not just some lucky swine who owes everything to his father. Well, I'll be better than him. Who was he, anyway? A womaniser and drunkard, that's what he was, but there's no shame in that. I can't be held responsible for what my father did. I'll make something of myself and with my own two hands. I'll be better than my father, better by far, better than anyone.'

'You're really determined in this?'

'I am.'

'In that case, I'll help you all I can. What can I do?'

'If it comes to war and I have to go to England to fight Harold, then you must keep the children safe. If something were to happen, Robert would succeed me. I'll leave some good men behind to protect you.'

'But I must do more, something special, befitting the Duke of Normandy.'

'Befitting a king.'

'Yes,' she laughed, 'befitting a king.' Her laughter broke the tension in the cold atmosphere of the room.

'I have been told that besides an army and a navy, I'll need a miracle.'

'Perhaps you ought to talk to the Pope. See if he can provide you with one.'

William looked at his wife incredulously. 'You know as well as anyone the Pope takes a dim view of Christians waging war on each other.'

'Then again, if the Pope thought it was Harold's fault?'

'What do you think he could do?'

'I'm not sure,' she answered. Their eyes met, he read her thoughts.

'I'll have a word with Lanfranc,' he said.

'Good. Do you feel better now?' Matilda asked.

'Yes. You're very good for me Matilda. You calm me when I'm feeling vexed.'

'And you feel calm now?'

'Yes.'

'Then it must be time for bed.'

William smiled as he looked at her. 'I was thinking the same thing too.'

ST. STEPHEN'S ABBEY, CAEN

In the privacy of the candlelit gloom of the Abbot's chambers, Lanfranc and Duke William were deep in discussion. The two men sat talking, taking the occasional sip of wine. William had called on the Abbot seeking help and inspiration. Before his eyes he saw the studious, olive-skinned Italian scrutinising the message delivered by Gervicus from London. The dark brown eyes set in his square face gave away not a single thought. William took the opportunity to study him more closely. The face, though middle-aged, had barely any lines. It was an intelligent looking face, studious and serious but when he smiled, which was rarely, the gap in between his front teeth gave Lanfranc an eerie, comic look. It was rather like seeing a snake smile. William could see the reflection of the flickering flames dancing like serpents in the Abbot's eyes. But William had respect for Lanfranc; after all, was it not he who had persuaded the Pope to bless his marriage with Matilda?

'Well, what do you think?' he asked Lanfranc tersely.

'The rumours are true, then. I think that Edward had a difficult life when he was young but later… '

'Not him! Not him! Harold. What do you think of Harold? He's stolen my crown! What are we to do?'

'Things have not turned out as we would have liked, it's true. Have you had any contact with him since his visit?'

'No, none.'

'And you still thought he would support your claim?'

'Well, I thought… ' William stopped short 'How are we going to get him to give up the Crown without the use of force?'

'I'm sure there's a way. But if we are successful, what then?'

'What do you mean what then?'

'Harold may have no right to be king but that's no reason to say that you have any right to depose him.' Lanfranc held up his hand to check William before he could disagree.

He continued, 'Although, my Lord, I am convinced of your claim, your relationship to Edward is a little, er, shall we say remote.'

'Remote?'

'It's true, is it not, that your aunt Emma, or more precisely your great-aunt Emma, was Edward's mother by her first husband, Ethelred?'

'What of it?'

'Well, your claim, based on consanguinity, has a major flaw. Queen Emma was never in the line of succession to the English throne. She was queen by marriage alone. Those of her relatives who are not descended from either of her husbands have a very tenuous claim. Some might say no claim at all.'

'I didn't come here to listen to this!' snapped William, infuriated.

'The heart of the matter is, my Lord, that it is not I who oppose you but the law. Now why fight the law, when you can make it your ally?' Lanfranc pressed on. 'Your claim is tenuous but it is still a claim, so we must find reasons to add weight to it.'

'Would the Pope believe that a man who swore falsely before God, a shamelessly self-seeking man, a man without honour, was the man God willed to be king? Is he suitable to rule over Church matters in England?' William asked.

Lanfranc, still nodding, was now smiling. 'I'm sure the Pope will do only what is best for the Church and its congregation.'

'Yes. Harold is a man of flagrantly corrupt morals, a fornicator who has brought up children outside a church-sanctioned marriage; he lives openly with some slut of a concubine. And then Stigand, his Archbishop, he's been excommunicated I don't know how many times and he is a bigamist to boot. Is this man an example of the sort of appointments Harold intends to make?'

Lanfranc sat back in his chair, now smiling his broad serpent smile. 'I think we're agreed, Duke William, that Harold is subversive to the Church's goals and that if left to his own devices he would allow and even cause great harm to befall the Church in England. It has become clear that my unavoidable duty is to inform Pope Alexander of the danger. Fortunately he's an old student of mine, from my days at Le Bec, so I'm sure he will listen to our case. I'm certain if the Pope deems them proper, he'll take the appropriate measures.'

'Mm. I'm sure there'll be a price to pay for it. There's a price for everything. Find out what it is and tell him I'll pay it.'

'I think I can tell you the price now.'

'Really. What is it?'

'As you know, Rome in recent years has undergone a great transition.'

'You mean there are now a lot fewer scandals.'

'Duke William, really.'

'All right, it has enjoyed a reformation.'

'Exactly, and its most ardent reformer is Cardinal Hildebrand.'

'Yes. I hear he's more politician than cardinal.'

'Probably the most skilful in the Vatican. Through Hildebrand's efforts, the election of the Pope has been transferred to the Cardinals and is no longer the business of the Holy Roman Emperor or anyone else. Only Rome can elect the Pope.'

'What has this got to do with my claim to the throne of England?'

'Everything. Only half of Cardinal Hildebrand's ambition has been fulfilled. You see, what Hildebrand believes is that kings should be appointed by the Pope.'

'That's an insane idea! Think of how much power that would give Rome… ' William stopped the instant the words came out of his mouth as he realised the magnitude of what he had just said. His penetrating gaze fixed on Lanfranc. 'Do you think he can do it?'

'If anyone, he can. We can ask for papal blessing for an invasion if you have something to offer in return. If we ask the Pope to adjudicate the dispute between you and King Harold… '

'Earl Harold, you mean.'

'Between Earl Harold and yourself, yes, it will set a precedent of great importance. Cardinal Hildebrand can tell the whole of Christendom that the Pope himself has appointed the King of England. And if the Pope can appoint the King of England he can appoint the king of any land.'

'Yes, but will he come down on our side?'

'Cardinal Hildebrand is someone I know very well; we were once close colleagues, and battled together against the heretics who denied transubstantiation.'

William was unimpressed by this kind of battle.

'So, Abbot, suppose we get the Pope's approval, where does this leave us? Do you think Harold will move aside and give way to my claim?'

'He may or he may not but if he doesn't, you will have the right to launch a crusade. Think how that would encourage the fighting men of Europe to flock to your side. Our aim should be something more than a squabble between earthly rulers. We must elevate your claim to that of a noble cause, a high ideal for which no sacrifice is too great. Naturally the rewards will be commensurate.'

Lanfranc added hastily, 'Our quest should be the restoration of Christian values to a corrupt and barbaric state: a holy war to bring back an errant Church into the fold of Rome.'

'You think that would work?'

'Of course, the English Church is corrupt. Most of its scholarship and pastoral work are in English. Why would they do that unless they were trying to hide something? As you so rightly said, the Archbishop of Canterbury is a bigamist and isn't even recognised in Rome!

'Think of this, Duke William, we have an opportunity to solve the problem of raising a large army. As a duke you can promise land and booty but the Church can promise something more, something everlasting; the Church can promise nothing less than salvation. Think how many will flock to your banner to join you on your crusade. If the Pope finds in your favour and offers his support, any soldier fighting your cause would be offered absolution.'

'And I offer them something a little more tangible?'

'There is one thing I would ask,' said Lanfranc.

'And that is?'

'You must assure the Pope that you have tried your utmost to solve this dispute without resort to arms. Perhaps if you sent an emissary to England with a view to persuading Harold to change his mind... '

'I've no reason to think Harold will give up the Crown.'

'Well, if he did, so much the better but as he won't, then at least you've done all you can in the eyes of the Pope.'

'I'll send an emissary to England immediately. I know the very man for the task.'

'Good. By the way, my Lord, if you are successful in your bid to depose Harold what do you intend to do about the errant Archbishop Stigand?'

'Replace him, of course.'

'Do you have a replacement in mind?'

'I thought you'd never ask,' replied William with a sly grin.

After his discussion with Lanfranc, Duke William sent Sir William Malet as his envoy to England. King Harold received his old friend with honour at Westminster. At the high table, after exchanging pleasantries, they talked.

'So tell me, old friend, what is the reason for your visit?'

'I have a message from Duke William, my Lord,' said Sir William, suddenly adopting a formal air.

'What's the message?'

'The Duke,' he answered, casting a fleeting glance at Edyth, 'wonders when you will set a date for your marriage with his daughter, Agatha, as promised by you, my Lord, to the Duke and Duchess.'

'I promised no such thing.'

'The Duke believes you did, as part of the arrangements.'

'Arrangements?'

'Yes. To seal the alliance between England and Normandy, you were to marry one of his daughters.'

The expression on King Harold's face froze; he knew too well where this conversation was heading. Sir William, ill at ease, continued.

'This is the Duke's final expression of friendship, my Lord. If you would still marry his daughter you would be free to rule England in his name. You would be as good as a king. The Duke himself would remain in Normandy, content in the knowledge his daughter would one day produce a son who would become England's ruler. In return you need simply forget your claim to the throne.

'The Duke understands why you wanted to make poor King Edward's last days on earth as comfortable and as free from suffering as possible. It was an act of kindness to him to agree to succeed but now that he has passed on, it's time to honour the oath you made on the holy relics when you swore before God.'

'That oath was forced from me, as well you know, Will.'

Sir William averted his gaze, before continuing, 'My lord has asked me to convey a reminder that the sacred promises you made in Normandy are totally binding, utterly irrevocable. If they are violated, the consequences will be grave.'

'Grave! Grave for whom?'

'The Duke is resolute, my Lord.'

'So am I.'

Sir William did not reply. He had delivered the Duke's message. All had been said that needed to be said. He remained sombre and silent.

'Will, you've done the Duke's business. Could he ask any more of you?'

'I'm not sure I understand your meaning, my Lord.'

'Why return to Normandy and an uncertain future? Why not send for your family and settle here in England? You already possess some fine land and I am more than happy to add more.'

'I can't do that, my Lord, though I thank you for the offer. I'm the Duke's vassal and fealty is a stronger bond than friendship.'

'Will, you know I've always thought God meant for us to be friends. I don't know where the blame lies for all this but I do know I feel betrayed, although not by you.'

Again Sir William remained silent.

Harold continued, 'I would have given everything to avoid this. Tell the Duke what I've said and if he would still have me make atonement for the oath, I'll pay him no less than Count Guy asked for my ransom in Ponthieu and even double it. If he would have my help in peace or war I would give it gladly. But I'll not, at any price, deliver up my country and its people as a result of an oath obtained by trickery and deceit.'

'I'll give him your reply, my Lord.'

'I'll have it put in writing but tell him this, too. I make my offer not because I'm afraid of Normandy or I think I'm in the wrong; it's simply that I refuse to let other men die over a quarrel between us. How do you think he'll react?'

'My Lord, last time I saw the Duke he was angrier than I have ever seen him. I beg you to reconsider; after all, your brother Wulfnoth is still his hostage.'

'Are you speaking for yourself or the Duke?'

'I speak entirely for the Duke, my Lord.'

'What will he do to my brother?'

'I can't say.'

'Will you take a message to Wulfnoth?'

'It's more than my life's worth to take a letter but I could take him word.'

So Harold gave Sir William a message, telling Wulfnoth that the family missed him and loved him and that he would have to prepare himself for a long stay in Normandy. In the meantime he would do all in his power to have him released.

'You will make sure he hears my words, won't you, Will? And if the Duke determines it shall be war between us then request he send another messenger.'

'That I will, my Lord.'

The two friends then parted, wondering whether their next meeting would be on the battlefield.

STORM CLOUDS GATHER

Shortly after William Malet had delivered Harold's reply to the Duke, another envoy left Normandy, this time for Rome, carrying the news that all diplomatic attempts to wrest the English throne from Harold had met with failure. Overlooking the Seine, at the pretty town of Bonneville-sur-Toques, Duke William called together a council of war to sound out his vassals as to their support for an invasion of England. Among members of his council were Robert de Mortain, Robert Count d'Eu, Richard Count d'Evreux, the aged Roger de Beaumont, Walter Gifford, Hugh de Montfort, Roger de Montgomerie, William FitzOsbern and the bellicose William Warenne, looking out of place, as usual, with his long grey hair.

The mood was tense. Standing on the dais, Duke William put forward his case.

'You all know why I called you here today. The honour of Normandy has been offended and I, Duke William, have been personally insulted by the perjuring blasphemer Harold, Earl of Wessex.' He slammed his fist on the table to demonstrate his anger. Everyone waited to see what he would say next.

'As you are all aware, my dear, beloved cousin, King Edward of England, was called by Our Lord on the eve of Twelfth Night. You know also that before his body was cold, Harold Godwinson organised a meeting of the ruling clique and with indecent haste unbefitting the sad occasion, named himself successor to Edward. Do you believe a man who would do such a thing can escape retribution? Do you think he can break the covenant and escape? No! He shall not get away with it.

'You are all good Christian men here and you all know the teachings of the Bible. Does not our Lord God say to us: "As I live, surely my oath, which he despised and my covenant which he broke, I will requite upon his head. And all the pick of his troops shall fall by the sword and the survivors shall be scattered to every wind, and you shall know that I the Lord has spoken".'

William paused for effect but could detect none. All the gathering but four sat with blank faces. The assembly remained eerily quiet.

The Duke continued, 'Earl Harold is guilty of three unforgivable sins: First, he is guilty of the murder of Alfred, King Edward's brother.

'Second, Harold and his father were also guilty of wrongfully driving Robert, the Archbishop of Canterbury, as holy a man who ever lived, out of England.

'Third, Harold is a perjurer who has broken an oath that was sworn on the relics of holy saints and usurped the kingdom that rightly belongs to me.

'My friends, have we not fought at each other's sides for many long years? Have we not heard the clash of our comrades' swords as we cut a swath through enemy lines? Has not our blood flowed on the battlefield and gained honour where others saw only defeat? Have we not seen the tears of our women when they've lost a loved one? Have we not defeated many brave armies when the odds were against us and returned from the field valiant and with honour when lesser men would have run away like rabbits? All I ask now is that you, you men of Normandy, you brave and mighty warriors, sail with me to England, and take revenge on the perjuring usurper who has made Normandy the laughing stock of Europe. I know you are warriors with brave hearts who would revel in the danger and bask in the glory of raising the name of Normandy to the lofty heights where she belongs. Are you with me, men, are you with me?'

'We're with you. We're with you,' cried FitzOsbern, Gifford, de Mortain and Warenne. The rest remained quiet and stared ahead, trying not to catch the Duke's eye. The hall was so quiet the Duke could hear his heartbeat. William stared around the room. Four of his best knights were on their feet with their fists raised and clenched, though they were now being slowly lowered; looks of incredulity were on their shocked faces.

'What do you care for me? What do you care for Normandy? You are not men who fight in armour but crabs that hide in their shells beneath rocks. You will not fight for me? You will not fight for Normandy? What are you? Who are you? You are not Normans. Cowards! That is what you are, cowards! Cowards!' The Duke paused in his ranting to take a breath.

'I made you what you are and how do you repay me? With this... this... this disloyalty. You bring shame on yourselves, your families, your country and me. You disgrace us all. You… ' At a loss for words, he paused. He was so furious, so overwhelmed with rage and disappointment he could hardly speak, hardly believe that for once he had lost support. He looked around the room searching for inspiration and caught the eye of William Malet.

'You. Yes you'

'Yes, my Lord.'

'Will you come with me to England to regain our honour?'

'I will not, my Lord.'

'You will not! You will not!' William seethed, 'Why will you not?' he shouted.

'My Lord, none of us here is obliged to provide service overseas and anyway England is too big and too powerful a foe for Normandy to become entangled with.'

'You think so?'

'Yes, I do, my Lord.'

'And the rest of you?'

D'Evreux came to the aid of his friend. 'My Lord, we must be realistic.'

'Realistic!' snapped William.

'Yes, my Lord, realistic. This expedition is beyond our powers to resource. Where would we find the ships? Where would we find the crews for such a venture? And as for land forces, we would need three times the men Normandy could muster. Who here is not afraid that this expedition would reduce this prosperous Normandy of ours to penury? It would take the resources of a Roman emperor to succeed in so hazardous an undertaking. And what if we failed? What would prevent the English invading Normandy? No, my Lord, this is too reckless an undertaking.'

'Really? And you Malet, presumably you agree with him,' accused the Duke, tossing his head to indicate d'Evreux.

'I do, my Lord.'

William simply stared wide-eyed and nodded his head while Malet put his case for staying in Normandy, saying why he thought they had no chance against the English. When he had finished, William stepped down and walked towards him, fury bubbling up within him, all the time spluttering, 'You do, do you? You do, do you?'

When he got right up to Malet, shaking with rage, just inches away from his face, he bellowed at him, 'That is why you are a chevalier of no importance, nor will you ever be, and that is why I am a duke and why I will soon be a king! And that goes for the rest of you.' He stood amongst his men, red-faced and out of breath. 'Where is your courage?' he yelled. 'Where is your faith?' he shouted, turning his head this way and that. 'Where is your pride and where is your honour?'

Now, quite calmly and with utter contempt in his voice he said, 'I pity you, you spineless rabble.' He turned his attention back to William Malet and looked him straight in the eye. To the amazement of the gathering, in a mock child's voice he said, 'We don't have to go, so we're not going to and anyway they're too big and we haven't got a navy.'

Duke William gazed slowly around the room, the contempt he felt for them all radiating from him, his rage about to explode. Then addressing the entire council at the top of his voice he shouted, 'You are not men, you are petulant children!' and he stormed toward the door, all eyes following him. Opening it he turned and bellowed, 'You disgust me, you piss ants!' Then he left them and as the echo of the slamming door subsided, the incredulous nobles were left drowned in silence.

After a few moments a murmur rose in the hall gradually increasing to a loud din. Shouting broke out as the four men loyal to William berated the rest. Accusations flew, as did justifications, denials and defences. The arguments ebbed to and fro, the cases for and against. Logic gave way to passion, calm to fury and although debate was heated, no blows were exchanged. Finally common sense prevailed and the council agreed, with half a dozen dissentions, that supporting William's claim to the throne of England by invading would be foolhardy.

As one by one they drifted out of the council, the Duke's men, feeling a little flustered and dismayed, thought they could rest safe in the knowledge that William's proposal was a passing embarrassment for them but soon to be forgotten when the summer arrived. No one was going to England.

But William had to proceed. What else could he do? As the last of the winter weeks passed, whilst his chevaliers took shelter in their lonely castles, he called on them one by one. Their fortress walls were thick and hard, their towers strong and sturdy. But those mighty castles were no match for William's guile. He penetrated them with aplomb. By direct

279

and personal interviews with his vassals, one at a time, by encouragement and cajolery but mostly with promises of conquered land and absolution, somehow William was able to persuade them to promise to double their prescribed quotas of men and arms. And ever present was a little clerk, who wrote down the promised help in a ledger. All the time the number of those who volunteered grew. Who could refuse? And so by the spring William had raised within his Duchy more than 1,200 mounted soldiers who promised to fight by his side. This was a third of what he needed. His mission was doomed to failure if he could not secure considerable outside help.

ROME

Gilbert de Lisieux was the man Lanfranc had chosen for the mission to Rome. The cleric was an earnest, studious, quietly spoken and eloquent man in his late thirties. Lanfranc had told Lisieux that the Pope owed him a favour and time spent with the primate would be both comfortable and rewarding. No one ever discovered what the favour was that the Pope owed Lanfranc but it ensured his full cooperation.

Gilbert's instructions called for him to seek an audience with Cardinal Hildebrand; the Pope could wait till later. The Cardinal received Gilbert warmly and Gilbert delivered his letter from Lanfranc, which the Cardinal studied carefully. When he had finished, he let Gilbert know he had been concerned about the condition of the English Church for quite some time.

'You know, one of the things that most bothers me about it is the English churchmen's insistence on writing in their own language, rather than Latin. This indicates a deplorably bad attitude. They are sheep wandering away from the flock and need to be brought back under the protection of the shepherd, otherwise who knows how many more will stray.'

'The shepherd they have now is deplorable. He is a fraud and an open and shameless fornicator,' Gilbert added.

'Quite right; Stigand is a disgrace and an embarrassment to the Church.'

'I wasn't talking about the Archbishop, Cardinal. I meant the King, Harold himself,' said Gilbert eagerly, before continuing to heap up the charges against Harold that Duke William and Lanfranc had concocted.

Hildebrand was delighted to hear how far Harold had strayed from the path of righteousness and indicated he would be prepared to help Duke William's petition to the Pope.

Gilbert assured Hildebrand that once William had taken his rightful place as king, he would appoint worthy men as bishops and archbishops and repay his debt to Rome.

'I can assure you, Cardinal Hildebrand, the Duke's intention is to hold the resources of England, not for his own use but for the greater cause. The Duke's victory would be God's victory.'

'Are you saying that if the Holy Father were to give Duke William his blessing, if successful he would agree to hold the Crown under his eminence?'

'Duke William has authorised me to inform you that such is his love of the Church, in return for the support of the Holy Father, he would gladly become his liegeman.'

By the time the papal court was in session, Hildebrand, with Gilbert beside him, had already thoroughly briefed Pope Alexander II. Apart from many cardinals, another former student of Lanfranc's was present: Anselm, Bishop of Lucca.

It was Hildebrand who made the presentation before the court. Only Erminfred, Bishop of Sudunum, took it upon himself to defend the English King but Hildebrand was a gifted speaker and put a strong case for the Duke, chastising Erminfred for his timorousness in a righteous cause.

Looking directly at Erminfred, his only real opponent in the court, Hildebrand summed up his case. Pope Alexander looked about to pronounce judgement when Bishop Erminfred rose slowly to his feet. 'Very eloquently put, Cardinal Hildebrand. Your case sounds convincing but I hear no argument to the contrary, of anything you have said to us today. Is there no one here to plead King Harold's case?'

The court remained silent.

'Holy Father,' Erminfred addressed the Pope. 'I ask you, how wise is it to give judgement against a man before you have heard him speak?'

Now Hildebrand stood up impatiently. 'Have I not told you he admitted swearing an oath!'

'Were you witness to this oath swearing?' Erminfred asked in an instant.

'Father Gilbert, do you have the letter?' enquired Hildebrand, trying hard to conceal his anger.

Gilbert handed over the letter Harold had written to the Duke and Hildebrand read it out. 'It says here quite plainly, "I do not deny I took the oath." So there you have it.'

'Surely that's not all the letter says?' Erminfred replied. 'Perhaps Cardinal Hildebrand would read the entire contents of the letter aloud so we may have the benefit of all that King Harold has to say.'

Hildebrand reluctantly read out all that Harold had written and when he had finished, Erminfred said, 'It sounds to me very much as though the oath was forced and therefore it should not be upheld.'

Hildebrand was growing impatient and annoyed with Erminfred. 'I can assure the Holy Fathers that's not the case. Father Gilbert, will you enlighten the court?'

Gilbert rose to his feet and gave his testimony, 'Holy Fathers, the oath was not forced. It was when Duke William conferred a title upon Earl Harold that he swore to be his liegeman and support his claim to the English throne.'

With those words Harold's fate was sealed; judgement was given against him. The Pope pronounced the Duke's campaign against Harold a holy crusade, the cause of righteousness against evil. Gilbert returned to Normandy, bearing not only the good news but also a sealed parchment on which was granted approval for the Duke's expedition, a consecrated papal banner and a ring with a hair from the head of St. Peter himself, contained in a special compartment. When Gilbert presented him with the ring, William put it straight on his finger. He said nothing but he smiled, as did Gilbert some time later, when he heard he was to receive a bishopric.

The Pope's support for his expedition drove William into a frenzy of activity. All across Europe his emissaries announced the forthcoming crusade against the English and their perfidious king. William having appeared to have won the moral high ground, support was begged, demanded and cajoled from all the Christian nations of Western Europe; of all the leaders of Europe only Eustace of Boulogne offered to come in person.

The first to wish Duke William luck with his campaign was Count Conan of Brittany, who informed him that if he should journey to England he, Conan, would take the opportunity to seize what was rightfully his – Normandy. Conan went to great lengths to point out to Duke William that he was, as everyone in Europe knew, a bastard. Conan, on the other hand was the legitimate great-grandson of Richard I, Duke of Normandy.

Conan's idea was a good one. There was every chance William would be killed in England but even if he survived, his forces would be too weak to repel an invader. A few months after Count Conan had made his promise to take Normandy, while he was besieging Angers, he sat on his mount giving orders to his chevaliers. They were shocked when he was suddenly stricken, as if by the hand of God, and fell dead from the saddle. It was belladonna that killed him, smeared on the reins of his horse. His observant assassin knew his habits well. The Count always held one of his gloves in his teeth whilst putting on the other. He always took off his gloves before he dismounted from his horse and so lay dead, a victim of habit. Brittany now had a new count, Alan the Red, friend and ally of Duke William. Such is fate.

IN ENGLAND

Just as William had been busy building support for himself in Europe, at home Harold was showing himself to be a fair and conciliatory king. All the leading Normans who chose to stay were still at court performing the same functions as they had under Edward, even though they were suspected by some of being Duke William's spies. In Wessex and East Anglia, where he was known, Harold's position was easily established. Mercia, home of the late Aelfgar, was proving problematic and in the North, where he was known mainly for being Tostig's brother, he faced great difficulties.

One evening, as Harold lay entwined in Edyth's arms, doubts and fears raked his mind.

'You're restless, my love. What's troubling you?'

'The North. I think Morcar and Edwin are up to something. Word reached me today that the people of Northumbria say they can't accept me as king unless formally requested.'

'Is that reason to believe they're plotting something?'

'Well, they are as thick as thieves with the Bamburghs. I must go there, Edyth. I have to see the lie of the land.'

'No King of England's been to the North for years.'

'I know. That should work in my favour.'

'When will you leave?'

'Tomorrow.'

'That soon?'

'The sooner I go, the sooner I can straighten this out and the sooner I'll be back to you. I won't be home until Easter, my love, and then I'll make you my queen.'

'Oh Harold, really?'

'Really.'

'That's more than I ever dreamed of.'

'Come here. I'll give you something to dream of.'

Early the next day Harold started his journey north. As King, it was expected of him to make the journey with at least a hundred housecarls but Harold wanted to travel fast and to demonstrate he trusted the Northumbrians. He let Gauti pick ten housecarls to accompany them to York. The saintly Bishop Wulfstan would travel with him to help him win over the North. As they made their way through the wintry countryside, conversation drifted to the subject of Tostig.

'Where did Tostig go wrong, Wulfstan?'

'I believe events conspired to bring about his downfall.'

'What do you mean?'

'He had courage and strength. No one would deny that. And as everyone knows, he practised his religion strictly and he was always a sober man. He never failed to observe the sanctity of his marriage vows but in Northumbria those virtues aren't looked upon with the same favour as in the South. Too many people saw your brother as simply rigid and stern. He could never really adapt himself to living up there, which is one of the reasons he spent so much time at court.'

'So, I'm to be flexible and prudent.'

'After you've visited Northumbria, what do you intend to do?'

'Marry Edyth in true Christian fashion and have her crowned queen.'

'That wasn't what I meant but it makes an old man happy to hear such news.'

'I'm going to ask Ealdred to officiate at the wedding.'

'He'll be delighted.'

Harold arrived at York, one of the biggest, busiest and wealthiest cities in northern Europe, on a chilly winter morning. As his party approached in the crisp frosty light, they could make out the old Roman city walls dominating the landscape. They could see an eight-tower frontage, which followed the banks of the river where wide bellied Scandinavian knarrs tied up to unload their exotic and valuable cargos.

Men were everywhere, struggling with fully laden baskets, loading carts, unloading ships, and hauling up sails. And as Harold grew closer he could hear the noise of the city; man and beast grunting and groaning under their burdens, the shouting of instructions, the exchange of insults and banter and the eternal squabble of merchants and traders, each vying to get the best deal.

Visible all along the riverside was the merchandise for which everyone flocked to York; amber from one ship; bear, wolf and seal furs from another, whalebone in crates here, whetstones in sacks there. Skins brought in from the Baltic and soapstones from Norway. Occasionally and available to only a few, were spices, silk and ivory from the Orient, taken to Samarkand by camel and from there, through the river ways of eastern Europe and the Baltic to York's bustling quaysides.

There was an enormous stir when Harold passed through the city gates. No one could remember the last time an English king had entered York. Within minutes word had reached Earl Morcar that Harold was in the city and a guard of honour was hurriedly turned out to meet him. Earl Morcar and Earl Edwin arrived on horseback, forcing their way through the rapidly growing throng. Morcar greeted the King with a cheerful, 'Good morning, my Lord,' looking very pleased with himself.

'Good morning, Earl Morcar. Earl Edwin.'

'This is indeed an honour. We hadn't expected a visit from you so soon.'

'It's I who am honoured, Earl Morcar, to receive such a hearty welcome.'

'Follow me, my Lord. We'll show you our hall and a true Northumbrian welcome.'

Morcar cast a perplexed glance along the length of Harold's column before asking, 'Is this all you've brought with you, a dozen men?'

'Why, should I need more? I'm amongst friends, aren't I?'

The answer produced a roar of approval from the crowd.

'Indeed you are,' replied Morcar, with a forced grin.

They made their way through the crowd. Harold thought the city quite Roman in character. The principia, where Roman emperors had sat in state, was still roofed and standing. Mixed in with and around the Roman buildings were the Viking parts of the city, densely populated and thriving with the industry of craftsmen of all types. Morcar led the way through the streets, off which ran labyrinths of narrow, crowded timber walkways. Everywhere the noise of striking hammers seemed to sound. Harold had never seen such activity, not even in London or Rome. Areas were identifiable as much by smell as sight or sound. Butchers, surrounded by cuts and carcasses, called out to passing shoppers. Close to them the candle makers, who used the tallow, plied their trade. Leather workers stripped hides and covered them in dung and urine to cure them. People with a strong sense of smell would do best to avoid that part of the city in the summer. Even in the winter there were plenty of foul odours to keep a person away.

Down another street, combs were being made from walrus ivory. Knives, axes and all manner of iron tools were manufactured in smithies, while the bronze foundries produced brooches, buckles and the like. Along a narrow lane, beads were being made from glass or chunks of amber. All the industry, all the produce made Harold wonder why he had not fully realised York's importance and why Tostig had never informed him. This city was the real gateway between Scandinavia and England. Harold resolved to pay more attention to Northumbria than previous southern kings, perhaps even to hold court there.

At last they reached the great hall, where Morcar led Harold to the dais and offered him the best seat, which he graciously accepted. Glancing around the hall it took only a moment to register its grandeur. It rivalled Winchester's great hall in size and if anything was a little taller. There was barely a piece of wood in the place that was not beautifully carved or decorated in some fashion. Columns were decorated with lizards and birds climbing through vine leaves pursued by all manner of creatures, some real, some mythical.

Morcar and Edwin sat to Harold's right, leaving a seat either side of him; one was for Wulfstan, the other had been left for Aldytha, who made an entrance as the last of the guests took his seat. All heads turned as she entered, dressed in scarlet.

'Welcome, my King,' she called as she bowed low. As she raised her head her eyes met his and seemed to fix on them for a few moments longer than was necessary. Breaking off from her gaze, she regally surveyed the great hall. Every man there thought she was looking at him personally. Every man there felt they shared some secret bond. When she had everyone's rapt attention she turned to Harold, whose eyes had been fixed on her since she had entered the hall.

'It is a surprise and a great honour to welcome our beloved King to our humble hall,' she said warmly. She continued, and although what exactly she said Harold could never recall, he would never forget the way she looked.

When she had finished her speech, Aldytha went over and sat beside him. Morcar and Edwin exchanged conspiratorial winks. Behind the scenes, servants worked at breakneck speed to produce a feast for the King. Luckily for them, the customary exchange of gifts, over which Lady Aldytha would preside, was yet to take place, giving them some extra time to prepare. Earl Morcar spoke to his King in hushed tones.

'It's such a great privilege to have the King of England honour our hall with his presence.'

'Earl Morcar, the honour is mine.'

'Tell me, my Lord; King Edward never ventured further north than Gloucester in his entire reign. Why do you take it upon yourself to visit us here in York, so soon into yours?'

'Because you said the people of Northumbria would not accept me as their king unless they elected me themselves. So here I am, up for election. Surely you expected me to visit?'

'Of course. Just not so soon, my Lord.'

'I must apologise if I caught you by surprise.'

'No apology is necessary, my Lord.

'How long will it take to organize a full meeting of your court? I thought we should hold a Witan.'

'It shouldn't take more than a week, my Lord.'

'Perhaps you can arrange it.'

'It's no trouble at all,' said Edwin, confidently.

While Edwin replied to his question, Harold noticed Bishop Wulfstan deep in conversation with Archbishop Ealdred. The two clerics seemed very happy in each other's company.

'Before the Witan meets, my Lord, perhaps we could show you a little more of Northumbria,' Edwin suggested. 'I'll be too busy myself organising things but if you have no objections, perhaps Lady Aldytha could show you round?'

Harold looked across the hall to where Aldytha was presenting the last of the gifts.

'That seems an excellent idea, Earl Edwin.'

There was a round of applause as Aldytha placed the final gift with the others. She raised her hand for silence, was handed a huge drinking horn and proposed a toast to the King. She took a sip and passed it on, everyone in the hall taking a sip in turn. Once they had drunk to Harold's health, the members of the court took their places and Aldytha joined her brothers and Harold on the dais. She took her place and Harold turned to see her eyes focused only on him. She smiled alluringly.

'Your brother, Earl Edwin, suggested you spend the next few days showing me round this part of Northumbria.'

'Whatever you'd like to do, it would be a pleasure, my Lord,' she said, with a flutter of her eyelids.

Harold noticed her broad smile, the generous mouth and the sparkle in her eyes. To say he found her interesting would be an understatement. For the rest of the evening, Aldytha gave Harold her undivided attention. She asked him about his journey and proceeded to praise his kingly qualities. They had to talk in whispers and sit quite close together so as not to spoil everyone's entertainment.

'Everyone's so impressed that you've taken the trouble to journey here, especially in winter. No English king has travelled this far north since Athelstan and that was years ago.'

'So everyone keeps telling me.'

'Was it your idea, my Lord?'

'It was, as a matter of fact.'

'Well, I must say it was quite brilliant,' she said, leaning towards him in order to whisper. 'I think my brothers are quite put out.'

Harold could feel her warm breath on his neck as she spoke.

'Really?' he replied.

'Yes. They thought you would stay put in London, perhaps venturing out to Gloucester and Winchester like all the others before you. I think they had designs of their own.'

Now it was Harold who was whispering in her ear. 'What designs would they be?'

'I don't know. They never tell me anything.'

As the evening passed, they got to know each other better and a mutual fascination grew between them. All too soon, the evening was over and the ladies made their way to the bowers. Once they had gone, Harold found he missed Aldytha's company and tried to fill his mind with the politics in hand. As what was left of the evening wore on, Edwin and Morcar grew friendlier and they seemed pleased to see Harold had enjoyed the company of their sister.

The next day, Harold discovered he would be spending the morning out hunting. Naturally, as hostess, Lady Aldytha would accompany him.

On this morning, as on all subsequent mornings, the two of them would enjoy the time they spent together. By the end of the week Harold would be revelling in her company. Each day they would make an excursion to one or another part of Yorkshire. She paid close attention to whatever he said, always asking thoughtful questions and making intelligent observations, neatly sprinkled with witty remarks. It seemed to him that she positively sparkled.

Each evening he would wait with eager anticipation until she came down to join him in the hall. After the customary toasts and formalities of the early evening, they were free to talk. Edwin and Morcar had a fine group of minstrels providing music and entertainment, which Harold and Aldytha used to full advantage, dancing with each other whenever the opportunity arose. Many of the northern nobles found this reassuring. Others thought their behaviour was verging on the scandalous but while Aldytha's brothers seemed happy for their sister to monopolise the King, nothing would be done to change things. Meanwhile, in the background, Bishop Wulfstan and Archbishop Ealdred worked on securing the support of the North. Wulfstan worked constantly on Edwin, Morcar and all the northern nobility present at the Northumbrian court. He was successful with the clergy and the common people alike.

Two days before the Witan was due to meet, Harold was out on the moors hunting with Aldytha and his housecarls. The sky had looked quite threatening when they were in York but Aldytha had assured them the weather would be fine and dismissed their concerns that they might get caught in a storm. Now the weather was closing in rapidly, growing cold and raw.

'We're never going to get back to York in time to miss this, Harold,' said Aldytha, riding by his side, looking around, concerned about the darkening sky.

'What do you suggest?'

'Well, we can't stay out here for long. It will most likely turn nasty very soon but we should be able to reach Guthrum's hall in time.'

'Who's Guthrum?'

'He's a wealthy thane and a friendly fellow. I'm sure you'll like him.'

Casting a glance to the horizon, Harold saw black wedges of rain pouring down from the dark heavens, which were looking increasingly threatening.

'Well, what are we waiting for?'

Aldytha put her horse into a canter and the rest of the party followed. By the time they had reached Guthrum's hall, freezing rain was thrashing down on them. With backs hunched against the wind, they dismounted and some of Guthrum's men led their horses to the stables. Guthrum himself was surprised when he recognised Lady Aldytha and was rendered speechless when introduced to a drenched King Harold, dripping water, like the rest, all over the floor.

Quickly recovering from his surprise, Guthrum ordered refreshments and led his guests to the hearth, where he introduced them to Whitgar, his youngest son, who still lived at home. Guthrum made a decent stab at small talk while they warmed themselves round the fire. As they stretched out their arms to warm their hands by the flames, Harold could not help but notice the glow of Aldytha's skin, the brightness of her smile and the way the occasional water droplet ran down her face.

Guthrum was quite a humble man, even though he was a considerable landholder and he was already looking forward, with excitement, to telling his friends and neighbours about the King's visit. The amount of prestige visited on his home was immeasurable. As he spoke, he knew he would dine off this day for years.

Once he relaxed, Guthrum was the perfect host. Soon everyone was warm and dry, the smell of roasting meat wafting through from the kitchen whetting their appetites. Noting his guest's hunger pangs, Guthrum ordered cold meats, smoked meat and pickles to be served immediately.

Although there was no wine, there was an endless supply of mead and beer. In the evening when the cooked meats arrived, the party could barely manage anything more to eat. At the end of the day, in the place of honour with Aldytha by his side, Harold was surprised when she leaned over to him and said in a whisper something that made his heart skip a beat.

'How are you enjoying our hospitality, my Lord?'

'Everything I've heard about northern hospitality is true. It couldn't be better.'

'You don't find the northern nights too cold?'

'Not at all,' he answered a little perplexed.

'I do.'

'Really?'

'Since I lost my husband, there's been no one to keep me warm through the cold winter nights. I've tried extra blankets but all to no avail. Can you suggest anything, Harold?'

'You know, I'm absolutely amazed none of the fine young men of Northumbria have found a solution to your problem, Aldytha.'

'I think it might take someone very special to make me warm.'

'You know, I think your problem that you just need the right man.'

'Well, if I'm cold I'll need someone hot to warm me, won't I? Do you think you're hot enough, Harold?'

Harold admired her boldness. 'I think you need to be the judge of that.'

'Oh, thank you, you're so kind. I didn't know how I was going to sleep tonight.'

She looked at him, her eyes all fire.

'I'm not sure what your brothers might think, Aldytha.'

'Well, if they don't know they won't think anything, will they?'

'Don't you think it'll be a bit obvious, the King prowling round the women's bowers at night?'

'No. All you have to do is wait until after I've left.'

'And then charge along the corridors after you?'

'Don't be silly. Leave a little time and then go towards your own quarters. I know Guthrum's hall very well. I've been coming here since I was a child. Along the passage there's a door that looks like a cupboard. Open it, step through and come up the stairs. When you get to the top, open the door quietly and you'll see my bedroom door opposite. Two steps and you'll be in my room and no one will be any the wiser.'

'Isn't there a guard?'

'No. The only guard will be at the bottom of the stairs to the ladies' quarters.'

That evening, not long after Aldytha had retired to bed, Harold made an excuse, eventually managing to prize himself away from Guthrum and his family before leaving the hall, finding the doorway as described by Aldytha and from there making his way to her room and a warm welcome.

She was in bed, waiting for him, the bedclothes tucked under her arms just like the time he had seen her in Gruffydd's palace. That time the thought of pulling back the bedclothes had crossed his mind but he had done the honourable thing and maintained her modesty. There was no need for that now. Completely undressing while she watched his every movement, her eyes darting up and down his body, he moved toward the bed and she pulled the bedclothes back. At a glance he could see she was everything he had hoped she would be; her body soft and warm as he embraced her.

The next day, in the cold chill of dawn, Harold slunk back the way he had gone the previous evening. Exhausted, he entered his room and climbed into bed to await the call to breakfast.

And so it was on a bright, cold, February morning, a week after he had arrived in York, Harold found himself standing on hard frozen ground, ready to address the freemen of Northumbria, who had gathered to meet at the Witan to decide whether or not they would pledge allegiance to him. Well over a thousand formed the crowd in the square and thousands more were jammed in the surrounding streets, hoping to see their king.

While Archbishop Ealdred ran through the formalities before introducing the King to his subjects, Harold took his place in the centre of the huge circle of men that formed the Witan and addressed them sincerely, almost reverentially.

'Good people of Northumbria, I thank you all for turning out on such a cold day, just to see me. They tell me no King of England has ventured so far north for many a year. I can't think why; the hospitality here is second to none.'

A cheer went up from appreciative crowd.

'I must admit, though, it's not just for the famed Northumbrian hospitality I'm here talking with you today. As you are all aware, our enemies are gathering against us. Now I know there are those who would like nothing better than to see a proud, independent Northumbria ruled by its own king, in its own way. Those of you who think that are looking back to the old days, which often seem fairer when time alters the memory. In those old days, when Northumbria was a kingdom, life was harsh. Norsemen raided the land and subjugated its people. It was only when England became united that we had the strength to fight off the foe. Now the foe threatens us once more. This time it is Duke William of Normandy who threatens us, to say nothing of my brother Tostig, who might yet return in an attempt to reclaim his old earldom.'

At this there was much muttering from the assembly.

'Never fear. I'm sure if Tostig returns, you'll have a warm welcome waiting for him, just as Wessex would have a warm welcome for Duke William, a welcome warmer than the fires of hell. But think about how much easier it would be if Northumbria and her neighbours fought off Tostig together. Or for that matter, how much easier it would be for Wessex to fight off Normandy with the help of her neighbours and fellow countrymen, for aren't we all Englishmen now?'

Now the assembly warmed to Harold and shouts of agreement went up from the crowd.

'Nobody in England wants to be ruled by a foreign king who would have no respect for our customs or laws. England needs but one king. Be warned, a house divided must fall.'

'The King is right and has my full support,' yelled Morcar, enthusiastically.

'And mine,' added Edwin, with a bellow.

'King Harold is wise, his words so true,' added Morcar before continuing, 'think of England, as it was, the separate kingdoms of Mercia, Northumbria and Wessex, powerful kingdoms but easy prey to enemies. Think of England as it is today, the powerful earldoms in the South, East Anglia and Wessex, united under one family, the illustrious House of Godwin. And here in the North we have the earldoms of Northumbria and Mercia, united under one family, the House of Leofric. Now think of the future. Think of all England and the earldoms, united under one family: think how strong we would be.'

There was a resounding cheer from the crowd.

Earl Morcar, with the Witan on his side, turned to address the King at the top of his voice. 'Then why not unite our houses and secure forever the future of our great country? King Harold, the House of Leofric proudly offers you its fairest daughter, Lady Aldytha!'

The crowd roared in jubilation; hats and anything to hand flew into the air. Harold knew instantly there was no way out of this trap. To refuse the hand of Lady Aldytha would be a gross insult to Northumbria as well as to Edwin and Morcar, to say nothing of the lady herself. He could afford no more enemies; he had enough as it was. His heart sank as he smiled at the crowd and accepted Morcar's proposal. Lady Aldytha was produced and escorted through the gathering to Harold's side. Their eyes met as she approached him and she held his gaze.

'I didn't know anything about this, Harold, I swear.'

'Really?'

Aldytha's bright blue eyes flashed. 'What do you think?' she snapped, affronted.

And yet like a perfect couple they held hands and kissed before the cheering crowd. Morcar and Edwin were obviously delighted and applauded for all to see. The picture was one of perfect happiness.

Two days later, Archbishop Ealdred presided over the wedding and crowned Aldytha Queen in York minster. Later that evening, after the wedding feast, Harold excused himself to the Aelfgarson brothers and rose to leave the hall to raucous calls from the guests. Harold was acutely conscious of the new sword that hung at his side; his brothers-in-law had had it especially made for him.

The royal couple bade goodnight and made their way to the bedroom, the cheers of the guests dying behind them. Swaying slightly, arm in arm, they reached the bedroom door. This was the first time they had been alone together since Morcar had made his proposal at the Witan. Since then, whenever the circumstances permitted, they had exchanged whispered words, accusations and denials and the occasional furtive conversation. Aldytha claimed to know nothing of Edwin and Morcar's plan. She claimed to have been duped as much as he. Harold believed her and everything between them was as it should be with newlyweds. Keener than most brides, Aldytha was already starting to undress before she reached the bedroom door.

Harold found her irresistible. Here was his legal wedded wife, his Queen, for whom he had renounced all others, yet to him she felt like the other woman, a concubine. But looking at her in the candlelight, seeing how much she wanted him, it was as though everyone and everything outside the room evaporated. The world was just the two of them.

In the morning, after once more making love, Harold presented Aldytha with a fabulous morning gift of seven bolts of the finest silk in an array of bright colours, some shot with gold thread.

'Thank you, Harold. You're so generous,' she said and planted a kiss firmly on his lips.

In raptures she ran all of the silks through her fingers, studying them carefully.

'They're beautiful,' she said, as though in awe of their colour and texture.

'So are you,' he answered.

'Do you really think so?'

'I thought that was obvious.'

'You know for me this is more than just a marriage of two families?'

'I did have that feeling, yes,' he teased.

'Don't be horrid,' she said, giving him a playful slap across his upper arm.

They kissed and putting the gift to one side, she arranged herself on top of him.

'I love you, Harold,' she said, sighing.

Harold kept his eyes closed and simply enjoyed her.

Later, as they lay side by side, Aldytha once more told Harold she loved him.

'Of course, I don't expect you to love me in return.'

'You sound quite forlorn, Aldytha. I would have thought you'd be happy.'

'Oh, I am. I'm the happiest bride there's ever been.'

Waltham and Edyth flashed though Harold's mind.

'Are you the happiest groom?'

'You know I am.'

'Then why don't you say it?'

'I'm the happiest groom there's ever been,' but Harold was not at all sure which wedding had made him so.

Aldytha thought she detected a note of sadness in his voice.

'Really?'

He was beginning to resent this pestering of hers. She was beautiful, it was true, and such good company. But he wished she would stop fishing for compliments.

'Really, Aldytha.'

She smiled and kissed him, stroking his face as she did so. As they broke off once again, she told him she loved him.

'And I you,' he replied.

Edwin and Morcar were thrilled. Harold had their sister but they had him. In the fullness of time they would have a nephew with a strong claim to the throne. By that time, Harold would be well past his prime, if not dead; they, on the other hand, would be at the height of their powers. What golden future lay ahead of them? In the meantime their sister and the King looked delighted with each other. For his part, Harold looked the happy groom. But there is always someone ready to spoil a party and with this in mind, Harold and the two northern earls discussed what strategy to employ if an invasion were to be mounted against England in the coming year. It soon became obvious that Edwin and Morcar's concerns lay in Northumbria, where Tostig might land to reclaim his earldom. If he carried out his threats, he might well do so while William was attacking the South.

'We need more men to guard the coasts,' urged Morcar.

'There are none to spare. They're needed in the South,' Harold replied.

'Against Duke William! What kind of an army can he raise? I'd be surprised if he could raise more than three thousand men and even then he's still got to cross the Channel. How's he going to do that? He's got no navy.'

'He'll find a way, I'm certain.'

'Well, I'm sure Tostig'll have no trouble finding his way here. He could raise just as many men as Duke William and he knows how to sail.'

'That's why we need to come to each other's aid if we're attacked.'

'So, how many men will you bring up here if Tostig turns up?'

'I'll have to leave a force behind to protect London; I can't leave it undefended. I could be here with six to eight thousand men in no time. How long will it take you to come south?'

'We could be in London in, say, eight to ten days from the time word arrived that we were needed.'

'We'll leave it at this then; if you are attacked in the North, I'll come to your assistance but whatever you do, don't engage Tostig in full battle. Delay him, distract or divert him but don't engage him under any circumstances.'

'You think we can't handle him?'

'You know his reputation.'

'We do and we're not scared of him.'

'It would be as well if you were.'

'Well we're not, are we Edwin?'

'We don't frighten easily in the North.' In a cursory way he added, 'My Lord.'

'Just as I thought. You'll keep cool heads then and not engage him.'

'We'll send for your help if we need it,' Morcar answered.

'Likewise, if William attacks the South, I'll send for assistance.'

'What if we're attacked at the same time?'

'Then the victor rides to the help of the other.'

'We'll remember that, my Lord.'

THE JOURNEY SOUTH

Three days after their wedding, Harold, with his new queen, made his way back to London to preside over the Easter court and to discuss preparations for the repulsion of William, should he ever attempt to invade. The news that the King had married Lady Aldytha had spread rapidly around the country. In Coventry, when she received the news, Lady Godiva gave a quiet smile of satisfaction. The future was looking rosy for the House of Leofric.

Harold sent word to Gyrth explaining the situation and requesting him to tell Edyth he had been duped. He was to tell her he still loved her and to wait patiently at Waltham for him. It was asking her to leave Westminster that filled him with dread.

Once again Bishop Wulfstan accompanied Harold but the Bishop's company irritated him now as it had stimulated before. His mind was in a whirl. On the one hand he was concerned with keeping Duke William and Tostig at bay; on the other, feelings for Aldytha seemed to have infused every part of him. He felt revitalised, yet still his thoughts wandered to Waltham and Edyth.

'You appear preoccupied these days, King Harold. I would have thought your young wife would have brought you happiness,' said Bishop Wulfstan. The question of Edyth remained unasked. 'What troubles you?'

'I've felt tremendous relief since you gave me absolution from my oath to William, as though a great burden were lifted from my shoulders.'

'Good. That's no less than you deserve. Since the sin was in the making of the promise, not the breaking of it, it was impossible to keep.'

'Though I am aware that I must still atone for taking it.'

'What else is bothering you?'

A little shamefaced, Harold answered, 'I feel I'm adding to my sins.'

Wulfstan looked a little startled. 'I think talking might be good for your soul.'

'I hope so. You see, I've told Aldytha I love her. She was upset and it seemed the best thing to do at the time.'

'Like swearing an oath to Duke William?'

Harold blushed and cast his eyes downward. 'I know. I feel as though events are conspiring against me.'

'Has it occurred to you that you might be conspiring against yourself, my Lord?'

'Yes, it has. You see, I am genuinely very fond of Aldytha ...'

'Very fond?'

'Well, more than very fond. I must confess I have a passion for her.'

'A passion?' repeated Wulfstan, as though he suspected something a little more carnal.

Harold ignored the retort and pressed on. 'It's Edyth I think of all the time. No matter how I try, I can't get her out of my mind.'

When Wulfstan failed to respond, Harold continued.

'Father,' said Harold, 'you can see how attractive Aldytha is; I can't help but desire her and after all, she is my wife, my queen. You see, the problem is, when I'm alone with her, I feel as though I'm involved in an adulterous affair. She told me she loved me and kept asking me if I loved her.'

'So you told her you loved her to make everything seem all right?'

'What else could I say?'

'You need to be honest with her, Harold. You need to tell her the truth.'

Harold looked lost for words.

'If I tell her the truth now, then the marriage could be for nothing. I need her brothers on my side. If I lose their support and lose England, everything could fall into the hands of the Normans.'

'You won't lose her, Harold and you won't lose her brothers' support.'

'How can you say that?'

'Because when you tell her, she'll simply forgive you.'

For a moment Harold stared incredulously at his old friend.

'It's true, my Lord.'

'Wulfstan, why on earth would she forgive me?'

'You don't respect my judgement?'

'I can't tell her. It wouldn't do any good. I'd just hurt her. I can't do it. She doesn't deserve it.'

'She does deserve to be deceived and she doesn't deserve the truth? Is that what you're telling me, Harold?'

'You're oversimplifying.'

'Am I? Life is as simple as you make it, my Lord.'

'That may be so in your world, Bishop, but not in mine.'

'King Harold, don't we both inhabit the same world?'

'It seems not.'

'Have faith, my Lord, have faith. God has not deserted you; He is here with us now.

Ours is to have faith and believe.'

'Sometimes I find that difficult.'

'Sometimes we all do. Just have faith. The Lord will take care of everything the way he intends and it is not for us to question the outcome.'

'If God is present in all things, can He send us messages?'

'Yes, He could if He so chose.'

'Are they easily understood?'

'What are you referring to, my Lord Harold?'

'The star.'

'Ah, you've seen it too.'

'Can it be a message?'

'Perhaps. But as for its meaning, who knows?'

'It must be a sign but what does it mean? What do I tell my people?'

'What you tell them and Queen Aldytha is up to you. You are the King and the best judge of that. My advice is simple: be honest in all things.'

Gyrth and Leofwine had organised a public reception to welcome Harold and Queen Aldytha to London and Harold's brothers led him through the crowded streets. The two positioned themselves on either side of Harold. It was Gyrth who started the conversation.

'Well?'

'I fell victim to a trick of Morcar and Edwin.'

Gyrth turned and looked Aldytha over while she responded to the cheers of the crowd. Returning his attention to Harold he said, 'Nice trick.'

'Never mind that. What did she say?'

Gyrth took a deep breath. 'She took it very badly,' he replied. 'She hadn't heard about the wedding. I tried to break it to her as gently as possible but it still came as a tremendous shock.'

'What did she say?'

'Well, she said quite a lot. None of it very flattering to you, I'm afraid.'

'Where is she now?'

'Waltham. She moved everything out of Westminster.'

'Get word to her I'll see her at Waltham as soon as I can. Why are you looking at me like that?'

'Like what?'

'There's something else, isn't there?'

'The boys didn't take it well, either. They've left home, all except Ulf. They've gone to Ireland. Edyth sent them. She was afraid they might kill you in a rage.'

Within two hours of his arrival at Westminster, Harold was addressing his war council.

'As I see it, William is going to need a long time to build up an army strong enough to invade England. He also has to find himself a considerable amount of ships and someone to sail them. To be honest, I'm not sure he can do it.'

'Leo and I came to the same conclusion,' added Gyrth, by way of support.

'I don't think we'll need to call out the fyrd until August but just to be on the safe side I thought I'd take the housecarls down to the coast just after Easter and post them in groups at all the likely landing sites.

'Eadric.'

'Yes, my Lord?'

'What do you think of moving the navy to the Isle of Wight just after Easter?'

'That would be the ideal place, my Lord. With the prevailing westerlies behind us we could be down on any fleet within a day or two at most.'

'Do you suggest we wait until William has landed or would you prefer to engage before they make land?'

'Engage them at sea, my Lord. It's unlikely they'll have any real sailors amongst 'em. If we can catch them on the open sea we could kill hundreds of them before they even get ashore and drive the rest up the Channel into the North Sea.'

'That's just what I was thinking.'

'My lord?'

'Yes, Gyrth, what is it?'

'Why wait for William to come here? Why not let him build up his fleet a little, then cross over the water and sink his ships before he can set sail? If we time it right we could delay his plans for a full year, perhaps even permanently. After all, if he builds up an army big enough to invade England, it would by its very nature be filled with foreigners. How long could Normandy feed and house them and how long would William be able to control them?'

'It's a good idea, Gyrth, and I would agree in an instant if it weren't for Tostig. If the English fleet leaves home to sink William's fleet, we might well find ourselves in serious trouble.'

'Do you think he'll come over on his own or do you think he'll join forces with William?'

'Tostig's the least of our worries. On his own he offers the least threat.'

'He could offer a serious distraction, though.'

'Yes, he could. We'll just have to respond in the way that seems most appropriate when the time comes. Is everybody clear about what we are to do?'

The commanders all responded positively, although Eadric seemed a little preoccupied.

'What is it, Eadric? Do you still have something to say?'

'Well, there is something that's been bothering me and I know it's been playing on the minds of some of my men.'

'Is this to do with the star?'

'Why, yes it is, my Lord. Some of the men reckon it's an omen. There's talk that the last time there was a star like this in the sky, it was a warnin' of a Danish invasion and that ended up with us havin' a Danish king.'

'Go on?'

'Well, it's gettin' bigger every day. Some say it's headin' straight for us, sent by God himself to strike us all down.'

'Tell your men from me, Eadric, it's an omen. They can see it in Normandy too and it's a warning to Duke William to keep away. There'll be no successful invasion of England while I'm on the throne. Do you understand?'

'I do, my Lord,' said Eadric, looking much relieved, 'an' I'll tell 'em right away.'

With that the meeting closed.

Harold made the journey to Waltham on the pretence of going to Bosham to make plans for the repulsion of the expected invasion. Just ten of his most trusted housecarls accompanied him.

Through the cold winter rain they rode, the mad March wind blowing wild around them, the rain lashing their faces and the damp chill seeping through their clothes. Miserable, they reached Waltham. Gyrth, with his and Harold's housecarls, went to the abbey where they could be sure of a bed for the night and certain not to become embroiled in an argument between Harold and Edyth. The King went straight to his home to seek the welcoming arms of Edyth. As he approached the door to the hall, Wynfrith appeared.

'Earl Harold, welcome home.' Catching Harold's eye he corrected himself, 'King Harold, welcome home. I'm sorry, my Lord, I was forgetting myself.'

'Never mind that, Wynfrith; is Lady Edyth home?'

Wynfrith looked considerably ill at ease.

'Erm, I, well ...'

'Is she or isn't she?'

'Sort of, my Lord.'

'What do mean, sort of?'

'Well, she says if it's you who comes calling, I'm not to let you in.'

Harold sighed and dismounted. 'Stable my horse, Wynfrith', he commanded, offering the reins to the servant.

'Where are you going with that horse, Wynfrith?' Edyth's voice cracked through the air like a whip. She looked stern walking straight towards the two men.

'Oh, my lady, there you are.'

'Edyth.'

'Give the Earl his horse back, Wynfrith. He's leaving.'

'I'm no longer an earl and I'm not leaving.'

'Well, you are leaving and if you're not an earl, then what are you?'

'You know very well. I'm the King of England and you will address me as such.'

'The King, are you? Then shouldn't I be the Queen or have I missed something?' she hissed.

'That's what I've come to talk to you about.'

'Oh, Harold, you're so kind. How thoughtful of you to make a special journey all this way just to tell me, behind my back, you've married another woman. Don't tell me, I'll guess, it's that slut Aldytha, Aelfgar's daughter.'

'Edyth!'

'Oh, I'm right. I wonder how I knew. Fed up of hopping into bed with Welshmen, is she? Been through them all, I expect.'

'Edyth, I didn't expect …'

'Didn't expect what? Isn't my welcome warm enough? What should I say? "Oh darling, welcome home. You've been gone a little longer than expected but never mind. I understand from your brother that you got married while you were away. The children were as delighted as I was when they found out. Are you disinheriting everyone or perhaps we can look forward to a violent early death, so our presence at court won't cause embarrassment." Oh, I forgot, we're no longer allowed at court. How silly of me to forget.'

'We'll never get anywhere like this.'

'We? We, Harold? We aren't going anywhere. You are. Now get out of my sight or I'll set the dogs on you.'

'They're my dogs. They won't hurt me.'

'You just want to humiliate me.'

'Really, I don't.'

'Well, if the dogs won't hurt you, I will,' she said, pulling her knife from its sheath on her belt and hurling it at him as hard as she could. He dodged to the side and it flew harmlessly past his head.

'Why don't we just talk, Edyth?'

'Because I hate you, that's why.'

'You can't hate me,' Harold replied.

'I can!' she screamed. 'I hate you. I hate you. Now get out of here. Get out and don't ever come back, you bastard.' She broke down and began to wail, tears streaming down her face. She turned and putting her head in her hands she broke into a run and raced back inside, crying mournfully, slamming the door behind her.

Harold called after her, 'I'll be here waiting for you. I'll wait as long as it takes.'

Wynfrith stood stock-still, unable to believe his eyes.

'What are you looking at?' Harold snapped. 'Take him to the stable,' indicating, with a nod, his horse.

Wynfrith led the horse away, leaving Harold on his own in the rain. After the clop, clop, clop of his horse's hooves striking the ground had faded, the King waited outside his home, the doors barred to him, alone except for the sound of the rain.

In the comfort of the abbey, having dried and changed out of his wet clothes, Gyrth Godwinson sat drinking wine in his room. He was reassured by Harold's absence. It could only mean he'd sweet-talked his way back into Edyth's affections.

The next day, in the bone-numbing cold of dawn, a shutter opened, just a fraction, on the side of the great hall. Harold thought he caught sight of some movement there but was not sure who it was; a servant perhaps. He curled and uncurled his toes as rapidly as he could in an attempt to warm them.

In the great hall, someone had put wood onto the fire; grey smoke rose rapidly skyward. Harold watched impassively as the house began to stir. A door opened and Wynfrith appeared. Cautiously, as though in fear of some sort of attack, he approached Harold.

'Good morning, my Lord. Lady Edyth will see you now.'

'Well, best not keep the lady waiting.' Harold walked across the courtyard and into his home to find Edyth waiting for him in the centre of a dimly lit room. Just two candles provided light. The shutters to the window remained closed against the cold morning air.

Their eyes met but no word was exchanged. Silence filled the room.

'Well, Harold, if you're not going to say anything, why did you bother to come?'

'It's hard to find the words.'

'I should think it is.'

'You're not making this easy for me.'

'You, on the other hand, are making it easy for me. Is that what you're saying?'

'No. No, not at all. I appreciate it must be difficult for you too.'

'You appreciate it might be difficult for me too? You've got no idea.'

'Think of what I've been through.'

'What have you been through? All you've done is marry some trollop.'

'She's not a trollop.'

'Oh, I see. Love her, do you?'

'No, of course not.'

'Why should I believe you?'

'Believe me, I'm telling the truth.'

'Do you say the same thing to her?'

'What?'

'Do you say the same thing to her? "Believe me, I'm telling the truth." Does she even know you're here?'

Harold looked down to the floor.

'I thought not. You'll tell her a lie and if she doesn't believe you, what are you going to say?'

'Edyth, this isn't fair.'

'Not fair! How dare you tell me what's fair. I'm your wife of more than twenty years; I've had your children and nursed you back from death's door. I've shared your trials and tribulations. I've always stood by your side; surely that's worth something? And now you reward me by casting me aside as soon as the fancy takes you?'

'I was trapped. I was forced into a marriage I didn't want. There was no escape. If I hadn't gone through with it I would have lost Northumbrian support, at the very least. Don't you see I had no choice?'

'Then why be king?'

'A king can't control everything. Just like anybody else, there are times when you have to make the best out of a bad lot.'

'So you made the best of it, did you?'

'I've always said that I would need to be free to take a wife for political reasons. You've always known that.'

'Knowing something is one thing, having it happen is another. A few months ago I had no reason to believe you would ever marry anyone else.'

'I didn't either. I just want us to be together.'

'Have you taken leave of your senses? You're married now. Aldytha is your queen. She has a hold over you, as do Morcar and Edwin. How strong a hold will they have over you if Aldytha has a child?'

Harold looked uneasy.

'Is she pregnant?'

Harold, looking even more uneasy, said nothing.

'You don't know, do you? But she might be?'

'Yes, she might be.'

'Well, it didn't take you long, did it?'

'Edyth, I had to consummate the marriage.'

'God, life must be so hard for you.'

'But it's you I want. It's always been you.'

'You've got a fine way of showing it.'

'I just want things to be as they have always been.'

'Do you really think that's possible?'

'I am the King and I have the power to do things no one else can but there are things expected of me which would not be expected of anyone else. Surely you can see that? This time next year everything will be different, you'll see. We'll be able to get on with our lives as before, I promise you.'

Edyth knew he was right; he could see it in her expression and he loved her, as he had always done. His love for her didn't intoxicate him as often as it once had but his love for her felt complete. His heart would skip a beat if he saw her by chance, or suddenly, for no apparent reason, he would miss her dreadfully.

'I don't know what to think, Harold.'

Harold's gaze drifted across the room and it was then his eye caught sight of the table and he remembered a time in the past when they first made love. Looking up, he caught Edyth's eye and realised the same thought was passing through her mind too. Stepping forward he took her firmly in his arms and kissed her on the mouth, pulling back her clothes as though peeling a rich, ripe fruit before devouring her.

It was still early morning; as in times past, the couple lay entwined on the floor.

'It all seems beyond us, Harold.'

'What do you mean?'

'Have you seen the star?'

'Yes.'

'What does it mean?'

'It's an omen. It means everything's going to be all right.'

WILLIAM PREPARES

Across the English Channel, Duke William was talking to Tostig and his sons, Skuli and Ketel. The Duke was sceptical, to say the least, as he listened while Tostig tried to persuade him an alliance between the two of them was just what he needed.

'Think how much easier it would be to take possession of England if you had my supporters behind you. All I ask is that, in return for my help, I be reinstated to my old earldom.'

William eyed Tostig coldly. 'How many ships do you have?' he asked.

'Twenty.'

'Twenty. That's not very many. By the end of the summer I shall have a thousand.'

'A thousand!'

'You sound surprised.'

'I am a little, my Lord.'

'You doubt my word?'

'Not at all, my Lord. It's just that that would be three times bigger than the entire Norwegian navy.'

'Do you see something wrong with that?'

'Not at all, Duke William. It just seems like a lot of ships.'

'We need them for the horses.'

'The horses?'

'We're taking our cavalry when we go to England, naturally.'

'Naturally,' replied Tostig, trying hard to visualise the scene.

'We Normans find cavalry indispensable to warfare. Naturally we will require transport to get them across the sea. That's why we need so many ships.'

'Can't you just capture English horses when you get there? That's what the Norsemen used to do.'

'These are specially bred and trained horses. English horses wouldn't be up to it.'

'I see.'

'We're building the ships ourselves. Can you imagine the amount of wood needed for such an enterprise?'

'I think I can.'

'I've had to cut down almost every tree in Normandy.'

'I can imagine it. When you have your thousand ships, my Lord, will you have the men with the experience to sail them?'

'We only need one.'

'I'm sorry, my Lord, I don't quite follow your reasoning,' said Tostig, concealing his astonishment.

'Any fool can sail a ship; you should know that. All you need is one man who knows the way and the rest will follow.'

Tostig could hardly believe his ears and even without looking at them, he could tell Skuli and Ketel felt the same way.

'It would be an education for you but I'm afraid you won't be there.'

'You think you can succeed without me?'

'Your offer of help is very generous but I don't think you or your men would cope with our sophisticated battle tactics. You're best advised to find another way of taking revenge on your brother.'

'Very well, my Lord,' replied Tostig, concealing his anger, 'I will.'

'Will you be staying with us much longer, cousin?' asked William in a tone that invited him to leave.

'As much as I find your hospitality most agreeable, I'm afraid I have pressing matters to attend to. I'm sure you'll understand, my Lord.'

'Indeed I do, Earl Tostig. It was a pleasure to meet you. Should you wish to visit us again, you'll be most welcome at court.'

'Thank you, Duke William, I'll remember that. Goodbye.'

'Goodbye, Earl Tostig. Skuli. Ketel.'

As the trio, accompanied by a few housecarls, made their way back to their ships Tostig, appearing agitated, asked his sons what was their opinion of the Duke.

'He's very confident. I should think he's very impressive on land,' answered Ketel.

'I'd agree with that,' added Skuli.

'Do you think his invasion plans will work?'

'I think he'll end up at the bottom of the sea.'

'And you, Skuli, what do you think?'

'He could end up anywhere. The bottom of the sea is as likely a place as any. If the conditions are perfect when he leaves port and they remain so for, what, a whole day, then there's a possibility it can be done. But if the wind changes or the sea grows rough, he could end up anywhere.'

In the Norman court the talk was of nothing but Tostig.

'Are you sure it was wise to turn down his offer of help?' asked William Warenne, slightly concerned.

'Oh, I accepted his help, sure enough.'

'I don't understand, my Lord,'

'Did you see how offended he was when I refused his offer? It really hurt his pride.'

'Yes, my Lord,' replied Warenne, none the wiser.

'He's bound to take it out on someone.'

'I see, my Lord. You think he might attack the English?'

'He'll soon be off the coast of England creating havoc, mark my words.'

'Yes, my Lord,' responded Warenne flatly.

'You see, if Tostig raids along the English coast the alarm will go out. Harold will call out the militia, or whatever he calls them. If he does, that means they might be waiting along the coast for months before we arrive. Who's going to work in the fields, bring in the harvest and all the other things that need to be done? And most of all, how can he feed the thousands of men he'll need to guard the coast? They'll last no more than a month, six weeks at the very most. After that they'll desert, turn on the local population and each other. Then, when they've finished creating mayhem, they'll go home. When we get there, they'll be exhausted, starved; they'll have deserted or simply returned to their huts.'

'Brilliant, my Lord.'

'I knew you'd think so.'

Leaving Normandy in a foul mood, Tostig headed not to raid along the south coast of England but to Denmark to seek the help of his cousin, King Swein. Sailing across the North Sea, he found the welcome less than friendly. Swein was not open to persuasion; how could he help one cousin without making an enemy of the other? Besides, as far as he was concerned, Harold was the rightful king. After a week of Tostig's best efforts to cajole him, Swein finally managed to make it clear he could expect no help from Denmark.

So it was that once again Tostig sailed north, this time heading for Norway. It was an act of desperation. When Tostig was refused help by Swein, he was quite despondent but then he had a flash of inspiration. The old Gota River Treaty had appeared in his thoughts, as though from nowhere. He left Denmark, setting sail for Norway with the hope of persuading its king, Harald Sigurdsson, that there were rich pickings waiting for him in the south.

Tostig arrived in Norway in low spirits, knowing this was his last chance to win to his side someone powerful enough to mount a successful invasion. Under a grey, rain-laden sky, he entered Trondheim. With Skuli and Ketel, he made his way with a small escort to King Harald Sigurdsson's great hall. On the way, they passed a rubbish heap, upon which lay stretched out, facing the sky, the decomposing body of a man, a young adult by the look of him.

Tostig noticed the sight had caught the attention of his sons.

'It's what they do with their suicides,' he said flatly, in an attempt to calm them.

'Thank heavens it's not what they do to unwelcome visitors,' Skuli replied in an attempt at humour.

'Oh, they do that sometimes, too,' replied Tostig dryly.

'I'm really glad we came here, Dad.'

'You might be, soon. In the meantime don't look at any of the men for too long and don't look at any of the women at all.'

'Anything else?'

'Yes. Whatever happens, don't show any fear.'

After being challenged by a guard, Tostig and his two sons were taken to Harald Sigurdsson, who sat impressively on his throne, looking every part the mighty Viking warrior. As he stood to welcome them, the full height of his six foot six inch frame was revealed. His blond hair hung loose, flowing down over the broad expanse of his shoulders. He was powerfully built and looked immensely strong. There was a resolution about his face too. His blue eyes sparkled with life, although something about them gave him, at times, a somewhat demonic look.

By his side sat his queen, Elizabeth, a young beauty from Kiev.

'Welcome, Earl Tostig,' said the King. 'I've been expecting a visit from you. Come here spying for your brother, have you?'

'If that's what your informants tell you, you'll need to get some more reliable spies.'

'Perhaps I'll recruit you.'

'You can recruit me if it's my brother you've a quarrel with, but to a purpose other than spying.'

'Tell me about it while you join me at my table.' Sigurdsson indicated for Tostig and his sons to be seated and called for food and drink.

'So, Tostig, why do you come to visit me?'

'Because you have a claim to the throne of England.'

'The Gota River Treaty,' Harald replied.

'Yes. I can make arrangements for the nobility of England to support your claim.'

'Why would you want to help me, Tostig?'

'Because by rights I should be Earl of Northumbria.'

'And why aren't you?'

'Because of my brother's boundless ambition; an ambition that would stop at nothing to grab the throne, even if it meant siding with his own brother's enemy.'

'I thought it was Edward who banished you?'

'It was, but he was forced by circumstance.'

'Couldn't the same be said of your brother?'

'No. It was just the excuse he needed to grab power for himself. He planned the whole thing, the rising in the North, everything.'

Tostig paused for a second. 'Why don't we join forces?' he continued, more calmly. 'An earldom for a kingdom, surely that's fair exchange? Think of it, if I were your ally, conquest of England would be an easy matter. Later, should matters of state bring you back to Norway, if you chose, I could rule the entire country for you in your absence. Soon, you would, as the King of two great countries, have the wealth and the manpower to finally overcome Swein and Denmark. Times would be the way they were under Knut, with all three countries united under one great king, one great emperor.'

Tostig could see how much the idea appealed to Sigurdsson.

Harald suspected Tostig had little support in England, but thought twenty ships and the crews to man them might come in useful. Besides, even if only a few people came out to help him, so much the better. He could easily take care of Tostig later, but for now the picture he had painted of Sigurdsson as the new Knut formed a dazzling vision in his mind's eye.

'Tostig, I will discuss this with my council. Now you and your sons are my guests. Eat and drink heartily.'

So Tostig and his sons did as the King bade them, while the court discussed their guest's proposition. First to speak was Ulf Ospaksson, the King's oldest and most trusted friend.

'My lords, I would commend you to forget any ideas Earl Tostig has about capturing the English Crown. He is, after all, an Englishman and it is well known that the English have a dreadful reputation for unreliability. Who is to say when our fleet arrives in England our esteemed guest would be there to meet us?

'If he has support in England now, who is to say he will have it in the future? But what if he does have support and his English allies turn out to support him? How many will there be? Will they stay if the fighting gets rough?

'As many of you will know, the English have many good fighting men; housecarls just like here in Norway. They have a formidable reputation and each one of them, it is supposed, is worth two of ours.

'Finally, if we are to launch an expedition against the English, our best chance is this summer. The English king is new to the throne and I understand has problems with Duke William in Normandy who is, as I speak, preparing to invade. Do we really want to raise a huge army to cross the sea in force and suffer all the problems that would entail, and with what chance of success?'

Ulf Ospaksson left the questions to hang in the air, looked around the hall then took his seat.

'Does anyone speak against Ulf Ospaksson?' asked the King.

'I do.' It was Skule Kongsfostre who spoke. Skule was a close friend of Sigurdsson's son, Olaf. He had taken a liking to Tostig and besides, he was a young warrior with a reputation to make. Now that the war with Denmark was over, he had to look elsewhere for glory.

'Everyone knows of Ulf Ospaksson's bravery, how he and Ragnvald Brusesson saved our king's life when he was a youth and took him on the great adventure, which led to his being our king today. Against all the odds they rose to power and position. Who could have seen when King Harald, no more than a youth, was dragged from a ditch, wounded and exhausted from fighting a lost battle, that he would one day be king?

'A warrior cares not for the odds; a warrior cares for glory. Ulf Ospaksson says the English are unreliable; if so, they will be so much easier to defeat. If no Englishman turns out to help us then how much greater will be the glory? And how much richer will we be with fewer to share the plunder?' Skule paused to let his message drive home.

A loud chorus of agreement greeted his last remark.

'It looks as though the court agrees with Skule, father,' Olaf remarked.

Sigurdsson replied, turning his attention to Tostig, 'It looks as though you'll have some company when you next return to England.'

'I'm glad that's your decision. When do you think you will be ready, my Lord?'

'Around August, I expect.'

'Good. That will give me plenty of time to raise men in Flanders.' And, he thought, my money won't have run out.

'Well, now we have decided, let me tell you of some of my previous victories in the Mediterranean,' said the King.

Sigurdsson liked nothing more than to tell of his adventures as a young man. Everyone at court knew them off by heart. Now Sigurdsson had a fresh audience, he could tell them all anew.

'You know, there was one time when I was a general fighting for the Emperor of Byzantium in Sicily; all the major towns were prepared for my arrival. They knew my reputation, you see. They were ready for direct attacks or sieges but there was one thing they were not prepared for. You know what that was?'

'No, my Lord. What was that?'

'Me,' Sigurdsson answered, laughing and striking the table with his fist, 'Me and my cunning.

'One time I had my army camped outside the enemy's city walls when I noticed small birds nesting in the thatch of the houses; pretty little things they were. It was watching them that inspired my brilliant idea. I had my men catch the birds and bind chips of fir, which had melted wax on them, to the legs of the little creatures. They set the chips alight then released them to fly home. Well, naturally the birds were in a panic and flew straight back to their nests and the next thing you know the city roofs are on fire. My word, you should have seen the place burn.' Harald burst out laughing, still delighted by his own cunning, even after all the years. The whole court laughed with him.

'There was barely anyone left alive when we entered and those who did survive wished they had died when we got through with them, ha, ha, ha,' Sigurdsson guffawed.

'Then there was another time when I was besieging some other town,' said the King, waving his drinking horn around before taking a huge gulp. 'I fell sick and took to my bed. Soon I was in a fever and having the strangest of dreams, the sort the gods impart to great men. In my vision I climbed from a coffin and took control of a town.

'When I recovered from my fever I sent some of my men to tell the townspeople I had died and to request a Christian burial for me in one of the town's local churches. Well, you can imagine it, can't you; every priest for miles around wanted the honour of burying me in the hope of making a small fortune out of my men.

'So, this procession of priests turned up at our camp, all squabbling among themselves they were, about who should do this and who would be paid that. Anyway, with my men marching behind them with my coffin, with me inside it, they went back to town. Once we'd passed through the gates my men dropped the coffin and sounded their horns. The priests were terrified. They ran this way and that, like chickens running for their lives.' Harald was slapping his thigh in delight. 'You should have seen their faces when I jumped out of my coffin, sword in hand, yelling like a berserker, ha, ha.'

'It sounds like a great adventure.'

'It was. We charged round the town attacking everyone in sight. Our raven-feeders,' he said, waving his now empty drinking horn as though it were a sword, 'gave their helmets a good battering and their shields were soon smashed to pieces. It wasn't long before we chopped them up too. The women we took back to the ships and as there were no longer any priests around, we took the liberty of helping ourselves to their treasure. What a glorious day that was,' Sigurdsson sighed and smiled to himself for a moment, as he silently reflected on a glory from his past. Then he spoke again. 'We left the eagles and the wolves plenty to eat that day. Ah, those were the days.'

'I see now why you are known as the greatest warrior under heaven.'

Always vulnerable to flattery, in response Sigurdsson smiled happily at Tostig.

The next day King Harald sent out a command to raise a levy of half of the men in the kingdom. While the Norwegians made their preparations, Tostig sailed to Flanders to see how Copsig had fared building up forces for the forthcoming campaign.

NORMANDY

'Have you seen it?' snapped the Duke.

Lanfranc had been called to Rouen to offer William an explanation. The Duke snapped out the question as soon as the Abbot entered court.

'Do you mean the star?' answered the inscrutable Lanfranc, stopping in his tracks, all the eyes of the court on him.

'Of course I mean the star!'

'It's a message from God. It means you are right and Harold is wrong,' said Lanfranc, sublimely confident in his reply, knowing it was exactly what William wanted to hear.

'Is it miraculous?' enquired William, anxiously.

'Yes it is, my Lord.'

'Well, get the word out and make sure everyone knows.'

And with that, Lanfranc left, having given William a boost to his already bursting confidence. The Pope had assured him God was on his side; now the heavens had sent him a sign to prove it.

WESTMINSTER, EASTER 1066

Having reassured Edyth that his love for her was as strong as ever, Harold promised he would return and at the earliest opportunity, he left for Westminster. Thoughts of Edyth and the children played through his mind. Aldytha would sometimes find him preoccupied. Somewhere deep inside, the seed of suspicion began to grow; she needed to know.

'Harold,' she said, almost in a whisper, as they lay in bed together. He failed to hear her.

'Harold,' she said, only this time a little more loudly.

'Yes, Aldytha.'

'Have you seen Edyth since we were married?'

'Since we came to London I've seen her just once and that was to discuss the children. Please don't be jealous of my children, Aldytha.'

'I'm not jealous of your children, Harold. I understand how you must feel but do you love me?'

'Aldytha, it's not a question of whether I love them more than you. A father's love for his children is different from the love for his wife. You know that.'

'Then tell me you love me.'

'You know how I feel about you. Here, I'll show you.' And he took her in his arms and kissed her passionately. When they parted she was breathless but not reassured.

'Tell me you love me.'

'You know I love you.'

'Then tell me.'

'I just have.'

With that, they kissed. Aldytha embraced him and pulled him forcefully toward her. Harold found her impossible to resist and soon they were joined in the hot throes of passion. As they reached the climax he called out a name, but was it hers? Was her mind beginning to play tricks on her?

Harold was lying beside her now, dozing, his arms around her. She turned to study his face. Harold seemed so genuine, so sincere in his lovemaking.

It must have been my name he called, she thought.

On Easter Monday, the fleet, with Eadric in command, would sail to the Isle of Wight. Harold, Gyrth and Haakon would take their housecarls to the south coast, leaving Leofric to guard London and the Thames estuary. At the Easter Witan it had been decided that the fyrd would be called out only if absolutely necessary; there was too much to do on the land. At the summer's end the navy would lay up in London, at the time of the autumn equinox. Naturally, if William tried to invade before then, the fyrd and navy would stand down as soon as he had been dealt with.

But it wasn't strategy that was playing on Harold's mind. It was the star; each night it grew bigger and brighter. Everyone was talking about it. Each night little groups of people would gather and stare skyward at the fearsome sight. Speculation was rife. Did the star presage an invasion, as in days gone by, or was it a sign of God's anger and if so, who was God angry with? As a safeguard, special prayers were offered in churches across the land. The star was seen as a sword and each night Harold prayed that it was the hilt that was being offered to him and the point directed at William. But for now, he would concern himself with observing Easter and celebrating the Resurrection.

MAY

On a bright early morning in the beginning of May, Harold lay in bed with Aldytha draped around him. Her head lay on his chest and he could smell the sweet scent of her hair. He enjoyed being with her more each day but he was astute enough to know that what he found most alluring about her was the physical. Nevertheless he found her witty, interesting and generous in many ways.

Harold had not seen Edyth since his visit to Waltham, just after marrying Aldytha, although messages were being smuggled to and fro. By the time he and the Queen had dressed, news arrived that Tostig was raiding the Isle of Wight, demanding money and provisions. It was Leofwine who broke the news.

'He has about twenty ships and he's forced some people from his old estates to go along with him. He hasn't had much of a welcome by all accounts.'

'Has anyone seen Duke William?'

'No. It's just Tostig, apparently.'

'Do you think this is just a diversionary raid?'

'I doubt it. William won't have had enough time to gather men and ships just yet.'

'We'd better call out the fyrd, though. Tostig could raid anywhere along the coast, so we need to be ready for him, wherever he goes. In the meantime, get your housecarls together and we'll go and pay him a visit.'

'What about Gyrth?'

'He can go up to East Anglia and prevent Tostig doing any damage there.'

'And there's something else you need to know about.'

'What is it, Leo?'

'A Norwegian emissary has arrived at court to see you. I suspect he's here to discuss Sigurdsson's claim to the throne. The Gota River Agreement. Remember?'

'Oh, bloody hell. Not that again.'

'Shall I tell him you'll see him?'

'Yes. In the meantime can you make sure everything is prepared for me to leave in a couple of hours?'

'Of course.'

Tostig, now sailing off the coast of Kent, was making his way north pursued by the English navy. Having no wish to engage with Harold's much stronger forces, he set sail for Northumbria, raiding as he went. Discovering there was very little support for him anywhere in his homeland, he became more and more disillusioned. Finally he made his way to Scotland in the hope of persuading King Malcolm to join forces with himself and Sigurdsson.

After sending a message to Morcar and Edwin, Harold arrived in Sandwich to discover Tostig had left it ravaged but far from ruined. Leaving some of his men to guard the port, he turned westward along the south coast. At every likely landing spot, housecarls were left behind; they would be joined by the fyrd later in the month.

When he reached Bosham, Harold established his temporary headquarters at his home. Edyth had travelled down and brought Ulf and young Gytha with her. Having Ulf for company made Harold's stay more pleasant. Thorkell was still training as a housecarl and would ready for initiation very soon. Having Haakon at Bosham was of more benefit than Harold could have hoped for. He and Ulf got along famously, unlike their fathers in the past. And for Edyth, having young Gytha with her now that she was a young woman made the days more interesting.

The comet had disappeared from the night sky and so Harold felt a little less tense, but still a restless spirit haunted him. Now, after months of separation, he was back with Edyth and at least some of his family. He had thought he would be happy again. But just as when he had been with Aldytha he had thought of Edyth, now he was with Edyth he found himself thinking of Aldytha. But he told himself it was the freshness and excitement of a new affair he missed. Occasionally he would catch himself looking at Edyth with a critical eye. It was unfair, he knew; she was still a fine looking woman and besides, in his heart he knew they were meant for each other.

As the summer wore on, Ulf and Haakon accompanied Harold as he toured the coast, inspecting his soldiers and the defences. If William was spotted, arrangements had been made to take Ulf to a place of safety. Haakon would fight alongside Harold. On the Isle of Wight they met Eadric and inspected the navy. The ships had been hauled ashore on rollers and the crews were clustered round cooking fires, making their meals for the evening. From the top of the white cliffs, Harold could see the same scene all over the little island. Scores of vessels lay in rows on the beaches and at night, from the mainland shore, the light of innumerable campfires mixed with the stars.

Over the next few weeks, the number of men awaiting the arrival of Harold's Norman nemesis swelled. They all found places to stay on the mainland. Some stayed with thanes in their halls, some with farmers, some in tents or makeshift shelters, but all close to the shore, where every day they would gather, quite a few of them enjoying the novelty of setting eyes on the sea for the very first time. There was a general air of excitement; every man thought that within days he would be called upon to risk his life in defence of his king.

Along with the fyrdmen there followed a great variety of people. From all over Wessex, farmers arrived with supplies, as did peddlers and purveyors of beer and cider. Musicians turned up, as did magicians and women who had innumerable ways to entertain a lonely young man. But no matter how attractive the distraction, each day, all day and every day, anxious eyes would scan the horizon in search of enemy ships.

May grew hotter and still no ships were seen. Days turned into weeks and still the finest summer that anyone could remember blazed on and the men grew accustomed to their new way of life. To keep them fit for the forthcoming fight, housecarls drilled the men daily in the arts of war and when they were not training, they were kept busy with competitions, running, archery, spear throwing and anything the professional soldiers could do to keep their comrades from the fyrd ready for battle. May gave way to June and still no fleet was sighted. But for Ulf this was a time he always remembered with great happiness. He made a great friend in his cousin Haakon and best of all, Thorkell had returned from training and was now a fully-fledged housecarl. The three spent most of their spare time together.

It was a good summer for other young men. Some had made friends with the local girls and the summer life was easy. For some, these were the days they wished would never end. For others, as June turned to July, feelings turned from ease to anxiety. Thoughts turned to the harvest and the winter that lay beyond. Grumbling fyrdmen counted the days now until their service was up. Their fears were allayed when gradually the new fyrdmen arrived to take the place of those who had turned up earlier in the year. As each man finished his two months' service, another arrived to replace him. The word spread quickly along the coast; yes, it had been difficult without them but work was being done and the harvest would be safe. Once more there was a holiday atmosphere along the coast as fresh fyrdmen arrived to complete their service.

At the heart of the army was Bosham, where Harold had his headquarters. From his window he could see the harbour he knew so well. The people here he knew as well as the place; some he had known all his life. Bosham was where he had caught his first fish, flown his first falcon. There was the church where Tostig and Judith had been married, the same church where just under two years ago he had prayed before he embarked on his fateful voyage to Normandy.

Harold's thoughts turned to Edyth and what he would do without her, he didn't know. He wondered if things would ever be the same. All the little things lovers share were still there, the way they slipped their hands into each other's. He still enjoyed the simple pleasure of the smell of her hair and skin, the feel of her next to him. Harold noticed, too, she always had a smile for him if they should unexpectedly meet in a room, a hall or a courtyard. Harold was wise enough to know that these little things, deemed insignificant by others, in fact were the essence of love. He relished them.

Looking through the window, the smell of salt air and the sound of birdcalls all around him, reclaiming the adventures he had had as a boy, he almost forgot the world and its troubles. Here in Bosham with Edyth, Ulf and Gytha, for just that moment life had become idyllic, a time to relax, a place to just simply be at peace under the hot summer sun, and to enjoy the cool, refreshing breezes blowing in off the harbour.

'Wouldn't it be marvellous if it were like this all the time?' was the thought going through Harold's head when he was disturbed by a knock on the door.

'Come in.'

A servant entered.

'A messenger for you, my Lord, won't tell me what it's about. Says to tell you it's Osred.'

Someone looking like a fisherman sheepishly entered the room. Unable to make eye contact with his king, he looked most shamefaced.

'What's happened, Osred?'

'I was discovered, my Lord.'

'Sit down and tell me all about it.'

Osred took a seat at the table and Harold sat across from him, studying him carefully.

'I'm not sure how they caught on, but they dragged me off to see Duke William and I thought that was it, a few hours' torture to entertain them before they got bored and chopped off my head, but Duke William couldn't have been kinder. He invited me to join him at his table for the evening meal with him and some of his friends. They didn't say much to me, just ignored me most of the time. When they'd all finished I was shown to a tent and slept there for the night. In the morning I was taken to Duke William again and I thought, this time I really am for it.'

'And?'

'And he said, "Give Earl Harold two messages from me. Tell him this; firstly, that it's pointless wasting money sending spies because I'll be in England before the year is out, so he'll see for himself the strength of the Norman army".'

'The second?'

'The second message is that Duke William has promised to give away all of your property and possessions. He says he knows you've made no promises to give away any of his things because you're too weak ever to do so and you know it.'

'How does he know what promises I have or haven't been making?'

The spy's expression changed imperceptibly. 'He must have his own spies here.'

'Just what I was thinking.

'Did you discover anything of his plans before you were captured?'

'Well, he doesn't have anywhere near enough experienced crew for his ships, so he intends to sail across the Channel at the front of a procession that will follow on behind. Because hardly any of them know how to sail, they're having lessons around the harbour at Dives. It's the

Duke's intention to wait for the wind to come from due south and cross then.'

'So if he ever comes, he'll end up somewhere round the Pevensey-Hastings area?'

'No idea, my Lord. If I was him I'd stick to the coast for as long as I could, then cross at the narrowest point.'

'Hmm. Do you know when he's likely to be ready?'

'It's hard to tell. In about a month, I'd say.'

'Well, should he ever arrive, we'll give him the welcome he deserves.'

NORMANDY, THE SUMMER OF 1066

As a result of papal support for William's crusade, more and more soldiers were making their way to Normandy, lured by the promise of absolution and loot. Many thought that whatever the result of their endeavours, they had nothing to lose and much to gain. Numbers were increasing closer to the amount William would need. Many from Brittany answered the call, as did men from Flanders, Anjou and Maine. Many of the crusaders believed William's propaganda and felt that as God-fearing Christians, it was their duty to fight Harold the Perjurer, as he had come to be known.

Some of the soldiers, or mercenaries to be more precise, were considerably wealthy by any standard but avarice drives a man to many depths. But the bulk of the men gathering from across Europe were landless younger sons, more interested in the prospect of a roof over their head and free meals, rather than any feud between Harold and William. Of all those who made their way to the Normandy coast, the worst were the freelancers, those who were there for the sheer love of violence and the opportunity to make fame and fortune. One of these was Ralph Pomeroy.

Pomeroy had spent the last two years fighting in Sicily and for his efforts he had accrued an excellent sword, two horses, a donkey, a servant who he described as his squire and an earthenware cooking pot. He was tired of hot slosh and the hot Sicilian sun and the flies that went with it. On hearing William's call for fighting men, Pomeroy and his squire left for Normandy without the money to cover the journey. Robbing a church of some of its plate soon solved the problem. A month later, after an uneventful sea voyage and a trudge across France, they arrived at Dives and enlisted.

They found town and countryside alike bulging at the seams with shipwrights, carpenters, carters, sail makers, blacksmiths and vendors. The town was also crowded with soldiers waiting to embark on the journey of a lifetime. After them came the followers, there to feed on crumbs from the table. For the locals, the days were filled with work, work and more work, but the money flowed freely. While the civilians busied themselves making and preparing the ships for the crossing, the soldiers crammed into the fields round about to practise their martial arts. Everywhere, archers and crossbowmen were shooting at makeshift targets. Infantrymen went through their exercises, as individuals or in formations. The cries of their captains carried grudgingly in the humid air. All along the river, the days passed in sultry heat, the nights in fevered merriment. Hot young men took their pleasure in taverns, putting the cares of the day aside. Wine and beer were consumed by the barrel.

As the strength of Norman army and navy built up, William's invasion plans grew clearer. As he had never been to England, its geography was a mystery to him; Sir William Malet was a great help and was included in all discussions, but once again it was from the Church that William was to receive invaluable assistance. Obviously, he would invade England's south coast, but where, precisely? The Abbot of Fecamp, who felt he had good reason to help the Duke, provided the answer. Fecamp had held two abbeys in England under King Edward. Harold had revoked the one at Steyning in Sussex and reclaimed it for the Crown. Although this was quite within his rights, the Abbot had taken umbrage. However, Fecamp still held the other abbey at Rameslie, also in Sussex, which ran to the coast from Hastings to Winchelsea, across the sea, due north of Dives. The arrangement the Abbot struck with the Duke was simple; he would supply William with details of that part of the country in exchange for the return of the estate at Steyning, should the Duke's invasion succeed.

The Abbot of Fecamp also brought William news that lifted his spirits: Harald Sigurdsson was planning to invade England to claim the Crown for himself. So William would wait until he had word that Sigurdsson had landed before setting sail. He might not be sure whom he would fight but he could be sure that whichever army he met would be depleted from a previous encounter. All he needed was a southerly wind after news of Sigurdsson's landing and his future would be assured.

NORWAY, AUGUST

Further north, Tostig's spirits were deflated. At the court of his old friend King Malcolm of Scotland, he was busy trying to persuade his blood brother to join him on the expedition to England. Malcolm advised Tostig to find another ally. Tostig, dismayed by his friend's reaction, sailed for Flanders to see how many men Copsig had raised. What he discovered dampened his spirits further. Most men who were willing to act as mercenaries had gone to Normandy, where the rewards were more plentiful than anything he had to offer. However, Copsig had found an assortment of pirates and outlaws to bolster the fighting force. With these, he made his way back to Norway, to meet with his only ally, King Harald Sigurdsson.

When Tostig arrived at Trondheim, he was relieved to discover invasion preparations were well underway. More than three hundred longships had gathered and although Harald's men were loyal in answering his summons, many had forebodings about the expedition. Men were having ominous dreams; some had dreamed of the Norse army being eaten alive by English wolves, others of giant trolls smashing their skulls before devouring their spilled brains.

While his men were nervously awaiting the time for departure, King Harald was in Trondheim with Tostig, finalising invasion plans.

'My plan is simple, Tostig. We'll storm York and make it my capital. You'll be reinstated as Earl of Northumbria. With your influence in the North, we shall raise a Northumbrian army, ready to join the rest of us when we travel south to take London.'

'It'll be easy,' Tostig assured Harald. 'I'll use my influence with my sister Edith to raise support in Wessex, or at least make sure there's little opposition.'

Before boarding his ship, which sat with an escort outside his palace on the River Nid, Sigurdsson paid a visit to the remains of his half-brother, the late saintly King Olaf. Alone, Sigurdsson made his way to St.

Clements's Church. Once inside the cool darkness of the interior, he walked as quietly as he could to his brother's elaborately decorated shrine, where gold, silver and precious stones sparkled in what little light pierced the darkness. He unlocked the gate, entered the shrine then knelt down beside his brother's vault. The old Viking warrior never felt comfortable in churches unless he was robbing them. His half-brother might have been a saint but for Sigurdsson it was Thor and Odin who ruled the heavens. Valhalla would be his final destiny, not some kind of Christian great hall filled with peace-loving effeminates playing harps. So he prayed now to the Norse gods, rather than any other.

Having finished his prayer, he took his knife from its sheath, cut off a lock of hair and placed it beside the vault. Then he trimmed his fingernails and put them in a little pile alongside his shorn locks; an offering to his brother to bring him good fortune.

Rising to his feet, he stared in silent contemplation at the vault for several minutes before leaving to rejoin Tostig and a small group of his commanders.

'Tostig, there you are. Are you ready to reclaim your earldom now?'

'Yes, I am.'

'Good, then follow me.'

Sigurdsson led them at a brisk pace towards the riverbank; he stopped and threw the key to his half-brother's shrine into the river. His luck would be safely locked away forever. Looking pleased with himself and ignoring the quizzical looks of his followers, he strode straight off to his ship, the Long Serpent. He leaped aboard with one bound and before his feet had even touched the deck, shouted at the top of his voice, 'Cast off!'

There was a brief moment of activity as lines were untied and cast aboard. The enormous sail was hoisted high up the tall mast and the biggest longship that ever sailed began to make its way out to sea with one hundred and forty-four men pulling on thirty-six pairs of oars. Soon he would join his fleet off the Solunder Islands. It was the end of the second week of August. With a strong north-easterly wind behind them, Harald and his berserkers left the land of fog and shadows, sailing swiftly in his pagan ships across a godless sea, to reclaim the land of his fathers.

NORMANDY

When each ship was ready, it was floated downriver to Dives. Gradually, as the summer progressed, more and more ships were to be seen there. By mid-August, William was ready to sail but word came back to him that Harold had still not disbanded the fyrd and he dared not attack while the English king lay in wait for him.

So more churches were robbed and food brought from markets miles away but still there was not enough. Word of William's problems reached Matilda and she made the journey from Rouen to be by his side. She was saddened to find him frustrated by events that kept him from launching his expedition.

Matilda's visit came as a real fillip to him; he was delighted to see her. In the privacy of his tent he confided in her.

'What can I do to raise your spirits, my love? Tell me, I'll do anything.'

'Thank you; you're such a comfort to me. I miss you so much – and the children.'

'Why not return to Rouen with me and spend a few days with us? It can't hurt.'

'No, I can't,' he said, looking downcast. 'If I left, the men might desert.'

'Then why don't I go to Rouen and fetch them back myself?'

William's face lit up with joy. 'What a marvellous idea.'

Early the next morning, Matilda left for Rouen. A few days later, when she returned with the children, it was to find the port empty and quiet, the last sail disappearing over the far horizon.

SEPTEMBER, ENGLAND, THE NATIVITY OF ST. MARY

Early in the morning of the day of the Nativity of St Mary, Harold woke from the depths of a deep sleep. Curled up beside him, Edyth lay dreaming, a thousand miles away. The nightmare was over. The army could disband and the fleet could sail home to London. William would not come, not now, probably not ever. For some reason, the Bastard had not taken the opportunity and had missed his chance. Very soon now the storms of the equinox would be upon them. The campaign season over, the men of the fyrd would start making their various ways to home and harvest. By nightfall the beaches, which had been home to so many, would be empty. A ghostly silence would descend on the seashore, empty of ships, laughter and the idle chatter of soldiers. The crashing of the waves and the calling of the gulls would be heard by none.

Gently, Harold nudged Edyth. 'Time to get up.'

'Umph,' she mumbled.

'Time to get up.' It had been a long time since Harold had woken up without some sense of foreboding.

'What time is it?'

'I've no idea but it must be late. Come on. We've got to see off the fyrd and I'd like to be in London before the fleet returns.'

'Are we travelling overland?'

'Yes, I thought so.'

'So you can get in a little hunting on the way?'

'That's a good idea,' he replied, good-humouredly.

'We're both going to London?'

The smile faded from Harold's face.

'I thought you might like to accompany me before travelling on to Waltham.'

'I'm to go to Waltham, then, am I?'

'I thought that might be best, under the circumstances.'

'What you mean is, out of the way.'

'It's not that. It's just …'

'It's just that you want me out of the way while your other wife has the baby.'

'I thought we'd gone through all this.'

Edyth sighed. 'We have. I'm sorry, Harold, it's just so hard for me.'

'I promise, as soon as I can I'll get everything back to normal, just the way it was before.'

'Do you really think things will ever be the same?'

'We can try, Edyth. We can try.'

Throughout the day, the soldiers packed up and left. Some of them gladly turned their backs on the coast and hurried home to their families. One or two left with promises to return to their summer sweethearts or girls with broken hearts who would forever remember the long hot summer of 1066 as the time they met their first love. A few would be married and leave to follow their new husbands to far-off shires.

The sailors, too, made ready to leave, pushing off to catch the morning tide, setting sail for London after bidding farewell.

Further north, Harald Sigurdsson was making for England. With him were sixteen thousand men. Many were Norwegians, including the formidable earl, Eystein Orri, who had been promised the hand of the King's daughter, the beautiful Maria. Madly in love with the princess, Orri was desperate to prove the choice of groom had been a good one.

Tostig, Skuli and Ketel, with twenty ships filled with mercenaries from Flanders, accompanied King Harald. Godfrey Crovan, son of Harold the Black of Iceland, had arrived with fifty ships full of men keen for a fight, and from Ireland was King Lachlainn, with his small army. These men, along with Paul and Erlin, sons of Thorfinn, the late Earl of the Orkneys, sailed with the biggest Viking invasion force by far that was ever to set foot in England. Even with these numbers there were still those who had reservations, so many of the men were having bad dreams. And there were those who, around midnight, had seen the dances of the spirits in the sky. Not that this was anything unusual at this time of the year; it was the malevolent appearance of the spirits that had unsettled them. The colours in the sky had formed the shapes of beasts and daemons. But Harald told them he, too, had seen the spirits in the sky and they were on the side of the Norsemen. He told them he, too, had had a dream. In his dream, Freya, the goddess of love, had told him that when the English next celebrated Christmas, it would be with a new king sitting on the throne. Freya had never lied, never let him down. Harald flattered himself that the goddess had a particular fondness for him.

NORMANDY

Before Matilda had had time to return with the children, word had reached William that Harald Sigurdsson had left Norway with a large fleet. He presumed that Sigurdsson would be sailing straight to England. Soon, William would turn his dreams into reality and more good news was on its way. Hugh Margot had arrived with news that the English army had stood down.

William turned to his brother. 'Well, Robert, what do you think?'

'The coast is clear, William but is it safe to cross?' Robert replied.

'Why wouldn't it be?'

'I'm no sailor, William, but surely this is not the right time to lead an invasion force across the Channel. They say the storms can be terrible at this time of the year.'

'Robert, it's now or never.' William had always thought Robert a little too cautious and dismissed his advice without consideration. 'You know as well as I do, we're almost out of provisions.'

Duke William looked at the south-facing wall of the tent blowing gently towards him.

'The wind is from the south,' said William, addressing Odo, who he knew was more inclined to his way of thinking. 'We must sail before it changes, don't you think?'

'You're right, William, we must go now. Go while the going's good.'

'Good. Give orders to your men. If the wind is still blowing from the south when we wake in the morning, we'll be on our way.'

It was still dark in the Norman camp when, before the sun rose the next morning, the order went out to rise and pack. There was a hectic scramble as tents were taken down and loaded onto carts, ready to be transferred to their designated vessels later in the day. Horses were led, protesting, on to ships, tied secure and given enough hay and oats to last them the journey.

Racks of chainmail, barrels filled with wine and sheaves of arrows were ready and waiting, loaded the previous day. There were even all the parts required for the building of four wooden forts. Poles, pegs, hinges and bolts were there and all the equipment to assemble them. Finally the men boarded; everyone knew his assigned place on the ship that bore its individual recognition mark. Everything was prepared, nothing left to chance.

The ships cast off and drifted down river with the current. The Normans, hopeful but apprehensive, were soon adrift on the sea.

All the ships headed for the *Mora* to be close to the Duke. Crews and passengers exchanged insults and curses as the boats careered this way and that, colliding here and there as novice steersmen struggled with the helms. There was confusion at first, as the faster ships passed the slower. The Duke gradually left them all behind.

Due north they headed, across the spume water; closer to England they crept, the sun and the southerly wind at their backs. Their hearts beating hard in their chests, the Duke's warrior army was buoyant on the calm, calm sea. To many, the salt air was a new sensation, the chill of the ever-constant whipping wind a surprise to the landsmen, here in a new element. The sea rocked the boats as a mother rocks a baby, as if to comfort them. Still there were those who were sick. Further north they went, out of sight of land for the very first time; their lives in the hands of William's helmsman. Would he sail a true course? No landmark, no place of recognition on the watery plain; just grey-blue water all around. The little ships bobbed about, each following the one in front. Anxious glances, hearty greetings, words of encouragement and jests were shouted from one to another. The Norman army was on the move, travelling without opposition from any foe. Their confidence grew as the ships headed closer to their destination. At the present rate, by nightfall they would be making camp in England. Then someone turned; a sailor it was, his expression giving away his thoughts. From one ship to another, now many a head turned back. The Norman army had company. Dark clouds were closing fast and the winds were veering in from the west. In the *Mora*, William looked grim. He had spent the first part of the journey emptying the contents of his stomach over the side of his ship. Now he felt famished, but the drone in his dizzy head warned him not to take anything to eat. This was for him the very worst way to travel, but he knew he had the Pope's blessing, so he had God on his side. Surely he would complete the crossing safely.

The wind was rising, as was the sea. Spray drenched the soldiers in the wooden ships which, as every minute passed, were tossed about ever more roughly. Without waiting for orders, steersmen pulled on helms and started to head east. They had no choice; the wind had changed. For the first time since he was child, William felt as though he had no control, as though he had taken on too mighty a foe. He felt so alone, so small, so impotent. The waves that rose around him held his future in their power and their power was truly awesome, pitching and rolling William's ship this way and that. The Duke felt as though he were riding on the back of some huge monster. Waves crashed down around his crew, who struggled with their oars to keep on course. Airard FitzStephen, the helmsman, clung on to the helm for dear life. Now, William wondered if he would die, here in the raging sea. Would water claim him when battle could not? The sea had turned from a silver plate, something barely animate, to this raging element whose anger grew fiercer as every minute passed. The sky, too, was black and raging, thunder and lightning flashing and crashing all around. Then there appeared a sight that struck fear into the very heart of him; it was a vision of hell, if not hell itself, he saw. Through the lashing spray, William saw the whole ship light up, rigging and all. Fire shot out of the mast; everything was alight, everything a bright blue blaze in the unearthly darkness. Even the sea burned green, blue and white. William turned his head to see his ship being followed by more ships all alight, hopeless decorations bobbing around in the in the pitch black of night. He thought he was sailing into oblivion. So did some of his men, who in horror jumped ship. William turned his terror-struck face to FitzStephen, who grinned back at the Duke like a demon.

'Saint Elmo's fire!' he called out.

The Duke stared at him.

'Saint Elmo's fire. It's auspicious. It's a good omen. You'll see.'

William could hardly believe it. Here in the heart of the tempest, FitzStephen was beginning to look more relaxed. The steersman could see William had doubts. 'I've seen it before. Don't worry. It'll all be all right, my Lord.'

The Duke thought he would best take the sailor's word for it; the alternative did not bear thinking about. 'I have every faith in you, Airard,' he said. He even forced a smile.

As the ships continued on their way to land William felt belittled by an enemy he had no idea how to fight. Then after an eternity the cry went up, "Land! Land!" It was FitzStephen calling.

'Where is it? Where are we sailing?' shouted the Duke above the raging storm.

'The wind is taking us to Ponthieu, my Lord. We have no choice,' came the answer over the din.

'All that waiting! All for nothing! When will we ever get to England? Then turning to FitzOsbern, he bellowed, 'Is this a message from God? Are we destined forever to be at the mercy of the elements?'

'Fear not, my Lord. We'll get there.'

William eyed his friend closely. In FitzOsbern's eyes he could see not the slightest glimmer of doubt. Reassured, he hung on to the side of the ship and prayed silently that they would make a safe return to dry land. His fleet was still far out at sea, its ships scattered in the blackness with their cargoes of horses and landsmen, each individual helmsman running before the wind following a fast-fading lamp, searching in growing desperation for the shelter of the shore. Most survived, their boats crashing on the shore with the breakers, making it to St. Valery exhausted and frightened. The storm marked the end of summer and for many, the end of William's venture. Under cover of the dark some of the men slipped away back to safety, security and home. The wind followed them, howling in from the west.

WESSEX IN SEPTEMBER

Along the roads of southern England, soldiers were making their way home. Harold's party was one of many. For company he had Edyth, Ulf, Gytha, Thorkell and his housecarls. Ordinarily, it would take two days to cross Sussex, then perhaps a couple more across the North Downs.

In the late afternoon, the stagnant air grew hot and sticky, draining man and beast of energy. Storm clouds gathered in the oppressive atmosphere. Lightning flashed in the sky to the south and the sound of thunder rolled towards them, unsettling the horses. Gusts of cooler air blew in and rain began to fall heavily. Luckily, they were not far from one of Harold's estates. Putting their mounts into full gallop, they found shelter but not before they were all drenched. While the men took care of the animals, the local thane arrived and organised the servants. Harold and Edyth found the privacy of a bedroom to change into dry clothes.

'I wonder if they're having this storm in Normandy?' she asked.

'Let's hope so.'

As Harold spoke, lightning and thunder flashed and crashed around the house. The flash was bright and the thunder deafening. Rain thrashed against the wooden walls and roof slats.

'Let's hope they are and their ships get wrecked,' Edyth said chirpily.

Harold smiled by way of reply. He had noticed the way a couple of stray raindrops ran down her face, reminding him of a time earlier in the year.

'You're very quiet, Harold. Tell me, what's going to happen when you get back to London?'

'You know I love you, Edyth and there's nothing I'd like more than to return to Westminster with you by my side as my queen and for us live like any other couple.'

'But?'

'I've thought about it these last few months. I know it's entirely my fault. I know I said I might need to be free to have a political marriage but that was just a device to get my father to agree to our handfast marriage. I never dreamed it would happen. I thought we'd always be together, just the two of us, and the children of course, but now there are complications.'

'So I am your mistress?'

'You are what you have always been. You are my love. My only love.'

'I wish I could believe you.'

'You can. I've just spent all summer with you. You must know how happy you make me. It's circumstance that drives us apart.'

They held each other tenderly for a while. When they broke away, all Harold said was, 'So?'

'Waltham it is, then.'

'Gyrth will keep an eye on you. If there's anything you need, let him know. I'll be out to see you whenever I can.'

'It's not what I hoped for.'

'It's not what I hoped for, either.'

'What happens when all this business with William is over?'

'We'll have to see. Don't worry, I'll think of something.'

Edyth gave Harold a studied look. Their eyes fixed on each other in silence.

'Oh, Harold,' said Edyth, grabbing hold of him tightly. She was in tears, her words a confused babble of mumbles and sobs.

'It'll be all right, you'll see, you'll see. Everything will work out in the end.'

Edyth put on a brave face that evening. Occasionally, eyes glanced her way, to read her. The men wanted the measure of her mind, only so as to know how it might affect their king. They wanted to know her mood, all the better to read his. They were happy to see her looking serene. The King, too, looked relaxed, as did his son, sharing a joke with his father as they sat in the hall, a fire burning in the hearth, fighting off the cold, damp air, the thunder and lightning subsiding but the storm still raging around them. They could hear the patter of the rain on the roof and the window shutters, closed to keep out the angry elements. The cry of the trees as the wind whipped through their branches seemed to give the storm life, the palpable presence of an unwanted guest. In the lodge, all seemed calm. Everyone was glad to be by the fireside, out of the wind and rain to enjoy the warm, dry interior and the company of their fellows. Food and drink were plentiful. What more could anyone want?

341

PONTHIEU

When the *Mora* struck land, expertly beached by its steersman, William felt an overwhelming relief to be ashore. Wandering around in the darkness, he found his way to the church of St. Valery. When he entered, followed by FitzOsbern, William threw himself in front of the altar and lay prostrate, praying to God, offering his thanks for saving his life and those of his men. He then offered gifts and made promises of more, if only the Almighty would give him a favourable wind to take him to England. To FitzOsbern this looked too pitiful for comfort, so he left his lord to make his peace with his maker.

So keen was William to offer his thanks, he spent the entire night in the church, only venturing out early next the morning. So worried were FitzOsbern and William Warenne about the Duke's state of mind, they stood sentry all night. It was they who greeted him at the start of the day. William immediately ordered an appraisal of the damage caused by the storm. He would discover later that he had lost fifty ships and about four hundred men were missing. Of the four hundred, only about two hundred bodies had been found washed up along the coast. Some two hundred men, it appeared, had deserted. None of the prefabricated forts had been lost but the Duke was out of supplies. Most of the hired troops thought William would give the word to disband. To dispel these rumours, William raided barns and increased their rations. Two burial parties were sent out along the coast, one to either side of the camp to dispose of any drowned bodies washed up on the beach. Any deserters were to be executed on the spot.

Outside his tent, William was failing to enjoy a late breakfast with his commanders. They were keen to know the Duke's mind.

'We cannot let this little setback stand in our way,' he told his lieutenants.

Odo was going to say something but thought better of it. Robert de Mortain, too, remained silent. Following the example set by William's brothers, FitzOsbern, Warenne and Guy de Ponthieu kept their peace.

'We have no choice. We must invade,' the Duke continued. 'I've always said we would and we must do so this year. If we don't, what will happen to us?'

Duke William surveyed the company slowly, through his cold blue eyes. 'I can't disband the army. I'll never be able to recruit one again next spring. If I abandon my ships here in Ponthieu, do you think I'll find them intact when I return?' William looked meaningfully at Guy when he said this. 'And finally, we have no money. So you see, we have to sail to England. If we don't, we're beaten men.'

'No my lord, we will never be beaten.' said William Warenne with all the bravado he could muster.

'Thank you for your vote of confidence, William.'

'We all feel the same way, my Lord,' FitzOsbern added his support.

'I know I can also rely on my brothers to support me,' said William, smiling at Robert and Odo, before adding, 'Count Guy, can I rely on your support?'

'Naturally, my Lord.'

'You seemed very quiet for one keen to offer his services.'

'That's because I took it for granted you would know of my unswerving devotion to your cause, my Lord. Forgive me, I've been most remiss.'

'Thank you, Guy; I knew I could rely on you. Perhaps you would like to demonstrate your support by supplying us with food for the duration of our stay?'

Count Guy visibly tensed at the thought of Ponthieu struggling to feed ten thousand men. He was not at all sure the little county could cope for more than three weeks.

'Delighted, my Lord,' answered Count Guy. After all, he thought, it would only be for a couple of days. But for nearly the rest of the month the wind blew in from every direction but the south. William wondered if it was a sign from God, like the comet earlier that year. Looking at the trees around him, the Duke could discern the early signs of autumn. Soon, invasion would be out of the question. He wondered what would become of him then.

IN THE NORTH

King Harold entered London to a hero's welcome and the loving arms of his queen. Even though Harold had not engaged, let alone defeated, the enemy, Londoners at last felt safe and for that, they were grateful. Harold and Aldytha waved to the crowds from the steps of Westminster. The cheers were deafening. Barely had he had time to take any refreshment when a messenger arrived, demanding an immediate audience.

'What is it that brings you here in such a hurry?'

'He's landed, my Lord. Killed hundreds. You must come, my Lord. You must help,' the breathless messenger replied.

'What?'

'He's landed and creating mayhem. We need your help.'

'Landed where?' asked a confused Harold.

'Scarborough. They've burned it to the ground and now they're heading to York.'

'York?'

'Yes. He's turned up with more than three hundred ships. Earls Morcar and Edwin are going after him now, my Lord, but they need help.'

'It's Harald Sigurdsson who's landed?'

'Yes, my Lord, and he's heading straight for York.'

As soon as he was able, Harold gathered together his war council to make plans for the swift journey north. Leofwine was left to guard Kent and Essex, should William attempt to land near London. The leaders of the fyrd in Sussex and Hampshire were left with instructions to harass but not to fully engage William, in the unlikely event of his arrival. Harold hoped they might prevent a landing but if not, the resistance should consist of raids on the Norman camp. At all costs a pitched battle should be avoided.

Gyrth left for East Anglia to call out the fyrd there and lead it, with his housecarls, to the Great North Road, where he would later meet Harold.

The frenetic days that passed in London before Harold could organise his forces left their mark. Each night he would endure the most terrible dreams. Viking longships would appear off the coast and then drive up on to the shore. Dragons emblazoned on the ships' sails would spring to life, pounce down and pursue him relentlessly across the country, through towns and villages, across fields and eventually into woods. Sometimes he would attempt to sail out in his own ship to meet his foe, only to discover his sail would unfurl to reveal thousands of holes and the oars would shrink and become useless. He would wake in a sweat to discover Aldytha, silent and serene, asleep beside him.

Just as preparations were complete, Skalpi arrived at court, requesting an audience with Harold, which was immediately granted.

'My lord, I came as soon as I heard Sigurdsson had invaded. I want to volunteer my services.'

'Skalpi, your offer is very welcome.'

'Permit me to fight beside you with the housecarls?'

'There's nowhere else I'd rather have you.'

'Thank you, my Lord. It's an honour.'

'I'm the one who's honoured, Skalpi. Perhaps you'd like to report to Gauti. I'm sure you know where to find him.'

'Thank you, my Lord,' Skalpi replied. In high spirits he left for the housecarls' quarters.

Within an hour, Harold was heading up Ermine Street with his troops following on behind. The clatter of thousands of hooves on the old Roman road was deafening. Onward they rode, covering as much as sixty miles a day, through Cambridgeshire and Huntingdon, meeting Gyrth and his men in Northamptonshire as arranged. Onwards they rode, always travelling at the speed of the fastest.

When they reached Tadcaster, they found the remnants of Morcar's little navy taking shelter from the Norsemen. It was here that Harold discovered the awful truth of the situation. Wilfred, Morcar's helmsman, gave him the news.

'Sigurdsson came with three hundred and thirty ships full of Viking scum. They burned Scarborough and Holderness to the ground then butchered and murdered everyone in sight. Then they came up river and left their ships at Riccall.'

'Where are they now?'

'Well, my Lord, the ships are still at Riccall but the Norsemen are in York.'

'York! What happened to Earl Morcar and Earl Edwin?'

'They're all right, last I heard, my Lord, but most of their men are dead.'

'What happened?'

'Well, the earls decided to take Sigurdsson on, like. Well, Harald and your brother, Tostig, left a big force behind to guard the ships and headed off towards York with about ten thousand men. When they were about a mile outside the city, at Fulford Gate, they came across Edwin and Morcar. The earls had their men lined up across the road. They stretched from the river on one side to the bog on the other; there was no way past.'

'So Sigurdsson just charged through them?'

'No. It was Edwin and Morcar who did the charging.'

'Go on.'

'Well, they charged Sigurdsson's right flank with great success.'

'Don't tell me, the attack carried all before it, and then suddenly Sigurdsson's left flank caught them off guard.'

'That's exactly what happened, my Lord. Sigurdsson's lot forced Edwin and Morcar back into the marsh. It was a disaster. Those of 'em that weren't cut down were drowned. They reckon there were so many of 'em in the bog the Vikings could walk over 'em.'

'Did many get away?'

'Well, Edwin an' Morcar escaped unharmed.'

'And the men?'

'Well, there was about six thousand to start with and they reckon there was somewhere between a thousand and two thousand who made it back to York, my Lord.'

Harold's face revealed the anger and shock he felt. All they had achieved was to hold up the invaders by a few hours. The loss also raised the concern that there would be so many fewer to engage Sigurdsson when the time came.

'So York has fallen?'

'Oh yes. Once the earls were beaten, that was it. Old Sigurdsson just walked in.'

'Presumably he's still there now?'

'No, my Lord. Last I heard he'd gone back to his ships at Riccall, but he'll return to York for hostages.'

'Do you know when?'

'Tomorrow, I think.'

Harold turned to his men and ordered them to ride to York.

Just outside the city, Harold and his men passed through Fulford Gate. There were bodies everywhere; in the marsh, on the roadside and along the riverbanks where they had fallen, their weapons and valuables taken from them.

The English army rode into York and on Harold's orders, some of his housecarls raced through the streets to close the rest of the city's gates. No one was to leave town. The King was greeted with a rapturous applause. He dismounted from his horse outside the great hall and strode in, demanding to see Edwin and Morcar. A man shuffled forward, apologetically.

'I'm sorry, my Lord, the earls are elsewhere.'

'Elsewhere?'

'After the battle, some of the survivors came back here; the rest ran off, my Lord. They were afraid, you see. King Harald had won such a handsome victory so quickly and so easily; what chance did we have against him?'

'I suppose you're right. So what happened to Edwin and Morcar?'

'I'm sorry to say, when they heard Earl Tostig was looking for them, they left to join the others.'

'The others who had run away?'

'Yes, my Lord.'

'So what happened then?'

'We had a meeting with King Harald where we promised to be obedient to him, just as if he were our king. To prove we meant it, we had to hand over hostages. They're all the sons of the foremost men of the city. Earl Tostig told us himself who they were to be. We are to hand them over tomorrow at Stamford Bridge, my Lord.'

'Thank you. Who are you?'

'I'm Thored and I'm an ealdorman, my Lord.'

'Well, Thored, for the time being you're in charge here.'

'It's an honour, my Lord.'

'Arrange accommodation for my men and their horses. And arrange for a feast to be served here in the hall as soon as possible.'

'Yes, my Lord.'

'And arrange for a bigger feast for tomorrow night.'

'Tomorrow?'

'Yes. To celebrate our victory over the Norsemen.'

'Yes, my lord,' replied Thored with a smile.

STAMFORD BRIDGE

Sunrise, and the city of York stirred. Horses were saddled and chain mail byrnies donned, ready for the clash with the Norsemen. Through the streets of York the army hurried, with Harold and Gyrth at its head, old friends and comrades like Azur and Ansgar at their side. The army was twice the size that it had been when it left London. All along the Great North Road, riders had been sent out to gather volunteers; every man was needed. From towns and villages along the way, many men had joined Harold. And on this sunny morning, many volunteers from York, out for vengeance or to restore their pride, attached themselves to the King's army.

By the most direct route they headed to Stamford Bridge. With the sun beating down on his head, the creases in the back of Skalpi's neck showed white against the red- brown of his sunburn. Sweat ran down his neck, where damp hair clung to his hot skin. Sweat stained leather and cloth alike.

'Aren't you worried the men might be too tired for this, Harold?'

'We have the element of surprise, Gyrth. Sigurdsson doesn't know we're anywhere near here. By the time he realizes what's happening, it'll be too late. We have him where we want him and his forces are split. We might not get another chance.'

'Shouldn't we be more cautious? They say he is a great warrior; the Thunderbolt of the North, they call him.'

'Thunder box, more like. If Sigurdsson is such a great a warrior, why has he never beaten cousin Swein?'

'He won many battles for the Byzantines.'

'That was all years ago.'

'My lords,' it was Thored of York, accompanying them as guide, 'We are approaching Stamford Bridge.' He nodded towards the top of a ridge in front of them, beyond which the land fell away.

In the Viking camp at the side of the river, the Norsemen were in good heart, enjoying a glorious late summer's morning. The scene was bathed in a golden light that lifted the spirits. The earth was still dry and cracked, even so late in the year. Most of the men had finished breakfast and were waiting for the hostages to arrive. Some of the soldiers were playing board games, some idly chatting and exchanging banter. A small group gathered on the riverside were throwing stones at a washtub which had jammed itself in some reeds on the far riverbank, upstream from the bridge.

'King Harald, after we have the hostages, what do you intend to do?' asked Tostig, chewing on the last of his bread.

'We'll take them to Riccall, and then we'll go to London.'

'When you've ….'

'What's that,' Harald interrupted, 'on the ridge up there?'

Tostig looked across the river to the top of the valley. There on the skyline, underneath a cloud, he could see bright flashes and glints.

'Does that look like ice to you, Tostig?'

By now most of Sigurdsson's soldiers could see what their king was looking at but none could make it out.

'No, it's sunlight catching on something,' said the earl.

'It looks like ice.'

'It can't be; it's much too hot. It's metal. It's the sun catching on metal.'

'That cloud is dust. That's the dust kicked up by an army. The sun must be catching on their swords and armour. This means trouble, Tostig.'

'Well, it might be trouble but then again, it might not.'

'That's not very helpful, Tostig,' growled Sigurdsson, glaring at him.

'It might be some of my kinsmen come to welcome you. The word must be out that York fell easily into your hands; perhaps they've come seeking mercy and friendship.'

The Viking camp looked full of statues as everyone stopped and stared at the horizon; as they did so the vision on the ridge grew bigger.

'King Harald,' said Tostig, looking concerned, 'I think that's the English army. Why don't we retreat to the ships at Riccall?'

'I didn't come all this way just to run away at the first sign of trouble. We can handle this lot. What we'll do, Tostig, is send three men on our fastest horses to Riccall to fetch help. It'll be the Englishmen who'll have the biggest surprise of the day.'

'It's your decision,' Tostig said. 'I've no wish to retreat, either.'

Sigurdsson gave him a cutting look, then ordered three men to ride to Riccall and a dozen more of his finest berserkers to cross to the York side of the river to defend the bridge. While his men donned their armour, Sigurdsson planned to cross the river to pay King Harold a visit.

The horses were brought up and Tostig mounted effortlessly; Sigurdsson lost his footing in the stirrup and fell to the ground with a thud. Embarrassed but unharmed, he rose to his feet and with his second attempt climbed into the saddle. With a small troop around them, he and Tostig made their way across the bridge and rode boldly to where the English army lay poised on the ridge.

On his side of the river, Harold saw Sigurdsson fall from his horse.

'Does anyone know who that man is, the one in the blue tunic wearing the fancy helmet?

'That's Harald Sigurdsson himself,' answered the ealdorman.

'He's certainly a big man,' said Harold, 'but I don't think this'll be his lucky day.'

He then rode out in front of his army with a dozen men, close enough to the Norsemen to talk to them.

'Is Earl Tostig in your army?' he shouted across the gap.

'What if he is?' someone answered.

'I'd like to talk to him, if I may.'

'You can find him here.'

Tostig came forward; the two men confronted one another.

'Your brother sends you greetings,' Harold said, without giving away his identity. 'He offers you peace and an earldom. Rather than have you refuse and give battle, he'd make you a gift of a third of the kingdom.'

Tostig replied, 'Well, that makes a change from the trouble and disgrace of last winter. If I'd had this offer then, many a man who is now dead would be alive and England would be a better place. I thank my brother for his offer but I have a question to ask before I can accept his generosity.'

'What would that question be?'

'If I accept, what will my brother offer King Harald for all his efforts?'

'Your brother says something about that, too,' Harold replied. 'He offers him six feet of English earth, or a bit more as he is so much taller than most men.'

'Then King Harold must be ready for battle,' Tostig said. 'I can never have it said that Earl Tostig deserted his friend King Harald in the face of a fight. We shall stick together; die with honour or win England by victory.'

He turned his horse and rode away; Sigurdsson, who understood very little English but read expressions very well, followed after him.

'Who's that who spoke so boldly?' enquired Sigurdsson.

'That was my brother, Harold.'

'If I'd known, I'd have killed him on the spot.'

'I could never be the murderer of a brother who had offered me friendship and an earldom. If one of us had to die, I would prefer it if Harold killed me.'

Sigurdsson gave Tostig a sceptical look, then grunted and remarked rather patronisingly, 'King Harold stands very well in his stirrups for such a small man.'

Once they had returned to their side of the river, King Harald had his standard, the Landwaster, set up, a black raven on a red background. Tostig had his, a black leopard on a red background, placed beside it. The horses were sent packing and the King and Tostig took their places next to their banners in the centre of a circle of Norsemen, while the rest of the men struggled to dress for battle.

King Harald called out a few words to his men. 'Fight well today, men, and you will be rewarded richly: if you live, with land and gold; if you die, with a place in Valhalla.'

The English army advanced at a steady walk towards the bridge. Harald's berserkers steadied themselves.

'Let my men take the bridge, will you, Harold?' Gyrth called out. 'They're all keen to prove themselves.'

'Very well, Gyrth. Good luck.'

Gyrth gave the signal and a hundred of his housecarls broke into a steady run, moving ahead of their comrades. As they approached the bridge, they heard one of the berserkers, the biggest one standing in front of his comrades, call out, 'Good morning, Englishmen. Welcome to Stamford Bridge.'

No one replied and the battle to take the crossing began. It was a bloody affair. The Norse vanguard was there to give Sigurdsson's men time to put on their armour and to form a respectable defence. Each Viking knew from the moment he set foot on the bridge that this would be his last day on earth and by nightfall he would be feasting with the gods.

Gyrth's men, knowing this, ran screaming wildly at their foe, hoping their ferocity would see them though. It did not. In less than two minutes forty-three of them were dead, hacked and slashed to pieces, some of them cut in two by the deadly axes of the berserkers, only one of whom remained standing. He was the one who had welcomed them just a short while ago. At seven feet he towered above everyone and now, drenched in the blood shed by his double-headed axe, he looked even more formidable. No one in the English army was keen to make his acquaintance.

'What do you want to do now, Gyrth?' asked Harold.

'Get some archers and shoot him. I don't think we can afford to risk any more men.'

'We can't do that; it'll bring dishonour upon us. Let's offer him clemency.'

'Very well, then. It can't hurt.'

'Gauti!'

'Yes, my Lord.'

'Go down there and offer our warrior friend clemency. Tell him it's a mark of our admiration for his valour. Tell him he can either leave the bridge and rejoin his friends or go home. Tell him he can do whatever he likes as long as he gets out of the way and lets us pass. If he fails to comply, tell him we'll kill him.'

'Yes, my Lord.'

Gauti turned and walked down the ridge toward the berserker, who was waiting for him with a grin on his face and an axe in his hands. He wore his ginger beard and hair long and in plaits. His helmet was of blackened steel with polished brass trimmings and nose guard. Over his chain mail he wore a black leather sleeveless tunic, covered in brass studs. A giant of a man, he made an impressive sight standing amongst the dead. Everyone's eyes were on him; those that were not were on Gauti. No one noticed Bondi slip quietly away down to the riverbank.

Gauti stopped a few feet short of the berserker, well out of range of his axe. The berserker was still waiting at the end of the bridge, axe in hand, smiling.

'My king sends you a message.'

The berserker continued to smile.

'He says, as a mark of his admiration for your valour, he is willing to show clemency. You may leave the field if you choose or you may rejoin your comrades.'

The berserker remained motionless, his manic expression fixed.

'If you don't leave the bridge, you'll die.'

The berserker's grin broadened and he beckoned Gauti towards him, inviting him on to his axe.

'I take it your answer's no?'

The berserker beckoned, reaching out with his left hand, palm upward, welcoming Gauti on.

'I'll see you later,' said Gauti, taking a few paces backward before turning to walk back up the hill.

Upstream, still unseen, Bondi had climbed into an old washtub.

'What did he say?' Harold asked Gauti.

'He didn't say anything.'

'What, nothing?'

'Nothing. I think he's more interested in his place in Valhalla.'

'Send twenty men down there to deal with him, then.'

Gauti ordered twenty housecarls down to deal with the lone Viking. They made their way cautiously towards him. The English looked on. Sigurdsson's army on the other side of the bridge was still preparing itself.

The housecarls fanned out, planning to attack their foe from all sides simultaneously, but the berserker attacked them. Like a whirlwind he spun this way and that, his deadly axe finding its mark and leaving its mark with every swing. His superhuman strength and energy were too much for ordinary men, too much even for the housecarls. One after another was slain. The vicious, thin-lipped axe bit deeply into many a man, swung with such force it smashed shields and tore through byrnies as though through naked flesh. Screams echoed round the shallow valley. How the berserker enjoyed his work, playing like a puppy with a bone.

There were now only three housecarls alive and in one piece. The crazed warrior laughed again and beckoned them down for more, taking his place on the bridge as before. As they moved forward toward him, he remained perfectly still, grin fixed on face, axe in hand. He had done just what Bondi hoped he would; stood on the bridge focusing his entire attention on his enemy. As his washtub floated beneath the bridge he thrust his spear up through a gap in the planks, deep between his enemy's legs. The berserker let out an almighty scream as he was skewered and squirmed on the spear. The English army let out a cheer and Harold gave the signal to attack. The three housecarls charged forward as one and chopped up the Berserker with hefty blows from their axes.

It was not until the heat of noon that the English rushed across the bridge, in so much of a hurry to engage the Norsemen that a few of them ended up in the river, forced there by the crush. Under the Golden Dragon of Wessex and Harold's own banner, the Fighting Man, they charged straight towards Sigurdsson. Furious hand-to-hand combat followed. As housecarls led the attack, the English archers let fly a volley of arrows which crashed down into the Norse army just as the mighty warriors reached them. After the housecarls came the King's thanes and the earl's thanes and finally those ordinary, decent men of the fyrd who had been called out or volunteered on the way north. In the thick of it were Harold and his bodyguard. Outnumbered and many still without their armour, the Norwegians began to fall back but were soon surrounded, dying in their hundreds and with nowhere to go except their graves. Soon, they would dwell in Odin's great hall but for now all they could hear was the thud of sword against shield, war cries and death screams, the clash of steel against steel, axe against helmet. These were the sounds that filled the air around a riverside more used to the call of bleating lambs and birdsong. All the while the grass turned red.

After an hour of bloody fighting, Sigurdsson's shield wall was breached and Gauti led a wedge of housecarls through the gap, isolating a group of about six hundred.

'Take that lot, Gyrth,' yelled Harold, as he used his axe to clear a way toward Sigurdsson and Tostig.

Sigurdsson was enraged and attempted to lead a counter-attack to save his beleaguered forces but a keen eyed English archer shot him in the throat. Clutching the arrow, the Norse king fell to the ground. Desperately he tried to struggle to his feet to continue the fight but soon realized the futility of his actions. Resigning himself to his fate, he stayed on his knees, a wide-eyed, pale-faced miniature of himself. Around him the battle ceased as two armies, aware of the forthcoming demise of a great leader, waited to see what would happen next.

Sigurdsson beckoned his scribe to come closer.

'Remember this, my last great poem,' spluttered the dying king.

'Yes, my Lord.'

We march forward in battle array without our corselets to meet the dark blades.

Helmets shine but I have not mine,
For now our armour lies down on the ships.'

Sigurdsson looked to his scribe for approval. The scribe looked blank. 'You're right, that was a bad poem,' he croaked with a strained voice. 'That'll never inspire the men. Try this.

We do not creep in battle under the shelter of shields before the crash of weapons;
This is what the loyal goddess of the hawks had commanded us.
The bearer of the necklace told me long ago
To hold the prop of the helmet high in the din of weapons
When the Valkyrie's ice met the skulls of men.'

'That was excellent, my Lord.'

Before the scribe had finished his reply, Harald Sigurdsson, the last great Viking warrior king, fell dead. An awed silence fell over the battlefield.

Without their leader, the Norsemen were at a loss as to what to do. While they hesitated, Harold stepped up to his standard. Seizing the opportunity to avoid further loss of life he addressed the Norsemen in their own language.

'Listen, all of you. You have fought bravely here today and brought honour on yourselves and your king. It will never be said that any of you is anything less than a hero. But your king, Harald, is dead and his dreams have died with him.

'You have done for him everything that any king would hope for from loyal followers but for you, the fight is lost. So I say to you, leave the field with honour, for there's nothing for you to gain here this day.'

'Only if we lose!' yelled Tostig, standing proudly, waving the Landwaster defiantly. 'You know it's you who's beaten, Harold. As I speak, men are rushing to our aid. So why don't you leave the field, or would you rather spend an eternity here, buried beneath the grass?'

Tostig's men roared their defiance and the Norwegians joined in support. Every man prepared to fight to the death. Tostig saw the Crown of England within his reach, never to be so close again.

'So be it, Tostig. But remember, it was you who offered up these men's lives to satisfy your own vanity and selfish ambition.'

'Harsh words for someone prepared to see his own brother live in exile if it meant he could wear a crown; a crown that is rightfully mine.'

'You can't believe that.'

'It won't be your crown much longer. Enjoy it while you may. Let battle commence!'

A roar went up from Tostig's supporters.

Harold raised his axe high in the air for all to see. On the signal, they charged on the group of men who had surrounded their dead king's body.

As Sigurdsson had done just a few days before, the English did now with equal skill. Housecarls and thanes forced the Norwegians back towards the river. Desperate, the Norsemen tried to force their way back to the bridge; it was their only means of escape. During fighting that was bloodier than ever, the Viking army lost nearly all of its men to the blade or the water but they made the English pay a high price for their victory.

Falling back on the bridge, the Norwegian survivors put up a gallant defence; their leaders stayed in the thick of it even when they knew they would surely die. And die they did. Gyrth hacked down Tostig. The brothers fought with such passion, such fury, they were blinded. Not until the fatal blow was struck did Gyrth recognize his own brother. Not until the ice-cold instant before death did Tostig recognise his slayer.

In Wilton, in the nunnery where Queen Edith now lived, as she walked along a corridor, she felt a pain in her heart in the same instant that Tostig fell to the ground.

There were few Vikings left to fight now, so few that many a man on the English side sat down to rest in whatever shade he could find out of the heat of the sun. Content to let the remnants of the Norse army escape across the bridge, Harold gave the order to his men to stand down and take a rest. As the last of the Vikings made their way up the side of the valley, those of Harold's men who were still fighting broke off to recover, wherever they could find a welcoming place. Now in complete possession of the battlefield, the English relaxed.

'I'm sorry, Harold,' said Gyrth, looking down at Tostig's corpse. 'I didn't even know it was him until I'd dealt the final blow.'

Harold looked down at his dead brother; there was a deep wound from his neck down to his chest, where Gyrth's axe had struck, chopping him almost in half.

'Would it have made any difference?'

'I don't know, but it feels like I've committed a dreadful sin.'

'It was his choice, Gyrth. What alternative did you have? You were fighting for your king and country. You were defending yourself and your lord.'

'I know, but ...'

The conversation was interrupted by war cries. From behind them, Eystein Orri was leading a charge of the Norsemen, just arrived from Riccall.

As soon as Sigurdsson's message had arrived from Stamford Bridge, Eystein Orri had given the order to his troops to don their chain mail coats. In the sweltering afternoon sun he marched his men at the double to Sigurdsson's aid. It took them over three hours to cover the distance. His men arrived exhausted, only to discover they were too late to help their king but not too late to avenge him. Even though they were tired to the point of exhaustion from the long march and the sweltering heat, the Norsemen launched their fearsome charge, catching the English by surprise.

'Form the shield wall!' bellowed Harold to his troops.

He need not have bothered; even as he shouted the command, housecarls were taking their positions.

The initial attack almost succeeded in breaking Harold's men but the English stood firm and the line held. After that, the dreadful battle continued until late afternoon, by which time Eystein Orri and his commanders were all dead. The several hundred Vikings left on the field, realising they had nothing left to fight for, began to break away and run for their ships at Riccall.

'Gauti! Take the housecarls. Follow them; hunt them down. I'll go with the rest of the men for the horses.'

'Yes, my Lord.'

As the housecarls chased the remnants of Sigurdsson's army one way, Harold, accompanied by Gyrth, his thanes and the volunteers raced back for their horses. Within fifteen minutes they had caught up with Gauti and the rest of the housecarls. All along the way a trail of dead bodies lay.

'We'll take over now, Gauti. Go back for your horses. We'll finish off the rest. Take your time. We'll see you at Riccall.'

'Very well, my Lord.'

'And Gauti ...'

'Yes, my Lord.'

'Well done. This has been a fine day's work.'

The English army, once mounted, pursued the Norsemen without mercy, ruthlessly cutting down any stragglers they encountered. By the time Harold arrived at Riccall, Gauti and the housecarls had rejoined him. As the sun set at the river junction, they found a panicked Viking army trying to make off in their longships. Half a dozen were moving quickly and quietly down river. Tired men, made strong by fear, pulled heavily on the oars.

'Fire the ships,' called out Harold.

Just as soon as they were ready, flaming arrows shot through the twilight air. First one ship, then another was consumed by fire.

As Skalpi and Gauti raced toward one of the stricken ships, Gauti was shot in the arm with an arrow. It struck high, almost in the shoulder and although his byrnie absorbed a lot of the force, the arrow had still penetrated an inch or two into him. It was enough to make him yell in pain and fall to his knees. Skalpi looked up to see a golden-haired youth staring down at him from the deck of the ship. He looked as fierce as the dragonhead prow of the ship.

'Keep away or I'll kill you all!'

'You can't take us all on, lad.'

'That's what you think. Come up here and get me if you dare.'

'All right, I will.'

Skalpi glanced around and called some men to him, keeping an eye on the Viking archer all the time.

'Spread out and on my command, rush him.'

The archer fired off another arrow, which harmed no one. Skalpi gave the command and the housecarls rushed the ship; he arrived on the deck to find a dozen men standing around the archer, who was leaning back against the prow, his eyes filled with tears.

'What is it?'

'Look,' said Whitgar, son of Guthrum, who had so recently entertained Harold and Aldytha when they had needed shelter from the rain. Whitgar nodded down to the youth's feet. They had been cut off.

'What happened?' Skalpi asked the youth.

'They left me to guard the ship and to keep you away long enough for them to escape. They chopped my feet off to stop me running away.'

'Jesus Christ.'

'Won't you help me?'

'What do you want us to do?'

'Finish me off quickly. Do it, please. Just let me die with a sword in my hand. I won't give you any more trouble, I promise you. I just want it over with.'

Skalpi looked from one man to the next; none of them looked keen to be the executioner.

'Come on, one of us ought to put him out of his misery.'

Skalpi looked at the young thane's sword. It was still unbloodied.

Noticing the glance from Skalpi and anticipating the housecarl's next question, he responded with a simple, 'I'll do it.'

'Good. Then you'll have drawn blood.'

'No, I forbid it.' It was Guthrum, the young thane's father.

'Why?'

'He should kill his first man in battle. There's no honour in this.'

'There's no honour, father, I'll grant you, but at least I'll draw blood.'

'Will you lot just get on with it?' cried the wounded warrior.

'I'll do it now,' said Whitgar.

'Very well,' his father replied.

The Viking turned on his knees, falling on all fours, his hair falling over his face.

'Don't cut off my hair,' he pleaded, pulling the golden locks off his neck.

'Why are you bothering with your hair at a time like this?' asked Whitgar, baffled.

'Just don't cut it off.'

'I'll hold it out of the way,' volunteered Guthrum.

The old thane gathered up the Viking's hair and pulled it up over the youth's head, away from where his son's sword would strike.

Now the business was at hand, Whitgar looked pale; he shook like a leaf from head to foot. The young Viking on the deck was mumbling frantically. Whitgar raised the sword in his trembling hands and took aim at the warrior's neck. He guessed they were the same age. Gathering his strength he brought his sword down, closing his eyes as he did so. There was a deafening scream as the sword struck. It continued even as Whitgar's sword rested with its point on the deck. Something was horribly wrong; he could still hear the Viking talking. He opened his eyes, expecting to see the decapitated head of the Norseman cursing him as it rolled on the deck but what he saw was much worse. His father writhed in agony; it was he who was screaming as he stared in horror at the stumps of his arms where his hands used to be.

There was commotion all around as the housecarls tried to deal with Guthrum. The Viking was moaning and begging to be dispatched into the next world. Skalpi brought his axe down with a well-aimed blow, sending the young man on his way. When his head came to rest on the deck, a lock of golden hair floated down beside it.

Skalpi looked around to see Bondi and some others racing toward a burning ship. When they got there all Skalpi could see was a silhouette reaching for a burning piece of wood before racing back to put it to Guthrum's stumps, sealing his wounds forever.

The young Viking was the last man to die at Riccall. Once he realised fighting was futile, the fifteen-year-old Olaf Haraldson, who was now in command of what was left of the Norwegian army, begged for terms. Harold, aware that the Norsemen no longer posed a threat, allowed Olaf to depart in peace with what ships he would need for the journey. In his turn Olaf promised that Norsemen would never again set foot uninvited on English soil. He sailed home with his men. They had needed three hundred and thirty ships for the outward journey; they were sailing home in twenty-four.

Harold and Gyrth, mounted on their horses, watched them leave.

After the battle, many of those who made it back to York were content to sleep, preferring to postpone celebrations until the following night when the stragglers and the wounded would join them. Tostig's body had been brought back from the battlefield for burial the next morning in the grounds of York Minster.

The following evening, Harold sat at the high table with his brother Gyrth, Ealdred, Archbishop of York, Merleswein, Sheriff of Lincoln, Azur and Ansgar. Once they had heard York was safe, Edwin and Morcar arrived to join in the celebrations. A guard announced their arrival.

'Won't you join us?' welcomed Harold, in a tone a little less than civil.

'Thank you, brother,' they replied in unison.

Harold asked people to make room for them on the benches.

'Are we not to sit on the top table?' asked Morcar.

'As you can see, the dais is crowded and there's no room. We are celebrating our victory over the Norseman; the top table is for the heroes of Stamford Bridge.'

'We ran them a decent fight at Fulford Gate,' replied Morcar. He was feeling most indignant now.

'Against my orders, you took them on in a head-on clash, lost most of your men then surrendered York.'

'We didn't surrender York.'

'So you weren't even here for the surrender. Where were you, exactly? And come to think of it, where have you been since?'

'We had to tend to our wounds.'

'I see no wounds.'

'I meant the wounds of our men,' replied Morcar, rather feebly.

'Why weren't you and those of your men who weren't wounded with us at Stamford Bridge?'

'We had other things to do.'

'Other things to do? What, exactly?'

Morcar was suffering acute embarrassment. He could make no convincing account of his whereabouts. He remained in a sullen silence. His brother came to his rescue.

'It's as we said; we had the wounded to treat.'

'I am your lord and you will address me as such.'

'We had the wounded to treat, my Lord.'

'That's not your job. Your duty is to protect your people. I didn't see you at Stamford Bridge and in the morning we will meet and you will tell my why. Until then, you will sit down on the bench there and enjoy our hospitality or you may leave.'

Edwin wondered glumly at his future. Looking about the hall, he could see heads together talking in whispers; the odd glance shot his way. He knew very well what they were saying; if he and Morcar could not defend them, what were they doing here? Harold's arrival had been warmly welcomed, so he understood. He also knew Harold's standing in the North was now higher than that of any English king, including even the great Athelstan. If he and Morcar were to maintain their positions in Mercia and Northumbria, they would have to think of something to rescue their reputations very quickly. While Edwin sat and dwelt on matters, the hall rang with celebration. As the feast livened up and soldiers boasted of their exploits, Harold and Gyrth talked quietly at the high table.

'What are you going to do about Edwin and Morcar, Harold?'

'Nothing, for the time being.'

'But they're a liability.'

'I think even they might realise that.'

'So what are you going to do?'

'For the time being, nothing; there's still the threat from William to consider.'

'He won't invade now, surely.'

'For all we know, he still has his fleet gathered on the other side of the Channel.'

'You're right there. He must know Sigurdsson invaded and if he doesn't, he soon will.'

'Now is the perfect time, in some ways.'

'The Channel is too unpredictable, though. Would you take an army across the sea at this time of year?'

'No, but I'm not William. I'm uneasy about this, Gyrth; William has no option but to invade. It's highly unlikely he'd be able to reform his army next spring and there's no chance of his ships still being serviceable after the winter.'

'Do you think he was waiting for Sigurdsson to attack?'

'It clears the way very nicely for him. Whoever won the battle would have depleted forces. If William lands on the south coast and bides his time, the victor will have to go to him.'

'Perhaps we ought to get back to London as soon as possible.'

'We'll have to stay here for a few days to celebrate while the men and the horses recover.'

'So, what about Edwin and Morcar?'

'I thought they could stay here for the moment. I don't think the time is right to deal with them just yet.'

'You trust them, then?'

'Well, they can't do too much harm up here. I thought I'd leave Merleswein here to keep an eye on them and if William tries his luck they can come down and give us a hand. It's the least they can do after Fulford Gate.'

Harold announced his intention to cut short his stay in York on Thursday evening in the crowded great hall.

'Men, I have something to tell you all. We have taught the Norsemen a lesson they will never forget. We need never fear them again.'

A cheer went up from the assembly.

'Although we need no longer fear the Norsemen, we still have an enemy who even now may be preparing to launch an assault against us.'

A murmur ran through the hall.

'In order that we are ready to respond to any attack, I shall return with my housecarls to London tomorrow. Those of you who joined me on the march north are welcome to accompany me on my journey south. Any of you who choose are welcome to come with me to London, where you will be accommodated at my expense, until the threat of invasion is over.

'As we must make all possible haste, there's no time to distribute any of the plunder captured from the Norwegians. All the plunder so far gained will be entrusted to the care of Archbishop Ealdred, until such time as our gains can be divided. And let me assure you, all the heroes of Stamford Bridge will have their fair share of the spoils.'

Another murmur ran through the hall, this time one of dissent.

'In my absence I will leave Merleswein, the Sheriff of Lincoln, to organize things. Follow Merleswein's instructions; he has my authority in everything he does.'

Edwin and Morcar exchanged glances. They would have words with the King later.

'For the time being I suggest you continue to enjoy the celebrations.'

As Harold sat down, the din of hundreds of men exchanging their opinions filled the room as each and every one discussed the King's speech with his companions.

'Edwin and Morcar don't look too happy,' remarked Gyrth. 'Are you sure it was wise to leave Merleswein in charge?'

'Well, I can trust him to hold the North and send men south if need be.'

'So you don't trust Edwin and Morcar?'

'After Fulford Gate, would you?'

'D'you think there's more going on up here than meets the eye?'

'What, are they separatists, you mean?'

'They might want to keep the North as a separate kingdom, while William has the South?'

'Yes. It's not beyond the realms of reason.'

'If William attacks in the South, do you think you can rely on them for assistance?'

'I'm really not sure, but their sister is queen and a baby is on the way. They won't do any better than have a nephew as King of England.'

'Perhaps they'd rather be kings of Northumbria and Mercia?'

'It's all a bit fanciful but they are young and headstrong.'

'So they are unreliable?'

'Not completely. They made a mistake at Fulford but they might have learned from it.'

'Well, if William turns up we'll find out.'

Just feet away, at another table, talking under their breath, sat Edwin and Morcar.

'What do you think he means by it?' asked Morcar. 'Is he leaving Merleswein in charge because he doesn't trust us?'

'Do you think he'll try to get rid of us entirely, like he did with our dad?'

'Who knows? Who would trust a Godwinson?'

'He dealt with Tostig when he had to.'

'I heard at Stamford Bridge he promised him his earldom back if he changed sides.'

'Do you think he would have? Given him the earldom back, I mean?'

'I don't know but what I do know is this, either way he can't be trusted.'

'But now he's married to our Aldytha, we're all kin.'

'I still don't trust him,' replied Edwin, cutting savagely into a piece of meat.

'But his son will be our nephew. There won't ever have been a king with such strong support.'

'Assuming he lives to wear the Crown. An accident could easily be arranged, I'm sure. Aldytha could be walking along by the Thames one day with the little one and before you know it they've slipped into the river and that's the end of them. And they'd get away with it too. Look at Cospatric; no one ever got to the bottom of what happened to him.'

'But that wasn't Harold. It was Tostig and that bitch of a sister of his.'

'That's right, but look at it this way; Harold has half a dozen brats with Edyth Swan-neck. It's only natural for them to think they're going to inherit the Crown; it's only natural for Harold to want them to rule after him; if he had us removed from power and put his sons in our place, and if our sister and her baby met with an accident, his family would be stronger than ever.'

'When you put it like that it seems so obvious. What are we going to do?'

'We'd better think of something fast.'

The next day, shortly after a cold dawn, Harold left York with Gyrth and all of their housecarls fit enough to travel, together with several hundred followers keen to see London. They made their way south at an easy pace so as to spare the horses, still weary from the outward journey.

Making their way down Ermine Street, which cut straight through freshly ploughed fields, the army enjoyed the warm autumn sunshine and the weary soldiers took time to enjoy their journey. Gold-tinged trees stood scattered around the countryside, early heralds of the autumn grandeur to follow, the hawthorn a blaze of colour. And overhead, like them, birds were heading south for the winter.

The journey was uneventful until the end of the third day, when a rider was seen fast approaching. As he came closer, the rider looked more and more familiar to Harold, until to his amazement, he at last recognized him as his son, Ulf.

PONTHIEU

Outside Duke William's tent a war council gathered. The Normans and their allies had lingered at St Valery for more than two weeks, waiting for the word from the Duke to set sail.

'It's almost the end of September, my Lord,' said Odo. 'What are we to do?'

'I still have no news of Sigurdsson.'

Odo continued, 'Count Guy can't support us much longer. We either go to England soon or we pack up and head for home.'

William glared at Count Guy. 'Is this true?'

Count Guy was desperate to be rid of his guests. 'I'm afraid so, my Lord. The barns are empty.'

'God's Face!' snapped William. He took a moment to pause for thought. 'Gentlemen, I had hoped we would know the outcome of the battle between Earl Harold and the Norwegian king before we sailed for England. The men think we wait on a southerly wind, one that looks as if it will blow from that direction long enough for us to cross the Channel safely. I don't want to tell them we've been hanging around here waiting to see what someone else does. It looks hesitant and indecisive. We must do something more.'

Odo was the only one who dared respond. 'Perhaps if we all prayed together.'

'Make a show, you mean so the troops can see we're trying everything.'

'That kind of thing, yes.'

The Duke cast his eyes heavenwards as if in resignation but it was inspiration that struck him that day.

'Get down to the Abbey, Odo. Tell the parish priest to remove St Valery's remains and have them carried down to the flats by the river. Have them placed on a carpet or something. I'll muster the men and have them gather round.'

'When do you want to do this?'

'Now! Do we have time to waste?'

Two hours later, William's army was assembled in unit formations and a special service began. The army knelt around St. Valery's casket with Duke William and his brother Odo at the centre, on their knees, offering up prayers for a change of wind. Odo led the congregation. Once he had finished, William rose to his feet and indicated to Odo to have the venerable saint's casket returned to its shrine but only after every single one of his troops had filed past. The soldiers, as they passed the casket, had to make an offering, no matter how humble, to the saint. Ralph Pomeroy, who had survived the storm, cast a worthless foreign coin in with the others. He even begrudged that. It took until evening for all the soldiers to pass and make their donations but it lifted morale.

The following day, while Harold celebrated his victory in York, the Normans' prayers were answered. After enduring a cold, sleepless night, William ventured outside his tent. He was greeted by a beautiful golden autumn morning, the air bright, cold and clear but not quite still. He could feel the warmth of the sun on his face. A thrill of excitement ran through him. He looked at the weather vane; the wind was from the south.

'Muster the men!' he bellowed. 'Muster the men!'

Trumpets sounded, prompting sleepy-eyed barons to emerge from their tents to find the Duke snapping out orders this way and that. There was a rush as men, half asleep, hurried to carry out their duties. As at Dives, each man presented himself at his appointed ship and boarded. There were enough provisions for the crossing and that would be all. The next time they ate, they were told, it would be English food, captured in England.

It was early evening when William's ship left the harbour at the head of his forces, its dragon head facing England. At the stern a gilded boy blowing an ivory horn looked down on them. Following the *Mora* the way ducks follow their mother, in the deepening twilight six hundred and ninety six ships made their way out of the Somme estuary towards England.

On the *Mora*, William, sitting in the shadow of his ship's red-and-yellow-striped sail, spoke to his brother Robert. The oarsmen, all twenty of them, sat scattered around the deck enjoying the last of the day's sun. Matilda had taken the precaution of having the boat fitted out for oarsmen, the only vessel in William's fleet to carry them, just in case he needed to escape from the invasion beach in a hurry. But the *Mora*, even without the use of its oars, moved faster than any other ship in the fleet.

'Didn't I tell you we could do it? Didn't I?'

'You did, William,' answered Robert. 'You did. There's no arguing with that.'

'In the morning we will land unopposed on English soil. Mark my words.'

'You seem very sure, brother.'

'I am. The English will be too busy dealing with the Norwegians.'

'Well, we must trust that whoever wins the battle has little left of their army.'

'Just think, Robert, if the weather holds good for just twelve hours, England will be ours.'

As long as we don't meet the English navy or get caught in another storm, thought the Duke's companions.

At nightfall, a lantern was attached to the top of the mast so the other ships could follow their leader. Under cover of darkness the Normans crossed the Channel, the hunter creeping up on its prey while it slept. In the morning they would give the English a rude awakening.

Three hours after sunset the crescent moon sank below the horizon, leaving them in an iron-cold darkness. William's captain sailed by the stars; his followers steered towards the lantern. There were no storms to push him off course but the constant pitching and rolling of the ship was again making him feel ill. And the cold, the bone-chilling cold, bothered him too. The constant spray from the bow seemed to penetrate every layer of his clothing. He sat on deck near the helm by Airard, his back against the prow, the horn-playing boy looking beyond him, further than any human eye could see. William sat propped up there all night, only stirring to throw up over the side.

It was the warm morning sun on his face that woke him; that and the sounds of activity on deck.

'Good morning,' he called to his comrades, over the sound of the gulls, the sea lapping the ship's sides and the gentle wind slapping the sail.

'Good morning,' echoed the replies.

'She's a fine craft, the Mora, isn't she?' the Duke said to no one in particular.

'Very fine, my Lord,' replied Odo, with some obvious discomfort.

'I see you're feeling seasick too.'

'It's not that, my Lord. It's just that I feel a little uneasy.'

'Why do you feel uneasy? It's not like you.'

'It's the fleet.'

'What about the fleet?'

'Where is it?'

William looked around, this way then that. There was not a ship in sight, nothing in any direction. Everywhere were dark green-grey waves, each one identical to the other, but no land in sight. He could detect a look of mild panic behind the mask of calm, yet the oarsmen seemed genuinely unperturbed. Filled with foreboding, William looked to Airard for some assurance.

'Captain, I wonder, do you have any idea where the rest of the fleet might be?'

'Don't worry, my Lord. The *Mora*'s so fast the rest can't keep up with her.'

'Well, can't we wait for them?'

'If you like, my Lord.'

So FitzStephen gave the orders. The sail was lowered, the anchor was cast and the *Mora* simply bobbed about on the waves. An eerie gloom settled over the ship. William looked around to see everyone aboard scanning the horizon for their comrades. After half an hour there was still no sign and William's comrades grew more apprehensive. The Duke found a way to distract them.

'Why are we wasting time standing around gawping at the sea when we could be enjoying a fine breakfast?' His comrades turned to face him as if in shock. He then called out to his servants to fetch him something to eat.

'Which of you men will join me?'

'I will,' responded Robert, enthusiastically.

'And I,' replied Odo.

'Me too,' added FitzOsbern. Everyone else resumed scanning the horizon.

Food was laid out and the Duke called for spiced wine. He and his comrades tucked in heartily. Their stomachs were empty; wine and the salt air had combined to make them all ravenous. The oarsmen ate the breakfasts they had brought with them, just some bread and cheese. William and his brothers, even while they devoured their food, still stared at the vast, empty horizon, quaking in their boots.

Turning to the nearest oarsman, William commanded him to climb the mast for a better view.

'Well. Can you see anything?'

'No, my Lord, nothing,' cried the man.

The Duke concealed his disappointment well.

'You'd better come down, then. Have a look a little later when I'm sure you will have some better news for us.

Slowly the man descended while the Duke, his two brothers and FitzOsbern continued making a show of enjoying their breakfast. Fifteen minutes later the oarsman was ordered to climb the mast again.

'Well, can you see anything this time?'

The oarsman peered into the distance for a short while.

'Ships! Ships!' he cried.

'How many?'

'Four, my Lord. And they're heading this way.'

'Good. You see,' he announced to the crew, 'they're all as keen to get to England as we are. It's just that they're not so swift.'

But four ships are, after all, just four ships and a little while later, to reassure his men, he once more sent the oarsman to the top of the mast.

'And what, my friend, do you see now?'

'Masts, my Lord. Many masts.'

'How many masts?'

'Too many to count, my Lord. It's like a wood, no, a forest of masts. There are hundreds of them.'

'Good,' said William with obvious relief. 'This evening we'll celebrate a successful crossing by drinking English beer.'

Eventually England appeared on the horizon, its white cliffs growing gradually taller. FitzStephen could make out Beachy Head and set his course further to the east in the hope of landing at Hastings. Soon it became apparent to him that they would miss their destination.

'We will have to land at Pevensey, my Lord.'

'Why can't we sail into Hastings?'

'Because the wind isn't blowing that way and we have to make land before the tide changes or we'll be floating off the coast all day. Pevensey is our best chance.'

'Pevensey it is, then.'

'Very well, my Lord.'

Between the coast and the Norman fleet, unnoticed by anyone, was a little fishing boat. Its owner had set out early in the hope of bringing in a good catch. Its small crew of three were busying themselves sorting out the net before casting. The boat's owner and father of the two other men cast a glance to the horizon. No matter how close to shore he was, he always kept a weather eye open. It was he who noticed them first, moving at speed towards him. There, coming over the horizon, were ships, more than he had ever seen in his life, more even than the King had when he guarded the coast over the summer.

Seeing their father motionless, staring out to sea with his jaw dropped open, the sons followed their father's gaze. The sight was awesome; ship after ship after ship disappearing into the distance, covering the sea like scum. As the fleet grew closer, they could make out brightly coloured sails and the grotesque dragonhead prows of war ships. Death was in the air. As one, the crew sprang to life; the little fishing boat turned sail and headed swiftly for port. They reached Pevensey ahead of the invaders to discover the town quite empty. Not even a dog lay sunning itself. They ran inland as fast as they could, praying that someone had sent word to the King. They need not have worried; a rider was already galloping toward London.

If they had stayed to watch the landing, the fishermen might have found their hearts filled with confidence rather than fear. The disembarkation was a shambles, even though the long, flat shingle beach was ideal for the landing force. William, on the *Mora*, sailed boldly into Pevensey harbour. The old, fortified Roman harbour would make an ideal base. Surrounded by a half-mile long wall was a network of docks, only recently vacated by ships of the English navy. A few unmanned merchant ships were tied to the quays; their crews vanished with the rest of the town. But the bulk of William's force crashed in with the waves onto the shingle.

Soldiers, some with green faces, many still feeling sick from the voyage, hurled themselves over the sides of their craft, staggering to shore, glad to be on land. One or two ships came in sideways, depositing their passengers and cargo into the shallow water of the shore. There was chaos and confusion as horses escaped the torment of the waves. Kicking, rearing and bolting in all directions, they too had been affected by the constant billow and roll of the crossing.

From one ship a group of archers crept, bows drawn ready to fire on any Englishmen who might spring forth in a surprise attack. From the next, a group of infantry was hurriedly unloading amour and weapons, well prepared for any danger there might be. It was they who spotted the Duke land ashore.

Stepping off the *Mora*, William walked like a drunk along the quay, the journey and the spiced wine making their effects known. No sooner did he step off the quay and onto English soil than he tripped, falling spread eagle to the ground with a thud and a groan. This was an ill omen. Ever the quick thinker, he instantly turned the accident to his advantage. As he lay stretched out he clawed up a handful of soil and shouted out, 'By the splendour of the Almighty, I have seized my kingdom; the soil of England is in my own two hands!'

A cheer rose up from the men, who watched as he rose histrionically to his feet, with a broad smile forced onto his red face, two handfuls of soil held above his head.

When all the ships were unloaded the masts were lowered and laid out along the decks to make the craft more stable on the beach. By midday Pevensey's barns and stores had been emptied to provide food for the troops, enough to feed them for a couple of days at least. As they had brought nothing with them they would have to raid the surrounding countryside.

Gathered around the port reeve's table that afternoon, William and his captains made plans for the following day.

'So far, gentlemen, providence has been kind to us; out of six-hundred and ninety-six ships that left St Valery we have lost only two. Now we must press on to Hastings. We can't stay here; it's far too stony for the horses and besides, the only decent road out of here leads not to London but to somewhere called Lewes. Tomorrow we'll make our way along the coast, where I am assured the country is more suitable for our needs and where friends are waiting to offer their assistance.

'Any questions?'

Warenne spoke. 'May I ask when we march on London, my Lord?'

'Marching on London is another matter. We will stay in Hastings until we discover who has won the battle in the North. If Sigurdsson is the victor, we'll march on London; they'll probably be glad to see us. It must be bad enough having Harold for a king but even he is preferable to those pagan dogs from the North. And if Harold is the victor, we'll stay until he comes for us.'

'How do you know he'll come for us?'

'Because,' answered William, with a certain smugness, 'it's in his nature to respond directly; he's a man of action. Besides, this is Wessex. Harold has many a private estate within easy reach and he must protect his people. Are there any more questions?'

This time there was no response.

SUSSEX

At dawn the Normans broke camp and started their journey east. The army divided in two as it left Pevensey, the infantry following the coast and the horsemen journeying further inland. Every encounter with the invaders brought the locals the same misery. Adults were tortured, raped and killed and their children impaled alive; every village was razed to the ground, bodies left where they fell.

The Norman infantrymen completely destroyed Bexhill. The good folk there were given no warning and shown no quarter. Years later, the only sign of the town's existence were piles of blackened beams lying at grotesque angles by the side of the road.

After destroying Bexhill, the infantry column continued its march, sweeping down on Crowhurst, Wilting and Filsham. The result was the same; mayhem and murder. The animals were driven off to Hastings to die at a butcher's hands.

Travelling inland with the chevaliers, led by Sir William Warenne and Robert Montgomery, was Ralph Pomeroy, feeling much better now he had recovered from the crossing. His stomach was full and he was enjoying the camaraderie of his countrymen. Burning down villages had put him in a good mood. They would destroy one more today before heading to Hastings for the night. Warenne and Montgomerie had it on good authority a village called Whatlington belonged to King Harold, so Duke William insisted on its total destruction. As a way of testing Sir William Malet's loyalty, the Duke ordered him to accompany two of his most ardent supporters. The Normans' first sight of their objective was the little church of St Mary Magdalene on their right. As they grew closer they saw an isolated cottage on their left. Sir William Warenne ordered some of the men to investigate. Within minutes the cottage was ablaze. Villagers working in the surrounding fields came running to help. Their neighbourliness was to prove fatal. The few that survived the immediate onslaught were pursued across a field into an alder wood. They were never seen again.

Montgomerie ordered Pomeroy to deal with St Mary's. With half a dozen men he approached the church where they dismounted and tied their horses to a yew tree before entering. Once inside they found Father Aethelweard, busy in conversation with one of his parishioners. The old priest was surprised to see armed men enter his church. The leader appeared to be a down-at-heel thane and as they approached him he caught a look in their eyes that he found disturbing. Perhaps they were King Harold's men come with some terrible news.

Pomeroy drew his knife and levelled it in line with one of Aethelweard's eyes, casually backing him against a wall, the priest protesting all the while. When the old man stopped, with nowhere left to go, Pomeroy continued an extra step until he felt his knife slice through the priest's brain and stop when it made contact with the inside of the old man's skull. Aethelweard was dead before he hit the ground. His parishioner fell beside him, screaming, disembowelled by one of Pomeroy's men. Pomeroy watched the man for a few moments as he writhed on the floor before ordering his men to take whatever valuables they could find. As they set about their task, Pomeroy watched the life slip away from the villager. Looking up he noticed the light shining down from above, through the two triangular windows in the tower. He had no idea why, but he felt a moment's discomfort.

'My Lord?' It was an infantryman.

'Yes,' replied Pomeroy.

'We've got everything we could find.'

'Good. Put a torch to this heathen temple, then.'

'Pleasure, my Lord.'

The men went outside, filled their saddlebags with stolen goods and then returned to set about burning the building.

As he left St. Mary's, the sound of shouting and screaming greeted Pomeroy's ears. Looking down Whatlington's main street he noticed all the cottages were on his side of the road; on the other side ran a small river, little more than a stream. His eye followed the river to a water mill at the end of the village on the other side of the road. It was the last building in the village except for a little stone bridge. Two soldiers had just cut a youth down in the street. Leaving him for dead they hurried into the mill. Too busy with their own tasks, no one else paid any attention to the scene.

Pomeroy unhitched his horse from the yew tree, climbed into the saddle and made his way along the street at a canter. Arriving at the mill he heard a rumpus from inside. His curiosity roused, he dismounted and entered the darkness of the building, which was illuminated only by golden shafts of autumn sunlight shining through windows and doors; dust mites and specks of flour circled idly in the air. Now that he was inside, all that Pomeroy could hear was the grinding rhythm of the mill's cogged wheels as they gnashed together; the sound of the millstone as it ground down seed and the ceaseless babble of the water as it flowed across the millrace towards the sea.

From somewhere above, the giggling laughter of a baby caught his attention. He felt excitement rise up within as he made his way up a ladder to the next floor. There he discovered a young mother clutching her baby, as she dodged round sacks of flour, attempting to escape from two men who were intent on ravishing her. Her infant thought it a game.

She saw Pomeroy enter the room like an apparition materialising in the air. He stood silent before her. The two men who recognised him froze as if unsure what to do. They looked to him for orders.

Pomeroy observed the scene for a moment. This part of the mill was brighter than the ground floor but the spokes of the mill wheel turning outside constantly broke the shafts of light. The room changed from bright to gloom from moment to moment. Like the soldiers, the young woman remained motionless holding her baby. Pomeroy thought that by the look of it, he was a boy. The infant was still giggling, still enjoying the game. He had a smile across his little pink face and when the light struck it, his fine, blond, curly hair glistened like gold.

The woman, whose name was Aelfryth, looked to the newcomer for protection; perhaps he would save her? Pomeroy smiled and stepped forward towards Aelfryth; he held out a hand of friendship. Briefly she felt relief but as he smiled more broadly she was no longer reassured. Something in the eyes gave him away; she felt in terrible danger. Her baby began to cry. Now she realised her mistake; she had let him get too close. There was nowhere to run as all three soldiers made for her. As the two men grabbed her arms, Pomeroy pulled the baby from her. In a couple of strides he was at the open window, the shadow of the millwheel flickering across his features. A lascivious grin spread across his face as he held the baby a little way back from the window. He looked Aelfryth up and down and nodded to the two soldiers who ripped off her clothes. To protect her distressed infant she made no attempt to stop them. Pomeroy thought it was something in her that would make him do it but as he gazed at her face he realized it was something in him, something that he had felt before and it was here again, with him now in the mill; a strange power that filled him, overtook him. A daemon, as it had so often done before, had possession of his soul. So when Aelfryth was naked he laughed and threw her tiny son out of the window. The little boy's crying stopped abruptly.

Aelfryth wailed the pain of deepest misery, her love, her heart destroyed. She gasped in horror as Pomeroy turned his attention to her. In her ears she could hear the laughter of his comrades.

As he grew closer, the deep reddish brown of her nipples against the white skin of her milk-filled breasts, drew Pomeroy's attention. Terror was now shuddering uncontrollably through her body. Aelfryth felt powerless. Pomeroy stood before her feeling as potent as a god but really much less than that; he was capable of nothing but destruction. He looked her in the eyes and smiled again. She knew instantly he was the kind of man who loved other people's fear. He lived to kill; he loved to kill. In death he found life. The dread in her eyes thrilled him. All the signs he knew so well were there. He knew she realised he would be merciless. The thrill of her fear excited him to the centre of his very being. Now he reached out and took one of her breasts in his hand and fondled it so very gently. She cried and struggled and begged him again and again to leave her alone, not to hurt her. He carried on as though he had not heard her but he savoured her fear.

He reached up with his left hand now and fondled both breasts. The soldiers were hooting with laughter and already looking forward to their turn. But still they held on tight to the struggling girl, egging their master on to greater deeds. He began to squeeze her harder, as hard as he possibly could. Pain as well as humiliation and helplessness seared through the young woman. Her screams joined those of others in the village who were meeting a similar fate. Tears poured down her contorted face.

Pomeroy's heart was pounding now. Her screaming made him euphoric; her writhing body delighted him; her futile struggle was pure ecstasy. Breathless, he released her and stepped back, drawing his sword, holding it vertically before his face as he did so, the light shining on its cold, silvery blade. Stepping forward again he held it flat under her breasts. She recoiled from the chilling touch of the steel and begged for mercy.

'What's the matter? Do you think I'm going to cut your tits off?' he laughed. 'No I wouldn't do that to a handsome wench like you. It would be such a waste.'

What Pomeroy relished as much as violence itself was the knowledge that inside his victims' terror lived the faint, foolish hope that complete submission might lead to their lord sparing them. How little they understood his sport. What he liked best in this moment before death was to prolong the anticipation of agony. Let the victim imagine the supreme pain of his probing blade before the deed was done. In this world between life and death he was more than a just a warrior; he was king. A regular visitor to this world, he knew the landscape well. He enjoyed its views, its strange perfumes, its urgent sounds that screeched louder than any bird and, of course, the feel of warm blood on his hands. But what delighted him most was the pleasure of feasting his eyes on his victims' faces as they realised they were about to die and the fascinating fading away of the light in their eyes as their life drained from them. Terror filled a void in his life.

Pomeroy indicated to the soldiers to force the woman down on the floor, which they did, stretching her out before him. Stepping between her splayed legs, he dropped to his knees, then staring into Aelfryth's eyes, reeled in depraved rapture as he set his sword about its work. Obedient it was in his well-trained hands and it performed its bestial butcher's business with a zeal unsurpassed in any abattoir. Her deafening screams echoed in his head long after the business was all over. The skull that housed his bulging eyes, the manic grin, the pale face, held motionless above Aelfryth's now calm corpse. She was finally free of her tormentor.

He let out a sigh. Now he felt replete, he could relax and enjoy a moment's calm. He noticed the flickering light and the sound of the mill stream brought him back to earth. There was no time for rest. He had the Duke's work to continue. He wiped Aelfryth's blood from his sword in her long blonde hair and as he did so he examined her flowing locks more closely. He couldn't help admire the way they caught the sunlight and revealed lustrous gold. It was truly beautiful hair. Odd though, how it still felt the same whether they were dead or alive. If you had to say if someone were dead or alive just by feeling their hair, you'd have to guess, you wouldn't have a clue. Funny that.

The two soldiers watched him in silence while he cleaned his weapon, concentrating intensely on the task in hand until once again he had a bright, clean, gleaming blade. Realising he was being watched, he rose to his feet and slid his sword back into its scabbard.

My God, I hope I wasn't talking to myself then, he thought, self-consciously. For a moment he looked at the two soldiers, then without a word, turned and left.

'You'd thought he'd a let us fuck her first,' said one.

'Yeah, selfish git. He's ruined her now,' replied the other.

'She's still warm, though.'

'You have her, then.'

'What d'you think I am?'

They released her body in disgust, left the building and walked away. Looking for more mischief, the three of them blended in effortlessly with their comrades. Heading back into the middle of what was left of the village, they passed a pale-faced chevalier heading to the mill, looking quite ill. He was the only one amongst the Normans who fully understood the cries for help and who was familiar with the names of loved ones called in anguish. Drained of all emotion and in a state of shock, Sir William Malet headed to the mill. Stepping round the body of a young man, Sir William entered the building. It was unnaturally silent inside. Over the sound of the babbling brook he could hear something dripping. He looked down and on the floorboards saw a dark pool spreading in a sunbeam. His eyes travelled upward and he saw the source. Like Pomeroy and the soldiers before him, Malet climbed the ladder and the sight that met his gaze made the battle-hardened warrior vomit. Skalpi's wife lay dead before him; it was obvious how she had died. Feeling the need for air and wanting to avert his eyes he stepped uncertainly over to the window. Looking through it, there he saw, trapped in the millwheel, the body of a baby. He retched again, this time more violently. Unable to bear being in the mill, he raced down the ladder and made his way outside where, in an effort to recompose himself, he took deep breaths and a few steps away from the building. Gradually, as his head stopped reeling, he became aware of the scene around him. Everywhere was butchery and bestiality. Every crime known to humanity was being committed with impunity. He felt so numb he could not even cry and Pope's absolution or no Pope's absolution, he wondered whether they would all burn in hell.

As he mounted his horse another Norman approached him on a big bay stallion.

'Missed an opportunity there, friend,' the stranger said in a Breton accent.

'I don't know what you mean.'

'It's the only building left standing.'

It was then Malet noticed, although he never knew how he could have missed it, that the chevalier carried with him a burning torch.

'Still, not to worry; I'll take care of it.' He smiled as he hurled the torch onto the thatched roof of the mill. 'That should burn nicely. Mills usually do.' He turned and rode away as Malet, still white-faced, not knowing what to do or say, stared as the torch rolled harmlessly down the mill's thatched roof and extinguished itself on the ground.

Upstream, peering through the undergrowth on the riverbank by the side of the bridge and unseen by the withdrawing Normans was a small group of villagers hiding out of sight. In all there were seven crouched under the bridge, including two children and a baby. When the Normans left, the villager who had been watching signalled his neighbours to join him. From under the bridge six came out alive, the baby having joined the other children of the village in eternal rest. Her father had gathered her up when he saw soldiers running amok and carried her beneath the bridge to safety. Unlike Aelfryth's baby she did not think this was a game and being frightened cried for her mother. Terrified of giving their position away, in his fear, the father had hugged her close to his chest. Still he could hear her crying; it sounded deafening. Neighbours, the panic-stricken look of their stares glaring down on him, demanded a solution. Soldiers were approaching. Two horsemen actually came to a halt on the bridge right over their heads. As they approached the man placed his hand over the baby's mouth, stooped down and placed her gently and respectfully beneath the water. Soon there was no life left in her little body and her father could hear nothing and see nothing, simply conscious of the terrible weight of his burden and the fearful pounding of his own heart. Tears ran down the father's cheeks and fell from his face to mingle with the water and run downstream through the millrace over Aelfryth's baby's body to the sea.

The Normans, their day's work complete, headed to Hastings, riding hard along the road. When they left Whatlington, it was shrouded in silence; almost nothing could be heard, not even birdsong. The world screamed out in silence.

At twilight, Duke William arrived at Hastings. Assured that they had nothing to fear from well-disciplined Norman soldiers, the townsfolk had stayed and opened the town gates for him. The Normans were especially glad to be there; it was beginning to rain.

William was very happy to reach his destination. Hastings was a well-protected, strong defensive position. A range of hills ran down to the sea with high ground commanding the beaches to either side. William's men helped themselves to what they wanted from local supplies. With Harold and his army miles away, there was no one to stop them. Before dining that evening, Duke William had discussed with Sir Humphrey de Tilleul en Ague exactly where he would erect his castle next morning. This was not to be a temporary stay.

LONDON

Two days after William had landed, a messenger from Pevensey arrived at Westminster's great hall. This was just an hour after a messenger had arrived from York with word of Sigurdsson's defeat and the great victory for the English. A heavily pregnant Queen Aldytha sat on the throne presiding over victory celebrations, which were in full swing. Leofwine, whose responsibility it was to guard London while Harold was away, was a little the worse for wear, then, when he received the second message and had difficulty absorbing the facts. The Queen promptly fainted and was carried off to her chambers by her attendants. Ulf, the only one of the family present in a fit state to respond, volunteered to get word to his father. Ulf was a fine horseman and Leofwine had no reservations in sending him on his way. After two days' hard riding, Ulf met his father on the Great North Road.

'Ulf! You have news and I can tell it's not good.'

'It's Duke William, father. He landed on the coast at Pevensey four days ago.'

'What's he doing now?'

'I've no idea. As soon as we got the word I came up here to warn you.'

'How many men does he have?'

'Somewhere between ten and twenty thousand.'

'Well, we'd better go and pay him a visit.'

Orders were passed down the line: proceed to London with all possible haste. The King would see his soldiers there. Word was sent to all the counties to warn them and to raise the fyrd. They were to meet in Sussex at the old grey apple tree on Caldbec Hill.

Harold's arrival in London on the 6th of October was one of great jubilation. The city was welcoming the victor of Stamford Bridge and the king they saw as their saviour. If Harold could so easily defeat a Viking army, what chance did the Duke of Normandy have?

Edgar Atheling rode out to meet him, as did the Bishop of London and the burgesses. They were surprised to see how weary the victorious army appeared and how small it looked. Harold had led the English to a great victory but at a high cost. Now back in London, he did his best to show a cheery face. The comet had been a good omen after all and now Harald Sigurdsson had been dealt with, it was William's turn. Tonight he would feast in Westminster; tomorrow he would make plans. Now he would acknowledge the cheers of the crowd who loved him so much it took two hours for him to get from the city gates to the great hall.

News of his arrival had spread through the city and when he finally arrived at Westminster, it was to find the great hall in chaos. Earl Leofwine, with the help of Archbishop Stigand, was doing his best to keep things in order. Harold took his place on his throne.

'Christ Almighty, Harold, I thought you'd never get here!' exclaimed Stigand in a fluster.

Ignoring the Archbishop, Harold asserted himself immediately. 'Who are all these people and what do they want?' he demanded of his brother.

'Refugees from your estates and men who've answered the call to march with you. Oh, and finally there is a messenger from the Bastard.'

Harold barked his orders. 'All you men who've come to join me, make your way to the soldiers' quarters. I'll talk to you later.

'The emissary from Duke William, it's not Sir William Malet, is it?'

'No, my Lord, it is I,' answered a priest who Harold had not noticed. 'What's the Duke's message?'

'Duke William would once again remind you that by right the throne of England is his and you swore an oath to ...'

Something about the tone of the priest's voice prompted Harold's memory, 'I've seen you before, haven't I? At Bosham before I sailed to Normandy, or should I say Ponthieu? I've seen you in Rouen and Steyning. You're Hugh Margot. I'm looking at the face of Judas. Get out!'

'But the Duke's message?'

'You can tell Duke William that whatever either of us thought at the time, no one has the right to promise a crown, not even the King.'

'I must deliver Duke William's message. He pleads with you to have your rival claims assessed by an independent commission. Or failing that, trial by combat.'

'Independent commission! What independent commission would

that be?' snapped Harold, rising to his feet. 'When would it be held? He's in England now. Where will he wait till this commission meets and if by some strange chance it found in my favour, would William simply pack up and go home, saying to his men as he went, 'Well, I'm sorry, but I made a bit of a mistake. The promises I made of booty and rewards simply aren't going to materialise?'

Harold approached the trembling Margot and stood within inches of him. 'I'll give you my answer,' he seethed in his most forceful way. 'You may return to Duke William with this message. Tell him that the oath I made has no value because it was extorted from me by force and trickery. As for any promise, real or otherwise, that has been cancelled by Edward's deathbed nomination. This has been the unbroken custom of the English and has been recognised by law since the time St. Augustine was preaching the faith in this country hundreds of years ago.'

Harold took a breath and calmed himself before he continued. 'However, as a concession, I offer Duke William my friendship. If he goes quietly back across the Channel, then our friendship will remain unbroken, but if he is bent on forcing a decision by battle, then England is ready.'

'But the Crown of England is the Duke's by hereditary right!'

'Can't you hear me?' Harold shouted in the face of the priest. 'Haven't you heard a word I've said?'

'I have, sire but you are mistaken if ...'

'Mistaken! I am mistaken? You tell me, the King of England, I am mistaken. Do you think you understand English law better than I?'

'But it is not just English law that is of consequence in these matters, is it, my Lord?'

'What?' roared Harold. 'This is England, what other law prevails here?'

'The Pope himself has already made his decision.'

The shock of this announcement produced a silence that spread through the court like the plague.

'Didn't you know,' Margot continued sneeringly, 'Duke William is fighting under the papal banner? His Holiness has pronounced his blessing on the Duke's campaign and declared it a holy cause. On his finger, Duke William is wearing the holy relic of St. Peter and suspended round his neck are the very relics on which you, sire, swore the oath in

Normandy. The Duke's brother, Bishop Odo, is bearing a papal bull and his holiness the Pope is excommunicating you. A hearing has been held in Rome and you have been judged guilty.'

Hugh Margot leaned forward, smiling smugly at the dumbstruck king. 'This being the case, you will not be fighting a mere man; you will be fighting the Church, the Pope and even the Lord God Almighty. If you fight William, you are damning yourself and what's more, you're damning all those who fight with you,' he added, looking around the room in a self-satisfied way.

Harold stood white-faced, staring in disbelief before the contemptible little monk. Silence, like a lead weight, had dropped into the room.

'What shall I say to the Duke now, Earl Harold?'

Addressed by his former title, Harold flew into a rage and grabbed the monk by the neck with both hands. Now it was Margot who was speechless. All he could do was cough and splutter. Gyrth and Leofwine hauled Harold off as he shouted at the monk, 'Get out, you fool. God will decide whois the rightful claimant to the Crown and he will deal justly.'

As Margot was being dragged out of the room, he shouted back at Harold, 'Repent! Repent! Repent before it is too late. The Duke is a merciful man, he might still forgive you.' The court was still and silent; Margot's voice grew quiet, lost in the still night air.

Stigand stepped forward. 'You don't really think the Pope has excommunicated you, do you?'

'You know, I've honestly no idea.'

'Of course he hasn't. This is another Norman trick to undermine you. Duke William knows you have no time to verify what Margot has told you. Whatever the Pope said, assuming he said anything at all, the Normans have exaggerated in order to strengthen their claim and to demoralise you. If you see them riding into battle under a papal banner, it'll be one they knocked up themselves.'

Harold thought for a moment before replying. 'May God decide between the Duke and me. Let Him pronounce to the world which of us shall be king. Summon the members of the war council!'

Even before he had time to see Aldytha, Harold was presiding over a council of war. With him were his brothers, Gyrth and Leofwine, his nephew, Haakon, and Earl Waltheof, who had accompanied him from York. Harold's housecarls, Finn and Bondi, were present, as were Skalpi, Azur, Ansgar, Sheriff of Middlesex, and the gigantic Godric, the new Sheriff of Berkshire. Harold's aging uncle, Aelfwig, brother of Earl Godwin and Abbot of the minster of Winchester, had also reported for duty, bringing twelve men of his order with him. Edgar Atheling was present, as was Ulf; the two young men were ostensibly there as observers but begged the King to take them with him.

'No, I need you both here to guard London and to meet Edwin and Morcar when they arrive.'

The two were disappointed but reluctantly agreed.

Ansgar was also keen to go south with Harold but was ordered to stay in London and charged with organising the care for all the horses that came back from Stamford Bridge. Gauti, recovering from his wound, was also ordered to stay behind.

'I would add, should I not survive, I'd like Edgar to be my successor. Is that agreed?' Harold enquired of the council.

In a subdued atmosphere, the council gave its assent.

Harold had been keen to do battle with William. After talking with Margot he had another reason to engage William's army at the first opportunity; he did not want any rumours of his excommunication, true or false, to spread through the country for fear of frightening off supporters.

Gyrth then made a suggestion. 'Why don't I lead the army? No one would be damned for following me. The threat of excommunication doesn't hang over my head.'

'For all we know, the Pope hasn't excommunicated me, either,' Harold replied.

'Well, we just don't know and there's no time to find out but if your great sin is that you swore on holy relics to support William's claim, then why don't I oppose him? I've made no vow binding me to William.'

'Neither have I,' chipped in Leofwine.

'Neither have any of the rest of us,' added Godric.

Gyrth continued, 'If I'm defeated, you'll still be able to raise another army and engage William. On the way to Hastings, I could lay waste to the countryside. The locals could be compensated later but William and his troops, even if they won the initial battle, would starve. If we gamble everything on a single cast of the die and lose and worse still, you get killed, then England will fall into chaos. If I lead the army and get killed, England has only lost a general.'

There were murmurs of agreement from all around; there was no voice of opposition to his plan, save one – Harold's.

'Gyrth, I appreciate your thoughtfulness but I can't stand by while English villages burn and I certainly can't sanction the destruction of lands or property of Englishmen. How could I harm the people who I'm supposed to govern and protect? How could I impoverish those who I wish to see thrive under my rule? Besides, if William escapes from the Hastings peninsula he's free to roam wherever he chooses and then what would we do? I've seen how the Normans operate.'

'Very well,' Gyrth said, with a sign of resignation. 'When do you intend us to leave?'

'Tomorrow.'

'Tomorrow? Surely that's too soon. We've lost so many men and the survivors need a rest before another big battle. Why don't we wait a week or two? By then Edwin and Morcar should be here with their men. There might even be a chance of using the fleet to blockade Hastings, so William can be neither supplied nor reinforced.'

'But we have to move quickly.'

'Do you think using the tactics that were so successful against Sigurdsson will work against William?' Gyrth asked gently.

'They worked well enough at Stamford Bridge.'

'And haven't you ever stopped to wonder whether Harald and Tostig simply let their attention wander and dropped their guard, handing us victory on a plate?'

'Listen, William can't keep his men there much longer; he'll have to break out. When his men grow hungry, he'll have to move. We must go down to Hastings soon.'

Harold looked at the grim faces of his council one by one before announcing, 'Very well then, we leave not tomorrow but early Wednesday morning. Send riders out with the message for the fyrd to gather at the old grey apple tree on Caldbec Hill as soon as they can.'

Garth breathed a sigh of relief. At least he had brought some time to allow the army to form and the housecarls to rest.

HASTINGS

Under a slate-grey October sky, a building such as had never before been seen in England, made its way heavenward, like a plant in search of the sun. The construction was built on a hill, totally dominated the town and the countryside and appeared to offer protection only to its defenders, not the townsfolk. It seemed foreboding and somehow unnatural to the locals but the Normans appeared to know what they were doing.

Duke William had appointed Sir Humphrey de Tilleul en Ague to take charge of building castles during the campaign. Sir Humphrey had brought partly-assembled wooden forts in sections eight feet wide. Each fortification would be of the motte and bailey type, consisting of a wooden structure sitting on top of an earth mound, surrounded by a ditch and a rampart topped by a solid fence. Using hundreds of soldiers as labour, he could complete the fortifications in two days. Now on the second day, with the earth mound and ditch finished, the fence was being erected.

Duke William had been in Sussex a week now and there was still no sign of Harold. Rumours were spreading through the lines. Some thought they had fallen into some deadly English trap; others that plague stalked the land, leaving the country beyond the horizon still and dead. Would they be next? William needed intelligence. He had sent Hugh Margot to offer terms to Harold, hoping he would be provoked into an early attack. Although he knew Sigurdsson had landed in the North, William still did not know if Harold had engaged him. But the answer soon presented itself when Father Hugh returned from his mission and was escorted to William's quarters in the great hall at Hastings.

'Well, Father Hugh, what news do you have for me?'

'I gave Harold your message, my Lord'

'He's still alive then?'

'The barbarian is still with us, my Lord, yes.'

'What about Sigurdsson?'

'Killed, my Lord, as was Earl Tostig. It was a decisive victory. '

'Well, it was hospitable of Harold to rid us of a hostile neighbour.' Turning his attention back to Margot, the Duke asked him how Harold had received his offer.

'The ingrate rejected it out of hand.'

'Tell me, Father Hugh, what's the condition of his troops?'

'He has lost about a third of his housecarls, which leaves him with about two thousand but they're mostly exhausted from the battle and the long journey back to London, my Lord. Their horses are in a sorry state too.'

'Good,' said the Duke, sitting back in his seat to take a sip of wine. 'He'll be even more tired when he's marched his men down here.'

The Duke then tossed the cleric a small bag of gold coins before summarily dismissing him.

As he watched him depart, William became conscious that his brother was leaning over to him. He turned his head, the better to hear.

'How should we best break this news to the troops?' enquired the bishop.

'What do you mean?'

'Well, on the one hand this news will be a fillip to them but on the other they will know Harold has defeated, arguably, the greatest warrior king in the world. How will that make them feel?'

'We'll say it was unnatural.'

'In what way unnatural?'

'We'll say it was wicked. Harold sold his soul to get the throne and now it's cost the life of his brother, a holy and pious man.'

'What an excellent idea! We could say Harold killed him with his own two hands.'

'Yes. Chopped off his head.'

'And stuck it on a spear.'

'Then cut his heart out.'

'And ate it,' added Odo, breaking into a raucous laugh.

'That's going a bit too far, don't you think?'

'Very well, we'll stick to mere fratricide and decapitation.'

There was enough food left on the peninsula to last the Normans until the beginning of the third week of October. After that time they would have to move away from the fort and the sea, into an alien and hostile countryside. Until then they could afford to wait.

WALTHAM

While waiting for the fyrd to arrive in London, Harold made a pilgrimage to Waltham Holy Cross, accompanied only by Edmund. There they met Brother Thurkill and Harold requested a cell in which Edmund could spend the night. Thurkill walked with them into the abbey, where they placed gifts Harold had brought upon the high altar of the church. When he had finished making some final adjustments, Thurkill said to Harold, 'Come, my King, let's join the brothers in prayer. And let's not just pray for victory in the coming battle. Let's pray you rule justly and piously for years to come.'

'Yes, let's,' the King replied.

In the eerie darkness of the church, Harold and Edmund joined Thurkill and the other monks; their prayers rose upwards with the smoke of incense and candles climbing up into the heavens. When they had finished praying, the holy men formed in procession before the still-kneeling Harold, then passed down the nave, leaving the King alone. Edmund, remaining in attendance, witnessed the most miraculous scene of his life.

Harold, thinking he was alone, bowed and lay prostrate before the Holy Cross; the same Holy Cross which all those years ago Tofi had dug up and transported across England and which Harold and his men called upon in battle.

In the cool quiet of the October evening, while the flames flickered silently, Harold and his friend were alone in the church. Edmund looked on while Harold lay before Christ upon the cross, stretched out on the stone floor, humbled in prayer; above him the figure of Christ, carved in black flint, his head held high, staring out into the vastness of eternity.

Hidden in the shadows, Edmund looked on and in the darkness thought he detected a movement, although he had heard not a single sound. Everything was familiar, yet something was strange, and there in the dim light he saw it. No longer was Christ standing proud on the cross; his head now hung in sorrow, his chin upon his chest. His eyes, full of pity, gazed upon the prostrate Harold. Edmund felt a shiver run through his body; his spine tingled and his stomach tightened. Nausea swept through him. Suppressing the urge to faint, he looked on as Harold rose to his feet and made his way to the door before leaving for the great hall. Edmund looked once more to the figure on the cross and noticed a trail of tears running down the face. As tears streamed down his own cheeks, he silently made his way to his cell, avoiding all others so as not to betray his secret.

Outside the abbey, Harold, all alone under the stars, made his way to Edyth. As he passed under the tower, its high double windows seemed to look down on him. He was disappointed not to find her at home; she had left to join him on his journey to Hastings.

Early on Wednesday 11th October, even as the last of the stragglers from Stamford Bridge were still making their way down the Great North Road, Harold led his army out of London. In the cold early morning small crowds gathered to say farewell, cheer and shout encouragement. But the leaving was a sombre affair; no housecarl was mounted, as the King's horses were still recovering from their journey. The few horses fit to use were pulling the carts in the baggage train. The soldiers, on foot, ambled slowly by, tired before they began. True, as their journey progressed, fresh soldiers from Sussex and Kent joined them, so they consoled themselves with the thought that at least some of them would feel fresh when the battle started, but three days' march lay ahead.

Harold rode, as usual, at the head of the column with his brothers. Haakon rode with them, looking every bit the English noble warrior, holding the banner of the fighting man proudly aloft. By Haakon's side rode Skalpi, the golden dragon of Wessex flying above his head. Edmund, Harold's friend and spiritual mentor, was by his side, as always in times of trouble. Behind them were his own housecarls with Finn and Thorkell at their head, followed by Azur and his men. After them came the thanes he had recruited in London, including sheriffs and abbots from Berkshire, Buckinghamshire, Oxfordshire and Kent; then there were the men raised by the fyrd, mainly from southern England, including a few from East Anglia. Bondi would join Harold at the old apple tree with men from the southwest. Behind the column came the camp followers – wives and lovers, girlfriends and daughters and unrecognised in her veil, Edyth Swan neck with Lady Gytha for company.

Leaving London had been a sorry affair. Aldytha begged him not to go. Ulf and Edgar begged him to take them with him. Stigand and Wulfstan blessed him and his troops and were there to see them leave, watching as the procession turned over London Bridge to cross over the river, disappearing from view, snaking southward.

Harold hoped to reach Rochester by nightfall but his hopes were in vain. Twenty-eight miles were a few miles too far for his tired foot soldiers; they slept at the side of the road in tents, hastily made bivouacs or under the stars in their leather sleeping bags.

The following day was a struggle. After breakfast and an early start the army made its way into the arboreal depths of the Andredeswald. The leaves on the trees ranged through every hue of gold, red and yellow; there was still some green amongst the ferrous colours of autumn. Underfoot was wet and muddy. For those in the rear the conditions were made worse by the thousands of feet in front churning up the ground.

The journey to Hastings, though shorter than to Stamford, was no less arduous. Any man without a horse, and there were many, had to walk, carrying his own weapons, equipment and supplies. They covered much less distance in a day than they had done on the way north, but felt much more tired. The forest unsettled them. Every man present had heard tales of beasts and hairy men with no necks that killed travellers and ate their children alive. Some said there were people who had lived in the forest since before Roman times and would murder an Englishman on sight. None looked forward to passing the night there, with who knew what lurking in the shadows, ready to spring out and savage a man at any moment. But at least there was plenty of firewood to keep the fires burning big and bright once the sun went down.

FRIDAY, 13TH OCTOBER

After a restless night, Harold's army began the final leg of its journey, leaving the quiet forest behind them; the army began to encounter evidence of the Norman presence.

By late afternoon, the head of the column arrived in what was recently Whatlington. This was one of Harold's villages, a place he knew well, where his late father was still fondly remembered. There was an eerie stillness about the place; even the wheel on the water mill hung rigid. It was obvious for all to see that the horror stories they had heard from refugees were all too true. Skalpi, without thinking, handed his banner to Haakon, dismounted and raced over to the mill. He stopped in his tracks when he came across the body of Aelfryth's brother lying outside the doorway, in the street where he had fallen. Tentatively, he made his way into the building where he found the stench overpowering. He felt himself heave and instinctively made for the nearest window; leaning through as far as he could, he retched violently. It was only after he had emptied his stomach that he noticed the body of a baby, his little son, trapped in the mill wheel. Staggering back in shock he noticed the congealed blood all over the floor. He looked up to see dark stained wood above his head. Stiff limbed like a cadaver, Skalpi made his way up the stairs. When he got there the sight that greeted his eyes made him wail; he knew it was his wife, his true love.

The instant he heard the soul-searing sound of Skalpi's scream, Harold realised his friend had stumbled upon something terrible. He entered the mill to hear Skalpi whimpering upstairs. When he entered the room, his comrade was on his knees beside Aelfryth's body. Tears streaming down his face, his mutterings incoherent, he surely wanted to hold his wife once more in his arms. What husband would not? But decay and its fragrant accomplices kept them apart.

'There's nothing we can do for her, Skalpi. Come with me. I'll send a party in here and we'll give her a proper Christian burial in the church grounds.'

'And the baby?'

'The baby?'

Harold looked around for a baby but saw nothing.

'He's trapped in the mill wheel. They must have thrown him there.'

Harold helped Skalpi to his feet and guided him to the top of the stairs. The housecarl moved slowly down the steps of the mill that he had worked so hard for.

Harold turned and took a last look at the body. In the silent mill the only sounds he could hear were Skalpi's footfalls and the buzzing of flies.

'Edmund,' called the King, his hand placed gently on his old friend's back for comfort, 'I need you to form a burial party. I'd like you to start with Aelfryth.'

'Oh no. They didn't …'

'I'm afraid so. Would you take care of her?'

'Yes, my Lord.'

'The body of their baby's trapped in the mill rush.'

'Oh God, poor Skalpi.'

'Her brother's body is lying just outside the mill where they killed him. Would you see that they're all buried together?'

'Of course, my Lord.'

While Edmund pressed members of the fyrd into helping him, Harold rode to the remains of the church. Its walls were still standing and a few roof beams remained. The body of Father Aethelweard lay where it had fallen, as did his parishioner's. Like the roof beams, they were charred. Three crows perched in a line upon the body of the parishioner, helping themselves to a free meal.

As Harold stared at the remains of the priest, struggling to come to terms with the emotions he felt, his brothers rode up beside him. Leofwine, extremely agitated, looked this way and that, pointing, swearing; giving voice to his rage, anger and grief. But Gyrth sat white-faced and silent astride his horse. He was the first to speak.

'Let's get down to Hastings right away and teach the bastard a lesson.'

His speech was calm and measured but he did not look directly at anyone. He stared into space as though talking to himself, in a quiet but determined kind of way.

'Yes. You're right,' replied Harold, eager to prevent another massacre. He then gathered the men together, leaving Edmund to direct the burial party. Lady Gytha stayed with the priest in order to see what could be salvaged and to give help and comfort to those few villagers who remained. Scouts were sent up to Caldbec to check for the enemy. The English army left more resolute in its purpose to destroy the invader. Weary limbs had been infused with vitality by Norman barbarity.

Making his way across Sussex, Harold came across more evidence of savagery. Each village he came to had been wasted. At each one a party was left to take care of the dead and any survivors brave enough to show themselves. Exhausted, the tired army marched on towards the old apple tree, were it would camp. Tomorrow the soldiers could rest and probably on Sunday too, for now they would concentrate on reaching their destination.

All around them the sun shone, picking out the colours of autumn in the trees, a truly glorious celebration of nature. All around, falling leaves would spiral to the ground, sunlight making them flicker as they fell. The sun also brought out the rich, sweet scent of the warm, damp earth.

At twilight that Friday, Harold led the English army to the old grey apple tree high on Caldbec Hill. When they saw the skeleton of the tree against the skyline, almost every soldier to a man gave a sigh of relief before taking heart and pressing on with renewed vigour. The first men to arrive were the least weary, but even these men were fatigued. Ponderously they went about lighting fires, setting up tents, building shelters and preparing food for the pot, watched by three horsemen further down the hill, hidden in the dark shadows of the woods. The horsemen were Norman scouts returning from patrol. Their leader, Vital, had stopped to relieve himself against a tree. Idly looking about him, he heard, and then saw, his enemy approach. His heart skipped a beat and then pounded a little faster with the excitement of knowing they were entirely unaware of him and his men. Within a minute Vital had finished his business, mounted his horse and with his comrades, quietly dissolved into the darkness. Within an hour he would appear in Hastings to tell Duke William, who would order his men to stand to until dawn. He informed his commanders that in the morning they would ride out to meet Harold. While William made plans, priests heard confessions all through the night.

In the swelling English camp there was a relaxed atmosphere. The men had achieved their objective; they had blocked the road to London and trapped Duke William in the Hastings peninsula. Now they could look forward to a good night's sleep and wake in the morning at their leisure. If the Normans should spot them tomorrow, what would it matter? It would take at least three hours for Duke William to bring his men to face them. It would be noon at the earliest before he could fight and no matter how good the Normans were at fighting, no matter how brave, how determined, it would take more than an afternoon to beat the English.

Yes, tomorrow should be an easy day, each man told himself. William would probably stay hidden behind his palisades. Sunday would probably be quiet too. The English had heard how the Normans were reluctant to fight on the Lord's Day. So after a nice rest, Monday would see them busy.

Harold entered his tent, fastening the flaps behind him. Inside, already curled up in bed, lay Edyth. She had never accompanied him on any previous campaign, but he was glad she had come with him this time.

'Hello, I didn't see you come in,' he said, when he saw her.

'I can be sneaky when I choose.'

'I'm glad to hear it,' Harold replied, sitting on the bed to take off his boots.

They were both thinking of the day's journey, although it was not the ride but the horror they had seen that had taken its toll; hellish visions of devastated villages ran through their minds. Harold was acutely aware that as much as they had disturbed him, for Edyth, who had never seen such sights, the effect must be so much worse.

Harold climbed into the bed made warm by his lover. As they embraced she held him firmly and said, 'We have to destroy him, Harold, we have to. We have no choice.'

'I know, Edyth, I know. Don't worry. This time next week we'll be back in London.'

But, she thought, they would not. He would be in London; she would be in Waltham.

Harold read her thoughts in her eyes. 'All this will work out, you'll see,' he assured her as he leaned over to blow out the lantern to prevent their silhouettes showing on the wall of the tent.

As they made love, the English army, full of tired men lying in the darkness under a cloudy sky, struggled to sleep on the cold, hard ground and in the chilly night air.

14TH OCTOBER, 1066

Harold woke in the grey light of dawn; beside him Edyth lay sleeping. Quietly, without disturbing his lover, he rose from his bed. Shivering, he peered out through the tent flap to see the ghostly sight of the dew-sodden English camp. He was surprised to see no sign of frost. Mist was all around, hanging in the air, joined by the eager smoke from a few fires. He decided to dress and make an inspection of the camp.

Enjoying the warmth of his heavy winter cloak, Harold made his way through tents and bivouacs. It was a little lighter now and the sun was warming the soldiers, who through the long cold night had had difficulty sleeping. Comfortable at last, they slept on while Harold sneaked stealthily round the silent camp, totting up their number. There was much guesswork. Some men slept in the open but those who had the shelter of cover he had to estimate. He needed to know how many men had arrived during the night. By the time he had finished, he guessed seven or eight thousand men, perhaps enough to do the job, perhaps not, but he reassured himself with the knowledge that more troops were on their way to join them. Most would be with him before nightfall and many more the day after that.

Satisfied, Harold began to make his way back to his tent. The sun felt warm on his face as he returned to Edyth. On the roof of his tent the dew drops had collected like jewels, sparkling brightly. As he pulled aside the door to enter, many of them slipped to the ground. Once inside he found Edyth still asleep. He sat down on the bed, leaned over and kissed her. Slowly she stirred. Harold looked at her in the early morning light, surprised to see the face of the girl he had first seen all those years ago. In all that time she appeared not to have aged at all.

Six miles away in Hastings, Duke William had already attended mass and was now astride his horse, addressing his men before preparing to lead them into battle. He made an impressive sight on his black charger, his noblemen ranged behind him. Around his neck he wore the relics on which Harold had sworn his oath, a reminder to all that the oath was broken and for Harold, the saints' protection was forfeited.

As the troops filed by, William began to make a speech designed to raise morale. 'This is the day on which you will show the English your strength and your courage. Remember, victory is sweet but defeat is bitter, bitter as death. Today you will fight for your very lives, but victory will be yours and with victory comes honour and fortune. But should your courage leave you, should you find emptiness instead of boldness in your hearts, then you may expect to be butchered by the merciless barbarians.

'Look around you. Behind you is the sea, where an English fleet waits for anyone cowardly enough to desert the field of battle. Ahead, the English army blocks our way to London. But, you must ask yourselves, what kind of army is it that stands before you? I'll tell you: it is an army that has been cut to pieces by our kinsmen, the Norsemen. It is an army whose best men lie dead in Yorkshire; an army exhausted from its long marches. There is no escaping destiny. Today we will be victorious. Only be bold! Be bold!' William waved his mace above his head as he spoke. His men cheered in response.

'Onward! Follow me!'

The Duke jabbed a spur into his horse's side and moved off, his nobles and his men following in jubilant mood. After a few paces, William FitzOsbern moved up to his side.

'So, the day has finally dawned,' announced Duke William.

'Finally, my Lord. Finally.'

'Oh, I knew this day would arrive, FitzOsbern. You knew it too, even when we were stuck on the Dives, even when the fleet was washed up on the shores of Ponthieu.' Then the Duke focused straight into FitzOsbern's eyes. 'But I knew it even before Godwinson set foot in Normandy. I've always known it.'

'Ah, you mean the dream.'

'Not so much a dream as a prophecy, eh? But it's not just that; it's a question of will. You simply decide what you want and then you grasp it with all your determination. You do not flinch; you do not allow yourself to be distracted. You disregard criticism, you dispose of enemies and discard those who call themselves your friend but simply get in your way.

Of course, you need to be favoured by God as I am. I know I can rely on divine intervention. Do you know why?'

'Why, my Lord?'

'Because my faith is unyielding.'

'Yes, my Lord.'

'The Pope must think so; he's given me his blessing. And do you know what else, FitzOsbern?'

'What, my Lord?'

'Tomorrow I shall be King of England,' said William with absolute certainty.

Twenty miles to the west of Duke William, Bondi was eating breakfast with eleven hundred men from the western counties. They were mainly thanes, but volunteers had joined them on their journey. None of them had been at Stamford Bridge; all of them were fresh, well equipped and eager for battle.

In good cheer they broke camp, mounted their horses and formed a column, which started to snake its way through Sussex at a brisk pace. They were making good time and expected to join Harold at the old grey apple tree well before sunset.

Also heading toward the old grey apple tree were the earls Edwin and Morcar. After resting their men and horses for a day in London, the brothers were leading what was left of the northern army to Hastings. An assortment of housecarls and volunteers, two thousand men in all, were crossing London Bridge while Duke William was addressing his troops. The northern earls were certain they would reach the old apple tree by noon on Sunday.

Four hours' march from Caldbec, three hundred and fifty Danish housecarls had also just finished breakfast and they were now marching briskly to join Harold. They had been sent by King Swein, who wanted to help his cousin. Before them and behind them came the stragglers of Harold's army, still marching down from London. In all, up to two thousand men would arrive at the old grey apple tree at varying times throughout the day.

Harold, having left Edyth in the tent chatting with Lady Gytha, was eating breakfast with Gyrth, Leofwine and his captains. In the air the smell of wood smoke mixed with the musky fragrance of autumn leaves and birdsong mixed with the voices of the men. It was a perfect autumn morning. Then a commotion broke out in the camp as a scout approached the King at full gallop shouting, 'Normans! Normans!'

The rider jumped off his horse before it had completely stopped and took a few bounds forward, bowing to the King as he ran. Coming to a halt and out of breath, the scout delivered his message: 'Duke William, my Lord, he's just over the other side of the hill.' The rider indicated, with a wave of his arm, a hill on the other side of a nearby ridge.

Harold ordered his men to form a line at the top of the nearby ridge. Most of them had already grabbed their war gear and some were on their way even as he spoke. Senlac Ridge had a commanding view over a small valley to Telham Hill. If he could gain possession of this piece of high ground, he would have a fine defensive position. The top of the ridge was only half a mile wide with thick woods and undergrowth on either side; to the west the ground rose quite sharply, making it easily defendable.

Those who were still sleeping were woken by the kicks and shouts of their comrades. A clamour broke out as men fresh from dreams stirred themselves to rush straight from their beds to form a shield wall.

Harold shouted to Edmund, 'Take Edyth and Gytha. I'm entrusting them to your care. Wait with them by that oak,' he called out, as he indicated a tree three-quarters of a mile or so away. Mounting his horse, he raced for the top of Senlac to be with his troops who had already arrived and were busy forming a shield wall.

On the other side of the valley, William had ordered his archers to clear the ridge of the English, in the hope of making the high ground his. His plan was that the archers would throw the enemy into confusion and if the cavalry could organise itself in time, they would charge the thin English line and make the high ground theirs.

Harold, aware of the danger this manoeuvre posed, signalled most emphatically to his men to join him. In spite of their weariness and the surprise of the attack, the English reached the ridge first, but the fast-moving Norman archers had covered the ground quickly. Closing in, the crossbowmen in the middle of the Norman ranks fired a volley at their enemy. Behind and below them the cavalrymen were donning their armour, making ready to join the battle. Firing as many arrows and crossbow bolts as they possibly could into the unprotected legs of the

English, the archers felt safe, staying just out of spear throwing range. Some fyrdmen, never having seen a crossbow, were terrified by the speed of the bolts and the accuracy of the shot; in a panic some of them left the field.

William hoped that the archers would be able to keep the pressure up for long enough to enable the cavalry to charge in and take the ridge. But as the depth of the English line increased, the archers, still unsupported by their cavalry, retreated down the hill. Two hours would pass before fighting resumed.

Harold instructed Gyrth to take command of the left flank and Leo the right. The brothers went to their appointed places, watching patiently as the Normans below them prepared for the coming battle.

The English stood on the ridge, facing south, watching the Normans fifty feet below. Harold was beneath his standard viewing the army below; he estimated William must have about eight thousand men with him, all of whom would be seasoned professionals. His own army possessed no cavalry and most of the archers were still struggling down from London. The infantry was a mix of housecarls and fyrdmen. Looking along the ridge in either direction, Harold felt pleased. He could see his army in close formation, protected in front and at the flanks by the housecarls' shield-wall.

'See the effete Normans and their French friends. See how they scuttle about, pretending they're preparing to do battle but really delaying the moment when they march to their deaths. They may have mounted soldiers who will race their horses towards you but they can't break a shield wall. They have archers but what good are they? Arrows will fly aimlessly over your heads or land harmlessly at your feet but none will hurt you. As for their infantry, by the time they've walked up these slopes they'll be exhausted. And remember, as much as you've never fought against Normans, they've never fought against you. Who have they fought, you might wonder? What kingdoms has the Duke of Normandy conquered? None, save for a few puny counties belonging to his neighbours.

'And what are they fighting for, these dogs who dare to set foot, uninvited, into our homeland? Are they men come to liberate us from some tyrant whose rule is so despotic it's intolerable to the world? No!

'They are men come to take our land, our riches and our women. Remember well the villages we passed through on our journey here.

Every village in England will look like that if William has his way. Unlike the Normans, we are fighting to keep our homes, our women and our children. We are fighting for freedom, for life itself.'

Harold shouted the last words as he waved his axe above his head. The gesture earned him a rousing cheer.

'Remember, men, all you have to do is stand firm and by nightfall we'll be supping in Hastings.'

Another cheer went up from his men but soon silence fell over the ranks. The Normans had started their advance. William approached astride his black charger. At his side, carrying the papal banner, was Turstin, son of Rollo. At William's other side was Ralph de Tosny, carrying the Duke's standard, the Leopards of Normandy flag and a raven emblem. William's half brothers, Odo and Robert were there, as were Walter Gifford, Roger de Bigod, Montgomerie, and looking like a man whose worst nightmares had become grim reality, the ashen-faced William Malet.

Behind the Duke in the centre of the army were his fellow countrymen, the Normans, the largest contingent of men totalling about four-and-a-half-thousand. On his left were some two thousand Bretons, Poitivins and troops from Maine under the command of Alan of Brittany. On William's right was a mix of two thousand French and Flemish mercenaries under the command of William FitzOsbern, with Eustace of Boulogne and Robert de Beaumont under his command. The vanguard consisted of the archers and crossbowmen; in the second rank stood the infantry and finally the squadrons of chevaliers whom he would later be joining to lead the attack. From their vantage point on the ridge, the English soldiers paid particular attention to this last group. They were fascinated by their shields, kite-shaped, not round like those of the infantry. They could see the heavy swords, long spears and maces that would soon be used against them. To their relief, they also noticed the horses' lack of armour; the animals wore no protection at all.

It was then William rode forward a few paces ahead of his comrades. Holding the attention of both English and French armies, he began to taunt Harold, all the time playing with the relics round his neck. He shouted up to where he could see Harold's standard: 'You might believe in God and you might think God is on your side, but God is with me and I have the banner to prove it.'

No one in the English ranks understood a word. What William had shouted, only heaven knew but the relics and the banner were clear for all to see and a rumour started to spread amongst the English that their king must have been excommunicated. Every man knew, that if this were true, then the same fate hung over anyone who fought with him. Surreptitiously, one or two thanes slipped quietly away and left the field.

Even at the distance William was from the English line, he could see his display having impact. He was winning the confidence of his own men while Harold's men were losing faith in him. With a smirk on his face, he turned to his troops. What he saw surprised him; they looked obviously fatigued. A night spent praying had left them tired and jittery. Their morale concerned him. He knew he could win the battle but his men would need to be in good spirits to face the ordeal ahead.

Riding along the length of his troops, the Duke racked his brain to find some dramatic way of starting the proceedings that would be to his advantage. He wanted some way of unsettling the enemy, some way of disturbing them. His answer came in a flash.

'Is there any man here who would challenge a Saxon to single combat? Is there a man who would demonstrate to the enemy our Norman prowess and strike fear into their barbarian hearts?' he called out.

'I'm your man, Duke William. I'll slay a Saxon for you,' answered a young warrior 'Just say the word.'

It was Taillefer, a military adventurer and minstrel, grown weary of his normally menial role and hungry for glory.

'I praise your courage, young man, but are you sure you know what it is I'm asking?' enquired the Duke, as Taillefer halted in front of him.

'I beg you, my Lord. May I be the one to strike the first blow?'

'You may, Taillefer. God be with you.'

Taillefer put his horse into a walk, heading out between the two armies, in high spirits, sure that fame and glory awaited him. At a gentle pace he headed up the hill to the centre of the English line, to the sound of his comrades' cheers following on the air behind him. As he went, he sang the ancient songs of long-dead heroes like Roland and Charlemagne. Thrilled by the thought that from this day on, songs would be sung about him, his spirits rose. With supreme confidence he flung his sword high into the air, watching it turn before catching it again. The minstrel chevalier was in his element, performing before his biggest ever audience.

Gradually silence fell over the Norman army gathered at the foot of the hill. On the ridge the chant of English soldiers could be heard: 'Out! Out! Out!'

The noise grew louder and the housecarls in the front line smashed swords and axes against their shields in time to their shouts. The sound was deafening.

Skalpi looked up to Harold, who nodded in response to the unasked question. The housecarl handed the Fighting Man standard to Finn and stepped forward through the ranks to meet his enemy. Walking confidently with his shield over his back and his axe held almost casually in his right hand, he took his position twenty feet in front of his comrades and waited for the Norman.

Taillefer stopped and turned his horse towards his comrades. He would milk this occasion for all he could. 'For William, Normandy and the Lord God Almighty!' he cried. There was an instant roar of support from those gathered below.

Taillefer made minor adjustments to his shield and reins, and then unable to resist putting on a display, once more threw his sword high into the air. It twisted and turned as it flew upwards, stalled, then made its way earthward to be caught with aplomb by the great showman. A roar of appreciation greeted his ears from his comrades.

With a grin on his face, Taillefer turned his horse to the enemy and put it into a trot. His heart was now racing, the sound of his comrades' cheers growing dim in his ears; just the thud, thud, thud of his horse's hooves. Then at a canter, he headed toward his glorious fate. Silence fell on the battlefield as both sides awaited the outcome. Soldiers saw the contest as symbolic of the forthcoming battle; it would be a good omen for the winner.

Skalpi, noticing Taillefer's acceleration, started to swing his axe in a figure of eight. The Norman, with his sword held high, now riding at full gallop, bore down on the Englishman.

'Out! Out! Out!' chanted the English army.

Faster and faster Taillefer rode his horse, eyeing the precise spot on Skalpi's neck where he would land his blow.

The housecarl's nerve held; he too had picked a spot to place his axe. He would aim at the rider's right hip; the horseman would be fit to fight no more and could be finished off at will. Skalpi swung his axe with careful aim; timing was crucial. He had no defence except to sidestep the deadly sword but his axe gave him the reach he needed. Then the horseman was on top of him and in one deft movement, a little sideways step at just the right time, the precise timing of the swing and the contest would be as good as over.

Taillefer had Skalpi in view at all times and thought it would be relatively easy to cut down a man armed with only an axe. The young man underestimated the skill, the courage, the reach and the power of the man and his weapon. Too late he saw his opponent's sidestep and the grey blur of the axe head; then the feeling of insufferable pain.

Each step his horse took was agony for the young chevalier. Every jolt of the fine charger's body put him through the most excruciating suffering. His scream was so loud it seemed to fill the heavens. He struggled to control his horse; it was all he could do to stay in the saddle, his right leg held on only by skin and a little muscle, the smashed bone clearly visible through the blood and tissue. The horse came close to a halt by the shield wall and as the white-faced Taillefer tried to turn he vomited, dropping his sword to the ground before falling after it with cries of pain echoing in a head so light it seemed to float. The charger turned for home, confused, no master's hand to guide him.

Taillefer's world was reduced to the immediate awareness of the present, to the precise here and now, to one huge mistake. No future. No past. The world on its head. King, Duke and armies had vanished. He was aware of unbearable pain, his helplessness and the smell of earth and damp grass. His vision consisted of no more than the housecarl above him and his leg lying at a distorted angle by his side. Even so he could not help but notice, as his head lolled back on the ground, how blue was the sky and how pretty the fluffy white clouds looked as they sailed above. What a beautiful day. Then the glory that was to have been his vanished in the grey blur of an axe.

When Skalpi picked up Taillefer's head, the helmet that still protected it fell to the ground revealing the hairstyle that the English often mistook for that of a monk. Facing his friends, he raised his trophy high and the army gave out a deafening cheer. The opening clash had gone their way. The omens were good. Skalpi had not let them down. Taking a spear from one of the men in the front line, Skalpi drove it hard into the ground before sticking the head of his challenger upon it.

'Come and see your friend,' he shouted to the Normans below. 'He's waiting for you.'

The army, impressive though it was in its orderly sections, now somehow seemed less threatening. He could see Taillefer's horse still cantering homewards, its tail held high, panic in its eye and stirrups jangling empty by its side, heading towards the subdued Norman soldiers who looked on as he stuck their comrade's head on a spear. They failed to hear the words he shouted down to them before he picked up his axe and returned to take up his place in the line.

The Duke, maddened by losing his champion in such a way, cursed himself for not picking someone more experienced, someone who would have at least taken an Englishman with him. He now addressed his men.

'You saw the valiant Taillefer,' he yelled, his mace held high in the air. 'You saw how courageously the young man faced the enemy without the slightest hesitation, without any second thoughts, gladly giving his life for our cause. He was a hero with the heart of a lion, made stronger by his faith in God, slaughtered like a lamb by a barbarian. Let us avenge our brother and repay the English for this atrocity. Let us advance!'

Clarions rang. To the sound of drum and trumpet the Normans advanced. The infantry, with the archers following on close behind, marched forward, forgetting their fear in an outburst of rage. William's soldiers started to make their way determinedly up the slope, singing, as they went, the *Song of Roland*, in Taillefer's honour.

When the distance between the two armies closed, a fusillade of missiles from both sides took to the air, arrows shooting uphill and spears, hatchets and stones hailing down. The Norman archers could make no impact upon their enemy. Once within stabbing range of the shield wall, the Normans were skewered, impaled and scythed down by the dozen; they were making little impression. They were chopped up or run through and their corpses thrown back with the exultant cry of 'Out! Out! Out!' William's losses were truly terrible.

The Bretons were getting the worst of it. The ridge they advanced up was steeper than the eastern side. They were breathless when they arrived at the crest and they had no match for the axe. The Normans in the centre were also experiencing dreadful losses but stoically they drove on. The mercenaries on the right flank were holding back, demoralised by Count Eustace's insistence that they had fallen into a trap.

'This ground favours Harold too much for this battle site not to have been picked in advance. And look, more men are joining him all the time!' cried Eustace in alarm.

He was right; parties of Englishmen were arriving every few minutes.

After half an hour of the bloodiest combat the Normans had ever experienced, the assault petered out. Atop his charger, William read the situation well. Already he knew this would be a battle that would last longer than the usual two or three hour affairs he had fought at home. He knew, as well as anyone present, if they did not win the battle that day, he would have no future. The English had to be congratulated. They had stood up well to the infantry but it remained to be seen how they would cope against cavalry.

Signalling his commanders, William watched as groups of between five and twenty horsemen charged the English. The impact was not what he had hoped for. The axe men made easy meat of them. Although the spears his men hurled caused some casualties, the greater loss was on his side.

From his vantage point, Harold watched as his men came out from behind the shield wall and placed blow after blow of well-aimed axe upon the Norman riders and their mounts. In front of his very eyes, Finn took the head off a horse and killed its rider with one blow.

As he looked over to the west, he saw the Bretons were making heavy going of it. Leofwine was laughing, enjoying the sight of the struggling foe. To the east, he saw Gyrth, shouting encouragement to his men whilst he was himself fighting in the thick of the action. Harold took comfort from the fact that the shield wall was holding steady. His confidence rose. Looking toward the Bretons, it seemed to him that as one, their nerve cracked. They turned tail and streamed down the ridge like leaves before the breeze. Harold saw someone on the Norman side fall from his horse; it was a black charger. It was William! The Bretons, thinking their lord dead, were now in full panic. Then, in defiance of strict orders to hold the line, a horde of fyrdmen rushed after the retreating Bretons. Leofwine ran forward to drive his men back and caught a crossbow bolt right in the middle of his chest and he fell dead on the spot. The housecarls called the fyrdmen back but in their excitement they ran on.

In the chaos and confusion that reigned on the Norman side, Harold saw a chance to snatch victory. If the entire army were to swoop down now, they could drive their enemy from the field. He looked across to Gyrth, who he could see was thinking the same thing. But Leo had just fallen and there was no one to receive the command or lead the right flank. Looking across to the right, his heart sank as he saw William remount his horse and remove his helmet so his troops could clearly identify him.

'Are you all madmen?' cried the Duke, racing across the path of the retreating Bretons. Like Harold, he knew if the entire English army fell on them now they would be lost.

'Can't you see victory?' he called to them. 'Run away and you'll only find death! Look at me: I am alive and by the grace of God I shall be the victor this day. Why are you running? Where can you go? You're allowing yourselves to be beaten by men who you could slaughter like cattle. You're throwing away victory and lasting glory, for what? None of you can run fast enough to evade destruction. Only if you fight on can you live.'

Unconvinced, the Bretons kept on running. Grabbing a spear and ignoring the protestations of Eustace of Boulogne that retreat might be the best policy, William whacked and prodded the fleeing men. His half brothers Odo and Robert joined in, as did William Malet and Montgomerie. Very soon the Bretons were forced into turning around. What they saw brought the light of hope back into their eyes. Only some of the English had pursued them. The vast bulk of the opposing army was still high up on the ridge. Some of their pursuers had run far ahead of their comrades. The Breton cavalry turned and charged back up the hill, picking them off as they went.

Now it was the turn of the English to run. Some of them made it back to safety but most were killed. A few hundred ran to a small tree-topped hillock. There they fought a losing battle against overwhelming odds. From the top of the hill their comrades watched helplessly as their numbers were depleted. Some of the soldiers who had so bravely charged down their enemy only minutes ago were now seeking the shelter of the tree by climbing up into its branches. William's archers and spearmen made light work of them all.

Hurriedly reforming the shield wall, Harold's men prepared to receive another vicious attack. Despite their losses, morale was high and their discipline held. They continued to maintain close order and took heart from the Norman losses, already twice their own.

The Normans, who had been losing heart, now saw an opportunity to deal the English a savage blow. William led another ferocious attack directly in front of Harold. The two men were just feet away when William hurled a spear directly at Harold, who neatly sidestepped it.

'I will kill you myself, Godwinson,' the enraged Duke shouted.

'You'll have to try harder than that,' was the laconic reply.

The Duke turned away to collect another spear but fell from his horse for the second time that morning. Seeing him topple, the housecarls surged forward in the hope of killing him where he lay. It was all William's bodyguard could do to hold them back. Flustered but uninjured, the Duke scrambled to his feet, calling for another horse. There was no response. Catching sight of Roger de Beaumont, William ordered him to give up his mount but Sir Roger refused. With his bodyguard falling back and the housecarls coming ever closer, William started brawling with Sir Roger, striking him several hard blows on the leg with his mace before dragging the hapless cavalrymen to the ground. Leaving him to his own devices, William rode off on his horse.

He heard Harold shout loud enough for everyone to hear, 'How are you going to kill me, William, if at every opportunity you run away?'

Embarrassed, William left his bodyguard behind as it tried to disengage itself from Harold's housecarls. He rode along the line, busying himself by encouraging his men to fight harder. Feeling a little shaken by his fall and still trying to compose himself, William paid little attention to the immediate battle. He was shocked to be knocked straight out of his saddle. He crashed on to the ground, winded. Looking up, he was confronted by the sight of Gyrth Godwinson, scrambling to his feet and making to head straight for him. Gyrth had the most murderous look the Duke had ever seen on anyone's face. The Earl held a long knife and was only two paces away. Still gasping for breath, the Duke was struggling desperately to get to his feet. He was seconds away from death and he knew it. He put out his arm to protect himself. But as Gyrth prepared to strike, the Duke was amazed to see a bloody spear point protrude from his assailant's chest. With a look of shock and horror on his contorted face the Earl collapsed to the ground.

'Everything all right, my Lord?' It was a cheery William Warenne.

The Duke, still fighting for breath and barely able to speak, looked up to his rescuer and simply nodded. His attempt to smile was made in vain. Still on all fours and breathing with difficulty, the Duke watched the life flow out of his assailant, who lay beside him writhing in agony. He had no idea who his enemy was but had, in those few brief seconds, formed a deep respect for him. It was out of respect, as soon as he was able, that he slit Gyrth's throat, releasing him from unendurable pain. By the time he had his breath back, his bodyguard had caught up with him and Warenne had retrieved his spear. Remounting, William rode with his men down the hill to the Norman camp, leading an orderly withdrawal back to his own lines, where archers sat around discussing the battle. Such had been the ferocity of their attack they had run out of arrows. The English, having few archers, had returned very few for the Normans to reuse, so William sent to Hastings for more.

Away from the English line the air smelled sweeter. Here, freshly cooked food greeted the nostrils of the hungry. On the ridge was the smell of death. A little past noon and half a mile away, four thousand men and several hundred horses lay dead. Most of them were Normans.

William gathered his captains around him and they retired to his tent where they would eat and make plans for the afternoon. A feeling of doom hung over them. Looking up to the top of the rise they could see the half-mile wide line of housecarls still standing proud. As they surveyed the English line they saw a straggler, most likely a young chevalier trying to make a name for himself, ride along the shield wall and throw a spear into the ranks. He turned to see what damage he had done. He failed to see Thorkell bring a pole-axe down hard onto his horse's neck. It was a bizarre sight to see the horse, whose head was almost severed, lolling and flopping wildly as his master still held the reins, trying to control the animal as it cavorted madly along the line. The rider screamed as blade after blade cut into him from axes, swords and spears. The witless beast fell to the ground, unseating its wounded rider; he crashed face first to the ground at the feet of the English, who made short work of him. Watching from the bottom of the ridge, William and his comrades knew that unless they came up with some good ideas, a similar fate awaited them all.

In the inner sanctum of his tent, William and his close friends sat down to talk and eat. No one said a word. Everyone avoided the Duke's eyes. Servants served platters of skewered meats, cheeses, roast fowl and bread. Still they sat in silence.

411

'This should be a banquet,' announced the Duke, sternly. 'We should be celebrating a victory, not moping about because half the day's gone and we're worse off than when we started.'

Still no one spoke.

'What's happening out there? I have the biggest army I've ever had at my command. I have the finest soldiers money can buy and the biggest cavalry force to set foot in England since the Romans. It should all have been over in an hour or two.' The Duke took a deep breath and sighed. 'Don't any of you have anything to say?'

The Count of Boulogne cleared his throat.

'Yes, Eustace, what is it?'

'Have you noticed the reinforcements that keep turning up?'

'I don't think we need concern ourselves with them.'

'But there must have been three or four hundred at least.'

'I saw them. There were fifty, a hundred at the very most.'

'Well, my Lord, however many there were, they keep arriving. Perhaps it's best if we retire to Hastings and send for reinforcements from home. Or better still …'

'Eustace, this battle will be won today and it will be won by me. Now I want some good ideas. Who has one?'

'My lord?'

'Yes, Monty.'

'When the Bretons retreated, the English came straight after them. I wondered; why not employ the feigned retreat?'

'Thank you, Monty; I thought the same thing. We'll try that tactic on the left flank first.'

The Duke continued, 'The tactic is most likely to have success there. If it works, we'll see how it works with those on our right.'

'What if the tactic doesn't work?' Count Eustace asked.

'Eustace.'

'Yes, my Lord.'

'Shut up.'

'Yes, my Lord.'

'I think we might very well be able to draw them down from the left or the right because their respective leaders are dead.'

'Really,' said William, his eyes lighting up with excitement. 'Are you sure?'

'I'm absolutely sure. Earl Leofwine was shot with a crossbow bolt just as his men started after the Bretons. Sir William Warenne killed Earl Gyrth sometime after that.'

'Did I?' said Warenne, quite surprised.

'He was the man who knocked Duke William out of his saddle.'

'Was that really Earl Gyrth?' asked Warenne, pleased with himself.

'I'm sure of it. I'd know him anywhere. Did you not hear the cry of dismay from the English lines when they saw him die?'

'I'm sure Sir William was too busy to notice anything like that,' interjected the Duke, before enquiring, 'so, of the Godwinsons, only Earl Harold is still alive?'

'Yes, my Lord.'

'Who else is up there with him?'

'It's hard to say, my Lord, but I didn't see anyone else I recognised. But Earl Harold is in the centre and his housecarls are too well disciplined to break order.'

'Very well then, we'll feign retreats on the left and the right. We'll work away at the flanks until we can get cavalry on the ridge and attack from the sides as well as the front. We'll keep the pressure up till the flanks collapse, then we'll go for Harold himself.

'Does anyone have any questions?'

Count Eustace wondered if they would be able to do all that by nightfall but thought better of voicing his concern.

'Very well, my friends; let's eat.'

On the ridge above them, Harold was taking stock of the situation. From the oak, Edyth could bear to watch no longer and went over to see if she could assist. Lady Gytha went to help the wounded. Edyth met her husband in mixed spirits.

'Is it over, Harold?'

'No, my love, not yet. Can you believe it? They've broken off for dinner.'

'Well at least it gives our men time for a rest. Where are Gyrth and Leo?' she asked innocently.

'Dead.'

'Oh, no. I'm so sorry, Harold.' Unable to hold back the tears, she cried.

'I'm sorry,' she said once more. 'These tears will do you no good. How can I help?' she said, pulling herself together.

'Help the wounded. God knows there are enough of them.'

'Very well.'

'The men will carry them over to the baggage train. You can treat them there.'

She wanted to ask him if he were winning, if he would take the day, but something stopped her. She felt hesitant, unsure. And then she was aware of his speaking to her.

'It should keep you busy most of the afternoon,' he was saying. 'I'll see you by the old apple tree when this is all over.'

'Will it take long?' What a stupid question, she thought; how would he know?

But he was trying to reassure her. 'It'll be over by sunset. They can't budge us off this ridge and they can't fight us in the dark. They won't dare to camp here overnight so they'll have to go back to Hastings. When tomorrow comes we'll have more reinforcements.'

She hugged him tightly, hoping his words were true.

'You'd better get on and help the wounded.'

'Bye, Harold.'

'See you later.'

As she made her way to the baggage train, three hundred and fifty Danish housecarls arrived to take their places with the others. There were joyful shouts of greeting from the English to their new comrades. Edyth felt relief sweep through the length of her body and she walked with a lighter step.

On the ridge Harold appointed Godric, Shire Reeve of Buckingham, as commander of the left flank and put Abbot Leofgar in command of the right. He thought they would do an admirable job of standing in for his brothers

Just a few miles away, at Ninfield, Bondi and his men had come to a halt. The sight before them had stopped them in their tracks. It was a village laid waste.

'There's nothing we can do here except bury the dead,' said Bondi.

But there was nothing with which to dig. Everything had been destroyed. Bondi's men began looking for anything they could use to turn the earth. They met with little success, so a party was sent back to the village they had stayed in the previous night, where they found the tools to do the job. In the meantime, Bondi and the rest of the men headed on to Harold's encampment. After the delay, Bondi calculated they would, if they hurried, reach the King sometime around sunset.

Duke William and his captains, replete after their midday meal, made their way back to their horses. The Duke made a point of separating Sir William Warenne from the others.

'Thank you, William, it was a close thing out there; I owe you my life.'

Warenne was thrilled. Never before could he remember the Duke having thanked him for anything. It would be something he would tell his sons as they warmed their feet by the fireside on long winter nights. The Duke never mentioned the incident again.

Looking around him, Duke William estimated there would be about three hours of light left in the day, which might just give him enough time to win his victory. He was anxious to press on. Count Eustace had other ideas.

'Why don't we wait until the arrows arrive from Hastings before renewing the attack?' he suggested rather feebly.

'Get on your horse and prepare your men,' was William's curt reply. 'Send up the infantry. The cavalry will press up right behind them, hurling spears into the English. When I give the signal, Count Alan, I want you and your men to run down the hill as fast as you can. When the infantry begins to turn I want the cavalry to break off. If the English fall for the ruse, I want you to wait until they are as far from their lines as you can draw them. Then turn your cavalry round and wipe them out. I will be observing. If the English follow you, I'll break off with my cavalry and charge down on them from above. Is that clear?'

'Very clear, my Lord,' replied Count Alan.

Alan the Black rode over to his men and gave the orders. Duke William rode to the front of his men, signalling them to advance. Trumpets sounded and drums began to beat. What was left of his infantry, now depleted to eighteen hundred men in all, began the long march up the hill, holding a perfect line. The cavalrymen held their horses in check until it was their turn to engage their enemy. All the while the archers, having no arrows, looked on.

In a perfect line William's troops advanced. Their discipline masked their fear. Every step forward brought them just that little bit closer to the time of reckoning. Each soldier knew in his own mind that if the slaughter continued at the same rate as it had that morning, by evening not one of them would be left alive.

'*Dieu Aide!*' went out the call.

'*Dieu Aide!*' was the chant taken up by the hapless soldiers.

Up on the ridge the English took up their chant, 'Out! Out! Out!' It went accompanied by the clash of sword and axe smashed against shield.

As the distance between them grew less and less, more and more became the evidence of the morning's carnage. Infantrymen had to step round piles of bodies. The higher up the ridge they climbed, the worse grew the smell, the grislier the sights. Arms, legs and the occasional head lay on the slope. The closer to the shield wall the Norman infantry advanced, the higher the mounds of bodies were piled up to make obstacles for them.

Norman timing, born of desperation, was perfect. Just moments before the infantry made first contact, the cavalry, in groups of twenty, raced along behind them throwing their spears hard into the English lines. Barely had Harold's men had time to recover when the infantry arrived. But the axe men were undaunted. Just as they had cut the Normans to pieces in the morning, they started to repeat the process in the afternoon.

From his vantage point Harold could see the battle progressing well and took comfort from the knowledge that the Norman infantry could not continue to take many more casualties; by nightfall there would be nothing left of them. The shield wall crossed the ridge as it had done earlier in the day, although it had not escaped his attention that the housecarls were taking the greatest losses, as evidenced only feet away by the ever-closing distance between himself and the Norman front line.

Again, even behind the chain mail and helmet, Harold could see enough of his beetroot face to recognise William, just outside spear range, encouraging his men forward in an attack upon the English standard. The Golden Dragon wriggled gently in the breeze, as if taunting the Normans. The Fighting Man waved his club from his banner. Harold could pick out William Warenne from his long grey hair, hacking away at the shield wall. And he could see hand axes flying to defend their lord.

Even in the din he could recognise Haakon's voice trading insults with Normans who were once his captors. Looking round to the left, Harold saw the giant Godric in the thick of the fighting, his new double-headed axe mincing French mercenaries with all the precision of the grim reaper. To his right, Abbot Leofgar was shouting encouragement to the men under his command. Then, as so often happens, just when we think all is going well, the worst befalls us. William made the pre-arranged signal to Alan the Black and the Bretons turned and fled as though in panic. Norman prayers were answered. From behind the housecarls, less well-disciplined members of the fyrd forced their way through the shield wall to pursue the retreating Bretons. Leofgar and the others shouted for them to stop but it did no good. Down the hill they ran, their hearts pounding with excitement, their faces full of glee.

In all, about five hundred fyrdmen broke ranks to pursue the Breton infantry down the ridge. The fyrdmen never bothered to look behind; why should they? They did not see William signal the Norman cavalry to move in behind them, cutting off their retreat. They only realised their mistake when the Breton cavalry wheeled round to charge them and by then it was too late. Like their comrades in the morning, they rushed for the shelter of the little hillock and its protective tree. Like their comrades before them, they were hacked down, speared or, if they climbed the tree, shot by crossbowmen happy to shoot such easy targets. On the ridge, spears, axes and even stones were hurled at the Bretons to keep them at bay, but all in vain. No one survived.

Harold, powerless to help, looked on as five hundred of his men died within a few minutes and the Bretons, emboldened by their success, attacked again with vigour. Once more the entire stretch of the hillside was engaged in the fight. Then on Harold's left flank William's mercenaries ran screaming from the battle. Once more fyrdmen broke through their own shield wall to give pursuit, only to be cut off and isolated by the same manoeuvre that had led to their comrades' deaths only minutes before. They gave a good account of themselves before they were scythed down.

William's ruse had worked well. In little under a quarter of an hour, Harold had lost a thousand men to the Normans and fear had got the better of some of the others. Sensing a turn in the tide of fortunes one or two fyrdmen disappeared but most stood firm, as did all of the housecarls

– as yet their losses were not critical. It was just as well; the Norman cavalry attacks were beginning to succeed in weakening the lines. For half an hour wave after wave of cavalry attacked; one group after another rode along the shield wall hurling spears at the defenders. At the bottom of the hill the infantry recovered, ready for another attack. Then, in the golden light of the October afternoon, the cavalry assaults stopped, giving Harold and his men some respite.

Godric's cheery smile greeted Harold as he looked over to his left, the big shire reeve beaming as he held high his blood-drenched axe. To his right, Abbot Leofgar also looked happy. He called both men over so they could report the damage.

Harold guessed that at most only one and a half hours of light remained until sunset. As the wounded crawled or were carried back behind the lines to helping hands in the baggage train, Harold looked to see how his bodyguard had fared. Everyone appeared to be all right. Then he noticed someone missing.

'Where's Haakon?' he called out.

No one replied.

'Skalpi, have you seen Haakon?'

'Not for a while, my Lord. The last time I saw him he was charging towards Duke William. I think someone hit him on the head with a mace, my Lord. But it's hard to say.'

'Take some men and see if you can find him.'

Finn and Thorkell took some of the men to look for Haakon. They made a macabre sight searching amongst the dead for the King's nephew. Turning bodies, scrutinizing smashed faces. As they went they piled up the dead to make more obstacles for the Normans, being careful not to slip in the gore. Search as they might, they failed to find Haakon.

Under his standard, Harold talked to Leofgar and Godric.

'I have a question for both of you; will your men last out till dark? 'Abbot Leofgar, what do you say?'

'If we keep our discipline, my Lord, we should easily last out.'

'Sheriff Godric, will your men last till dark?'

'Easily.'

'Good. Then we'll win the day.'

It was then that Harold noticed a change in Godric's expression.

'What is it?'

'Down there. The Normans, they're up to something.'

Harold looked to see a group of Normans on horseback making their way up the hill. There were about twenty of them. Something about their movement struck him as odd. They did not look like cavalry about to make an attack. Then he noticed they had someone with them on foot. His hands were bound behind his back and his legs were tied together in such a way he could only take small steps. He was being prodded with swords and spears to encourage him to keep moving. Then Harold recognised him. It was his nephew, Haakon.

It was William Warenne who had picked him out and with the help of Walter Gifford and a few others, he had managed to capture him in the last foray. The party came to a halt just out of spear range. An unearthly hush descended on the battlefield.

'Do you want your nephew to die, Earl Harold? Why should this young man pay the price for your avarice? Surrender. Give to the Duke what is rightfully his; his kingdom.'

Harold looked Warenne in the eye. 'I'll make no gift of this kingdom to any man. It's no possession of mine to give away. England and I are one and made so by King Edward and the Great Council.'

Warenne grabbed Haakon by the hair and pulled him forward. With his face only inches from his prisoner's he yelled, 'Did you hear that? Did you hear what your beloved uncle had to say?' Then turning to Harold he shouted just as loudly, 'It seems your uncle cares for you less than you thought. He's betrayed you. Still, what do you expect of an oath breaker?'

Sir William then kicked Haakon's legs, forcing him to his knees.

'It must be difficult for you, Haakon, to have to gaze on the face of your betrayer, but I'm not a man without feelings. I'll spare you the pain of looking upon such an unpleasant sight.'

Positioning himself behind Harold's nephew, Warenne grabbed hold of the boy's head, forcing him back against his thigh before using his fingers to gouge out both eyes. The screams were terrible. The English army looked on the ghastly spectacle, readying themselves for their King's command, while Haakon's screaming, eyeless face stared blindly upward at an unseen sky.

Harold gaped in horror, his nephew's screams ringing in his head. He started to move forward but Skalpi and Finn held him back as Warenne pulled out a knife and held it to Haakon's throat, all the while grinning at Harold, tempting him forward.

'There, Earl Harold, look what you've brought on your family. All your brothers are dead; your nephew's blind. If you can't protect your own family, what chance do your men stand?'

Once more Warenne turned his attention to his victim. 'Now you're blind, your life really isn't worth living. Allow me show you some kindness.' Looking directly at Harold, the old man slowly cut the youth's throat, stood up and kicked the corpse face first to the ground.

Harold rushed forward now, the housecarls by his side, all of them wanting revenge. But Warenne had anticipated their move and in a moment had remounted his horse and with his comrades was galloping back to the Norman line, the housecarls behind throwing axes spears and insults at him.

On their way back down the hill, Warenne and his men passed the infantry heading up towards the English. Within a minute, once more the battle was raging.

William repeated the tactic of the feigned retreat, first with the Bretons on his left flank, then with the Frisians on his right but the English held firm, refusing to be tempted by the thought of easy victory. After half an hour of hard fighting William had the retreat sounded and his men gladly broke off from the fight. The Duke was growing more desperate by the minute. 'We can't let the English off the hook now, Monty,' he said to his friend. 'There can only be an hour of daylight left.'

'Have you seen what's arrived?' asked Count Eustace, galloping over to join them.

Duke William looked in the direction indicated by Count Eustace and was pleased to see four wagonloads of arrows being shared out like sheaves amongst the archers. There was a rush as hundreds of bowmen hurried towards them. The Duke shouted over to their commander to open up an attack immediately.

The men in the infantry and cavalry saw this new turn of events as more of a nuisance than a real threat to the English. Archers were viewed with disdain; they inflicted the least damage and took hardly any risks.

'They'll give the rest of us a break,' the Duke said resignedly.

'Do you think a few archers will make any difference to the outcome, my Lord?'

'Do you have any better ideas, Count Eustace?'

'If we had the same amount of men in cavalry, now that would make a difference.'

'But we don't have any more cavalry or any men at all for that matter. At least the men we have are well armed. We can't ask for more than that.'

'But what's the point of archers? They shoot their arrows and the English just lift their shields and stop them all. It's a pity there aren't more archers to shoot them when they're holding their shields so high, that'd sort them out.'

The Duke's expression froze as a vision flashed before his eyes.

'What is it, my Lord?'

'You know, Count Eustace, you've just given me an idea.'

Three thousand rearmed archers began marching up the hill. At a comfortable distance they stopped and prepared to shoot their arrows. Duke William's inspiration was about to pay off; he ordered the infantry to attack the enemy line. Amongst them, making up for the number of fallen comrades, were chevaliers whose horses had been killed under them. The cooks were there, too, and so were the wagon drivers and anyone else William could find for the final, desperate push.

The bowmen were instructed to hold fire until the Duke gave the command to shoot; this would be just before the infantry clashed with the English. The creaking of thousands of bows being drawn gave William a great deal of satisfaction; a smile appeared on his lips. He had told the bowmen to aim high so that their arrows dropped on the English from above while in front of them spears and swords would probe undefended flesh. The English would fall to either arrow or sword.

Once more the Normans trudged up the hill, while again the English started their chant of 'Out! Out! Out!' Like hailstones in a heavy summer storm the arrows fell hard on the English, who held high their shields for shelter from the vicious downpour. Protected from arrows from above, they were vulnerable to sword and spear, to which many victims fell.

A particularly fierce volley was aimed at Harold's standard, wreaking havoc and causing concern for safety of the King. In the fading light, both sides cast ever more anxious glances towards the centre of the ridge, one hoping to see the Fighting Man fall, the other hoping to see him battling on. But the centre held firm; it was the right flank that looked in danger of giving way. Bravely though they fought, the men under Leofgar had lost many of their number; fatigue was overtaking them, arms were tired, hearts were aching, desperation was taking hold. Arrows had stopped falling, it was true, but now cavalry and infantry were attacking as one; men on horseback as well as on foot were attempting to force their way through the line. Still the shield wall held.

The Duke's men were closing in on the Golden Dragon and the Fighting Man. William himself could be seen barking orders at his bowmen. Once more they let fly their arrows; high into the air they shot before turning earthward, screeching like a flock of angry hawks, diving on the men below. So intermingled were the soldiers of the opposing armies that some arrows fell on William's own troops, but many more fell amongst the English. By the time the last volley of arrows struck, the bowmen had already turned to search amongst the bodies of the dead, looking for booty or souvenirs. Some of the bodies were so recently slain their wounds steamed in the chilly air.

On the ridge, behind the English line where Harold and his men were fighting a furious defence, there was a metallic ring as an arrowhead struck Skalpi's shield boss. The deflected arrow shot straight into Harold's eye. The instant he heard the scream, Skalpi knew the King was hit. He turned to see his lord down on his knees, his hands to his face, his axe lying by his side. Blood and vitreous fluid oozed between his fingers. Skalpi barked orders to the housecarls around him and shouted that the King was all right, not dead but injured. The rumour spread that the King had gone down. Worried soldiers glanced at the standard to see if it still stood.

'Are you all right, my Lord?' enquired Skalpi, urgently.

Harold's pain was so intense he could barely reply. When the arrow struck, all he saw was a blinding light and all he felt was searing pain. Instinctively putting his hand to the wound he found what he took to be an arrow. Because of the trajectory on which it had been shot, the arrow had fallen almost vertically. Skalpi's shield boss might have slowed it a little but it had travelled behind the eyebrow, through the lid, split the eye and entered the bone of the lower eye socket. He knew it would have to come out so pulled hard, tearing it out of the bone and back through the flesh the way it had entered. It felt worse than the initial strike. What was left of the tattered eye lay useless in its socket. But word spread along the ridge that Harold had fallen dead. Some of the fyrd, brave enough to fight for their king, lacked the courage to fight without him and slunk off in the twilight.

With Skalpi's help, Harold groped around until he found his axe then staggered to his feet. Even with one eye he could see the situation was dire.

At the oak where Edyth watched, she could sense all was not well. Something was different about the way the housecarls fought and about the way they gathered round the standard. There was something, she was sure. What it was she could not tell, but the feeling that there was something dreadfully wrong with Harold would not leave her.

Out in the field, in front of the scavenging bowmen, William had the same feeling but he knew the battle was not over while Harold still lived. Suddenly he saw him on the top of the hill, with the remnants of the housecarls still grouped around the Golden Dragon and the Fighting Man.

Alan the Black led the first attack to break through the shield wall, isolating the extreme right of Harold's flank. Mauling their way up the slope, the Bretons fed more and more men onto the ridge. The Normans, knowing this was their last chance to win the battle and sensing the English resistance crumble in the failing light, possessed a new lease of life. The knowledge that they had to be victorious before the sun set spurred them on further. English spirits, seeing the shield wall crumble, began to fall.

With a quarter of an hour of sunlight left, William began the attack on Godric's section of the ridge. Encouraged by the success of the Breton attack and realising victory just might be theirs, the Frisians fought with a wild fury. Wave after wave of cavalry charged along the eastern side of the ridge. Just behind the infantry they rode, hurling spears into the ranks of the English. The foot soldiers, pressing hard, finally pushed through with the cavalry charging amongst them. Ralph Pomeroy was there, fighting on foot against men whose shields, he was surprised to see, were covered in arrows, hedgehog-like. Seeing a huge fellow swinging a double-edged axe, Pomeroy started heading in his direction, flailing his sword at all comers. The giant with the double-edged axe was fighting like Thor himself, single-handedly cutting swaths through the mercenaries. Bodies lay all around him. Pomeroy knew in an instant he would kill the man. He would be seen killing the man and claim the glory.

Now outflanked on both sides, Harold had all but lost the crucial advantage of the high ground and was having to fight off attacks from three directions at once. Driving hard at him was William, cursing him as he came. The Breton infantry was slowly making its way toward him from the west and in the east he could see Godric and his men fending off cavalry as well as infantry; they were fighting a losing battle. Daylight was rapidly fading but if their luck held, the Normans would have to give up the fight because it would soon be too dark to continue. As if to remind him time was indeed running out, at that moment Finn screamed in agony as he was crushed by the fall of an enemy's dead horse. His ribs put up no more resistance than dry tinder. The sound of splintering bones was drowned out by his short-lived breathless scream. Squashed under the equine weight, his guts burst out of him, splattering others from head to toe. A few feet away, Azur cried out and fell to the ground disembowelled.

Revitalised, William rode round the battlefield calling for Count Eustace. Even though William had claimed to be willing to meet Harold in single combat, now that he saw him close to he remembered his Samson-like strength from the Brittany campaign and he thought better of it. He thought he had found a way of killing two birds with one stone. Unwilling to lead an attack against Harold in person, he could rid himself of Harold and a cowardly bore at one and the same time.

'Eustace, how would you like to cover yourself in glory?'

'Me, my Lord?'

'Yes, you.'

'Well naturally …'

'Good. Take half a dozen men and take the English standard. Don't worry about Harold, he's dead.'

'Dead?'

'Yes. I saw him go down a moment ago. Now get in there and capture his standard and then show it to the troops.

'Well, what are you waiting for?'

'Nothing, my Lord.'

'Well, get on with it!'

Eustace began rounding up men to help him with his task. As far as he could tell, Harold was still standing. Half a dozen men might not be enough and so he went out to gather twenty more men who would be keen to share the honour.

Along the length of the ridge the shield wall was collapsing. The defenders were desperately trying to close the gaps. Tripping over the gouged and gaping bodies of their comrades, each group of Englishmen desperately fought to rejoin the main body of men around the standard. This meant giving up ground on the flanks, making more room for the exhausted Norman horses to manoeuvre and charge.

Around Harold the Normans were getting closer. He was in the largest group on the ridge in the middle of a thousand men. Their number was being rapidly depleted.

Just over a mile away, Bondi and his men reached a fork in the road known as Henley's Down and the housecarl took heart, knowing that they had less than an hour's journey to the old apple tree. They looked forward to warm campfires and a hot meal. Those who had never met him were looking forward to the honour of meeting their king for the first time. An air of excitement hung over the group as they hurried though the twilight.

In the eye of the storm the King fought on defiantly. The searing pain in Harold's head had not abated; if anything it was worse but he would not leave the field.

'My lord,' pleaded Skalpi, 'you must get away from here!'

'I can't leave the men.'

'There's nothing more you can do.'

'I can do my best. What'll happen if I run away now, when they need me most? It's almost dark. If we're still here at nightfall, William will have to give up. We can fight him again tomorrow. We'll be stronger then, we'll have more men.'

'But my Lord ...'

'I must stay by the standard, Skalpi, I must. What sort of king would I be if I left the field now?'

'Then I'll not leave your side.'

'Edmund, I fear for the safety of the women. Leave us now and protect them.'

'My Lord, I cannot leave you.'

'Would you disobey your king when he most needs your loyalty?'

After a moment's thought Edmund replied, 'God be with you, my Lord.' He turned reluctantly and left.

Beneath the Fighting Man, the King, with Thorkell on one side and Skalpi on the other, prepared for the next onslaught. Around them the housecarls pressed together, forming a human shield. All they had to do was protect the King, just a little while longer until darkness fell.

A quarter of a mile away, Count Eustace had formed two groups. The biggest was made up of twenty mounted men, led by Robert FitzErneis. The Count had told him the Duke had selected him for the honour of taking Harold's standard and that he would be in the company of handpicked men whose mounts were not too tired to charge.

'Good luck, Sir Robert, I know you won't disappoint us,' Eustace had said to FitzErneis as he departed on his deadly mission.

'Thank you, Count Eustace. I'll return shortly with a gift for you.'

FitzErneis was thrilled to think the Duke had enough faith in him to bestow on him such an honourable task. With his head filled with dreams of glory, he put his horse into a full gallop and followed by his men, raced straight for Harold's standard.

Holding their horses in check were Eustace and three others. They were Walter Gifford, Hugh de Montfort and Hugh de Ponthieu, son of the man who had held Harold prisoner two years before. They were all hard men and seasoned warriors. They would charge straight in behind FitzErneis and his men, taking advantage of the confusion. They watched impassively as FitzErneis heroically threw himself straight into the mayhem.

For FitzErneis and his men, it was like entering the mouth of hell. They crashed through the shield wall and there followed terrible scenes of carnage as they forced their way toward the standard. They were only a few feet from the King. They could see him, axe at the ready, waiting for them. The din was terrible as exhausted housecarls and thanes were forced aside. Steel clashed against steel; the thunderous blows of axes shattered shields. Wounded men and beasts screamed in agony, some victims of an enemy blow and some trampled to death or crushed as they fell under horses. Some men, as in a scene from Hades, ran round blindly in distress, clutching at their wounds and yelling in rage at the world.

Skalpi was quick to spot the attack and immediately alerted the other housecarls to the danger. The weight of the charge was overwhelming and furious fighting raged around the standard. The twenty handpicked men were trying to fight their way through and taking serious losses for every foot they travelled. Axes bit deep into their flesh. Swords slashed into them. Spears penetrated hard chain mail and soft flesh. By the time he reached the standard, FitzErneis was the only man left from the twenty who had started out less than a minute before. He saw a man with a ghastly face wound, his eye a grisly mess in its socket. He felt his horse go down under him before he was thrown off, landing on his shield. He was on his feet in an instant but not fast enough. The one-eyed man brought an axe down hard through his shoulder. He fell in two separate bloody halves to the ground.

Thinking the strike over, for just a few moments the defenders lost concentration. Before they knew what was upon them, four more riders were in their midst, charging at full gallop.

With Eustace in the lead, the four riders bore down on the standard. With no one to defend him, Harold made an easy target. Enduring insufferable pain and afflicted by clouded vision, Harold was aware of the second strike too late. It was the thundering hooves that alerted him to danger. He turned from FitzErneis' body, staring up at the horsemen charging through the twilight. It was as though they had appeared from out of the earth itself.

It was Count Eustace who struck the first blow, running the King through the chest with a spear, piercing his heart, drenching the earth with his blood. The same hand that threw the spear snatched the Fighting Man from the earth and the Count galloped, deliriously happy, away along the ridge toward the Duke.

Harold tottered helplessly before falling; his one seeing eye stared but saw nothing. Walter Gifford's unseen blade sliced off his head. Bringing his horse up sharp, the Norman turned it round, grabbed the Golden Dragon and rode off to find his master. As Harold's decapitated body struck the ground the sun dipped behind the trees shrouding the battle in darkness; his soul took flight, ascending to heaven like many that day, lightly and gently, blown like a feather on the breath of God.

Hugh de Montfort, having nothing to fear, leaned right over in the saddle and disembowelled the headless king as he lay stretched out on the bloody ground. And last, Hugh de Ponthieu, Count Guy's brother, looking for glory, threw his spear, which pierced Harold's body and stuck pointing skyward.

It would be nightfall and the battle over before Harold received his final wound. Count Guy's son, Ivo de Ponthieu, searching by torchlight in the darkness, found the King's body amongst his slain housecarls. And there, Ivo, no victim's eyes to shame him, looking for a trophy, by taking away added an unspeakable wound of his own.

When the King fell to the ground, despair and dark desperation had struck the housecarls. Norman infantry, seeing the King fall, charged the housecarls and a ferocious fight ensued. The housecarls were overrun and many killed and wounded. Thorkell decided to leave the field when he saw Bishop Odo strike Skalpi down. With the King and it appeared, all of his friends dead, this seemed the best policy. He thought he would make his way to the watch oak. Perhaps he could protect Edmund and the ladies.

After Harold had fallen, Sir Walter and Count Eustace made straight for the Duke to give him the good news. William, when they handed over the two standards, could not conceal his disbelief.

'Well done, Sir Walter. Well done, Count Eustace, I wasn't sure you'd succeed.'

In those few short words he had betrayed his plan and already Eustace was wondering when the time would be right for him to make a move on the English throne. After all, he told himself, it was his by right. He had a claim and he had killed Harold. Where had the high and mighty warrior been then?

'I had a good plan, my Lord. You should know above all others the value of a good plan. The greater the plan, the greater the success.'

'Yes indeed, Count Eustace. And do you have any plans now?'

'Naturally, my Lord.'

'I'd love to know what they are.'

'You will see. Watch me, my Lord. I'll finish the English and proceed with my battle.'

'I'll do just that, Eustace.' And as the Count disappeared into the night, William thought he would certainly need to keep an eye on him.

On the English left flank, more and more of Godric's men were being cut down by merciless Norman swords. Pomeroy, along with dozens of William's men, had fought his way along the ridge, leaving the hilltop strewn with corpses. Sheriff Godric, who had as yet failed to rejoin the main group of men with the King, was fighting like a berserker.

After running his sword through a young thane, the blood-spattered

Pomeroy found himself on the edge of a group of men that had surrounded the huge Englishman. Now up close, Pomeroy, like most of the men present, was thinking twice about attacking the axe man. He weighed the danger against the honour and decided patience was a virtue. He knew there would be a younger man there, someone eager to make a name for himself, someone who saw an opportunity for glory. Pomeroy would wait for him to strike and make his own attack while the Englishman was occupied. Sure enough, a young man lunged forward but he was dispatched before Pomeroy could act. Worse still, it was the Englishman who was on the offensive; flailing this way and that; it seemed impossible to get near him. It was hard for Pomeroy to pick his moment.

But his moment came; Godric turned to face Pomeroy and as he did so, an infantryman stepped forward to deal him a blow. Godric, quick as ever, never staying still, turned and brought his axe down with awesome force, splitting the man's helmet and head alike but the blade was stuck. Quickly he put his foot on his victim's head and pulled hard on the axe's handle. Pomeroy saw his moment, stepped forward behind Godric and brought his sword down hard as the sheriff struggled to free his axe. The blade caught Godric in his side. It was a painful blow that cut through his tattered byrnie, penetrating deep between his ribs. Pomeroy had no problem withdrawing his weapon and struck a second blow, this time bringing his sword down hard into Godric's shoulder, close to his neck. The sheriff let out a fearsome scream as he fell back clutching at the wound. A spear hurled by a Frisian drove deep into his chest. Pomeroy brought his sword down hard across Godric's stomach. The big bear crashed to earth, dead before he hit the ground. Below his chest was a deep red gash, a wide, silent mouth speaking of pain and helplessness.

On the right flank, Leofgar had fared little better than Godric. He had received several wounds, two of them serious. He was taken from the field to where he could receive treatment. In the meantime the monks from his abbey and those men left on the English right kept up the fight, knowing darkness, if nothing else, might save them. Already the Normans were bringing up torches, their light casting ghostly shadows across the field.

It was as Eustace left William that Bondi and his men eventually reached Oakwood Gill, just on the edge of Dunniford Wood, not far from the battle. Bondi was at the head of the column leading the men along a track on the edge of a ravine and was the first to hear the dreadful news. He heard people rushing toward him through the dense woods. Men were shouting, crashing into each other, falling headlong in their attempt to escape the carnage. His own men shouted for them to join them. It was one of these fleeing men who ran headfirst into Bondi's horse. The housecarl dismounted, grabbed the man's tunic and questioned him.

'What's happening? Where are you going?'

'Get off. Who are you? Why should I tell you anything?' He replied breathlessly, still struggling to escape.

'Stand still and answer me. I'm with the King's bodyguard and I demand to know what's going on.'

'If you're with the King's bodyguard then you're out of a job. The King's dead.'

Bondi was shocked into silence but a moment's glance into the man's face convinced him he had heard the truth. He felt overwhelmed. It did not seem possible.

The clatter of hooves broke the conversation.

With contempt, Bondi threw the man to the ground. 'Dismount and spread out along the edge of the gorge, men,' he commanded.

The men obeyed and as they were doing so, more of the remnants of Harold's army, heading for the relative safely of the treacherous gullies and the hidden ravine, appeared out of the darkness and joined them. It was here they made their stand. Dozens of horses charged out of the darkness, their riders hoping to find the odd hapless Saxon running for cover. Without exception all of them plunged to their doom in the abyss. Dozens more came charging after, losing their footing, breaking their legs or hurtling to their deaths down the steep banks of the ravine.

Those at the rear were oblivious to the trap and galloped at full speed after their comrades until the ravine was a mass of dead and dying men and beasts. Many riders suffered an instant death, breaking their necks or smashing their skulls. Bondi's men quickly put others, who lay trapped or were too stunned or injured to move, out of their misery. What brought the slaughter to an end was the Normans' realisation that there was an impassable wall of their dead in front of them.

Eustace arrived leading a group of fifty chevaliers. Sending scouts forward to investigate on foot, they returned to report a second English army dealing out havoc and slaughtering hundreds of Normans at no cost to themselves. At this point Eustace flew into a panic and was about to sound the retreat when a stone struck him hard between the shoulders. He was carried off wounded, while his men fell back. He was speechless and blood was pouring from his nostrils. He had been about to send word to Duke William that they should withdraw to Hastings, away from the new English army. As it was, he was able to present himself as a hero of the Malfosse, as the fifty survivors of the massacre came to be known. The other heroes of the Malfosse, all three-hundred-and-seventy-six of them, would be burned in a giant pyre where they had died.

With the night came a terrible darkness; the moon would not rise till midnight. Realising there was nothing he could do for his king; Bondi led his men into the black woods to take shelter, as did other survivors of the battle. On the battlefield, disembodied moans and screams penetrated the still blackness of the cold autumn night.

AT THE WATCH OAK

While Duke William was dining with his comrades, Edmund, stumbling through the darkness, finally found Edyth and Gytha waiting in a cart beneath the vast oak tree. Even in the darkness where he found them, Edmund could see their anxiety.

'My ladies?'

'Edmund, is that you?' enquired Lady Gytha, in the gloom.

'Yes, my lady, it's me, Edmund.'

'What's happened, Edmund? Where's Harold?' asked Edyth urgently. But she knew, even though she could hardly see his face, what he was going to say. Even in the darkness she knew. Lady Gytha also knew.

Edmund started to speak. 'I wish it weren't so,' was as far as he got. The two grief-stricken women, as one, burst out crying. Edmund desperately tried to console them but to no avail, he had never seen either of them so distraught. Inconsolable, they wailed with grief and the tears flowed in streams down their faces. The few words either of them managed to speak Edmund found incomprehensible. The two women held each other in a tight embrace, the harder to drive away the pain. They soaked each other's shoulders with their tears. Edmund lost the fight to hold back his own; the three of them, like babies, cried beneath the unseen boughs, the chill air through the branches shushing them like a mother.

His concern for the safety of his charges helped Edmund compose himself. He knew it was unlikely the Normans would come their way but he remembered what had happened to other women the Normans had encountered. He also knew the women would fetch a pretty ransom and his priority should be to get them far away from the battlefield.

'Ladies, please, we must find somewhere for the night.'

They heard someone call out; it was a voice they all recognised. Thorkell had found his way to them. When their eyes met, not a word was said. In silence the party climbed into the cart and headed off to Mountfield in search of a place to spend the night.

SUNDAY MORNING

After a restless night spent in an old crone's hovel, Lady Gytha stirred, looked around the room and jolted when she realised everyone was awake. It was she who spoke first.

'What are we going to do?'

'Go to London and elect a new king,' Edmund replied wearily.

'I want Harold,' stated Edyth flatly.

'I'm afraid you'll never see King Harold again, my lady.'

'I want to see him, if only to give him a decent burial.'

'So do I,' added Gytha.

Realising just how determined the two women were, Edmund acquiesced. 'Very well, then.'

'But I'll not be coming to London with you,' Gytha added. 'I have no business there. I'll have no influence at court and frankly, I've little care for whoever is chosen. I intend to go to Bosham and then to Winchester to rescue my possessions and as much of the treasury as I can.'

'Surely that will be the property of the next king, my lady?'

'Be realistic, Edmund. They'd probably choose Edgar but who will support him? Edwin? Morcar? I doubt it. They'll be too busy trying to feather their own nests. Look how they let Harold down. Do you think they'll show any more loyalty to a boy? No. We need to get hold of the treasury in order to pay for an army to rid the country of the Duke. If we don't do it, who will?'

Edmund did not answer; instead he turned his attention to Lady Edyth.

'Lady Edyth, will you be travelling to London or Winchester?'

'Winchester is where I'd like to go but I have Ulf to consider. I must go to him first.'

'If that's your decision, my lady, then may I accompany you on your journey?'

'And me too,' added Thorkell.

'Will you two be staying at court?'

'I promised the King I would look after you. I know I can offer only you limited protection but such as it is, I would offer it,' said Edmund dutifully.

'Then you must accompany me. You too, Thorkell.'

'Thank you, ladies, you honour us,' replied Edmund for them both. The four then headed back to the old apple tree.

The journey to Caldbec was a silent one. No one spoke, each of them in their own world, travelling in silence, except for the squeaks and creaks of the cart. In the cold and wet they all felt the need to huddle in their cloaks. The fine autumn drizzle shrouded everything in grey. A weight sank in each one's stomach as they made their way to the battlefield. About a quarter of a mile from the scene of the catastrophe, a Norman scout came into view through the murky rain. He approached them and brusquely asked who they were and what they were doing.

Lady Gytha answered in perfect French, 'I am Lady Gytha of Wessex. I am the mother of King Harold. This is Lady Edyth, his wife. The priest is our chaplain and the young man is our escort. Now take us to Duke William.'

Such was Lady Gytha's demeanour, the horseman became quite deferential.

'Yes, my Lady. This way. Please follow me.'

Making their way across the ridge towards William's tent, they passed amongst heaps of naked dead. Here and there they could pick out someone they knew, not yet stacked in a pile with the rest. Here and there across the field were Normans throwing more bodies on heaps and dotted about the place were poor wretches who had come to find a body. Some were looking for a brother, some a son, others looking for a lover or husband. Some were looking for several family members. Like the crows they searched amongst the slain. At least the Normans were civilized enough to bury their own dead. They arrived at the Duke's tent and were surprised when their cart was put in the charge of a midget. The Duke appeared with a dozen men, all of them looking pleased with themselves. Sir William Malet and Count Eustace were the only ones familiar to the English. The Count smirked but Malet could not meet their gaze.

The Duke looked the four up and down. 'What do we have here?'

'I am Lady Gytha of Wessex, the mother of King Harold. This is …'

'Earl Harold,' snapped Duke William.

'This is Lady Edyth, my son's wife. This is …'

'Concubine, you mean.'

'I beg your pardon?'

'I said concubine. Unless this is Lady Aldytha, then surely this slut is one of Harold's whores.' He turned his head to his comrades, who were all laughing heartily, all except William Malet, who remained stone-faced, hiding his anger at the Duke's cheap remarks. William added, 'Getting a bit old for that game too, by the look of her.'

'It's strange to hear such harsh words from one born so noble,' snapped Lady Gytha.

The Duke found himself staring into the most penetrating gaze he had ever seen.

The laughter subsided in an instant.

The Duke, the smile wiped from his face, was a little more restrained. 'Did you come here for any purpose or have you just called by to exchange insults?

'We have come to claim my son's body.'

'Why should I let you have it?'

'Because it is the decent Christian thing to do.'

'Really?'

'Perhaps I can recompense you for the inconvenience. If I gave you his weight in gold, would that suffice?'

William was visibly shocked. Racing through his head was the thought that if Lady Gytha could make him an offer like that on the spur of the moment, then she alone was in possession of enough gold to make his expedition worthwhile. The prospect of having such a treasure trove thrilled but angered him too. As much as he wanted to accept her offer, he would appear ungallant and could not bear the loss of face in his comrades' eyes. For a moment he said nothing but he could feel behind him, in his men, the same astonishment at Gytha's proposal. Against his will he had to refuse. The offer hurt him more than any insult.

'My good woman, I'm not a mercenary who fights for reward.' The lie fell easily from his lips and even as he spoke, he was trying to work out where Lady Gytha kept her treasure and how he could get his hands on it.

'I came to claim my rightful crown,' he continued. 'I have no need of your trinkets; please keep them. Certainly I'll permit you to look for your son's body but remember this, I'll not grant Earl Harold the honour of a descent Christian burial, because he, and he alone, bears the responsibility for the deaths of so many good men.

'Malet!'

'Yes, my Lord?'

'Go with these people and see if you can find Earl Harold's body. When you find it, take it to the coast and bury it there; make sure it's in unconsecrated ground.'

'Yes, my Lord.'

'Take them away.'

'Very well, my Lord.'

'Oh, and Lady Gytha, it might help you in your search to know that Harold was decapitated.'

Lady Gytha paled and the tears once more began to pour from Edyth's eyes. Edmund put an arm round her for comfort. As they turned to follow William Malet, Duke William, feeling especially malicious, called after them, 'You see, in battle it doesn't pay to lose your head,' before bursting into laughter, raucously accompanied by his friends.

As Gytha and Edyth began to look for Harold's body, Edwin and Morcar, with a couple of thousand men, met some of the survivors of the battle, led by Bondi, who gave them the news of the demise of their king.

'So the Normans hold the field?' asked Edwin, unnecessarily.

'Yes, they do, what's left of them,' Bondi replied. 'At the most there can be only four thousand on the hill. Apparently there's another two thousand down in Hastings, too far away to help should William run into any trouble.'

'What do you mean?'

'Well, you are going to attack him, aren't you?'

'We haven't the men.'

'What do mean, you haven't the men?'

'We haven't the men. There are only a couple of thousand of us.'

'And there are five hundred of us. We can do it. They're exhausted. They won't expect it. A lot of them are already making their way back to Hastings. We could easily surround the few that remain. They wouldn't be able to use their cavalry and without their cavalry they're useless. What do you say?'

Morcar stepped in with a reply: 'We would need to elect a new king first.'

'Elect a new king? There's no time for that. Let's go and get him now and whoever's king in the future will be eternally grateful to you.'

'It's not our decision to make. The decision to go to war is for the King to make.'

'We haven't got a king,' Bondi replied, raising his voice, 'that's just the point!'

'Then my brother and I will return to London and call the Witan ...'

'Call the Witan? Most of the Witan are dead.'

'May I remind you whom you address? My brother and I will return to London and there the next King of England will be chosen. It will be he who decides whether or not to attack the Duke.'

With that the brothers turned their horses and led their men back the way they had come. Bondi stayed where he was, silent for a moment before shouting abuse at them as they left. They assured each other they were doing the best thing in returning to London. Their ignominious defeat at Fulford still haunted them and if Harold had met his match, what would be their fate if they confronted the Duke?

Grim-faced, Gytha, Edyth, Edmund and Thorkell, with Sir William, started the search for Harold's body. Slowly they passed the naked bodies of their countrymen, stripped by eager Norman hands.

But not everyone found being on Caldbec Hill an unpleasant experience. In the cold, fine drizzle, amongst the carrion picking the corpses clean with many others, was Ralph Pomeroy. In spite of the inclement weather he was having a fine day. His squire had rounded up a couple of horses that had once belonged to comrades now dead and held them secure. From bodies they had looted some fine gold rings and amulets as well as weaponry and armour. For Ralph Pomeroy, the decision to join William's expedition was to be the turning point in his life. His heroism on the battlefield had been noted and before a year had passed, he would find himself knighted and presented with a handsome piece of Devonshire land. He married the widow of an English soldier and gave her some children to add to her own two boys, who later died in an accident.

Also on the hillside were those who were hoping to find someone they loved amongst the dead, and yet hoping to find no one. Did no corpse mean that he had escaped into the night? Was he even now safe at home, warming himself, cosy by the fireside? Or would a stool stand empty by the hearth?

On the ridge, the eerie grey silence was too often disturbed by the sound of heartache, as a grief-stricken woman discovered the remains of a loved one. Edyth joined the ever-rising number when she caught sight of her lover's body. She ran over to him, quickly followed by Gytha, Edmund, Thorkell and Sir William. Though he was headless she recognised him, knew immediately and her long legs, like a newborn foal's, crumpled, unable to support her. Gytha fell to her knees and wailed.

Edmund climbed down from his horse to confirm in his own mind that they had indeed found the King. There was no doubt. The tattoos on his arms were easily recognizable; undamaged and as bold as ever, she had seen them a million times before, but never so lifeless as now.

Edmund lifted Edyth's shoulders so she was sitting up and he supported her until she came round. Sir William went to comfort Gytha. When she realised who it was she screamed at him, 'Don't touch me! He was your friend. He was your friend and this is how you treated him. Look at him! Look at him!'

Sir William looked at the blood-drenched body.

'My lady, it couldn't be helped. Like anyone I have to obey my Lord. Forgive me, but the decision was not mine to make.'

'And that makes it all right?'

'No, that doesn't make it all right, my lady. It makes it God's will.'

'That bastard duke's will, more like.'

Sir William remained calm and chose his words carefully. 'It's a sad business,' he said, 'but it has happened. It was fate that brought Harold here and that being so, Duke William's conscience must be clear.'

Lady Gytha glared at him but said nothing.

Edmund had brought a purple silk sheet from the cart.

'Sir William, will you help me?' he asked.

The two men had carefully wrapped Harold's mangled body when twenty or more Norman foot soldiers arrived, following their captain and an empty wagon. The captain addressed Sir William.

'The Duke has ordered me to escort these people from here, my Lord.'

'But I'm to bury this body.'

'The Duke says you know what the arrangements are; you're to bury him by the sea. This lot are to come with me to the London Road, where I'm to see them on their way. You're to put the bodies in the wagon there and take them to the coast. I'll return later to act as your escort.'

'This is outrageous!' yelled Lady Gytha, 'we were promised we could have my son's body.'

'The Duke told me you'd say that. He said to tell you he'd made it clear that you could look for the body. He said nothing about your taking possession of it. Now be on your way!'

'We will do no such thing.'

'I think you'd better do what he says, my lady,' Sir William intervened. 'I'll make sure Harold, and for that matter, Leo and Gyrth, have a decent burial.'

'What, in unconsecrated ground?'

'If that's what the Duke ordered.'

'We can do it. Edmund can say a prayer for them.'

At this moment the captain's patience ran out, 'Go now!' he barked, nodding to his men who surrounded Edmund, Thorkell and the ladies.

'You can't do this to us. Order your men off now!'

'Begging your pardon, my lady, don't tell me what to do,' said the guard, matter-of-factly, walking his horse towards Lady Gytha.

Sir William saw the danger of the situation. 'Please do as he says, my lady.'

Seeing no choice, Lady Gytha, Edyth, Edmund and Thorkell climbed into the cart and were escorted to the London Road.

Sir William was as good as his word. He continued the harrowing search for Leo and Gyrth, whom he eventually found. Leo had to be pulled out of a heap of dead housecarls, clinging together in death as they had in life. Gyrth lay where he had fallen. All the time the light drizzle fell; occasionally those on the hillside slipped over on the greasy, sodden grass.

When Sir William had collected the bodies together and he had them secured in a wagon, he headed to the coast with the escort to bury them. His escort consisted of the captain and his men who had returned from the London Road; they were to dig the graves and to protect him should he come under attack.

Sir William led the wagon to the coast. A warm yellow sun shone down on the white cliffs and seagulls soared overhead just as they did on any other day. A few feet from the cliff's edge, the party halted. Sir William gave instructions and the soldiers set about digging a grave, all except one whom he ordered to engrave an inscription on a large flat stone. When the graves were dug, without ceremony the bodies were carelessly thrown into the ground while Sir William quietly observed the proceedings. As his mind wandered, he drifted into the past; the sound of the wind buffeted around him, the sea crashed on the shore below and the birds called as they circled in the sky above. The sounds took him back to Bosham. Sir William thought back over the years and his memories of Harold and felt regret as he thought of his part in destroying a man he had so admired. What brought him back to the present he was never sure but it was most likely the movement on the top of a nearby ridge that caught his eye. Something about the movement told him it was someone who did not want to be seen and he knew it must be Thorkell and in the same instant he knew exactly why he was there.

Before the chalky soil could be tipped over the bodies, Sir William interrupted the proceedings.

'Captain, it's getting late in the day and you really ought to be getting back. I'll take care of the burial. Leave now; I'll catch up with you in a short while.'

'My orders are to supervise the burial, my Lord.'

'And you've done an admirable job. Look, I don't quite know how to say this, but I knew these men well. It's bad enough that they're buried in unconsecrated ground. Couldn't you just give me some time to say a prayer over them?'

'Very well, my Lord,' replied the captain and without further ado gave orders to his men. Within five minutes they were out of sight.

Full of a sadness he could not name, Sir William, without filling in the graves, put in place the headstone, the legend of which read, 'By command of the Duke, you rest here a king, O Harold, that you may be guardian still of the shore and sea.'

After saying a short prayer over the graves and without turning back for a last look, he rode away to rejoin the Duke. Behind him the setting sun cast its colour on an ocean turned red.